# THE UNQUIET DEAD

# THE UNQUIET DEAD

## STACIE MURPHY

PEGASUS CRIME
NEW YORK LONDON

THE UNQUIET DEAD

Pegasus Crime is an imprint of
Pegasus Books, Ltd.
148 West 37th Street, 13th Floor
New York, NY 10018

First Pegasus Books cloth edition April 2022

Interior design by Maria Fernandez

Library of Congress Cataloging-in-Publication Data is available.

ISBN: 978-1-64313-893-0

10 9 8 7 6 5 4 3 2 1

Printed in the United States of America
Distributed by Simon & Schuster
www.pegasusbooks.com

*For my mother.*

# 1

*Mid-August, 1893*

Washington Square Park was never deserted, even at half-past four in the morning. The feeble glow of the streetlights lining the sidewalk faded just inside the gates, and Amelia strained to see through the shadows. The heat wave that had been baking the city for weeks showed no sign of abating, and the air was oppressive despite the early hour. Sweat dampened her temples as she picked her way along the path. Jonas followed, his expression stony above his wilted collar.

In the daytime, shop girls strolled here with their sweethearts and paused for stolen kisses beneath the new marble arch. At night, however, the grounds were the domain of those seeking less licit pleasures. Most hurried past, their faces averted, intent on their own business. One man slowed, and Amelia's stomach tightened as his gaze slithered over her body in frank appraisal. He drew breath to speak, no doubt to inquire about the cost of her company. The words died in his throat when his eyes reached Jonas's face, and he turned and slouched away more quickly than he'd approached, disappearing into the dark.

Jonas stopped to watch him retreat, then turned back to her with a baleful look. "Are you sure this is a good idea?"

A ticklish bead of perspiration rolled down Amelia's spine as she studied the wisps of fog rising from the damp ground. "Truly? No."

She turned off the main footpath. Behind her, Jonas heaved a sigh. Amelia recognized it as the sound of capitulation and relaxed a fraction. She hadn't been sure he would go along with her plan. If he had balked or demanded they leave, she would've had to agree. She couldn't have risked running into another of the park's nighttime denizens without him. Jonas's sheer size was enough to deter most harassment. Paired with his flinty glare, all but the most desperate criminals would decide to seek other prey.

He'd nearly been killed by just such a desperate criminal several months before, near the conclusion of their investigation into a series of murders at the city insane asylum on Blackwell's Island. One of the perpetrators, fearing his role in the scheme was about to be uncovered, had followed Jonas into an alley, shot him, and left him for dead.

Jonas had largely recovered, though his left arm still ached and spasmed when he overused it. The doctor who had treated him assured them the weakness would fade with time. Eventually, he said, it would be as though the injury had never happened.

The doctor was wrong. Amelia knew it, and she suspected Jonas did as well, though he avoided the subject. The arm might heal, but Jonas's brush with death had changed him. He'd always been watchful, but in the past few months there had been a new, brittle quality to his vigilance, and he was more snappish with Amelia—as well as with Sidney, the young lawyer who had been his lover for the better part of a year.

But it was the drunken brawlers at the fashionable nightclub where they worked who bore the brunt of his shortened temper. In his role as bouncer, Jonas had always been willing to deal in violence when necessary, but what had been carefully measured and coolly delivered was now sometimes disproportionate and driven by wild anger.

Amelia and Sidney had discussed the changes, each confirming what the other had observed: nightmares, a skittishness when approached from behind, and, most recently, the smell of alcohol on his breath at inappropriate times. The man they both loved was still there—brilliant, vain, droll—but there was no denying he was altered.

Fortunately, they didn't meet anyone else as they neared their destination. Amelia's heartbeat quickened as they reached the bridge. The ground here dipped where a little stream bubbled up from beneath the earth. It tumbled through a stony channel before disappearing again twenty feet later. In the early morning silence, the water rushing over the smooth rocks sounded like a chorus of whispers. She shivered despite the warmth and stepped onto the bridge. Jonas followed. Their footsteps on the boards echoed through the hollow place in her stomach. On the other side Amelia slowed, creeping forward one small, measured pace at a time, until a familiar sensation prickled against the inside of her chest.

Her mouth went dry. The spirit was still here.

In the months since the fight at the club that had resulted in her head injury and left her with the ability to channel the dead, Amelia had gained some control over lesser spirits, maintaining a foothold inside her own mind as they spoke through her. But too many of them still managed to push her aside entirely, leaving her with no control over her body and no memory of what had occurred. There had been several incidents, the most recent only two nights before. A man had come to her, hoping to speak to his lost fiancée, and gotten more than he bargained for. Very nearly quite a bit more. Amelia's face heated at the memory. Such things couldn't keep happening. She had to learn to manage it.

The spirit that clung to this spot was the first one Amelia had ever encountered, and it remained the most powerful. If she could learn to channel this one without being overwhelmed, she should be able to handle any others. She needed to practice.

The theory was sound. Still, Amelia hesitated, aware of the risk she was taking. This wasn't a being to be trifled with. The last time she'd encountered it, she'd been labeled mad and shuttled off to the asylum.

But Jonas was with her this time. He wouldn't let it happen again.

Amelia took a deep breath, glanced back at him, and nodded once, confirming the spirit was present. Jonas grimaced. She turned back to the path, lowered her chin, and forced herself to take another step. The familiar itch behind her breastbone grew.

Twenty feet ahead, an outline began to form, misty and barely distinct from the lightening sky and shadowed ground surrounding it.

Amelia didn't turn. "She's coming. Remember what I said. If she takes me—"

"I know. Get you away from this spot and do whatever I have to do to bring you out of it." Jonas's voice was tight.

Her palms damp and her heart thumping against her ribs, Amelia eased toward the specter. It coalesced as she approached, and by the time she was ten feet away, the same young woman she'd seen months earlier stood before her, translucent and gray, all eager eyes and ragged clothes—and, half-buried in the swollen flesh of her neck, a knotted rope.

Amelia suppressed a shudder. Her breath caught in her throat as the shade began to drift closer. The woman reached a hand toward her, naked hunger on her face. Amelia fought the urge to step back. She had to do this. Her head buzzed. She lifted her own hands, palms up. A gesture of offering. Of welcome. Do you want me? Here I am.

Amelia closed her eyes and let the spirit consume her.

# 2

A drop of water splashed off her nose. Amelia blinked it away as the branches of a pine tree came into focus above her. Her back felt damp. Something spiky—a pine cone, if she were to hazard a guess—prodded her between the shoulder blades.

Amelia tilted her head an inch to one side, just far enough to see Jonas, who sat with his back against the trunk of the tree, cutting slivers from an apple and eating them from the point of his pocketknife.

He looked up at her movement, his expression wary. "Amelia?"

She blew out a careful breath before she answered. "How long was I gone?"

Jonas tossed the apple core aside. "About twenty minutes." He folded the knife and tucked it back into his pocket. "We ought to be getting home as soon as you're able."

Amelia started to ease herself up, then thought the better of it as her stomach lurched and her head began to pound. She lay back, taking deep breaths of pine-perfumed air and feeling like the butt of a cosmic joke: whether it was whiskey or ghosts, the stronger the spirit, the worse the hangover. She eyed Jonas.

"What happened?"

"You told me the girl was still here. Ten seconds later you were on the ground, clawing at your throat and making choking noises. You fought me when I tried to pick you up." He held out his hand. A neat semi-circle of punctures, livid against his pale skin, marred the flesh at the base of his thumb.

Amelia winced. "I did that?"

Jonas examined the bite mark. "Your teeth did, anyway. I dragged you off the path, and you went limp. I didn't want to carry you out of the park unless I had to—even here, at this time of night, it might have attracted attention."

Amelia gave herself another minute, then rolled onto her side, her hair falling across her face. She pushed it aside with an irritated noise. It had grown since her involuntary shearing at the asylum, and was now at a particularly inconvenient length. She wore a knot of false curls when she worked, but for this outing, she'd merely pinned the sides back—not securely enough, obviously. She pushed herself into a seated position and began searching the thick carpet of pine straw around her, hoping she'd lost the pins there, rather than while being carried from the path.

Amelia recovered three of them before giving the rest up as lost and trying to stand. She wobbled, and Jonas moved to help her, keeping an arm around her waist as they made their way back toward the park's entrance.

She leaned against him. "Do you want to tell me you were right and I was wrong?"

"Do I need to?" The words were chiding, but the tone was gentle.

"I suppose not." She couldn't help but look back at the place where she knew the girl's spirit still lingered. "I'm coming back," she called. "I'm not going to give up."

By the time they reached the gate, the morning sun was already heating the sidewalks, which were beginning to fill as the city's laboring classes headed to work. A pair of young women—housemaids, judging from their plain black dresses and white caps—tittered as Jonas and Amelia stepped onto the sidewalk, and a man with the roughened complexion of a dockworker glanced at Amelia, then gave Jonas a knowing wink.

Amelia shot them a sour look as she pulled away from Jonas and reached up to re-pin her hair.

Jonas caught the direction of her thoughts. "Never mind them," he said, then stopped, a frown creasing his forehead. "How are you feeling?"

Amelia stabbed the third pin into place. "Hungry," she said in surprise. Her stomach had already calmed.

"And your head?"

"It's not bad." It was true. The dregs of the headache remained, but the insistent throbbing had faded.

Jonas looked thoughtful. "A few months ago that spirit left you unconscious for the better part of a day. Now barely half an hour after the encounter, you're walking on your own and ready for breakfast. You're getting stronger."

Amelia looked back into the park, then quirked an eyebrow at Jonas. "What was that about one of us being wrong?"

He grinned and held up his bitten hand. "I'm still right. I said it was too dangerous, and look—I'm wounded. I'll probably have a scar." He gave a mock shudder. "My looks are my livelihood, you know. I might starve."

Amelia laughed and shoved him. "We can't have that. Come on, let's find some breakfast."

They reached the corner just as a newsboy was cutting the twine on his bundle of papers. An inch-high headline blared "POLICE RELEASE HOLLOWAY SUSPECT WITHOUT CHARGE." Jonas fished in his pocket, then flipped the boy a nickel and waved away the change as he plucked a paper from the top of the stack. The newsboy, who, like most of his peers, had an under-washed and underfed look about him, flashed a gap-toothed grin in their direction before turning away to begin hawking his wares in earnest.

Jonas caught Amelia's look. "Two cents means more to him than to us," he said with a shrug. He was already reading the lead story as they crossed the street. Amelia tugged him out of the path of a laundry wagon as he relayed the newest details of the kidnapping case that had enthralled most of the city.

Five-year-old Virginia Holloway had vanished from her parents' Fifth Avenue mansion four days earlier, the same night her family was hosting a lavish party celebrating her father Edwin Holloway's fiftieth birthday. When the girl wasn't in her bed the following morning, her parents first assumed she'd crept from her room to watch the partygoers and had fallen asleep elsewhere—something she'd apparently done before. This time, however, a search of the house and grounds failed to locate her.

The Holloways, frantic, summoned the police, who first interrogated the servants, all of whom insisted they'd seen nothing. Reluctantly, they turned to the party guests, sending detectives to politely question some of the city's wealthiest citizens, many of whom bristled at such disrespectful treatment. Inevitably, the existence of these sessions leaked to the penny press, which reported the supposed details with undisguised glee.

The addition of a trio of ex-Pinkerton agents, hired by the distraught family when the police failed to produce immediate results, added a new dimension to the story. Their leader was a reporter's dream, a bombastic man who opined—at length and always on the record—on the many shortcomings of the police department.

Spurred on by the criticism, the police eagerly embraced every theory. When one of the guests' footmen was overheard confidently asserting that the girl had been taken by white slavers, they wasted no time in hauling him in for questioning.

The man acknowledged seeing the girl that night, dressed in a white nightgown and peeping from a doorway to the side yard where the carriages were parked. But, he maintained, he knew no more than that. After more than a day, the police finally released him, now out of a job and with the taint of suspicion still clinging to him.

"Poor fellow," Jonas commented as they sat down in their favorite café. "He's ruined, even if he didn't do it." He tossed the paper on the table and signaled the waiter.

"He's an idiot who should have known better," Amelia said, picking up the discarded pages. "I wonder what really happened to her."

"We might never know," Jonas said as the waiter arrived.

"Maybe," Amelia replied, looking at the etching of Ginny Holloway printed on the front page. The look in the girl's eyes and her pointed chin gave the impression of a mischievous spirit. Her hair was a mass of curls. Auburn, according to the description that had been in every article.

As Jonas turned away to order, Amelia surreptitiously brushed her hand across the photo. "Where are you, child?" she murmured, hoping for one of the flickers of intuition that sometimes came to her. She got nothing for her effort but a smudge of ink on her fingers.

⁊

"I' was the damn Freemashuns that took her," the man slurred, listing to one side as Jonas maneuvered him down the club's front steps some twenty hours later.

"Just a little further, Mr. Hahneman," Jonas said, not bothering to mask his impatience. "Your driver is waiting right over there."

Hahneman looked blearily in the direction Jonas indicated and lurched toward the waiting carriage. Jonas kept a hand on his elbow as he clambered inside, belching a cloud of whiskey fumes. "Poor lil' angel," Hahneman mumbled.

Jonas had already turned away and exchanged an exasperated glance with Tommy, the club's Negro doorman. The Freemasons. Honestly.

Back inside, he took a slow circuit of the main floor. The band was halfway through its final set of the night. The musicians' shirts were soaked with sweat, but they played on, gamely trying to inject some gaiety into the lethargic crowd. The relentless heat had sapped the patrons' energy, and despite the lively music, the dance floor remained deserted. Roughly half the tables were occupied, many by men nearly as drunk as Hahneman. Jonas eavesdropped on their talk as he passed. An astonishing amount of it was about Ginny Holloway. He'd never seen a story capture the city this way.

Everyone had a theory. The Jews had taken her. Paul Kelly and his Five Points Gang were holding her for ransom. It was a plot by the mayor's political opponents to hurt his chances for reelection. Speculating about the identity and motive of Ginny Holloway's kidnapper was at the forefront of seemingly every affluent New Yorker's mind.

Their fixation was maddening. They lived in a city where poor children perished in droves. They died of disease and malnutrition. They were caught beneath carriage wheels and scalded by steam in factories. They were beaten to death by drunken parents and fell—or were tossed—from tenement windows. Unwanted babies—the lucky ones, at least—were abandoned on doorsteps every single night. But most people hadn't cared until someone dared to snatch one of *their* children.

A child who mattered.

His mood soured, Jonas mounted the stairs and made his way toward the back room where Amelia worked, hoping she wasn't going to insist on going to the park again. He agreed, in theory, that practice was a good idea, but playing with that particular spirit was too dangerous. She'd scared him half to death last night. And his hand still hurt.

Cigar smoke wafted from the open doors of the gaming rooms lining the hallway. He glanced into one as he passed. Even without the pile of chips at the center of the table, he would have known it was a high-stakes hand by the set of the players' shoulders and the way their eyes followed the dealer's movements. Jonas paused to exchange a glance with Gunnar, the newest member of the club's security staff, who stood along the back wall. Sabine had been forced to hire the broad-chested Swede a few weeks before, after a sweating steamship magnate lost a thousand dollars betting on a pair of nines, then vented his frustration on the unfortunate waiter who served him the wrong brand of gin. Jonas had managed to intervene before the waiter suffered more than a bloody nose, but the incident had highlighted the club's need for more muscle, as well as the growing tension enveloping the city.

The Holloway kidnapping might not have shaken Society so deeply had it not been for the fact that it was the second blow to their sense of invulnerability. The first struck against the very foundation on which it was built: their fortunes.

Throughout the late winter and early spring, Jonas and Amelia had been otherwise occupied, to put it mildly. For much of the country, and certainly for the segment of the population that made up the club's clientele, the nation's faltering economy was a source of rapidly mounting anxiety.

A major railroad company failed. Then a pair of steel mills. Nervous banks began calling in loans, and over-leveraged businesses found themselves unable to pay. Thousands were out of work. The stock market fell, taking a significant portion of the net worth of New York Society with it.

The club was starting to feel the strain. Its atmosphere of gleeful debauchery had thinned into desperate gaiety. The club's coffers remained full as ever, but the word was several of their most reliable spenders were fiddling as their fortunes burned. The well-publicized suicide of a bank president a few weeks before—a longtime client of one of the dancers—had cast a pall and left everyone delicately questioning their own regulars about their current state of liquidity.

Sabine was on edge, which put everyone else on edge, too. Jonas felt it all the time now, that coiled dread in his gut. The sense of balancing on a knife's edge.

In the gaming room, the dealer revealed the final card. One of the players threw down his hand in disgust. Gunnar tensed, but when no further outcry erupted, he settled back into his watchful posture. Jonas gave him a small nod of approval and continued on his way. He was a worthwhile hire, even if Sabine fretted over the additional outlay.

As if thinking her name had conjured her, the door to Sabine's parlor swung open, and the club's owner stepped into view, frowning at a sheet of paper in her hand. A tall woman of middle years, one look at her was enough to know she'd never been a ravishing beauty, but strong features and a velvet voice made her a commanding presence.

She caught sight of Jonas, and there was steel beneath the velvet when she spoke. "Why aren't you on the floor?"

"There's barely anyone still here." It was precisely the wrong thing to say. Jonas wished he could snatch the words back as Sabine's frown deepened. She glanced down the hallway, where a man waited outside Amelia's door.

"What about her? How many has she seen tonight?"

"I'm not sure," Jonas hedged. "I haven't been keeping track."

Sabine's eyes narrowed. "How many?"

Jonas sighed. "Three or four."

Sabine's frown became a scowl. "She's going to miss her quota. Again."

His own control slipping, Jonas's voice was cold when he replied. "It's harder now. Riskier. What do you want her to do?"

"I want her to make me money the way she used to. I hired her to tell people's fortunes, not send them away. And I hired you to work the floor, not to be her nursemaid."

The waiting man had turned his attention toward them. Jonas stepped closer to Sabine and lowered his voice. "You know I have to watch her now. I told you, if I hadn't gone in when I did the other night—"

Sabine snorted. "You should have let her fuck him. He'd have paid more." She turned on her heel and stalked away.

Jonas took a deep breath, mastering the impulse to spit a reply at her back. Sabine didn't truly understand. She didn't really believe in Amelia's gift, didn't understand that Amelia had been overtaken by the dead woman and hadn't been the one initiating that encounter. And she didn't understand what it would have meant to Amelia to return to herself and find she'd slept with a client.

He fought down his anger and continued down the hall. Sabine was crude, but she had a point about the money. Neither of them was as valuable to her as they had previously been. Jonas took fewer clients upstairs lately. Partly it was his own preference; random encounters were less appealing now that he had Sidney. But partly it was because of the greater need to watch over Amelia as she worked. There was a weeping irony to the whole thing. Before her injury, Amelia had been ninety percent fraud. Now she was a far better psychic, and all of them were the poorer for it.

Even in his more limited role, Jonas hadn't exactly covered himself in glory recently. The club attracted a fair number of would-be card sharps, and it typically fell to him to handle them. No stranger to their tricks, he usually nabbed them before they'd done too much damage. The previous week, however, one had taken more than a thousand dollars off of a table of regulars before they caught on. There'd been an altercation, and one of the regulars wound up with a broken arm. Sabine, fairly or not, blamed Jonas for not preventing it.

He grimaced, then smoothed the expression from his face as he approached Amelia's door, where the waiting man still stood watching him.

"Trouble with the boss?" he asked, curiosity plain.

Jonas forced a smile. "Nothing worth worrying about." He nodded toward the door. "When Miss Matthew's done with this one, I'll need to speak to her for a moment before your session, if you don't mind."

"I'm in no hurry," the man said affably.

Just then, the door swung open, and a well-dressed, hollow-eyed man emerged, clutching a crumpled white handkerchief. Jonas had time to note the half-dried tracks of tears on his face before the man brushed past him with a muttered apology and a tiny metallic clink. Jonas looked down at the man's right hand. The crumpled cloth he held wasn't a handkerchief, after all. It was a tiny white gown, fine threads still looped around a pair of knitting needles.

His chest tightening with worry, Jonas hurried through the open door and eased it closed behind him. Amelia sat behind the narrow table, her Tarot cards in a stack beside her right hand. She looked exhausted, her breathing ragged and her face strained and tear-streaked. She looked up at his approach.

"Who was it?" he asked, his tone grim.

Amelia let out a shuddering sigh. "His wife."

Jonas made a sour sound, then hesitated before he spoke. "There's another one waiting."

Amelia took a deep breath and scrubbed at her cheeks with the heels of her hands. "Send him in."

"Are you sure? I can tell him you're done for the night."

Amelia looked at him, her eyes red from crying a dead woman's tears. "I can do one more."

Jonas sighed and crossed back to the door. He poked his head into the hallway, but the man who'd been outside was now halfway down the hall, huddled with one of the waiters. The waiter was shaking his head as the man spoke. He held something in his hands. Jonas frowned. It looked like—

"Gentlemen." Jonas made his voice hearty as he strode toward them. They turned, the waiter looking relieved and the other man moving hastily to conceal the small notebook and pencil he held. Before he could tuck them away, Jonas clamped one hand around his upper arm.

"I didn't tell him anything, Jonas," the waiter said.

"That's fine, Sam," Jonas said. "You can go on back to work."

He hauled the other man toward the stairs. "Who are you and what do you want?"

"Peter Rhodes, *New York Sun*," the man said, scrambling to keep pace with Jonas's longer stride. "Lot of important people seem to like this place. Thought I'd come see what all the fuss was about."

A reporter, damn it. Now that Jonas looked at him, Rhodes's evening wear was poorly tailored and had shiny spots of wear at the elbows and cuffs. Second-hand, at least. He should have noticed earlier, but he'd been distracted. He hustled the man down the stairs.

"You're Jonas Vincent, right?"

Jonas ignored him.

Rhodes persisted as they crossed the main room, drawing a few interested eyes. "I'd love to talk with you. Or with Miss Matthew. Both of you must see all sorts of things. I pay for information, and I'll keep your names out of it. Anything you want to tell me—"

They reached the front door, and Rhodes's voice cut off as Jonas tightened his grip. "This is a private establishment. You aren't welcome." He opened the door and marched the man past Tommy and down the steps, letting go of his arm and giving him a shove when they were several yards down the sidewalk.

"You'd do better to talk to me," Rhodes said, rubbing his biceps. "I'm going to get what I'm after eventually."

"Not from me."

⁂

Amelia unpinned her hairpiece and dropped it on the dresser. "Another one? How did he get past Tommy? I thought he knew them all," she asked, massaging her scalp with a sigh of relief. No matter how careful she was, there was always at least one pin that felt as though it was on the verge of poking through her skull and into her brain. She combed her hair with her fingers, then secured the sides with a pair of tortoiseshell combs—they'd be easier to find than the pins if they came loose. She'd already exchanged her blue and russet brocade evening gown for the same gray cotton dress she'd worn for their trip to the park the previous morning. The back wasn't too badly stained, and there was no point in creating more laundry.

"Tommy says he never saw him. Rhodes might have mixed in with one of the larger groups." Jonas leaned against the doorway of her bedroom, his own change of clothing having been less complicated than hers. "Or else someone let him in the back door," he added, scowling.

"I wouldn't worry too much about it," Amelia said. "Sabine knows you can't catch them all. Now that you've seen him and we know he's poking around, we can all be on the lookout for him."

Jonas stepped out of the doorway and followed her into the main room of their apartment in the old carriage house behind the club, still looking disgruntled.

"Do we have to do this right now? She's not going anywhere."

Amelia hesitated, the thought of falling into her bed undeniably more appealing than confronting the hanged woman's spirit again. But . . . "Yes," she said firmly.

Jonas made a face, but followed her outside, grimacing at the foul, stagnant air.

Amelia ignored him. There was nothing to say. Everyone who could had left the city weeks before, decamping to summer homes in the mountains or on the coast. Those who remained behind did their best to withstand the unrelenting discomfort. Women took cool baths and powdered the insides of their corsets—ladies with scented talc and women of lesser means with common cornstarch. It made no difference. By the end of the day, mistress and maidservant alike would find their shifts all but glued to their bodies, the flesh beneath whitened and shriveled after hours swathed in wet fabric. Dockworkers went shirtless, while gentlemen sweated through their coats. Sunburned, naked children splashed in the river and took turns standing beneath public water spigots.

There was barely an hour in the day without a traffic jam caused by a carthorse dying in its traces, the corpses blocking streets all over the city until another ragged, sweating team could be sent to tow them away for disposal. Everyone in the city had complained about it until there was hardly anything more to be said. Everyone was miserable. The heat would break eventually. Until then, there was nothing to do but endure.

"I'll bet the asylum is one of the coolest places in the city right now," Jonas remarked abruptly as they reached the sidewalk. "All those stone walls and river breezes. Andrew's probably looking for any excuse to sleep on that old cot in his office."

"Probably," Amelia replied, trying not to look as jolted as she felt by the mention of Andrew Cavanaugh. Jonas persisted in bringing up the asylum doctor's name at odd moments, and she refused to give him the satisfaction of asking him to stop.

"Sidney's seen him a time or two. Says he's asked about you."

Amelia didn't reply.

"I'm sure if you wanted to talk to him—" he began, and her stomach tightened.

Whatever Jonas was about to say was preempted by a sudden flurry of shouts, followed by the unmistakable trill of a police whistle coming from one of the side streets. Such sounds were unremarkable in the rowdy neighborhoods around the club, though usually everyone had settled down by this time of night.

Grateful for the interruption, Amelia stopped to listen. "Sounds like it's coming from Houston."

Tommy lived down that way, along with his mother. He was likely walking home even now. They glanced at one another and turned in wordless agreement in the direction of the noise.

They weren't the only people drawn by the commotion. By the time they turned onto the narrow street, a ragged knot of perhaps twenty people had gathered halfway up the block. Something white lay on the ground beyond them.

Amelia hung well back as Jonas shouldered his way through. In every group, there was always someone marked by death—someone who'd either survived its touch or was soon to feel it. If she so much as brushed against their skin, Amelia was likely to be plunged into an overpowering vision of the experience. It was another of the "gifts" she'd received from her injury, an ability less useful—and even less pleasant—than channeling the dead.

Bitter experience had taught her to stay out of crowds.

Jonas returned, his face tight. "Let's go."

"What is it?"

Jonas shook his head. "It's nothing to do with us. You don't need to see it."

It was a body, then. Not so shocking. They'd both seen bodies during their time on the streets. But there was something in Jonas's expression Amelia didn't like. Something about the fact of this particular body bothered him. She hesitated, then tucked her hands into her skirts, put her chin down, and wove between the bystanders, ignoring Jonas when he protested behind her.

A pair of police officers stood over a sheet-covered bundle.

Too small to be an adult.

Amelia stopped her forward movement as one held up a hand. "Stay right there, miss. This is police business."

It didn't matter. She was close enough to see the small, bare foot protruding from one end. Her gaze locked on that foot, Amelia nearly gasped when a matching pair of feet stepped into view. Her fists clenched. Reluctantly, she dragged her eyes toward the newly appeared figure, already knowing what she would see. A little girl stood barefoot in the street beside the body, almost solid. Almost alive. But not.

Starched white nightgown. Pointed chin. Curly red hair.

Something in Amelia's chest, a hope she didn't even know she'd been clinging to, crumpled.

Ginny Holloway had been found.

# 3

Amelia's heart ached as she took in the expression of mingled fear and confusion on the girl's face. Ginny's gaze fluttered lightly as a moth over the crowd around her body, never lingering for more than a fraction of a second.

Until it found Amelia.

The sound of the crowd faded to a muted buzz in Amelia's ears as Ginny's eyes locked on her own. She felt the familiar pull deep inside her chest and, without intending it, took half a step forward.

She jerked to a stop with a gasp as a gentle hand closed around her upper arm. Amelia blinked and found Jonas at her side, his own expression guarded.

"Come on," he said. "There's nothing you can do. And Tommy's here. He says he needs to talk to you."

Shaken, Amelia glanced back at the place where Ginny's spirit had stood. It was gone. She released a breath and allowed Jonas to shepherd her away from the scene, unspeakably grateful that he'd interrupted. Surely Ginny couldn't have taken her against her will. Could she? Her guard had been down, yes, but even so, surely a new spirit, and that of a child to boot, couldn't be powerful enough? But the pull had been undeniably strong.

Amelia still didn't know what it was that made some shades more powerful than others. Some of them were thin, vaporous things, barely coherent enough to be channeled at all. They had to be coaxed, and their voices, when they managed to speak, were like the brush of cobwebs against her mind. Others . . . Amelia glanced involuntarily in the direction of the park and suppressed a shudder. If Ginny was like that one, then nothing good could have come from the encounter.

Tommy stood on the sidewalk, carefully removed from the crowd, as if trying to remain unnoticed. He was at a disadvantage, since he still wore the black tailcoat and white cravat that constituted his uniform at the club. He fairly hummed with anxiety as he greeted her.

"Miz Amelia." He nodded toward the body. "Terrible thing."

Amelia nodded, waiting for him to go on. "Jonas said you wanted to talk to me," she said finally.

Tommy hesitated, looking at the crowd around the body. "Not here," he said in a low voice.

He turned and set off without waiting to see if they followed. Amelia and Jonas exchanged a glance. There must be something very wrong for Tommy, whose manners were usually impeccable, to be so terse. They hurried after him. With each block, the sidewalk grew darker as the islands of light cast by the streetlamps grew further apart.

Amelia stayed close to Jonas. This was not a neighborhood where a woman wanted to look as though she were alone. They were surrounded by a mix of one- or two- family houses that probably dated to before the war and multi-story tenement buildings in various states of completion and repair. Most of the latter had half-story basements, a disproportionate number of which seemed to be occupied by saloons. Outside one, a man was slumped over near the top of the stairs, a puddle of vomit beside his head and one hand out-flung into the middle of the sidewalk.

With a sour grunt, Tommy nudged the offending appendage aside with the toe of his shoe as they passed. "This used to be a decent neighborhood," he said apologetically as they passed another man relieving himself against a wall.

Grateful she hadn't worn her good boots, Amelia lifted her skirts and stepped over the runnel of urine trickling across her path as Tommy went on. "Families and such. People worked. Now it's at least half trash. I've been trying to convince Momma to move for years now. We could afford something better. But she won't do it. Says she was here before 'em, and she'll be here after 'em."

"Is that where we're going?" Amelia asked as they approached the end of the block. "Your house?"

"No," Tommy said. "We're headed to Miles's place."

"Miles," Jonas said, sounding surprised. "I didn't know he lived over here, too."

Miles Alston was one of the dozen Negroes working as waiters at the club. Jonas spoke highly of him, but Amelia didn't know him well. She spent little time on the floor, and unlike some of the other staff, Miles had a family. He wasn't one to linger when his shift was over.

Tommy glanced back. "Miles's private. Don't talk much about his personal business. We cross here," he added, gesturing to the intersection, which appeared to be covered in a thick layer of dark, rutted mud.

Amelia knew better. The street sweepers had higher priorities than neighborhoods such as this, and several weeks' worth of horse manure and other offal had mixed with God only knew what—it certainly wasn't rain—to produce an ankle-deep mire. She grimaced and lifted her skirts again as they picked their way across.

As they reached the sidewalk, Amelia drew a breath to ask Tommy why Miles had chosen this neighborhood. Sabine paid her staff well, and Miles, unlike Tommy's mother, surely couldn't have any decades-long attachment to the place. Before she could voice the question, the faint sound of whoops and shouts reached them, and Tommy abruptly stopped walking. Amelia glanced up at him, then followed the direction of his gaze.

Rolling slowly through the intersection at the far end of the block was a police wagon. A gaggle of boys ran alongside, pounding on it with their fists and shouting words she couldn't quite make out. As it gathered speed, one of them bent to scoop up a handful of muck. He straightened and flung it at the wagon's side, where it landed with a splat as the vehicle passed out of sight.

The pursuers lingered for a moment, shaking their fists at the departing van, then began to disperse in little groups of three or four.

One such band walked down the middle of the street toward them, scuffling with one another and exchanging excited and ungrammatical commentary.

"Stupid bastid thought he could hide."

"Run home to his mama like a pansy when he got caught."

"Shame the cops got to him so fast. 'lectric chair's too good for 'em." The boy spat into the street. "Baby-rapin' piece of shit."

Amelia's eyebrows went up at that. They weren't talking about a brawler or pickpocket. She exchanged a glance with Jonas, who stepped into the street and snagged the nearest boy by the arm as he passed. With a curse, he tried to twist away, throwing a wild punch. Jonas rolled his eyes and leaned back to avoid the fist.

"Stop that," he said. "I only want to ask you a few questions."

The boy got a good look at his captor and went still, the progress of his thoughts playing out over his face with comical quickness. He wasn't fool enough to antagonize a man of Jonas's size, but neither did he want to look weak before his friends. He settled for a posture of insolent unconcern.

"The fuck do you want?"

"The police arrested someone?" Jonas asked. "For killing the Holloway girl?"

"Yeah," the boy said. "Just now."

"How do they know he's the one?" Amelia interjected.

"Cause they found him standing over the body, that's how. Miss," he added hastily, after a warning shake from Jonas. His tone was a shade more polite when he went on. "Everybody's talkin' about it. Patrolman turned the corner and found him hunkered over the body. He took off runnin', but they caught up to him pretty quick."

Jonas turned him loose, and he slouched away with his friends. Their voices faded to nothing as Amelia and Jonas turned back to Tommy, who looked grim.

"I guess it was lucky they had a wagon close by," he said. "They would have killed him—a Negro boy they thought killed a white girl."

"Wait," Amelia said. "They didn't say he was—You know, don't you? Who they arrested?"

Tommy hesitated. "It was Amos Alston. Miles's son. He didn't do it," he went on quickly, beginning to walk again, this time at a pace that had Amelia almost trotting at his side in an attempt to keep up. "There's no way. He's a good boy. Fifteen. Works at Steele's—that big laundry over on Vestry Street. Never been in any trouble. I heard they were after him on my way home. When I saw you two in the crowd, I thought maybe you could help."

"Help how?" Jonas said.

"I don't know," Tommy said, running a hand over his face. He sighed and glanced at Amelia, an expression of desperate hope on his face. "You helped Momma back in the spring. And I've seen how some of those people look when they come out of your room at the club. I don't know exactly what it is you have, but you know things. Someone has to help Amos. I thought maybe you could." He swung around again before Amelia could reply, and they turned onto the street where the police wagon had been.

It seemed the entire neighborhood was out in the street. Those who hadn't already been up for the day appeared to have been woken by the commotion, their hair unkempt and wearing whatever clothing had been near at hand. Amelia caught snatches of their conversations as they passed, and it was obvious word of Amos's identity and supposed crime was spreading rapidly.

Tommy cast a contemptuous look at the gossiping neighbors as he led Amelia and Jonas toward a neat little house in the middle of the block. The sidewalk was conspicuously clear of people for ten yards on either side of the door, and light leaked around the edges of windows shut tight despite the warmth of the night.

The door opened almost before he finished knocking, and a girl's worried face appeared in the crack.

"Mr. Franklin," she said in a tone of surprise. "I thought you'd be Dr. Landry. We sent for him." The sound of sobs filtered past her, and she cast a nervous glance over her shoulder. "Mama's . . . she's upset."

"Sarah. Can we come in?" Tommy said. "I've got some people here can maybe help."

Sarah seemed not to have realized he wasn't alone. She glanced behind him, and her eyes widened as she took in Amelia and Jonas. She stepped back and held the door open wider, revealing the toddler balanced on her hip. She hitched him higher, gesturing them inside, then hurried to shut the door behind them.

"Sarah," Tommy said, "this is Miz Amelia and Mister Jonas. They work with your daddy."

Sarah looked at them warily. She appeared to be about twelve years old. Her skin was lighter than Miles's, but her features were a smaller, feminine copy of his. She wore a long nightdress and her hair in two braids down her back. She was barefoot, and Amelia had a momentary flashback to the sight of Ginny's bare feet standing in the street. She blinked away the thought and extended her hand to the girl. "It's nice to meet you."

Sarah shook her hand, seeming both pleased and startled at the greeting.

"And who do we have here?" Jonas asked.

"This is Silas," Sarah said.

Amelia was terrible at guessing babies' ages, but she would have bet Silas was no more than two. He was darker complexioned than his sister, with pudgy cheeks and close-cropped hair. He stuck his thumb in his mouth as he regarded Amelia with wide, dark eyes.

There was a blanket on the floor, and Sarah moved to set him down. Silas began to whine, reaching up for her.

"Stop that," Sarah said absently, but without heat. She handed him a carved wooden horse and brushed a fond hand over his head as Silas began to gnaw on it with determined interest. "He ought to still be asleep," she said, "but all the ruckus woke him up. I can't get him down again. He's teethin'."

"You're doing just fine, lookin' after him," Tommy said, giving her shoulder a reassuring squeeze as he moved past her into the small, cozy-looking space. A rag rug covered the floor, and a pair of worn armchairs sat against one wall. The far back corner was dominated by a coal stove and cooking range. Tommy's mother stood before it, using a folded cloth to lift a kettle off the top. Mrs. Franklin's seamed face turned toward them, and she nodded a greeting to Amelia and Jonas before turning to pour coffee through a strainer into a row of mugs sitting on a battered table. A spindly chair stood at each end, and a pair of backless benches ran along the sides. On one of the benches, a woman sat folded over the table, sobbing into her pillowed arms. Only the top of her head was visible, dark, curly hair twisted into a rough bun.

"She can't stop crying," Sarah said quietly from behind them.

Tommy exchanged a somber look with his mother, who picked up one of the mugs and set it in front of the crying woman with one hand, rubbing her back with the other.

"Polly," she said, "here's coffee ready. You've got to stop this crying, now. It's not going to do Amos a bit of good. And look, you've got company."

With a visible effort, the woman choked off her sobs and raised her head.

Amelia blinked in surprise. Polly's face was swollen and tear-streaked. And it was white.

"Polly," said Tommy, gently, accepting another mug from his mother. "Is Miles here?"

Polly shook her head, fresh tears welling in her eyes.

Sarah answered. "He was here. He'd just gotten home when all the trouble started."

Polly began keening, a low sound in her throat. "They took him. Oh, Mother Mary help me, they took Amos."

The Irish lilt in her voice was evident, even in her distress.

Amelia felt useless. She struggled to think of something to say, but nothing occurred to her. She had no idea why they were even there.

Another knock sounded on the door, and Sarah hurried to answer it, again opening it only a crack. "Dr. Landry," Sarah said, relief apparent in her voice. She swung the door open to reveal a tall, slender, neatly dressed Negro man holding a worn Gladstone bag. "Look, Mama, Doc's here," she said in a falsely bright tone.

Amelia had known there were Negro doctors, but she had never met one before. She tried not to stare at him too obviously as he entered. For his part, Landry barely spared them a glance as he hurried across the room toward Polly. "Polly, how are you feeling?" He spoke in a slow, soothing voice, his words marked by a trace of an unfamiliar accent.

Polly put her hands flat on the tabletop and struggled to her feet as the doctor neared, and Amelia drew in a surprised breath. Miles's wife was heavily pregnant.

Landry waved Tommy's mother away as she moved to help Polly rise. "No, Mother Bea, you know very well you ought not to be lifting anything heavier than that kettle." He glanced around the room, his gaze settling on Amelia. "Miss, if you could help me with her, please."

Amelia was taken aback at the note of expectation in his voice, but moved to Polly's side.

Together, they guided the now silently weeping woman down a short hallway into a neat bedroom. There was a double bed covered in a bright quilt and a heavy cane rocking chair beside the window. Based on the sounds leaking through the closed shutters, it faced the street, and the parts of the neighborhood that hadn't been woken by the earlier clamor were now rising along with the sun. Wagon wheels squeaked and juddered over the rutted street outside as Amelia helped maneuver Polly onto the bed.

"Thank you," the doctor said, in clear dismissal, then turned his attention wholly to his patient.

Amelia stepped back into the hallway, feeling the vaguest tinge of offense at his tone. As she headed back to the main room, she heard the doctor ask, "Have you had any more bleeding?"

"Some. Less than it was, and mostly when I overdo. Miles's been . . ."

Polly's voice grew fainter as Amelia got further away, and the end of her sentence was lost as the front door opened and the din of the street spilled in. Amelia hurried the rest of the way into the main room.

Miles had returned. "I lost the wagon at Broadway," he was saying, his attention on Tommy, "but—"

Amelia's movement must have caught his eye, because he stopped, glanced at her, and frowned, before seeming to realize Jonas was there as well. He straightened and looked at Tommy.

"I brought them," Tommy said. "I thought they might be able to help."

"I don't see how," Miles said, his voice making plain he was struggling to remain polite. He, like Tommy, was still wearing his work clothes. His face was strained, and the collar of his fine broadcloth shirt was dark with sweat, the subtle stripes in the cloth now starkly defined.

"I told you how they helped Momma," Tommy said. He lowered his voice as he went on. "And you've heard the same things I have."

Amelia and Jonas exchanged a glance. What things?

Miles shook his head. "You know I don't believe in all that nonsense. Begging your pardon," he said to Amelia, who waved away the insult. He was hardly the only one to disbelieve. As long as people weren't rude about it, it didn't bother her.

Miles glanced between them, his voice and posture gone stiff. "Thank you for coming, but this is a family matter."

"We understand," said Jonas. "And we don't want to intrude. But truly, we may be able to help, even if it's only in a purely practical way. Amos's going to need a lawyer—a good one. Do you know where to find one who'd take a case like this? One you could afford?"

Miles looked stricken. "Lord, no, I hadn't even thought that far." He rubbed his forehead and looked up. "You're saying you do?"

"I know where to start, at least," said Jonas. "If you'll allow us, we'll go over there once it's likely someone will be in the office. In the meantime, can you tell us what happened?"

"I don't rightly know," Miles said, slumping as his fatigue began to cut through the agitation. "I'd just gotten home. Usually I get here about four o'clock. If Amos isn't already up, I wake him. He's got to be over at the laundry by five, most mornings."

"You didn't realize he was already gone this morning?"

"No," Miles said. "First I knew was when I heard the shouting out in the street. Amos was on the sidewalk with two big policemen holding him down." Miles put a hand over his eyes. "They had his arms all up behind him like they were about to break them, yellin' at him not to move."

"Did he say anything?" Jonas asked.

Miles shook his head, his face tight. "Didn't get a chance. They told him they knew he was the one who killed that little girl. The wagon was already coming down the street. They dragged him over and threw him in. They took him away. My son." Miles struggled to remain composed, but tears stood in his eyes and thickened his voice when he spoke again. "They took my son."

∽

Jonas asked a few more questions, but it was clear to him none of the family was in a position to tell them much more at the moment. They lingered long enough for Amelia to drink a cup of coffee. Jonas had already finished his first and politely declined a second, fearing it might make his eyes pop from his head. The Franklins were clearly of the "float a horseshoe in it" school of coffee-making. Tommy had three cups, and his mother was draining her second as Dr. Landry emerged from the bedroom to tell Miles he'd given Polly a mild sedative and would return to check on her later. In the wake of his departure, Jonas glanced at Amelia, an eyebrow raised. She gave him a minute nod, and the two of them rose and excused themselves as well.

The street didn't look any better in the daylight. Jonas hadn't paid attention to exactly where they were going earlier, but now he recognized where they were. The Alston family lived on Minetta Lane, in the middle of an area known as Little Africa. He'd once had a fascinating discussion with an only slightly inebriated patron at the club, a man who said his work involved documenting the history of such things. The street's pronounced curve, he said, had come about because it was a good deal older than many of the city's other, straighter streets. Minetta had been the name of a long-since buried creek, and the road had grown up along its path. The neighborhood had been a Negro enclave for decades, home to many of the domestic servants who worked for the wealthy residents living just north of Washington Square. But when those people moved further north, the jobs went with them, and the area began to decline. As the city's population swelled, so did Little Africa's, with much of the growth coming from an influx of desperately poor Irish and Italian immigrants looking for cheap rent. As a result, it was one of the most racially mixed neighborhoods in the city, home to the infamous "black and tan" saloons, which served black and white customers together.

It was also, Jonas thought as they walked back toward Houston, a neighborhood that appeared to be at war with itself. The houses that had not been replaced with tenement buildings were split between those that remained individual residences and those that had been chopped up into boarding houses. Some of each had neatly swept yards and window boxes bright with flowers. Others had sagging porches and broken windows with newspapers stuffed in the holes. A pair of women—one black, one white—were chatting amiably on the steps of a tenement house, while in the building next door the basement saloon appeared to be doing an impressive business for a Monday morning.

"I hadn't realized Miles was married to a white woman," Amelia said as they approached the streetcar stop. "I suppose that's what Tommy meant when he said Miles had his reasons for living around here. It's probably one of the only places where no one bothers them."

"About their marriage, at least. Plenty of other things to worry about. It's not the most dangerous neighborhood in the city, but it's not far off," Jonas said, as the streetcar approached. It was horse drawn, rather than one of the new electric ones with an overhead cable.

Beside him, Amelia made a little sound of relief, and he glanced down at her with a grin. In early June, an electric streetcar had careened out of control when the mechanism intended to cut the power failed, sending the car speeding along the track and smashing into several other cars before someone managed to interrupt the circuit and bring it to a stop. The shaken passengers had been unharmed, but the incident had made an impression on Amelia.

"You're going to have to get over it eventually," Jonas said as he paid the dime's fare and they climbed aboard. "All of them are going to be electric before long."

"So you keep saying," she replied as they settled into seats near the back.

They rode silently for a few blocks. A man in front of them left a newspaper on the seat as he exited, and Jonas leaned over to grab it. Amos's arrest had come too late to make the morning papers, but there were no doubt extra editions being printed at that very moment. Jonas grimaced. When his name inevitably leaked, it was going to be very, very bad for Miles and his family.

"Do you think Sidney can do anything?" Amelia asked, looking at the paper.

"I don't know," Jonas said. "He'll try." Sidney would want to help. Whether he would be able to or not was another question. Any Negro accused of such a notorious crime—guilty or not—would have an uphill fight.

Amelia pulled the cord to ring the bell as they approached their stop. She was quiet as they stepped down to the sidewalk, and Jonas assumed she was thinking of the case until he looked down and found her pretending not to watch him. He glanced around them, and a sudden chill swept up his spine. He hadn't had occasion to approach Sidney's office from this direction recently. They were nearing the place where Jonas had been shot earlier in the year.

The moment of recognition felt like a boulder landing in his gut.

"Are you—" Amelia began.

"I'm fine," Jonas said abruptly. The words sounded only a little breathless. With an effort of will, he set off down the sidewalk as if his chest didn't feel tight. As if the hairs on the back of his neck weren't standing up. As if he never woke in a cold sweat from dreams of running footsteps behind him as he walked alone along this very street. He passed the place he'd fallen without breaking his stride, his eyes straight ahead. He fought the urge to glance down to see if the bloodstain still lingered. That was foolishness. It was long since washed away.

Jonas refused to allow his turmoil to show as they reached Sidney's office, though his legs felt as if he'd run ten miles. He reached for the bell, hoping Amelia didn't notice the slight tremble in his finger. "It's not even eight yet. He may not be there," he said casually, proud that his voice was steady.

Sidney was not, but a clerk at the front desk confirmed that his secretary, Morris, was.

"Miss Matthew," Morris said as he emerged from a hallway to greet them. "How nice to see you again. And Mr. Vincent. I don't believe we've actually been introduced. I'm David Morris, Mr. White's assistant. You're looking a great deal better than the last time I saw you."

"Having been unconscious and on the verge of death then, I'm glad to hear it," Jonas said heartily, shaking the hand Morris offered as he looked the man over. Sidney spoke of him as an invaluable and trusted subordinate.

Not so trusted that he knew about the two of them, of course. "I've been told you were a great help that night. I'm glad to get the chance to thank you in person."

"Merely doing my job," Morris said. "What can I do for you this morning?"

"I don't suppose you know when Sid—Ah, Mr. White will be in? We need to speak with him about a matter of some urgency."

"He should be here shortly," Morris said. "Could I offer you coffee in the meanwhile?"

They both declined emphatically enough that Morris blinked before he recovered and led them to a waiting area with a pair of heavy chairs upholstered in dark green velvet. Amelia took the one that put her back to the front door, leaving Jonas the one against the wall. She did it so casually he would have thought nothing of it, had it not been for the swift glance she darted at him before choosing her seat.

Over the next twenty minutes, the firm's employees drifted in, giving them polite but curious looks as they passed. Most had the shiny, open look of privilege, the sleek, well-fed confidence that came from thinking their place in the world was natural and secure. But there were a few whose bodies and faces spoke of childhood deprivation. There was a wary intensity to them, the sort that came from having to strive for your position, and being aware that it could be taken away if you didn't fight to keep it. Their eyes inevitably found Jonas's, and he exchanged small nods with them, like recognizing like in a way that couldn't have been explained to the others.

When Sidney stepped through the front door, a flash of surprised pleasure washed over his face as he saw Jonas before he hastily rearranged his expression into one of polite welcome. Jonas felt the little upwelling of happiness he always experienced in Sidney's presence, marred only slightly by the constant need to not show it. When they'd first met at the club, Jonas would never have guessed that this quiet, unassuming man would become one of the two most important people in his life.

"Jonas. Amelia," Sidney said, stepping forward to shake their hands. "I wasn't expecting the two of you, or I'd have been here sooner. I hope you haven't been waiting long?"

"Not long. But we need to talk to you," Jonas said, standing. "It's important."

Sidney nodded at once. "Come to my office."

He led them down a long, dark-paneled hallway. Solemn-faced portraits glowered from the walls. Jonas glanced through a doorway as they passed—a single big room, with at least a dozen desks. Those near the front of the room were notably smaller, hardly larger than schoolhouse desks, and most were already occupied. Clerks and lower-level associates, Jonas surmised. Best to already be hard at work before the boss arrives. Early birds, scratching for worms. Three of the nicer desks toward the back of the room remained empty.

The room across the hall was twin to the first, in size if not in function. A single long table sat in the middle, surrounded by chairs. Bookshelves lined the walls, filled with impressive, gilt-limned volumes.

The hallway opened up into another foyer with a pair of doors in the back wall. Morris sat behind a desk outside the right-hand door.

"Good morning, Mr. White," Morris said.

"Good morning, Morris. Please see we're not disturbed," Sidney said as he led them into his office.

It was easily the same size as the room where the herd of associates toiled cheek by jowl. There was a large window on the back wall, covered by heavy silk draperies tied with gold cord. Beneath it was a wide velvet sofa. A sparkling crystal decanter full of amber liquor sat beside a quartet of glasses on a long, dark table flanked with bookshelves as large and laden as those in the conference room. The center of the room was dominated by an enormous desk, which in addition to the normal office paraphernalia held a bronze lamp with an elaborate shade made of bits of stained glass. A pair of dark leather chairs sat before the desk. The room spoke of vast wealth, impeccable breeding, and, above all, power.

Jonas, who had never had occasion to see it before, turned in a full circle, taking it all in with a low whistle.

"I know," said Sidney in the tone of one harassed by a circumstance he cannot help. "It's ridiculous. The five other associates share the office down the hall with half a dozen clerks. All of them are older than me and have been practicing longer. I warned my father they'd all hate me, but he insisted. And I was right," he added as he sat behind the desk. "Not a one of them is more than civil to me. Now, what's going on? What have you done that you need a lawyer first thing Monday morning?" It was clear he was only half-joking.

"It's not what we've done," Jonas said, tearing his attention away from the decor. Quickly, he explained everything that had happened that morning.

"My god," Sidney said when he'd finished, steepling his fingers under his chin.

"Can you help?" Amelia asked. "There's no way the family can afford a good lawyer for him. And he's going to need one."

"Too right he will," Sidney said, frowning. "We're not a criminal defense firm. Although we have done some work for existing clients. Quietly. More a courtesy than anything. But something like this . . ." He shook his head. "It will be anything but quiet." He sat, staring at nothing for a long moment, then stood with a sigh and reached for his hat and briefcase. "Let's go."

"Now?" Amelia asked.

"Yes," Sidney said, moving past them and putting his hand on the doorknob. "The sooner the better. But let's don't talk about it until we're on the way. Right now, the fewer people who know what I'm doing, the better."

They followed him back through the door, where Morris looked up, curiosity plain on his face.

"I'm going out, Morris," Sidney said. "I shouldn't be more than a couple of hours."

"I'll move your first meeting," Morris said, making a note. He hesitated. "And if your father asks—"

Sidney sighed. "I'd rather you told him you hadn't seen me yet today. But of course," he said with a sour look toward the room where the associates worked, "one of them would certainly contradict that story. Tell him I didn't say where I was going, just that I would be back in time for our lunch."

They attracted some curious glances from the associates' room as they passed, but Sidney paid them no mind. On the sidewalk, he raised his hand for a cab, looking anxiously in both directions before his shoulders dropped in apparent relief. "I'd rather not run into my father just yet."

"Better to ask for forgiveness than permission?" Jonas said.

"Something like that."

"What are you going to do?" Jonas asked as a cab pulled to a stop and they climbed in.

"I'll register as his counsel, at least for now. I'll demand to see him and make sure he knows not to talk to anyone except his lawyers, whoever they turn out to be. And I'll make sure the guards know there's someone paying attention to what happens to him."

The city was fully awake, and the morning traffic meant it took them a full forty-five minutes to travel the mile and a half from Sidney's office to the city block occupied by the Halls of Justice. Situated on the edge of the notoriously violent Five Points neighborhood, the complex housed both the city's municipal court system and its main prison. Before the state began sending the condemned to Sing Sing for electrocution three years before, hundreds of men—and more than a few women—had their necks stretched in the building's courtyard. That fact, as well as a rumor that the building's designers had been inspired by a photograph of an ancient Egyptian mausoleum, had given rise to its more colorful sobriquet: The Tombs.

Jonas couldn't suppress a thread of unease as they mounted the broad, dark stone steps of the Centre Street entrance, Amelia fidgeting beside him. It was impossible not to feel as though they were entering a massive stone vault, and that once the doors closed behind them, they'd be trapped forever. Or perhaps it was only impossible if one had lived, as he and Amelia had, the sort of criminal youth that could have easily landed them here. Sidney, Jonas noticed, climbed the stairs with the relaxed confidence of a law-abiding citizen.

At any rate, thanks to a combination of luck and skill, neither Jonas nor Amelia had ever been inside. But they'd heard the stories from those who had. The building had been constructed on ground that had once been the site of a freshwater collect pond. A main water source for much of New York City in its early days, by the beginning of the century it was a stagnant, filthy mire. City planners decided to fill it in. They did a lackluster job, however, and the entire area remained prone to seepage and subsidence. Constructed in 1838, the building had begun to sink as soon as it was completed, and it was notorious among the city's criminal classes for its damp, squalid conditions. More than one associate of Jonas and Amelia's had returned from a stay vowing to do whatever was necessary to avoid repeating the experience.

Once inside, Sidney strode through the corridors as if he owned them. "They should have Amos in the boys' cells," he said. They followed him to the entrance, where an unshaven, bored-looking guard sat behind a desk.

"I'm here to register as counsel for Amos Alston." Sidney's tone was that of a man who expected to be obeyed. "I want to see my client immediately."

The guard looked him up and down, unimpressed. "And who're they?" he asked, jerking his chin at Jonas and Amelia, who stood behind him.

"My associates." Sidney spoke as if it were entirely unremarkable that he would turn up in his fine suit accompanied by two people—one of them a woman, no less—in rough, rumpled clothing.

"Associates," the man repeated, his tone making clear what he thought.

Sidney appeared to be about to object, but the man forestalled him with a raised hand. "It don't matter to me who they are, or you either, for that matter. Alston ain't here."

"What do you mean he isn't here? Where is he?"

"Killed a little girl. We couldn't put him in with the rest. Wouldn't be safe. For him, you unnerstand. He had to be somewhere more secure." The man spoke with a faux virtuosity that grated against Jonas's nerves.

It appeared to have the same effect on Sidney, who looked at him through narrowed eyes. "You cannot deny me access to my client."

"I'm not denying anything. You want to see Alston, you go on over to the main cells. They've got him over there."

"They put a fifteen-year-old boy who hasn't been convicted of anything yet in the men's jail?" Jonas blurted.

Sidney and Amelia looked as horrified as he felt, but the guard only smirked. Sidney didn't waste time with a rebuke, only spun on his heel and led them away with the sort of rapid stride that indicated real alarm.

The men's prison was a building within a building, linked to the outer facility only by a raised metal walkway. Jonas had heard former inmates call it the Bridge of Sighs. Their footsteps echoed off the heavy stone surrounding them as they crossed. The bridge, kept in constant shadow by the angle of the buildings, was cooler than any other place Jonas had been in weeks. There was even a faint breeze in the middle.

Jonas paused in the center and looked down into the courtyard, at the area where the gallows had once stood. When he'd been shot, he'd had no time for deep consideration of his mortality. Instead, the only thing he'd felt was a flash of distant amazement that it was actually happening. Jonas had thought himself more comfortable with death than most, but in that moment he had discovered that was self-delusion. He hadn't believed death could happen to him. Perhaps, deep down, everyone felt that way. After all, throughout one's entire life, death only ever happened to other people.

How many had met their end in this place? How many people had been led out, forced to climb the scaffold and stand as the ropes were looped around their necks and pulled taut? What had they thought about as they waited through the droned prayers? What had they felt as they waited for the drop, knowing it was coming, knowing they could number their remaining breaths?

And what of the men charged with tightening the noose and pulling the lever? How many men had stood where Jonas stood now, watching? Did they even hear the prayers for the souls of the condemned, or did such things eventually become nothing more than mundane background noise? And the sound of the drop. It must have echoed off these walls. He imagined pointed toes swaying above the paving stones and shuddered.

There were so many different ways to die.

The others had reached the door to the inner building, so Jonas pulled himself away from the railing and followed after them. The door swung open, and they stepped inside. The space was grimy and cramped. It reeked of damp, of filth, of men confined. Another guard stepped forward, his appearance a match for the room. He was greasy-haired, with a florid complexion and a stained uniform straining over his soft middle.

Sidney drew himself up and spoke before the guard could. "I am Amos Alston's attorney. I want to see my client at once."

The man grinned, revealing a blackened front tooth. "Attorney, huh?" He made a disgusting sound in his throat and spat a gob of something on the floor. It landed a bare inch from the toe of Sidney's shoe, but he didn't flinch, and Jonas felt a flash of pride.

"You can see him if you want, but it don't matter."

Sidney's voice was cool. "Why is that?"

"Because he's already confessed."

# 4

"onfessed?" Amelia blurted, her heart plummeting.

"Yep," the man said, clearly relishing her dismay. "Told us everything. How he grabbed her outside her parents' house during the party, how he kept her hidden." He leaned forward and lowered his voice, as if his next words were only for her. "How he had his way with her." The salacious way he looked at her as he spoke that last phrase turned her stomach. Evidently, it showed on her face, because he leaned back with a pleased grin as he finished. "Then choked the life out of her and left her in the street like trash."

Jonas stepped forward, threat clear in his posture, but Sidney stopped him with a hand to the chest. "Be that as it may," he said, and his voice sounded completely unaffected by what he'd just heard, "we're not leaving until we've seen him."

"I ain't tryin' to stop you," he said. "But I can't leave my post. You'll have to wait til someone's free to take you down. Sign yerselves in here." He thrust a dirty clipboard at them.

They signed, then drew to one side. Amelia drew a breath to speak, but Sidney stopped her with a gesture. "Not here."

After a long ten minutes, another guard emerged from a heavy metal door behind the first. The noise that came with him was atrocious. It cut off when he closed the door with a loud clang.

"Got a visitor here for Alston," the first guard said, before the second had made it two steps in their direction.

"I just climbed all the way back up here," said the second guard with a grimace. "Why don't you take a turn?"

The first glowered back at him. "I'll take a turn putting my boot in your ass if you don't get moving."

With a beleaguered sigh, the guard turned and gestured for them to follow him, fumbling with the ring of keys on his belt and opening the door again. They stepped through behind him, Sidney first, then Jonas, and finally Amelia.

The stench was like running into a wall. Amelia breathed through her mouth trying to avoid it, then remembered what Jonas had once told her about odors being particulate. She closed her mouth and covered her nose with her sleeve instead. The guard didn't seem to notice as he led them down a staircase. It grew worse the further they descended. They must have been lower than street level by the time they finally left the staircase. The walls were slimy with wet, and the mingled smell of rot and sewage was overwhelming. Amelia couldn't keep herself from gagging. There were drains set in the floor every few yards, but they were useless, either clogged or too far beneath the grade to work. Cloudy, stagnant liquid pooled above the grates, greasily iridescent.

They passed through a narrow corridor with stark electric lights overhead and cells along one wall. Most seemed to be empty, though Amelia could make out a few wretched occupants huddled on low cots as they passed. She had a brief, sharp memory of being led down a similar, if notably less filthy, corridor on her first day in the asylum some six months before. A moment later, the thought was driven from her head as a dirty hand darted out of a cell and snagged at her sleeve. She jerked away with a gasp.

The men turned at the noise. Before Jonas could do more than scowl, the guard yanked a nightstick from his belt and slammed it across the bars, striking at the prisoner's hands until he fell back with a howl of pain.

"You'll want to stay well back from the cells," he advised, then turned to continue down the hall.

Amelia slid along the slime-covered wall, preferring the ruin of her dress to being grabbed by another of the ragged men. Ahead of her, Sidney got as far away from the bars as he could while still trying not to touch the wall. His suit was undoubtedly worth ten of her dress. Jonas remained solidly in the middle of the walkway, casting looks at the cells that warned of dire consequences if anyone else dared try anything.

The guard stopped at the last cell in the row, pulled another ring of keys from an inner pocket, and inserted one into the door. "Alston, wake up, you little sack of shit," he barked. "White folks here to see you. One of 'em says he's your lawyer." He glanced at them. "You can have five minutes."

"That's not—" Sidney began.

"Five minutes," the man repeated, his face hard. "I have better things to do than stand around down here all day while you fawn over murdering filth."

Sidney's face tightened, but he nodded and stepped toward the open door of the cell. Amelia and Jonas followed.

The light in the cell was even worse than in the corridor. As her eyes adjusted, Amelia made out a low cot at the back of the cell, with a dark shape like a bundle of rags piled on it. It didn't move.

"Amos," Sidney said quietly, "are you awake? Can you let us see you?"

The bundle moved and became a boy, tall and thin and dressed in rags. He pushed himself up with a groan of pain, and Amelia couldn't smother a cry of pity.

Even in the low light, it was obvious Amos Alston had been beaten within an inch of his life. He moved slowly, like a man of eighty rather than a boy of fifteen, one arm clutched across his ribs, the other in a makeshift sling, the forearm clearly broken, the ends of the bone bulging against the skin as if they would tear through at any moment. He'd torn his shirt into strips to make it, and the lower half of his battered torso was fully visible, dark skin with even darker patches where bruises were already forming.

But it was his face that broke Amelia's heart. Both eyes were blackened, puffed nearly shut. His nose was grotesquely swollen, and he breathed shallowly through lips split and crusted with blood. A ragged cut, the edges gaping and red, began at one eyebrow and continued nearly to his hairline.

"Well," said Jonas in a tone of disgust and barely contained rage, "we know why he confessed, at least."

"I was afraid of this," Sidney said heavily. He stepped toward Amos, who flinched away.

Sidney stopped. "It's all right," he said in a low voice. "None of us are going to hurt you. I know you're in pain, and I'm going to get you some help. My name is Sidney White. Your parents sent me. I'm your lawyer."

Amos made an incoherent sound, and after a beat it came to Amelia. It was a laugh of disbelief.

Jonas stepped around Sidney. "Amos," he said. "I work with your father. Maybe he's mentioned me. Jonas Vincent?"

Amos made another sound. This one had an affirmative quality. He sagged back against the wall, and his face twisted with pain at the contact. There was no way he could answer any questions now.

Amelia stepped forward. "Let me help you lie back down. We'll get you a doctor," she said, having no idea how she was going to keep that promise. She put a careful hand out, then hesitated, her habitual caution about touching people reasserting itself. This boy was accused of murder. At the very least, he'd been in close proximity to the corpse. She wasn't sure if touching him would trigger her gift. Amelia thinned her lips and deliberately placed a hand on the back of Amos's head, holding her breath. When nothing happened, she used her other hand to help guide him back down onto the cot.

She was as gentle as she could be, but Amos was still panting with pain by the time she withdrew.

"Try not to move," Sidney said. "I'm going to do everything I can. In the meantime, no matter what anyone promises you, don't talk about what happened. Not with anyone. Do you understand?"

The boy's chin moved half an inch.

As they stepped out of the cell, Amelia turned back to look one last time. There was no hope in Amos's eyes as they left him.

As they emerged from the cell, the waiting officer gave them a look of mock surprise. "Finished already?"

The tight rein on his temper that Jonas had been holding since stepping into the cell and seeing Amos slipped, and he could barely stop himself from lunging at the smirking guard.

Sidney anticipated him, speaking before he could do more than shift his weight. "Don't," he said, his voice sharp. "It's not worth it. We can't afford to waste the time."

Jonas seethed throughout the climb back up the stairs. The macabre thoughts he'd harbored on their first trip across the Bridge of Sighs were replaced with speculation about whether or not the drop to the courtyard would be enough to kill. He'd like to find the man—or men, he'd wager—who'd administered the beating to that boy and find out.

His fury had cooled enough for him to be rational again by the time they reached the warden's office, on the top floor of the outer building. In the hallway outside, Sidney paused—apparently to assure himself Jonas wasn't going to attack anyone—then marched through the door with impressive self-assurance.

The warden had a majestic view of Centre Street and an officious secretary, whose nose wrinkled at their approach. Jonas scowled, aware that the stench of the lower cells still clung to them. Amelia lifted her chin, the flush in her cheeks telling him she'd noticed the reaction as well. Sidney acted as though he noticed nothing wrong. At the news that Amos Alston's attorney had arrived and wished to discuss his client's treatment the secretary's eyebrows climbed toward his hairline. He directed them to a waiting area, then disappeared through a door, all the while with the air of a man going through what was clearly a formality. It was plain that he expected to return shortly with orders to toss them out.

The secretary returned a moment later, his astonishment apparent. "He'll see you," he said, gesturing for Sidney to follow him.

Amelia and Jonas took seats in the waiting area. Amelia perched on the edge of hers, clearly trying to spare the upholstery from whatever substances her dress had collected from the basement walls. A moment later, the secretary returned alone and resumed work, looking disgruntled.

With wry amusement, Jonas leaned toward Amelia and muttered, under the cover of the clacking typewriter, "I guarantee he was hoping he'd get to stay and listen."

She gave him a faint smile in response.

Sidney reappeared about twenty minutes later, his face strained and his lips pressed together in a thin line. Behind him was a well-dressed, prosperous-looking man with carefully groomed side whiskers and a distinct air of self-importance.

The man stopped beside the secretary's desk to issue a quiet instruction as Sidney rejoined them in their corner. Jonas made as if to speak, but Sidney shook his head—a tiny movement, but enough that Jonas cut himself off.

They waited in freighted silence as the secretary inserted a new sheet of paper into the machine. He typed in rapid bursts as the man spoke, apparently taking dictation. When he was done, he tore the sheet from the typewriter and handed it to his boss. The older man signed the bottom of the document with a flourish, folded it into an envelope, and strode toward them. He hesitated a moment before he handed it to Sidney.

"If you've set your mind on doing this, then so be it. This should get you what you need," he said. "I cannot say I think much of your choice, my boy, but I suppose you'll do as you wish."

Sidney tucked the envelope into the inner pocket of his coat as the man disappeared back down the hallway.

"What is—" began Jonas, but stopped when Sidney raised a hand. He didn't stop outside the office, but continued on until they were back on the wide granite steps out front. His back straight and his face impassive, he steered them out of the path of traffic, onto a far corner of the portico.

"What's happening?" Jonas asked. "Who was that? He's not what I expected the warden to look like."

"That wasn't the warden," Sidney said, his voice tight. "That was De Lancy Nicoll, the District Attorney. He happened to be in the warden's office discussing the Alston case when the secretary came to say I was there. He might not have been willing to speak to me, except . . ." Sidney's eyes closed. His shoulders slumped, and he sighed and pinched the bridge of his nose. "He knows my father. Damn it," he said, more to himself than to the two of them. "De Lancy is probably telephoning him even as we speak. He's not going to like it. I'd hoped to be able to tell him myself, but . . ." Sidney shook his head. "Well, I'll have to deal with that later. There's nothing to be done about it now. We have more immediate concerns."

"Such as?"

"They're in a rush. They're going to do the postmortem examination of Ginny Holloway later today, and they're holding the inquest tomorrow morning to bring charges against Amos."

"So soon?" Amelia said.

"That's not the worst of it." Sidney's voice was grim. "Murder is a state crime, and the trial won't be scheduled for at least a few months. Once Amos is indicted—and right now there's not a damned thing I can do to prevent it—De Lancy wants him out of the city. He's going to send him out to Sing Sing."

Jonas swore, loudly enough that a few passersby turned their heads in his direction. He ignored their censorious looks. The state prison at Ossining was notorious for its violence and brutality. The guards were hardly better than the prisoners. For a Negro boy accused of killing a little white girl . . .

"It's as good as a death sentence," he said, shaking his head.

Sidney looked tired. "I wouldn't give you a nickel for his chances of making it to trial. He's going to be notorious. He'll have a target on his back, and I guarantee someone will put a knife in it. He'll be lucky to last a week."

Amelia spoke. "When will they send him?"

If possible, Sidney looked even grimmer. "Friday morning."

"There must be something we can do," Amelia said, sounding as sick as Jonas felt.

"Precious little," Sidney said. "There's no chance I can stop the indictment—not when they're moving this quickly. Not when they have a confession from the person they found standing over the body. And if we want any chance of stopping the transfer, it's not going to be enough to raise doubts. We have to prove Amos absolutely did not do it."

After a long pause, Jonas said aloud what they were all thinking. "The only way to do that is to find out who did."

Sidney nodded. "And we have four days to do it."

# 5

There was an appalled silence in the wake of Sidney's declaration. Amelia opened her mouth, then closed it again, unable to think of anything helpful to say.

"I won a few concessions," Sidney said finally. "I convinced De Lancy to move Amos to the boys' cells and make sure he sees a doctor. And," he said, lightly touching the pocket where he'd tucked the envelope, "I got him to agree we could have someone there to observe the postmortem."

Amelia caught Jonas glancing at her from the corner of his eye. A touch of anxiety, unrelated to the morning's events, appeared in her stomach as she understood.

"Is that necessary?" she asked.

"Absolutely. Coroner is an elected position in New York City."

Amelia grimaced. Jonas let out a groan. Everyone knew city politics were utterly corrupt. Cronyism and connections were far more important than a man's ability or interest in serving the public.

"Precisely," Sidney said. "It doesn't even require a medical degree. Since the coroner system was put in place, there have been two who were saloon-keepers and one who was a butcher by trade. I don't know who's been assigned the case, and even if whoever he is knows his business, the politics of this whole thing mean there's no guarantee we can trust his report. We have to have someone in the room we know is both competent and honest. If the body offers clues, we can't afford for them to be missed or ignored."

Amelia spoke, knowing it was hopeless. "I'm sure Dr. Landry would—"

Sidney was already shaking his head. "I'm not sure even the letter would get him in, and even if it did, no one would listen to him. And we can't spend time hunting someone else. It'll have to be Andrew."

She waited for Jonas to offer to go. But a glance at his face told her he wasn't going to. Damn him. She fought not to scowl.

She must not have managed it, because Sidney sighed. "I can send a clerk from the office with the message, if you really don't want to see him, but—"

"No." Amelia avoided their eyes. "I'll go. He'll have questions." She put out a hand.

Sidney handed her the letter, along with some money. "Take a cab. You shouldn't walk alone through this neighborhood."

Amelia nodded, her shoulders tight.

Jonas flagged down a cab and took her hand to help her in, speaking in a low voice as she put one foot on the step. "You know, this could be a good thing. Maybe even—"

"Don't." She yanked her hand away, feeling herself flush. She didn't look at him as she settled into the seat. If she looked and found him hiding a smile, she would have to kill him.

Her stomach was tight as the cab began to move. The streets were choked with traffic, making their progress slow. Amelia's foot jiggled against the floorboards. Every muscle in her body felt like it was strung with piano wire. She took a breath and tried to make herself relax.

She wished with all her heart that they'd ignored the shouts that morning and gone ahead to the park as they'd planned. If they had, she wouldn't be here now, trying to master the turmoil in her gut as the cab headed toward the stately, leafy neighborhood where Andrew Cavanaugh's boarding house was located. Despite the friendship they had developed at the asylum—and the palpable sense that it might turn into something more—she had not seen the young doctor in nearly two months.

Their last meeting had been at an early July breakfast Sidney hosted for the four of them; a celebration, he'd said, of Jonas's recovery and a successful conclusion to their investigation. Amelia had been nervous at the prospect as Andrew had evinced a degree of discomfort after learning of Jonas's romantic proclivities. She'd fretted his unease might show at such an intimate gathering.

As it turned out, she needn't have worried. When she and Jonas arrived at the restaurant—tired and rumpled after their long shift at the club—they found both Sidney and Andrew already there, freshly dressed for their respective days and deep in animated discussion. They had, they explained after greeting the new arrivals, discovered they were both Harvard men. They'd already spent a pleasant twenty minutes reminiscing about favorite Boston haunts and identifying mutual acquaintances. There were apparently even some nebulous business ties between branches of their families. Far from being uncomfortable, Andrew appeared to be in his element as he chatted with the wealthy young lawyer.

It was disorienting.

Their unexpected rapport continued throughout the meal. Jonas seemed to enjoy watching them, but it left Amelia feeling as though she'd missed a step somewhere. She hung back, tongue-tied and awkward.

As they were leaving the restaurant—Andrew and Sidney bound for work and Amelia and Jonas heading home to bed—Andrew made his way to her side.

"I'm glad I got to see you," he said.

A warm rush of pleasure filled her chest, but cooled abruptly with his next words.

"I wanted to tell you I'm leaving for Philadelphia tomorrow."

"For how long?" Amelia blurted, unable to keep a note of dismay from entering her voice.

"A week. I need to be there. For the anniversary." He blinked hard and turned to stare out at the street, and Amelia's own throat tightened in sympathy as she laid a hand on his forearm. His sister's death nearly a year before had been a devastating loss. Amelia knew, better than anyone, how close they'd been, having channeled Susannah's spirit so Andrew might tell her goodbye. Amelia had felt Susannah's deep love for him, her anguish and regret at having to leave him behind.

Andrew covered her hand with his own and turned back to her. "You're the only reason I think I'll be able to bear it at all," he said in a low voice, and that warm feeling washed through her again. "But I've punished my family long enough for something that wasn't their fault. I need to go and try to make it right."

"I'm glad you're going," she said, meaning it.

He looked down at her. "When I get back, I . . . could I see you?"

Amelia took a deep breath before she answered, aware she was taking a step toward something new. "I'd like that."

"I'll send word when I return," he promised, squeezing her hand with a farewell smile.

Amelia played the morning over in her head in the following days. The way Andrew had looked at her brought a flush of pleasure every time she thought of it, but remembering bits of the earlier conversation left her uneasy. Andrew had mentioned on the island that his family was "prominent," but based on some of the things he'd said that morning, she suspected he had understated the case. She finally approached Sidney, who confirmed it, seeming surprised she didn't know. The Cavanaughs were, it turned out, one of the wealthiest families in Philadelphia. Andrew's mother was somehow related to the governor; his older brother was expected to run for the state legislature; and the family line could be traced back to some of the area's earliest settlers. "Prominent" did not begin to cover it.

All the anticipation she had felt turned to anxiety. Amelia spent the rest of the week imagining Andrew sleeping in his childhood home, which in her mind was a slightly smaller version of the block-sized Vanderbilt mansion on 57th Street. With the passage of a year, the family's mourning period would be ended. Perhaps his parents would host a dinner party to celebrate their return to society—and the return of their prodigal son. Or did wealthy Philadelphians leave the city for the summer the way rich New Yorkers did? She didn't know. She pictured white-gloved servants hovering beside his elbow, lifting domed silver covers from bone china plates. At the other end of the table, bank presidents and railroad investors negotiated deals as their wives chatted about whatever such wives discussed. How hard it was to find good servants, probably. Their charity work. Their children's accomplishments.

Amelia encountered wealthy men at the club on a nightly basis, but the women who accompanied them were never their wives, and from the conversations she overheard, few of them fell into the category of 'lady.'

After dwelling on it for a week she was feeling . . . not betrayed, exactly. Andrew hadn't lied to her. There had been no reason for him to outline his pedigree on the island. And he'd been estranged from his family, besides. But if he was reconciling with them, that changed things. Amelia felt as though she'd been walking a path and suddenly encountered an obstacle not marked on the map.

When Andrew returned to New York, he sent her a note inviting her to dinner at what she knew was one of the finest restaurants in the city. Amelia read it half a dozen times that day. And then, with a hollow feeling in the pit of her stomach, wrote a stiff little note declining. She sealed the envelope and sent it before she could change her mind.

He sent a second, more tentative missive, suggesting lunch and a visit to one of the city's museums. Her hand shook as she penned another polite refusal, and she had to copy it over when she blotted the page.

There was a short delay before his third and final note. It was a model of polite withdrawal, though Amelia thought she could see his hurt and bafflement in the strokes of the pen. Andrew wished her well and declared himself at her service should she have need of him.

And then there was silence. He didn't write again.

Jonas tried to argue with her. "Just talk to him," he said, his exasperation clear. "So what if his family is rich? He already knows where we come from, and he doesn't care. If it doesn't matter to him, it shouldn't matter to you."

"It does matter. You know it does." She refused to discuss it beyond that, no matter how he prodded.

It was for the best. There were some gaps that couldn't be bridged. They'd been brought together at the asylum under extraordinary conditions. They'd had to trust one another. It had created an artificial sense of intimacy. Of equality. But they weren't equals. And only a fool would let herself develop feelings—real, deeply rooted feelings, not the little green tendrils that had sprouted on the island—for a man she couldn't have. Better to root them out, to end it now, while they could continue to think well of one another.

And Amelia would never deny she did think well of Andrew Cavanaugh. He was one of the most essentially decent men she'd ever met. He cared about his patients, those lost, friendless women—many of them trapped as much inside their own minds as inside the asylum walls. His gentleness and patience were not things she'd often encountered—especially in men. Though, to be fair, gentleness and patience were not highly prized in the world she came from, where keeping your belly full every day was a struggle. The quieter qualities were expensive, and most people she'd known couldn't afford them. Jonas was the most brilliant person she'd ever known, but it would never have been enough to save him if he hadn't been able to hold his own in a fight.

Everything about Andrew belonged to a more civilized world. When he got angry, he used his voice instead of his fists. There was no swagger, no flash to him. Instead there was a solidity, a constancy. A comfort as plain as warm water and clean sheets at the end of the day. But he was not passionless. There had been a moment between them, the previous spring, when he had touched her and she had felt the intensity in him, heard his breathing grow ragged. The fingertip he'd trailed down the back of her neck and across her shoulder had left a burning trail marking its passage. They'd been interrupted, and nothing more had happened.

And now Amelia had chosen to make sure it never would.

It was for the best, she told herself again. She did not know how to live in his world, and he wasn't suited to hers. And despite the confidences they'd shared, there were still so many things he didn't know. Things that hadn't been relevant at the asylum, but would be if their relationship progressed. Things that would inevitably change the way he saw her.

The cab came to a stop with a little jerk, startling Amelia out of her thoughts before she could venture further down that path. She stepped down to the sidewalk on unwilling legs and focused on the house. The address was a good one, but the facade was somewhat shabby. Andrew had said his landlady was a widow, that she took in gentlemen boarders in an attempt to make ends meet. Looking at the house, it was clear she wasn't succeeding. Viewed beside its neighbors, there was a marked air of creeping decline.

Anticipation and dread warred in her stomach. Amelia wished she wasn't wearing such an old dress and sniffed discreetly at the sleeve, hoping the stink of the Tombs had dissipated. Finally, she gritted her teeth and forced herself to mount the stairs. This had to be done. Amelia raised a hand to knock. Before her knuckles made contact with the door, however, it swung open, and a neatly dressed man—not Andrew, she realized after a heart-stuttering instant—nearly bowled her over in his haste to exit.

Amelia clapped a hand to her chest as they reeled back from one another, wearing what were probably identical startled expressions.

"I beg your pardon, miss," he said. "I wasn't expecting anyone to be there. You're not hurt, are you?"

"No," she got out after a moment. "I'm perfectly well."

There was an awkward pause before Amelia started. She was still in his way. "I'm sorry," she said, stepping to one side. "I don't mean to keep you. But I wonder if you could tell me if Dr. Cavanaugh is at home."

"I haven't seen him this morning, but that's not unusual," the man said. "And I think Mrs. Danbury is out. But I'm sure she wouldn't mind you waiting in the parlor for him." He held the door open for her. "First door on your left. If he comes down, you won't be able to miss him, and Mrs. Danbury should be back soon. She'll go up to check for you, if need be."

She stepped inside. "Thank you."

He tipped his hat and left.

The house was quiet, the floors clean but not polished. The parlor was full of dark, heavy wood furniture. It had been recently dusted and still smelled of wood polish, but the velvet upholstery was worn and shiny with use. High standards and reduced circumstances. A difficult combination to bear. Amelia perched on one of the sofas and waited, her eyes on the doorway Andrew would have to pass on his way out. The only sound was the ticking of the grandfather clock on the far wall, the hour hand edging toward the gilt eleven on its face.

She fidgeted as the minutes passed, growing more concerned—or maybe more hopeful; she couldn't tell anymore—that he might not be here. He usually had Mondays off. But if he'd risen early, or his schedule had changed, or if he'd spent the night on the island, she could leave with her conscience clear. She waited five more minutes, watching the clock's pendulum swing and listening for any sign of an occupant, before standing with a noise of irritation. If he wasn't here, she was wasting time. If he was, and she left without speaking to him, it would waste even more.

The stairs were halfway down the hall. They creaked beneath Amelia's feet as she climbed. On the second floor there were four closed doors, two to a side, each with a small table standing outside and a hook on the wall beside it. Only one hook held a hat, indicating the occupant was inside. A basket of folded laundry sat on the table beside it, a freshly shined pair of shoes beneath it.

A fifth door stood open, revealing a white-tiled bathroom, and Amelia felt a sudden urge to duck inside. But it was only nerves, so she forced herself onward.

Before they could overcome her, she strode to the door and knocked.

"Thank you," a voice called from within. Andrew's voice. Caught between confusion and panic, Amelia said nothing. Footsteps came toward the door. Her mouth went dry, and she felt a wild desire to flee. Andrew wasn't expecting her. This was an ambush. It wasn't fair of her to suddenly appear this way, not after everything. She didn't know if he would be glad to see her or angry at the way she'd dismissed him. He might even refuse to help—she hadn't even considered that. Before she could move, the door swung open.

Andrew stood before her, wearing nothing but a pair of trousers.

Her eyes fell to his bare chest, and as heat flooded her face it was all she could do to drag them back up to meet his own shocked gaze. His mouth had dropped open. His hair was damp. Shaving soap covered one cheek, and he still held his razor in his other hand.

"Amelia?" His voice was faint. He sounded as if he didn't fully believe she was real.

"I'm so sorry," she babbled, feeling as though she barely had air enough for the words. "I wouldn't have—I didn't know you were—"

"No, it's all right," he said, flustered. He groped behind the half-open door and his hand came back into view holding an undershirt. He pulled it on, smearing the shaving soap without seeming to notice. "I'd never have answered the door like this if I'd had any idea you were—"

"Who did you think it was?" It was an inane question, but it popped out of her mouth before she could stop it. As soon as she heard her own tone, Amelia wanted to take it back. If there was someone in this house he frequently allowed to see him barely dressed, then it was none of her business. And she wanted to know who it was.

"My landlady." His own face reddened as he hurriedly went on. "I don't—We aren't—She knows I sleep later on my days off, so she saves breakfast for me. She knocks and leaves a tray. I thought it was her."

A beat passed as they looked at each other.

"What are you doing here?" he asked finally.

"Oh." The reminder of why she'd come sobered her. "I needed to talk to you. Something's happened."

A creak on the stairs and a quiet clattering of dishes announced the imminent arrival of the expected breakfast. Amelia wouldn't have thought Andrew's eyes could go any wider, but they did. He seized her by the arm and hauled her through the door, swinging it closed behind her.

"She can't see you up here," he whispered as footsteps approached. There was the sound of the tray being set on the table, then a quiet knock, and the footsteps retreated again.

Andrew released a breath when they'd faded. The look of relief on his face was so profound Amelia might have laughed, if she hadn't been struck by a complicated little bundle of feelings. He was trying to protect their reputations. She looked at the floor, a wry twist in her gut.

He was looking at her when she raised her eyes. There was another pause before Andrew seemed to abruptly remember he was still under-dressed. He reached around her and snatched a shirt off of the bed behind her.

"It's all right," she said. "I'll turn away if you want to finish shaving first."

After a moment, he nodded, and she crossed to the window, where a heavy curtain was pulled to one side, letting in a flood of morning light.

For the next few minutes, Amelia pretended to be looking at the street. Instead, every fiber of her being was focused on listening to him moving around behind her. The splashing of water in the basin. The scrape of the razor against his skin. An intake of breath and a muttered oath—he must have nicked himself. Finally, the rustle of cloth.

"All right," he said quietly. "I'm more or less decent."

She turned around, looking anywhere but at Andrew.

His room was square, with a neatly made bed and a stack of books on the nightstand beside it. On the opposite wall was a small writing desk, with more books and a stack of sealed and stamped envelopes sitting on one corner. The only other pieces of furniture were the dresser with its mirror and basin and an overstuffed armchair in the corner. Out of other things to look at, she faced him.

"Let me get my breakfast," he said, "and then we'll talk."

He retrieved the tray and set it on the desk. The smell of bacon reached her, making her mouth water. She hadn't eaten since her midnight lunch break, and her stomach gave a loud rumble.

Andrew huffed a laugh and pointed to the chair. "Sit, please. There's plenty."

Amelia sat, moving the mail out of the way so she wouldn't spill anything on it. The letter on top was addressed to Mrs. Thomas Cavanaugh. His mother, she assumed, glad for his sake that it seemed he'd repaired the relationship.

She lifted a strip of the bacon as he buttered a slice of toast. There was an undeniable intimacy to eating breakfast alone with him in his bedroom.

"I'm sorry there's only the one cup for the coffee," he said. "You're welcome to it if you like."

"I've had more than enough already," she said, taking a breath. As quickly as she could, she recounted the morning's events.

His face clouded when she spoke of finding Ginny's body. "I've been following the news reports," he said with a sigh. "I'd hoped . . . And her spirit? Did it try to . . ." He made a gesture with the fork.

"I think she might have if Jonas hadn't interrupted. I wasn't on my guard."

She went on with the story, and Andrew's eyebrows drew together when she described Amos's condition.

Finally, she arrived at the reason for her visit. "Sidney says we can't assume whoever is doing the examination is competent. He got permission to have an outside observer there, just in case. We were hoping you would be willing." She held out the letter.

He was silent for a long moment, then sighed as he took it. "I don't see how I could say no."

"Thank you."

Andrew shrugged. "It needs to be done. I have a few things I need to do this morning, but I'll make certain to be there on time."

When they were ready to leave, he opened the door and peered out, then gestured to her to follow. "Hopefully we can get out without being seen."

Amelia matched her steps to his as they went down the stairs. Maybe it would sound like only one person.

They were two steps from the bottom when a woman, obviously Mrs. Danbury, appeared in the doorway.

"Good morning, Dr. Cavanaugh. I don't believe I've met your companion." Her voice was cold. The censure was clear in every line of her body.

"This is Miss Matthew," Andrew said, very obviously trying to act as though he didn't see it, and equally obviously uncomfortable under her perusal. "She brought a message for me." He held up the letter. "A rather urgent case, in fact."

Amelia stepped around him, smiling. "I'm afraid no one was here when I arrived, and I couldn't afford to wait." She half-extended her hand, forcing Mrs. Danbury to decide in an instant whether to cut her or return the greeting.

Mrs. Danbury looked suddenly flustered. If Amelia were a tart, which she clearly suspected, the proper thing for a lady to do would be to refuse to acknowledge her. But if she was wrong, she would be offering a grave insult, both to a lodger she needed and to a guest in her home. She balanced on the knife's edge for a moment, then extended her own hand and grasped Amelia's fingers. "My apologies that no one was here to greet you. I'm afraid I'm a bit short-staffed at the moment."

"Oh, it's all right," Amelia assured her, and a moment later, she and Andrew were out on the sidewalk, his hand at her elbow as if she were an entirely proper young lady.

"I was afraid I was about to get tossed out." Andrew sounded relieved.

Amelia managed a shaky half-laugh. "You might have if we hadn't gotten out of there when we did. I threw her off balance for a minute, but it wouldn't have lasted."

"You're good at that," he said. "Throwing people off balance."

Amelia sobered. "I've had a lot of practice."

Andrew caught the change in her mood. "Well. It was well done." He hesitated. "It's good to see you. Even given the circumstances. I've—" He stopped abruptly. "I'm glad you felt you could come to me with this."

Amelia scoffed. "Who else? I certainly don't know anyone else with a pedigree like yours who might be willing to get involved with something like this."

"A pedigree like mine?"

She felt herself flush. "You know what I mean. No one would ever mistake you for anything but a gentleman. But you're willing to go out of your way to help the rest of us when we need it."

# 6

Sidney sighed as they watched Amelia's cab depart, her head, visible through the rear window, held resolutely upright. "I hope that isn't going to be too awkward for her."

Jonas snorted. "It's her own fault if it is. She's being ridiculous."

"Maybe so, but it was her decision to make."

"That doesn't mean I can't tell her I think she made the wrong one—or give her opportunities to change her mind."

"I suppose," Sidney said. "At any rate, it will be good to have Andrew aboard. He'll be able to—" He broke off as a voice came from the direction of the building's doors.

"Well, look who's here."

Jonas turned and barely suppressed an oath as Peter Rhodes strode toward them. "What are you doing here? Were you following us?"

Rhodes smiled blandly at Jonas. "I'm not following you, Vincent, I'm following the biggest story in the city. And it looks to me like it just got bigger. Word is," he said, looking them over, "that you just came from visiting Ginny Holloway's killer."

"Accused killer," Sidney said stiffly. "He hasn't been charged with anything yet."

"Indeed," Rhodes said, whipping out a notebook and pencil. "May I assume you are Sidney White? Your firm doesn't exactly seem the sort to defend indigent Negroes accused of heinous murders."

Sidney smiled without showing any teeth. "Can a lawyer not also have a keenly developed sense of charity?"

Rhodes barked a laugh. "Right, and I was born yesterday." He looked between them, his face intent. "Come on, counselor. I can confirm who you are easily enough. And if you can't give me a comment, then I might be forced to speculate. In print."

Jonas fought the urge to pick Rhodes up and toss him off the steps. "What do you want?"

"My byline on the front page," Rhodes said easily.

"And you think a story about who came to visit Amos Alston will get you that?"

"Oh no," he replied. "That's just an interesting sidebar. I already have the story."

"Which is?" Sidney asked, affecting disinterest.

"The fact that Virginia Holloway was at least this killer's fourth victim."

They both blinked at him for an instant, unable to process such a dreadful statement delivered in such a casual tone.

Sidney recovered first. "What?" His voice was a razor.

"There are at least three others, by my count," Rhodes said, clearly enjoying their stupefaction. "Children around the same age. All kidnapped, assaulted and killed. If Alston did this one, he did the others, too."

"You cannot possibly have any evidence of that," Sidney said.

"I suppose if you'd rather wait and find out about it when the paper comes out, that's your choice," Rhodes said. The lightness dropped out of his tone as he went on. "But I promise you this—I know far more about this case than you do. I started following it long before Ginny Holloway went missing, and I have sources all over the police department."

There was a long pause.

"And if I give you a comment, what do we get in exchange?" Sidney asked.

"I'll let you see what I have," Rhodes said promptly. "And who knows, you might even be able to convince me to hold the story for a day or so."

Jonas ground his teeth. "You'll want something for that, too, I suppose."

Rhodes gave him that same bland smile. "Of course. But there's no reason we can't both walk away happy. I'll tell you what. As a gesture of good faith, I'll go ahead and tell you one thing you don't know. The police searched every inch of the Holloway property. The only thing out of place was a broken stick of peppermint candy. It was beside the back gate. They think he lured her close with candy, then snatched her."

There was another pause.

"Give us a moment," Sidney said.

Rhodes made a "be my guest" gesture and stepped back far enough to give them the illusion of privacy.

Sidney pulled Jonas an additional few steps away and lowered his voice to barely more than a whisper. "If he does have anything, we need to know what it is. And we need to convince him to hold the story. This city is already a powder keg. If he writes something as inflammatory as a story that says there have been more killings, there will be mobs in the streets. It won't be safe for a Negro to leave his home."

"I don't trust him." Jonas's voice was flat.

Sidney scoffed. "Of course you don't. You're not an idiot. But we don't have a choice about this."

Reluctantly, Jonas nodded.

"All right," Sidney said, turning back to Rhodes. "After we've seen what you have on these supposed other victims, I'll give you a statement."

"I have to file a story this morning, but I can meet you this afternoon." Rhodes named an address. "Two o'clock. I'll expect you there, or I'll run everything I know, everything I think I know, and everything I suspect in tomorrow's paper."

With that, he turned and strode away.

"That certainly complicates things," Sidney said, moving to the edge of the sidewalk and lifting a hand for a cab. One appeared with surprising speed, and they climbed aboard.

They kept a decorous distance between them, and they were careful to keep their manner that of polite acquaintances. New York, for all its size, remained in many ways a remarkably small town. The cab had windows, and one never knew who might happen to glance through them as they passed. But on the seat between them, out of sight of passersby, their fingers entwined. Something inside Jonas relaxed a little at the touch.

Sidney glanced over at him. "You recognized that reporter."

"I caught him sneaking around the club last night. He's trying to get the staff to talk about the patrons."

"Not so surprising, I suppose. Plenty of stories there."

"No, but I don't have to like it."

"We need to know what he knows about the Holloway case."

Jonas snorted. "If he knows anything. He might be lying."

"Maybe." Sidney looked pensive.

Jonas squeezed his hand. "Thank you for agreeing to help. I know it was only because I was the one asking. There wasn't anyone else, and there's no way Miles could afford to hire anyone good."

Sidney sighed. "If somehow Amos does make it as far as a trial, he'll need someone with more experience than I have. And I doubt my father would allow me to keep the case anyway. But I can hold out for a few days."

Jonas leaned back against the seat of the cab and heaved a tired sigh. Mrs. Franklin's coffee was beginning to wear off, and he was suddenly aware he'd been awake for a long time.

"How have you been sleeping?" The question was casual, but there was an undercurrent to it that said otherwise.

Jonas considered lying, but it wasn't worth it. "Not well."

"The nightmares?"

Jonas nodded without looking at him. Over the last few months he'd been troubled by dreams—always of walking along, knowing someone was rushing up behind him and being unable to turn to face them.

"Are you still drinking before bed?"

This time Jonas did lie. "Not much." In truth, some nights whiskey was the only thing that quieted his mind enough to allow him to sleep at all. Jonas had no intention of becoming a sot, and he hated being hung over, so he tried to be careful about his consumption. Most of the time he got it right. It was better the nights they were together, when his mind was less occupied by the past and more diverted by the present. But over the past few weeks, Sidney's workload and Amelia's attempts to control her gift had kept them from spending much time together.

"As soon as all this is over, we should go somewhere for a few days," Sidney said, as if reading his thoughts. "The seashore, maybe. Somewhere private."

Windows or no, Jonas couldn't help but smile at what he saw in the other man's face.

That feeling lasted until they walked through the door of the law office and found Morris waiting for them, a look of anxious dread on his face.

Sidney heaved a sigh. "He's here, and he already knows."

Morris nodded. "He wants to see you at once. He told me that under no circumstances was I to let you leave again without seeing him."

"All right. I'll go now."

He didn't get the chance. Before they'd taken another step, an older man strode out of the hallway, wearing an expression of barely controlled fury.

"Good morning, Father."

"Don't give me that," he said in a low voice. "Who is this, one of your carousing friends?"

Jonas tried to keep his expression blandly polite, but his heart was pounding so hard he was lightheaded. He'd certainly never imagined he would meet Sidney's father, and he felt as though the man's scouring glare could see to his very soul, as if Jonas's relationship with his son could be laid bare at any moment.

Sidney's calm was astounding. "This is Jonas Vincent. I've hired him as an apprentice clerk. He's starting today."

Jonas barely kept the surprise off his face. The lie rolled so smoothly off Sidney's tongue even Jonas couldn't hear it. But then, he'd had practice.

Mr. White glowered at him. "Fine."

Sidney made as if to move past him. "I'm just going to get Mr. Vincent settled."

"No. That can wait. We have to talk. Now."

"Fine." Sidney walked past his father and down the hall to his own office, Jonas and Morris trading worried glances as they trailed behind. He left the door open a crack. Morris busied himself at the desk, but he seemed to be making an effort to be quiet. He wanted to hear, too. Jonas looked at him and moved deliberately closer to the door. Morris raised an eyebrow, but didn't object. Jonas got as near the door as he dared.

"—called me at home to tell me he'd just seen you. What on Earth are you thinking?" Sidney's father was saying in tones of purest outrage. "We cannot possibly be associated with this case. You will withdraw at once."

"I will not," Sidney said.

"What did you say to me?" Mr. White sounded as though he could not believe his ears.

"I said I will not withdraw. They've arrested a fifteen-year-old boy and beaten him bloody to make him confess. I was asked to intervene."

Jonas noticed he was careful not to mention who, exactly, made that request.

"This is the most notorious crime to happen in this city in years. To associate our name and that of this firm with something so . . . so sordid, was utterly irresponsible and shows an appalling lack of judgment. You are not a trial lawyer, and—"

"I have no plan to be involved in a trial. I was doing someone a favor, that's all. De Lancy is planning to transfer the boy to Sing Sing on Friday. I'll be off the case after that."

Jonas found himself impressed with how coolly Sidney was handling his father. Already, his anger seemed to be draining away in the face of his son's calm resistance.

"What am I supposed to tell people when they ask what you're doing defending this boy? Already this morning the Baxters sent their regrets about dinner tonight. Your mother is beside herself. She's convinced it's because they heard you took this case."

"Father, they can't possibly have heard that quickly. And if they had, they would have been even more eager to come. You said it yourself: this case is notorious. Most of New York would love a chance to hear the details. Tell me, have the Sheffields canceled, too?"

There was something in his voice, some quality Jonas couldn't quite identify, a tension he'd never heard there before.

Mr. White's response sounded equally odd. Stilted, somehow. "No. They haven't."

"They won't. We both know I'd have to do something much worse to take myself out of the running."

"Don't be crass. She's a lovely girl. Your mother and I are only—"

Morris cleared his throat, and Jonas had just enough time to step back from the door, his heart thudding, before another clerk appeared from the hallway. He handed Morris a stack of papers and lingered, obviously hoping to hear something interesting, before Morris sent him on his way with a pointed look.

The clerk had barely cleared the doorway when the door to Sidney's office swung open and Mr. White stepped through, looking slightly less ruffled than he had when he'd entered. He nodded once to Jonas, then crossed to the other office and closed that door firmly behind him.

Jonas wasted no time getting into Sidney's office, where the other man let out a shaky breath and slumped against the desk. Jonas made sure the door was completely closed before he spoke. "Are you all right?"

"I'll live."

"Why did you tell him I'm your new clerk?"

"I thought of it in the moment. I was going to hire someone. And this way you'll have an excuse for why you're in and out over the next week."

"How much does it pay?"

Sidney chuckled. "Much less than you make at the club."

"And what about the other thing?"

The humor leaked out of Sidney's face. "How much did you hear?"

"Something about a lovely girl." Jonas's voice was grim. "They're trying to marry you off, aren't they?" The thought of it roiled in his stomach. It was a possibility that always hung between them, though they'd never spoken of it. As a rule, men of Sidney's class did not remain bachelors. And he was an only child, with all the hope and expectation that carried.

Sidney looked glum. "They've been trying for a couple of years now. They've gotten more intense about it lately. Mother plans these parties, and they always happen to include a family with an appropriate daughter. I don't know how much longer I'm going to be able to put them off. They think I've had long enough to sow my wild oats and ought to be settling down."

Jonas snorted. "If they only knew."

"Indeed." Sidney sighed. "A few weeks ago my father asked me if I was keeping a mistress. He went so far as to suggest that getting married didn't mean giving her up, if I was really so attached."

"He said that?"

"Not in so many words, but the implication was there."

"And tonight's event?"

"The Sheffields," Sidney said. "They have two unmarried daughters, neither of whom I remember ever having met, though I must have at some point."

"And the Baxters? The ones who canceled?"

"A married couple and her younger brother, who is, conveniently, already engaged. My mother is the queen of this sort of thing. She always manages to build a guest list that contains no competition for me but is broad enough for her to pretend not to have any ulterior motive. She's going to hate looking so obvious tonight." Sidney half-grinned. "Actually, that part might be fun. She's so rarely off balance."

"Don't be too hard on her," Jonas said in mock sympathy. "Three empty seats at the last minute would be a challenge for any hostess. I don't doubt—" He went quiet as a wildly irresponsible idea occurred to him.

Sidney narrowed his eyes. "What? I know that look."

Jonas couldn't suppress a grin. "Just how far off balance would you like to push her?"

‿

Andrew stood watching as Amelia walked away, aware that he was hoping she would look back and annoyed with himself for it. When she rounded the corner and disappeared from his sight, he was struck by the fleeting sensation that the whole encounter had been some sort of bizarre hallucination. Surely Amelia had not appeared out of nowhere after all these weeks to knock on his bedroom door. And surely, he had not answered it while all but naked. His face heated. He ought to have apologized again before they'd parted, but he'd been so flustered by the run-in with Mrs. Danbury that he'd forgotten. Andrew grimaced. That encounter was likely to make his life awkward for a time, though Amelia had handled it well.

Letters in hand, he headed for the post box on the next block.

She looked well. Nervous at being there, whether because the circumstances were unconventional or because she hadn't wanted to see him, Andrew couldn't say for certain, though he tended to think it was the latter. It gave him a pang, but it was the only conclusion he could draw. Amelia was not much beholden to convention. That attitude, that willingness to do what was needed, convention be damned, was one of the things he liked most about her. It was refreshing, after growing up in a world where there was so much artificial distance between men and women. A great many of the conversations he'd had with her were about things he couldn't have even mentioned in front of most of the women he'd known. And not a one of them would have snuck upstairs to share breakfast in his bedroom while discussing their participation in a notorious murder case.

It wasn't her only appealing quality. Andrew also liked her bluntness and her unwavering loyalty. And her eyes. And the delicate shape of her profile. And—

He pulled himself back. Amelia had made plain that whatever had been growing between them—or might have grown, if it had been allowed—was over. And he couldn't claim to be surprised. She had made it abundantly clear on the island that she was skeptical of the whole notion of romantic relationships, though by the end she had seemed to be warming to the idea. Warming to him. The first time she declined his invitation, Andrew had mostly been puzzled. Her note had been so oddly stilted. With the second refusal, he understood. He'd made sure she knew it was up to her to decide what she wanted. Apparently she had.

He'd had to stop himself from writing to ask why. It didn't matter. When a lady made her disinterest clear, a gentleman didn't pry into her reasons. It was his obligation to step back gracefully, so he had. But it hurt. Andrew missed her. Before Amelia, he'd been so wrapped up in his work that he'd had little time for making friends anyway, and once he'd stumbled into the deadly plot at the asylum, his fast-growing friendship with Amelia had been the only port in the kind of storm he'd never experienced before. She was someone he could trust. The only one, in fact, since he'd been well aware that Jonas wasn't precisely a fan of his, at least at the beginning of their partnership. He had also seemed to be thawing. But then it hadn't mattered any longer.

Andrew reached the heavy cast-iron post box on the corner. He checked one last time to make sure there were stamps on all the letters, then dropped them into the box. His mother had written every week since his visit earlier in the summer, and he'd dutifully written back, aware of the need to reassure her that their reconciliation was real. Her hints that he might want to think about moving back to Philadelphia were growing less subtle with every letter. So far Andrew had avoided engaging directly. He liked New York, and he had plenty of reasons to want to stay—ones that had nothing to do with Amelia, he told himself firmly. But his job at the asylum wasn't going to last much longer.

He'd mistakenly accused the asylum's director of involvement in the murders of several patients during their investigation earlier in the year. It was only because Andrew had eventually helped uncover the killer's identity—and because it was one of his fellow doctors, leaving the already-shorthanded staff in dire straits—that he hadn't been tossed off the island at once. As it was, he was on borrowed time. A new doctor was starting in a few weeks, and it had been made clear to Andrew his services would no longer be required. He would have to make some decisions soon.

Andrew boarded a streetcar headed downtown. He wasn't too proud to admit he dreaded the autopsy. He was a physician. He had witnessed deaths from a hundred different causes and had studied every part of the human body, both inside and out. The sight of blood, the smell of disease and decay did not faze him, as a rule.

But it was always different with a child.

In his practice in Philadelphia, he'd seen several crib deaths, visited the bedsides of children dying of scarlet fever and measles, and, in one particularly distressing case, had been unable to save an otherwise healthy ten-year-old who scratched himself on a dirty piece of metal and developed a case of tetanus. All of them were heart-wrenching. Inconsolable parents, stunned siblings.

But he'd so far been spared the sight of a child lost to violence, and only the fact that it was Amelia who had asked it of him made him willing to expose himself to it now.

The coroner's building was a maze, and he had to ask several different people for directions until he found his way to the basement, where a long hallway led to the morgue. He pushed the door open. Inside, it was stark and modern, all tile and metal, with drains in the floor and rubber hoses dangling overhead. A wide tin sink took up most of one wall, and a pair of men in their waistcoats and shirtsleeves stood near a heavy steel door on the far side of the room. Both of them looked up as he entered.

"May I help you?" the elder of them asked, looking at Andrew over the top of wire-rimmed glasses. He was stout, with an imperious expression and a gray waistcoat precisely the same color as his short-cropped hair. The younger man was thin, sandy-haired, and had the jumpy, eager demeanor of a student.

"I am Dr. Andrew Cavanaugh," Andrew said. "I'm here to observe the postmortem on Virginia Holloway."

The older man looked surprised, then scowled. "By whose authority? I'm the coroner on this case, and no one told me about this. If you're another reporter, I swear I'll—"

"I have the authorization here." Andrew held up the paper.

The older man turned to the younger and spoke in a brusque tone. "Banning, go ahead and get the body while I deal with this." He came across the room with a self-important strut that put Andrew in mind of a pigeon.

"Humph," the man said after examining Andrew's authorization. "I suppose you can stay. Dr. Carver, you said?" He turned as Banning came back through the metal door, pushing a wheeled table with a sheet-covered form on top.

"Cavanaugh," Andrew repeated, without any confidence at all that the man was listening.

A puff of cool, malodorous air made its way across the room, and Andrew tried not to react. The morgue was a modern facility, with refrigeration for the bodies and adequate ventilation—nothing like the dark, fetid operating theaters of times past. But it was still a place to store the dead, and in a city like New York, there were always plenty of bodies that had lain too long undiscovered. Especially in such weather.

"Where do you want her, Dr. Houghton?" Banning asked.

Andrew bit back a sigh of relief. An actual doctor. That was a stroke of good luck.

"Right here is fine," Houghton said, pointing.

Banning locked the table's wheels in place, fetched a tray of tools, then opened a cabinet and withdrew a pair of heavy rubber aprons, handing one to Houghton. He hesitated, then, after an impatient wave from Houghton, withdrew a third for Andrew, who removed his own jacket and laid it aside. It had been a long while since he'd worn such a thing. His fingers felt sluggish, and he fumbled for a long moment with the ties at the back before he got it on.

Houghton waited with a look of mild disdain on his face, then turned a knob on an overhead light, bringing it up to maximum brightness.

"If we're all ready to begin?"

Banning nodded eagerly, Andrew with somewhat more reserve.

Houghton lifted the sheet and folded it back, revealing the small body beneath.

Andrew had always, since his first anatomy class, been struck by how empty a dead body was. Call it what you like—the spirit or the soul—once that animating force departed, a body was nothing but a shell. Ginny's lay curled on its side, wearing a voluminous muslin nightgown that matched the description of the one the girl had been wearing when she vanished. The skin of her right cheek, the only one currently visible, was nearly translucent. Her hair blazed around her head in the bright light, vivid and shocking against the flat gray steel of the table. Her feet were bare, and Andrew swallowed, recalling Amelia's description of the girl's spirit stepping into view. Though he knew he wouldn't see anything, he couldn't help but glance around the room, wondering if spirits ever lingered to watch what was done with their bodies. If so, did an examination like this horrify or comfort, since it was intended to help find their killers?

Andrew shook himself. He wasn't here for metaphysical musings. He was here to search for clues. He focused his attention on the body.

She did not appear to have been dead for long. There was no sign of decomposition. No swelling, no purging of fluids, nothing of what he would expect to see from a body several days dead, especially with the ferocious heat they'd been having. His stomach clenched. With no ransom demand, there were only a few reasons the killer might have wanted to hold the child captive for so long before killing her.

"The deceased has been identified as Virginia Holloway, white female, aged five," Houghton said. "She was found dead on Houston Street roughly halfway between Sullivan and MacDougal streets approximately seven hours ago, immediately brought here to the morgue, and placed in the cold room. The body is in full rigor mortis, which we will have to break in order to proceed."

Houghton nodded to Banning, who took hold of Ginny's legs and began straightening them. At times his motions were almost violent, and Andrew winced at the loud popping sounds that came from the stiffened joints and muscles. Straightening Ginny's legs dislodged a fold in her nightgown that had made a pocket between her knees, and it spilled perhaps a teaspoon's worth of coarse grayish powder onto the table. Banning paused to scrape it into a glass phial and push a black rubber stopper into the top before continuing.

Once the body was on its back, Banning removed the nightgown. Andrew tried to remain impassive as Ginny's small body was bared, but the sense of violation was acute. And this was only the beginning. There was no dignity on the autopsy table. The side of her body that had lain on the ground was a bright cherry pink. Andrew waited for Houghton to mention it, but the man's eyes only narrowed.

Beneath the gown, Ginny wore only a pair of long muslin underdrawers. The ribbon at the waist was tied in a neat bow—one Andrew doubted such a young child could have managed on her own. Someone would have had to tie it for her. His chest tightened in dread at the possibilities.

As if he, too, wanted to put off that moment of discovery, Houghton spoke. "Before we proceed further, Mr. Banning, would you please share with us your immediate impressions?"

Despite his unease, Andrew barely suppressed a wry smile, recognizing the signs of a student being tossed into the water to sink or swim. Banning jerked and straightened.

"Ah," he began. "Well. There are no obvious signs of injury or trauma. None currently visible, at least. The body itself looks relatively clean, though there is a bit of dirt on the nightgown, as well as more of that powder. She appears to be adequately nourished, so if someone has been keeping her for the last week, they must have fed her."

"What can you tell me about rigor mortis?" The question was open-ended, designed to force the young man to reveal how much he knew, or didn't know, about the subject.

"Rigor mortis is the stiffening of the body after death," Banning began, sounding as though he were reading from a card. "It typically begins within two to six hours after death with the small muscles of the face and neck. It peaks at twelve hours, and passes by around forty-eight hours after death."

"And the discoloration?"

"Livor mortis, sir."

"Which is?"

"Livor mortis results because once the heart is no longer beating, the blood ceases to circulate, and the effects of gravity pull it to the lowest parts of the body, where it becomes visible over time. The white areas within the pink are the places where the body was directly in contact with the surface beneath it, preventing the blood from settling there," Banning said, speaking rapidly, as if he wanted to get it all out before he forgot. "Livor mortis begins within a few hours after death and becomes fixed at around eight hours after death."

"And putting your understanding of those two things together, what is your estimate for the time of death in this case?"

"Rigor is complete, and lividity is fixed. She's been dead at least twelve hours. No more than two days."

It was a reasonable conclusion, though there were multiple factors that could alter the course of both conditions. It was inappropriate to make a firm determination of time of death without considering those factors and looking at other signs. And Banning had failed to mention another particularly interesting finding, one which Houghton was already moving to point out.

"What about the color?"

"The color, sir?"

Houghton waited, and Banning's own face turned pink as the seconds passed.

The doctor looked irate. "This is a murder case, boy. You've overlooked a significant indicator of the cause of death." He pointed at Ginny's cherry-pink cheek. "Lividity is typically purple or dark reddish. Bright pink lividity is atypical. And it's one of the characteristics of cyanide poisoning."

"Or hypothermia," Andrew said, thinking back to his own training.

"I beg your pardon?" Houghton said.

"People who die outdoors in cold weather also exhibit pink lividity," Andrew said. "Not relevant here, obviously, but important to know."

"Indeed." Houghton sounded ruffled, as if he thought Andrew had been correcting him instead of trying to help Banning. "Let's move on to the rest of the examination."

Houghton peered at Ginny's head, looking for signs of fractures or other injuries. He found something else.

"Forceps, please," he said, holding out an impatient hand. He pulled something out of Ginny's hair and held it up: a shard of something, striped in pink and white.

"Is that—" Andrew began, leaning forward.

"Peppermint candy, I believe," Houghton said. He dropped it into a glass tube, stoppered it and set it aside before moving on. "There is some redness around the nose and mouth," he noted. He used a small mirror to focus the light up into one nostril. "The interior of the nasal cavity is inflamed."

"May I look?" Andrew asked in his most collegial tone.

Houghton handed over the mirror without comment.

He was correct. There was a definite redness, though Andrew could not see any blistering. Intrigued, he forgot for a moment it was not his examination. He opened Ginny's mouth and peered inside. "The back of the throat is red as well. She must have been exposed to some caustic agent at around the time of death. Cyanide would certainly qualify, though it's interesting there's no sign of vomiting. And no smell of almonds. The tongue appears normal."

He looked up to find the other two men staring at him, Banning in round-eyed alarm and Houghton with a stony expression.

"My apologies," he said, straightening. He handed the instrument over and stepped back. Houghton's patience was obviously growing short. This wasn't his autopsy. He needed to mind himself.

"Quite all right," said Houghton stiffly. "Now then. There are no marks or bruising around the neck." He palpated the throat. "And I don't believe there was any crushing. She wasn't strangled. I suspect this is a case of poisoning, given the damage to the mucous membranes of the nose and mouth. I predict that testing that powder will reveal it to be some sort of cyanide salt."

Andrew made an involuntary sound.

Houghton looked at him, a challenge on his face. "You disagree?"

"Not necessarily," Andrew said hastily. "But given the damage to the inside of the nose and throat and the lack of irritation to the tongue or rest of the inside of the mouth, I would have thought if she were poisoned it was by a gas rather than a solid powder. But it's a minor quibble," he added. "The stomach contents should tell us more, as well as the condition of the lungs."

"Oh no," Houghton said without looking at him. "This is to be an external examination only."

"What?" Andrew exclaimed. "But this is a murder investigation."

"And they've already caught the killer," Houghton said. "He was standing over the body, for goodness sakes. And he's confessed. This child's family doesn't want her cut open, and I can't say I blame them. This whole business is distressing enough without such a violation."

"I understand that, but surely it's not—," Andrew said.

Houghton's eyes narrowed, and his tone indicated that his patience with Andrew was at an end. "When you are elected city coroner, you may decide to cut open every body that passes through your morgue if it pleases you, regardless of the sense in it or the families' wishes. My judgment is that in this case a full autopsy is unnecessary."

Andrew closed his teeth over a sharp reply. Getting tossed out on his ear wouldn't do any good.

Houghton looked at him for a long moment, then, seeming to believe he had quelled any resistance, went on with the examination. He removed

Ginny's drawers, and none of the men could suppress their relief when there were no overt signs of sexual assault. Whatever Ginny had endured before her death, she appeared to have been spared that much.

Andrew considered commenting on the fact that the lack of evidence conflicted with Amos's so-called 'confession,' then thought better of it.

His examination complete, Houghton stepped away from the table and began to remove his apron. "Banning, get the photographs taken, and then put her back in the cooler. I'm going to complete the paperwork so we can release the body to the family." Without even looking in Andrew's direction again, he left.

Banning looked at him awkwardly and began removing camera equipment from another cabinet.

"How long have you been his student?" Andrew asked in a casual tone, taking the opportunity to walk around the table and view the other side of the body.

"A few months," Banning said with a sigh, looking a great deal more relaxed now that Houghton had gone. "He's not a bad teacher. But he doesn't like to be questioned."

"Clearly," Andrew said dryly. He stepped back as Banning began to set up the camera. He'd have to remind Sidney to ask for copies.

Andrew removed his own apron, replaced his coat, and excused himself. The first flash of the camera lit the room behind him as he exited.

Once Banning was finished, the machinery of law would be done with the body, and the normal rituals of grief could begin. The washing, the dressing. Ginny could be laid in a silk-lined box, covered with flowers, wept over by her family, and finally laid to rest in an expensive patch of earth. Andrew knew, all too well, how little comfort that would be to her family as they said goodbye.

∽

After parting from Andrew on the sidewalk, Amelia walked aimlessly in the general direction of the apartment. She was unsettled by their meeting, on top of being exhausted by her long night and the morning's dramatic events. But there was no way she'd be able to sleep. And besides, she didn't want to go home yet. Jonas would probably be there. Maybe he would have gone to bed, but there was a good chance he was waiting up to hear how it had gone. And she didn't want to talk to him about it. Not until she knew how she felt about it herself.

There, at the end, before he stopped himself, it had seemed as though Andrew had been about to say he'd missed her.

Amelia wasn't sure if she was relieved or disappointed that he hadn't. She'd missed him, too. She could admit it. She didn't have many real friends, and, even though it was for the best, putting an end to their relationship had left a hole in her life. She'd grown used to it, but the hole was still there, and seeing him again was a reminder.

She also hadn't expected to see quite so much of him.

Her mouth twitched. They'd both been shocked, but on the whole, he was probably more embarrassed than she was. He would have been taught to never remove his jacket in a woman's presence, let alone his shirt. And it was not as if she'd never seen a naked man before. Once she'd left the orphanage where she and Jonas had grown up, she'd joined Jonas and the motley assortment of rogues he'd fallen in with. None of them had ever been overly concerned with modesty. They'd lived in quarters too close for that.

But she'd never seen—had never expected to see—Andrew's bare chest. His skin was pale, faintly freckled, the sort that would burn and peel if he'd had to work the docks instead of indoors. He was less heavily muscled than Jonas, but then most men were. She wouldn't call him weedy, though. There was a sort of litheness to him, a wiry-looking strength that—

She cut herself off. This was not a useful thing to be thinking about. Amelia blew out a breath. As she neared the corner, the dueling shouts of a pair of paperboys hawking extra editions of their papers reached her ears.

"Extra! Extra! Virginia Holloway found dead! Killer caught!" bawled a skinny, curly-haired boy as he waved a copy of the *New York Tribune*.

A snaggle-toothed child with a shaved head countered him in a piping voice, "Fiend found crouching over the body! Details in the *New York Sun!*"

Both boys were doing a brisk business, accepting coins and handing out papers while constantly jockeying against one another for the better position. The news hawkers weren't employed by the newspapers. Instead, they purchased bundles of 100 sheets and resold them, earning about a half-cent per copy. Every paper they didn't sell was an expense they wouldn't recoup. To that end, competition for the best locations was fierce. Violence wasn't unheard of.

Amelia bought both papers, handing over a pair of pennies, and skimmed the stories as she waited for the streetcar. Neither article named Amos, the *Sun* referring to him as "a colored boy of about fifteen years," while the *Tribune* called him "a mulatto youth." Both were light on details and heavy on lurid implication.

When the streetcar came—an electric one this time, to her dismay—Amelia surrendered another nickel and boarded. No matter what Jonas said about the science behind electrical power, a streetcar that appeared to move on its own was unsettling. It couldn't be safe. She rode in a state of heightened watchfulness and breathed a sigh of relief when she disembarked without incident. Still not ready to go home, Amelia turned instead toward the Alston house. Probably no one would have thought to update them on the morning's events; they would be desperate for news.

She would have found it easily, even if she hadn't been there before. It was still tightly shuttered, but its formerly tidy front was now streaked and spattered with gobs of filth. Someone had splashed red paint across the front. The neighborhood had rendered its judgment.

Dr. Landry stood on the sidewalk outside, looking at the house and shaking his head in apparent disgust. He glanced at her as she approached, then nodded a greeting. "I'm sorry, I didn't catch your name earlier."

"I'm Miss Matthew," Amelia said stiffly. "My brother and I work with Miles."

"I'm just on my way in to check on Polly again," Landry said, knocking on the largest clean spot on the front door.

"I came to let them know we've gotten Amos a lawyer and been in to see him," Amelia said.

Landry turned to her. "And how is he?" His gaze was direct.

She grimaced. "He's been beaten, badly. His lawyer made a fuss, and they're supposed to have a doctor in to see him."

"Will he check to make certain they do?" Landry's voice was cynical.

"Yes," Amelia said, vaguely offended. "Of course he will. But that's not the only thing."

Landry knocked a second time, harder, then glanced at her again. "What else?"

"According to the police, Amos confessed." Landry scowled, and she rushed on. "It's obvious they beat it out of him, but it's going to make clearing him more difficult."

The door opened then, Miles's exhausted face looking out. "Doc. Miz Amelia. Come on in." He swung the door wide for them. "Polly's still in bed. The rest of us are out back. I'm sorry it's so hot inside. It's wash day, and we couldn't afford to let it wait."

Indeed, pails of water sat heating on the stove, and the house was sweltering.

Amelia quickly told Miles what had happened that morning. He ran a hand over his face. "You need to go to Polly. She'll want to know you saw him."

"But don't say anything about the confession or the beating," Landry said. "I don't want her any more upset than she already is."

It was an instruction, not a request, and again, Amelia found herself mildly rankled. She left the papers behind and followed him into the bedroom, where Polly lay on her side, her face wan and her eyes red.

"Doc," she said in a flat voice as Landry entered, lifting halfway up.

"No, stay down," Landry said. "I'm just here to check on things. And Miss Matthew here has news. She's been to see Amos."

"You saw him?" Polly was abruptly more alert. "How is he?"

"Holding up," Amelia lied. "He wants to come home. He's worried about all of you. Wanted me to tell you to take care of yourself. We got a lawyer in to see him, and he's working on the case."

"My poor boy." Her eyes welled. "Will they let me send some things for him?"

"I'm not sure," Amelia hedged. "But if you put something together, I'll take it to Mr. White—that's the lawyer—and he'll see what he can do."

Polly moved as if she would get up and begin at once. "Some clean clothes," she said, more to herself than the two of them. "And some of those candy sticks he likes. Maybe Miles can run out and get some."

"You can worry about all of that later," Landry said, gently pressing against her shoulder to keep her in place. "I need to check on you and the baby now."

"I'll step out—" Amelia began.

Polly interrupted. "No, please," she said as Landry withdrew a watch from his pocket and found the pulse in her wrist. "I want to hear more about Amos. And what the lawyer said."

Amelia could hardly refuse, so she waited as the doctor moved through his examination, wondering how she was going to tell Polly anything that was remotely true while not upsetting her.

Landry asked a few questions and felt her abdomen. Then he opened his bag and withdrew a candlestick-shaped wooden stethoscope. He placed the wide end against Polly's chest and bent to listen. "Your heart sounds good. Now, let's check the baby's."

Polly pushed down the quilt, and Landry placed the instrument against her belly and repeated the exercise. "Everything sounds good," he said, standing. "But I don't like that you're still having bleeding this late. I want you to stay in bed as much as you can. You can sit up for short periods, but no lifting anything heavier than a fork." That directive tone was there again. Amelia stiffened, but Polly didn't seem to mind.

"I'm glad to get a chance to thank you for what you're doing, Miss Matthew," Polly said when he was gone. "Miles told me you were trying to help Amos. I can't tell you how much that means to us."

"Call me Amelia," Amelia said, pulling a rocking chair from the corner closer to the bed and sitting down. She patted Polly's hand. "And we haven't done much yet. I hope . . . I hope we can help."

Polly pushed herself up until her back was propped against the headboard. "I never imagined one of my children caught up in something so terrible." The tears, always close to the surface, threatened again, but Polly blinked them back. "But then, I suppose you never do, do you?" she went on. "Miles and I were reading about it in the papers, same as everyone else—he brings them home with him from work. I felt so terrible for her mother. Now all I can think about is Amos."

Her face was so pale her eyes looked like a pair of holes burned in a sheet of paper. She gripped Amelia's hand with desperate strength. "He didn't do it. He couldn't have. I'm up and down all night with this." Her voice shook as she gestured to her belly. "I would have known if he wasn't here. He was. All night. And Amos loves children. Usually I keep three or four little ones during the day while their parents work. And they love him—when he's here they all trail around after him like he's the Pied Piper. And when Sarah and Silas were born, why, Amos was so taken with them both. He would never hurt a child." She couldn't hold back the tears any longer, sobbing into her hands.

Amelia rose and murmured something about getting a glass of water. In the kitchen, she filled a glass from a pitcher in the icebox and took it back to the bedroom, condensation beading on the outside.

Polly had managed to compose herself. She drank deeply, and the ghost of a smile passed over her face. "Think someone's not so sure about the cold." She pulled her shift taut across her belly. Beneath the thin cotton, her stomach moved, lumps appearing and disappearing as the baby wriggled.

"I didn't know you could see it moving," Amelia said, startled. It was an odd feeling, knowing another being was moving beneath Polly's skin.

Both women were silent for a long moment.

"What else did Amos say while you were there?" Polly asked.

Amelia chose her words carefully. "We didn't have a lot of time this visit." Truth. "They're going to keep him in the boys' cells." Another truth, though cut paper-thin this time. "And Sidney—Mr. White—will do everything he can." Entirely true, but . . .

"What if it's not enough?" Polly all but whispered, her low voice an echo of Amelia's own thoughts.

Amelia couldn't lie to her, so she just squeezed her hand again. A few minutes later, she excused herself, telling Polly to rest and promising to come back the following day.

Out in the backyard, Sarah knelt beside a washboard, scrubbing a sodden bundle of cloth against its ridged sides. Miles stood beside her, cranking the wringer that squeezed the water out of the clothes and passing them to Mrs. Franklin to be hung on the line stretched across the small rear yard. The air was heavy with humidity, and between that, the hot water, and the effort, sweat darkened all their clothes in great swathes.

All three of them looked up as Amelia stepped outside.

"Miz Amelia," Miles said. "Let me get you a chair."

"No," she said. "There's no need. I just came out to—"

Amelia had intended to say she was just coming to say goodbye, but cut herself off as she got a good look at the three of them. Sarah, her face pinched and her arms shaking with the effort. Mrs. Franklin, who had heart trouble and should not be hauling heavy, wet laundry around in this heat. And particularly Miles, who looked exhausted. He'd been up all night, just as Amelia had. Add that to the enormous strain and worry—for his son, his wife, and the coming child—and it was no wonder he looked as though he were barely holding himself together.

Laundry was a grueling task. Water had to be pumped, heated, and hauled out to waiting basins. Every piece of cloth had to be soaked, scrubbed against the washboard with harsh detergents, then rinsed, wrung, and hung to dry. And if the family wanted to stay clean, it had to be done every single week. It was ironic: Amos worked at a laundry, but the family evidently couldn't afford to send their own wash there. Being assigned to help with that particular chore had been a popular punishment at the Foundling, and Amelia remembered the cracked hands and aching muscles of wash day all too well.

"I just came out to help," she said, unbuttoning her cuffs and suppressing a sigh. It wasn't a pleasant prospect, but she couldn't very well bid them goodbye and leave them to work themselves to the bone. All three made token protests, but she brushed them aside and sent Sarah to help Mrs. Franklin. Miles remained at the wringer, and Amelia folded her skirts beneath her as she knelt beside the washtub. She hesitated only a moment before pulling a shift from the basket and plunging it into the hot water.

"There was a man here earlier," Miles said quietly as they worked. "A white man. Big, dark-haired fella. Acted friendly, said he just wanted to ask some questions, didn't mean us any harm. I think he was one of those Pinkertons the Holloways hired."

"Did you talk to him?"

"No'm. He left a card. I'll get it for you." He set aside the sheet he'd just run through the wringer.

"No, don't worry about it now," she said. "I'll look at it later."

Amelia wondered about the family's visitor as her hands began to sting from the harsh lye soap. She'd have to soak them in aloe and lavender water before her shift that night. Still, she thought as she scrubbed, this way she could be certain she was actually helping. She couldn't say as much about the rest of their work.

# 7

Jonas arrived at the address Rhodes had given him and was surprised to find it was not a tavern as he'd expected, but a coffee house. The reporter was already waiting inside. He waved from a table in the back, where a pot of coffee sat beside an inch-thick brown folder stuffed with an untidy stack of papers. Rhodes was in the chair beside the wall, forcing Jonas to take the seat with his back to the room. Jonas tried to ignore the way the back of his neck prickled as he sat and waved away the waiter with a brusque motion before the man could do more than take a step in their direction.

He crossed his arms, his back rigid against the hard chair. "All right. I'm here, and I'll give you thirty minutes to convince me these other deaths are connected to Ginny Holloway's."

Rhodes gave him a sour look. "It'll take longer than that to go through everything I have here," he said, putting a hand on the folder.

Jonas looked at him. "Twenty-nine minutes left."

Rhodes sighed. "Fine. I suppose the easiest way is to show you the victims and hope you see what I do." He opened the flap of the folder and withdrew a photograph, laying it on the table facing Jonas. It was a formal portrait of a girl of about five, her hair in ringlets and her dress starched until it looked as though it could stand up on its own. Beside her was a little boy, barely more than a baby. Rhodes pointed to the girl. "This is Paulina Nowak. She went missing in Greenpoint a little over two years ago."

Jonas snorted. "Brooklyn? What makes you think a Polish girl going missing two years ago has anything to do with a girl kidnapped from Fifth Avenue?"

Rhodes ignored him. "She was found in an alley a week later. Assaulted and strangled. She hadn't been dead long." He reached into the folder again. "Markus Jankowski, age three when he disappeared seventeen months ago. Also from Greenpoint. His body was found in a vacant lot four days later. Again, assaulted and strangled." Rhodes laid a sketch, rather than a photograph, on the table this time. It was skillfully done, richly detailed and depicting a little boy with round cheeks and plump lips. Curls of hair corkscrewed around his face and spilled over his collar.

"Ina Rudlyk, age five," Rhodes said. He placed another photograph in the row, but it was distinctly different from the one of Paulina and her brother. Ina was alone, posed to look as though she was sleeping, but it was clear she was not. There was a darkish tinge to her lips and to the tips of the fingers folded together over her breast.

Jonas couldn't suppress a grimace. It was a *memento mori* photograph. This one was far less ghoulish than some he had seen, where the corpse had been made up and hung on a metal stand in a vain attempt to make it look alive. Sometimes family members gathered around it, dressed in their best, so the whole family could be photographed together. Open eyes would be painted on the corpse—either directly onto the closed lids or onto the photographic negative. The practice might be unnerving, but Jonas could hardly blame the families for doing it. For many of them, especially the poorer ones, it was the only photograph they would ever have of their lost loved one. He shifted uncomfortably in his chair as Rhodes continued.

"Greenpoint again, a year ago. Another vacant lot, eight days after she disappeared, too fresh to have been dead all that time. Assaulted and strangled." He sat back, evidently waiting for Jonas to respond.

"This is what you have to show me? Three children from Brooklyn. Three Polish children. All from poor families?"

Rhodes nodded.

Jonas waved an incredulous hand over them. "And for some reason you think the same person not only took all of them, but somehow also snatched Ginny Holloway from her mansion on Fifth Avenue?"

Rhodes's jaw tightened. "I know there are differences, damn it. Ignore that for a moment and look at these three children. Really look at them."

Jonas rolled his eyes but leaned forward, his eyes passing from child to child. He frowned, putting the sketch of Markus beside the photograph of Paulina. A little worm of unease wriggled in his gut. If the sketch was accurate, the two children had looked remarkably alike. The shape of their faces, the curly spirals of their hair. In fact, if you put a bow on top of Markus's head, he could pass for her younger sister. He reached for the photograph of Ina and looked more closely at her features, trying to see past the distracting signs of death. Yes, now that he focused on it, she did bear a resemblance to the other two. A strange, slow turbulence began in his mind.

Jonas looked up at Rhodes, who seemed to recognize what he was feeling. The reporter didn't speak. Instead, gently, almost reverently, he placed a fourth photograph at the end of the row.

Jonas glanced down at it and sucked in a breath. "Where did you get this?"

Rhodes smiled a thin smile. "I told you. I have lots of sources. I don't think the woodcuts that have been in the papers really capture her. Do you?"

Jonas stared down at the photograph. Rhodes was right. The woodcuts were close enough that he recognized the girl in the photograph, but they hadn't managed to show her as she'd looked in life. They hadn't shown that Ginny Holloway was, feature for feature, nearly a perfect match to the other dead children.

He sat back. There was something strange here. "All right," he said finally. Jonas reached into his pocket and withdrew a sheet of paper. He handed it across the table.

"What's this?"

"A comment for your story. From Mr. White. He told me to use my judgment about whether your information was useful."

Rhodes unfolded the paper, his eyes skimming across the few lines. "Statement from Mr. Sidney White, Esq for attribution: My client is a fifteen-year-old boy who was on his way to work when he came upon Miss Holloway's body. He was frightened, and when suddenly confronted by police, he ran, as any frightened boy might have done. His family have stated that he was at home the previous night and could not have been involved in this terrible crime. We would remind the public that he has only been accused, not convicted, and ask the citizens of this city to withhold judgment until the evidence has been heard." Rhodes looked at Jonas. "What about the confession?"

"What confession?" Jonas said blandly.

"Don't play games with me. I'm going to report it. This is your chance to rebut. You should take it."

Jonas hesitated. "They beat him half to death and threw him into the wet cells. He was afraid they would kill him. Anything he said was meaningless."

Rhodes wrote something on the bottom of the page. "I won't make that part of Mr. White's quote. It doesn't fit with the rest of it. I'll say it came from 'a source with knowledge of the matter.'" He finished writing and sat back, looking at Jonas.

The silence stretched between them as Jonas tried to formulate an approach that would somehow convince Rhodes not to write a story even he understood any reporter would kill for. The problem was that he had no leverage. Rhodes held all the cards, and both of them knew it. Finally, he blew out a frustrated breath and said the only thing he could. "What do you want?"

"What do you mean?"

"Now who's playing games? You said earlier we might be able to convince you to hold the story. You've got your statement and you're still sitting here. You're waiting for me to ask you not to write it. That means you're willing, but there's something else you want in exchange. Is it information about people at the club? Because I won't give you anything about—"

"Fine," Rhodes said. "Forget the club. I want to follow the investigation of this case."

"Why?" Jonas asked, caught flat-footed.

"The club will still be there later. I can find another way in. You're my way into this story," Rhodes said. "And there's plenty going on here. Sidney White is a fancy lawyer from a rich family. Why did he agree to take this case? Who's paying him?"

Jonas struggled not to let his alarm show. Sidney had taken the case because Jonas asked. But Rhodes absolutely could not be allowed to know that. He focused on the reporter, looking for a way to redirect him. And he found it. For all his casual words, there was a tension in Rhodes's shoulders. His breathing was shallow. There was something more he wasn't saying. Jonas was suddenly almost certain Rhodes, whatever his real reason for wanting into the investigation, wanted it just as desperately as Jonas wanted him to hold the story. Maybe more.

Only one way to find out. Jonas leaned back in his chair and threw the dice.

"No," he said, injecting his voice with confidence. "That's not it. You think there's some deeper story in an ambitious lawyer taking a case that could make him famous? And it's worth delaying a story all but guaranteed to make *you* famous? I don't buy it. Why are you really so interested?"

"My reasons are my own," Rhodes snapped. "It's personal, and it isn't relevant. All you need to know is I want in, and in exchange I'll hold the story. Yes or no?"

"There would have to be some ground rules," Jonas said.

Rhodes's jaw was tight. "Such as?"

Jonas looked at him for a long moment, trying to gauge how far he could go. "You don't print anything about this case without our agreement."

"My editor will want me turning in stories," Rhodes said.

That wasn't a refusal. There was room to negotiate. "We'll make sure you have enough to write about. But we see them before you send them in."

"Done. What else?"

"You don't print anything about me, Miss Matthew, or Mr. White without our permission."

Rhodes thought. "I'll agree for the duration of the case, but not beyond. If I find out who is paying Mr. White, and that's a story worth reporting, I'm going to report it."

"Fine," said Jonas. They'd all just have to be careful around him, which they would have done in any case. "And I want access to every single thing you know about these cases." He pointed to the row of pictures.

"I'll do better than that. I'll take you to meet the families myself."

"I know their names. I can find them without you."

"Eventually, maybe," Rhodes said. "But there are tens of thousands of people living in Greenpoint. Are you going to wander the streets asking strangers if they know the Nowaks? You realize that's like asking for Mr. Smith, don't you? And if you do find them, do you think they'll talk to you? How's your Polish?"

Jonas bit the inside of his cheek. Damn it all, the man was right. "And you can get them to do it?"

"I can."

Jonas took a moment to make sure he'd gotten what they needed. Best case, Rhodes would hold the story, and they would have a few days' breathing room from his prying. And as long as they were careful, even in the worst case they would only wind up where they had been, with Rhodes poking around the club and being rebuffed. Jonas didn't go so far as to offer his hand, but he nodded. "All right. We're agreed."

⁂

After more than an hour at the scrub board, Amelia decided she'd been a good enough neighbor for the day. Her arms were limp as noodles, and her exhaustion had finally caught up to her. She was working that night, so she needed to get some sleep before her shift at the club. Fatigue always made her gift harder to control, and she and Jonas had enough to worry about without inviting an incident.

Miles gave her the visitor's card, a crisp white rectangle with FRED-ERICK PATTERSON–INVESTIGATIONS printed in stern black type. Beneath it was a telephone number and an address on the edge of Hell's Kitchen.

Amelia tucked it into her pocket to give to Sidney, then headed home, looking forward to collapsing in her bed.

She'd been back in the apartment for only a few minutes when Jonas arrived, bursting to share what he'd learned from his meeting with Rhodes. The notion that Ginny was the fourth victim was enough to make her dizzy with horror.

"So you believe him?" Amelia said. "That whoever killed Ginny also killed those children?"

"If you'd seen those pictures, you'd believe it, too," Jonas said.

The apartment was stifling, and he'd shucked his jacket and waistcoat as soon as he entered. Now he unbuttoned his shirt as he disappeared into the washroom, his next words coming over the sound of the running faucet. "I'm going around to visit the families with him tomorrow. But it's good news, right? How could Amos Alston have had anything to do with deaths over in Greenpoint?"

"I suppose," Amelia said. It was hard to say there was anything good about this situation.

Jonas came out of the washroom, drying his face and hair on a towel. "What about your morning? Was Andrew at home? Did he agree to help?"

"Yes and yes," Amelia said, moving past him to take her own turn at washing up.

"How was it, seeing him?"

Not fooled by his casual tone, she made her voice intentionally bland. "It was fine."

"Not awkward?"

"No."

"That's good," Jonas said from behind her, "because we're having dinner with him tonight."

Amelia whirled to face him, unable to hide her shock. "What?" She listened in growing disbelief as he explained.

"So I suggested the three of us fill the empty seats," he finished.

"That is a terrible idea," she said flatly. "I'm not going."

"Then you're admitting it will bother you to see Andrew?"

It absolutely would, but there was no way Amelia was going to admit it. "That's not why. It's a terrible idea because of who they are.

And aren't you worried they might realize there's something between you and Sidney?"

"Not really," Jonas said. "We know how to be careful, and it's only for a couple of hours. We're both going. It will help Sidney. Besides, it will give all four of us a chance to talk about the case. We need to plan the next few days."

Amelia capitulated with a noise of irritation. "Fine." She stepped into the washroom and closed the door only slightly harder than necessary—there was no way it could be called a slam. She stripped to her shift and bathed, the cool water soothing her body if not her temper. She rubbed salve into her hands and retreated to her bedroom.

Despite her agitation and the afternoon heat, Amelia was tired enough to manage a short nap. She rose to bathe the sweat from her body once again, then stood before her wardrobe in her corset and a clean shift, tying herself in knots over what to wear.

She owned only a few plain, serviceable day dresses—not nearly nice enough for such an occasion—and even fewer of the extravagant, mildly risqué gowns she thought of as her work uniform. Those were suited to the club, but they were not the sort of thing a lady wore to a dinner party with strangers.

What colors did Andrew prefer? He'd hardly ever seen her in anything but the dull gray garb of an asylum inmate, and—She caught herself and swore under her breath. Finally, flushed, irritated, and on the verge of making them late, Amelia reached deep into the cabinet and pulled out a gown she'd bought several years before. Long-sleeved, made of claret taffeta with lacy cuffs and a high collar, it was one of the first "fancy" dresses she'd ever owned. She'd purchased it second-hand when she'd needed to pose as the daughter of a down-on-their-luck old money family looking to restore their fortune. The dress felt like something of a good-luck charm, given the role she would be trying to play tonight, so she shrugged into it, salved her hands again before tugging on her lightest summer gloves, and hurried out to the front stoop where Jonas waited.

On the way to Sidney's parents' home, however, Amelia was reminded of why she hadn't worn the dress more often. It was an inch too tight under the arms, and the hemline slightly too long. She had to be careful not to catch it under her toes when she walked. They had also bilked their would-be swindler in late fall, and the material was too heavy for the current weather. Sweat was running down the channel of her spine by the time they reached their destination, an elegant four-story row house off Gramercy Park.

The butler who answered the door showed them to the parlor, where most of the party were waiting. Sidney brightened as they entered, crossing the room to perform the necessary introductions. Mr. White was an older, balder version of his son. Sidney's mother was the epitome of the Society Mother, every ash-blond hair was in place, and her gown was fashionable and tasteful without being memorable. Both greeted them politely, though Mrs. White cast a cool look in Amelia's direction. Their other guests were a Mr. and Mrs. Sheffield and their two daughters. Emily, the elder, greeted them with disinterested courtesy. She had to be at least twenty-five, if Amelia judged rightly, with a plain, intelligent face and the air of one who has been dragged along to a tedious social engagement. The younger, Penelope, was vibrantly pretty. Blond-haired and blue-eyed, she was smooth and fresh as an apple blossom, with a daintily curved figure set off by a rose silk dress. She couldn't be more than seventeen, though her open, guileless expression and her way of speaking made her seem even younger.

Once the introductions were complete, Sidney filled a pair of glasses from a sweating pitcher on a side table and handed them over. "A summer cocktail before dinner," he said. Mint leaves floated in the liquid.

Amelia lifted it to her lips, but even before she tasted it, the alcohol burned her nose. Drinking made her gift unpredictable, so she merely took a sip to be polite, then set the glass unobtrusively aside as she joined the other ladies.

They were all dressed in the latest fashion, and as they regarded one another, Amelia realized, to her sudden mortification, that her gown, which she had originally purchased precisely because it was on the edge of being unfashionable—and thus exactly the sort of thing her character might wear—had, in the intervening years, moved over the line into dowdiness. Her skirt was too wide and the sleeves were too narrow. Worse, its imperfect fit screamed that she had no maid to see to such things. Cheeks flaming, she picked at a snag in the lace cuff until she realized it was only drawing attention to the flaw, then clasped her hands together, painted a pleasant expression on her face, and concentrated on fading into the background.

Jonas, of course, looked resplendent in evening wear of the most modern cut, with his snowy white collar and cuffs immaculate. Both mothers sized him up, Mrs. Sheffield with interest, and Mrs. White with barely concealed concern. She had designed this dinner with the aim of putting her own son on display, and here was a possible competitor for the young ladies' attention. The truth of the matter was there in front of them all, if they knew how to look, visible in the attentiveness with which Sidney refilled Jonas's glass and the carefully restrained nod of thanks Jonas gave him in return. But such a thing would never occur to either of the women. Amelia repressed a wry grin at the thought of their reactions. Most likely there would be swooning involved.

Her desire to smile evaporated a moment later as the butler announced Andrew's arrival. He stepped through the doorway, looking every inch as if he belonged in this room, with its silk wallpaper and velvet-tufted rosewood furniture. His evening wear was perfect, and his manners as Sidney made the introductions were smooth and elegant. Mrs. White looked as though she'd bitten into a lemon but was trying not to let it show as she welcomed him. Amelia couldn't help noticing that his eyes strayed to her several times, a fact she was able to note only because hers kept finding him as well.

Mrs. White excused herself to check on dinner, and returned to say it was ready. Etiquette dictated each man should escort one of the ladies in to dinner. Amelia immediately turned toward Jonas, but he swallowed the last of his drink, set the glass down, and offered his arm—along with a brilliant smile—to Penelope, who glanced at her mother for permission. Amelia could almost see the debate happening inside Mrs. Sheffield's mind.

A refusal would be a deliberate snub, and Jonas was an unknown quantity. Alienating him so early would be unwise. After a tiny hesitation, Mrs. Sheffield nodded, and Penelope tucked her hand into the crook of Jonas's arm.

Standing beside Sidney, Emily, who had been watching her mother, looked amused as she took the arm he offered. Which left Amelia with Andrew, who had somehow managed to wind up standing beside her. He raised an eyebrow in invitation, and she put her hand lightly on his forearm, her traitorous heart speeding at the touch.

They found their chairs—side-by-side, to Amelia's further consternation—flanked by Mr. and Mrs. Sheffield. Across from them, Sidney was seated between the two Sheffield girls, with Jonas at the end furthest from Penelope. Several of the place cards were subtly askew, and Amelia wondered if Mrs. White's abrupt need to check on the progress of dinner had been an excuse for a last-minute rearrangement of the seating chart.

Light shone from the massive chandelier overhead, winking off the crystal stemware and making the gilded edges of the china gleam against the deep red brocade of the tablecloth. A sudden remembrance of Amos Alston's bare gray cell flashed through Amelia's mind, and the contrast left her dizzy.

She blinked away the memory and surveyed the table. Each place setting consisted of four plates and the same number of glasses, all of different sizes and shapes, surrounded by an impressive array of silver cutlery. All but a few of the pieces were familiar from the club, though there were two forks whose purpose was a mystery.

She was acutely conscious of Andrew beside her. He smelled of shaving soap and clean linen, and she imagined she could feel the warmth of his arm only inches from hers. He leaned slightly toward her to allow the butler room to pour the wine for the first course, and his shoulder brushed hers. She forced herself not to react.

Ladies removed their gloves at the dinner table, so Amelia peeled hers off and placed them beneath her napkin in her lap. A moment later she caught both Mrs. Sheffield and Mrs. White looking at her hands and inwardly winced. First the dress, and now her hands. The salve had helped, but compared to those of the other ladies, Amelia's hands were rough and reddened. Mrs. Sheffield glanced down the table at Jonas, who looked like nothing so much as a young aristocrat, and then back at Amelia, a slight frown on her face. Her voice was pleasant when she spoke, but her eyes were sharp, clearly trying to puzzle out why a brother and sister should appear to be of different social classes.

She turned to Amelia as the soup was being served. "Did I hear correctly that you and your brother have different surnames, Miss Matthew?"

"Yes. We had different fathers," Amelia said, not mentioning that they had different mothers as well.

Both women nodded as if they understood. Amelia gritted her teeth. They thought she was some sort of poor relation. Mrs. White glanced at Sidney, who was smiling politely at something Penelope had said. Apparently reassured that her son had no particular interest in Amelia, she relaxed. Mrs. Sheffield, however, still looked concerned. She had daughters to consider. If Jonas was ungenerous with his sister, would he behave any better toward his wife? She had reason to probe further, but with Jonas not seated anywhere near her, there was no graceful way to do so.

Perhaps it was only coincidence, or perhaps it was that low-level mind reading that seemed to happen between some long-married couples, but at that moment Mr. Sheffield, seated directly across from Jonas, looked at him and said, "I understand you're working at the firm now."

"Oh, are you a lawyer?" Mrs. Sheffield asked quickly. A young lawyer could have prospects, even if his family was humble.

"No," Jonas answered easily. "I'm working as a clerk."

Before either of the elder Sheffields could follow up, he turned to Emily and asked how she liked the soup.

Thwarted, Mrs. Sheffield sat back. She wasn't done with him, but in the meantime, there was another unknown quantity at the table. She turned her attention to Andrew, and Amelia took the opportunity to observe the rest of the guests.

Penelope was still chattering brightly to Sidney at one end of the table. At the other, Mr. White and Mr. Sheffield were in deep conversation, their words too quiet for her to hear. Jonas, seated to Mr. White's left, wore a more strained expression than Amelia would have expected, and though she tried to catch his eye, he wasn't paying any attention, holding out his wineglass as the butler stepped forward to refill it. Amelia caught Emily looking at her, and she smoothed her expression. There was a surprising shrewdness in the other woman's face, as if she were performing her own private assessment of her new acquaintances. Amelia pasted on her blandest smile, confident that whatever Emily thought she knew, it wasn't the half of it.

∞

Andrew was on his second spoonful of consommé when his interrogation began. He was frankly surprised to have made it that long. After the autopsy, he'd gone to Sidney's office to share the results. The two of them had spent half an hour discussing the case and its implications. Andrew had been on the verge of departing when Sidney issued the dinner invitation, giving him fair warning of what to expect. Having been the target of such parental matchmaking dinners in the past, he had been on the verge of declining when Sidney added, in a diffident tone, that Jonas and Amelia would be there as well. Andrew had accepted without stopping to consider his motivations.

"My son tells me you're from Philadelphia," Mr. White said.

"Yes," Andrew said without elaborating. He might not be able to avoid it, but he intended to at least make them work for it.

Mrs. Sheffield, who had been watching him through narrowed eyes, looked more interested. "You're one of the Philadelphia Cavanaughs? The Awbery branch or the Rittenhouse branch?"

He suppressed a sigh. She might as well have come right out and asked if he was one of the rich ones or the very rich ones. "The latter," he said. Andrew's paternal grandfather had possessed a keen eye for good investments and enough money to be able to take risks. Most of them had paid off. There had been three sons, but the middle one died young, leaving two male Cavanaughs to inherit tidy fortunes. Andrew's mother had brought money of her own to her marriage, and access to two fortunes plus his own considerable business acumen meant Andrew's father was now an order of magnitude wealthier than his younger brother, who was in no danger of penury himself.

Mrs. White looked momentarily peeved to discover her son was no longer the only extremely eligible young man at the table, but hastily rearranged her expression into one of benign interest. "You were born in Philadelphia, weren't you, Della?"

"Yes," Mrs. Sheffield said, her voice and expression markedly warmer. "I was a Baird before I married." She affected a casual demeanor, but she was clearly eager to make certain he knew she was one of the so-called Old Philadelphians—the families who founded the city and, in many ways, still ruled it.

It was part of a tiresome ritual Andrew had spent his entire life performing. He'd once described his own family to Amelia as being excessively aware of their position. It was true, but he'd devoted a great deal of time to thinking about it and had concluded it wasn't entirely their fault. Humans had to have something to strive for. The wealthy, freed from the need to worry about the necessities of life, had to expend that energy elsewhere. Some concentrated on growing their fortunes, more out of habit than anything else. A few embraced philanthropy and even did some actual good—look at Mr. Carnegie and his libraries. But most went looking for other kinds of power. The men entered politics. The women set about climbing the social ladder.

The hierarchy was unspoken, but all of them knew the rules. Old money was superior to new, though enough new money might buy a spot on a lower rung, as long as the new money knew its place and remained properly deferential. If it married well and lasted long enough to become old money, it might be invited to step upward.

Almost as important as old money was an old name. For some unaccountable reason, which boat one's forebears had taken from Europe and how long ago it had departed figured into the calculation of one's current status. After money and pedigree came the more subjective measures: tastefulness in dress and decor, adherence to convention, and conscientiousness in guarding the perimeter against interlopers.

Andrew had never bothered to question any of it—it was a very comfortable life, after all—until his sister's death. The Cavanaugh money and position had not prevented Susannah's mental illness and eventual suicide, but it had done a fine job of covering them up and protecting everyone else from scandal. His grief and awareness of his own complicity had driven him to break with his family, end an advantageous engagement, and leave the city of his birth for a thoroughly disreputable job in New York City's municipal insane asylum.

Much of it was for the best. He had not been in love with his fiancée, nor she with him. His work at the asylum had been deeply meaningful, even aside from having helped put an end to a string of murders-for-hire committed by one of his fellow physicians. It had introduced him to parts of the world he had been shielded from growing up. It had given him greater empathy and broad-mindedness, made him self-reliant in a way he'd never truly been before, and taught him there was little he actually needed in the way of luxuries to be content.

And he had met Amelia.

But the total estrangement from his family had been an overreaction. For all their faults, his parents loved their children and had tried to do their best by them. Susannah's death had broken their hearts, and Andrew's subsequent rejection had salted the wound. Repairing that relationship had been necessary and healing, but he could not go back to being the person he had been before. He refused to go back to comparing pedigrees with new acquaintances and mentally evaluating everything he did for its potential effects on his place in some invisible ranking system. He would not play those games. Not anymore.

It felt especially grotesque given where he'd spent the afternoon. A child was dead. Another child stood accused of the crime. What did petty matters of rank and position mean when weighed alongside such realities?

So instead of doing as Mrs. Sheffield expected and asking a question that would allow her to talk about some illustrious ancestor or probe his own family line, Andrew merely nodded politely and said, "I'm familiar with the family."

Then he ate another spoonful of soup.

Thrown off balance by his failure to follow the typical script, she looked flustered for a moment before recovering. "What brought you to New York?"

Andrew found himself wondering, with a sort of devilish glee, how she would react to his answer. He suppressed a grin as he spoke. "I took a position at the city insane asylum."

The entire table was silent. Both mothers blinked at him, nonplussed.

"How . . . How extraordinary," Mrs. White said, a trifle breathlessly. "And commendable, of course," she added a beat later. "To want to help those unfortunate souls."

"Do you live there? Among the madwomen?" Penelope asked. Her eyes were round with curiosity and apprehension. "I'd be terrified. What if one of them decided she wanted to cut your throat in the night!"

"Penelope," Mrs. Sheffield said reprovingly. Bloody murders were not an appropriate topic of conversation for genteel young ladies.

"I'm sorry, Mother," Penelope said, abashed.

"Several of the doctors do live there," Andrew said, as the staff began to clear the soup plates. "But I board here in the city. And at any rate, most of the patients aren't violent. Many suffer from melancholy and other such afflictions."

"Drink and disease, I'd wager," Mr. Sheffield said from the other side of the table.

"Poverty," Jonas interjected, his voice louder than necessary. He seemed to hear it and adjusted his volume as he went on. "Mostly they suffer from poverty." He drained his wineglass and handed it to a waiting maid, who took the last of the used dishes away as the butler began to serve the fish course.

Emily excused herself from the table and whispered something to one of the maids. The maid whispered back—probably directions to the washroom. As the young woman left the room, Mrs. White took the opportunity to turn the conversation back to its original purpose.

"Do you intend to make a career of being an asylum doctor?" She sounded hopeful. Andrew would be quite a bit less attractive to the Sheffields if he meant to stay in such a low status position.

"I considered it," Andrew said truthfully. "But the job hasn't been what I'd hoped."

Jonas barked a laugh, turning it into a cough midway. His color was high, his glass already mostly empty of the crisp white wine they'd been served with the fish.

Andrew went on hastily. "I'm not likely to remain there much longer, in fact."

"And what will you do after that?" Mrs. White asked. "Set up a practice here in the city?"

"Perhaps. I've made no firm plans as yet," he said, then hesitated before he went on. "My mother has been after me to move back to Philadelphia." From the corner of his eye, Andrew caught the movement as Amelia's fork stuttered against her plate.

"Are you considering it?" Mrs. Sheffield asked.

"I may," he said, exquisitely aware of Amelia's sudden stillness beside him and forcing himself not to look at her. "My whole family is there, and I have . . . no strong ties in New York. I haven't made any decisions yet," he added, the words trailing off as Amelia rose from her chair and excused herself with a murmur.

"Well, I can certainly understand your mother's position," Mrs. White said in a hearty tone. "I would hate it if Sidney moved away. Fortunately, he's been content to stay right here, with his family around him. And, of course, we're so proud of him, working with his father. The firm will be his someday." Clearly, she was determined to drag the focus of the evening back to her own son.

Andrew was more than willing to let her.

&#8464;

Amelia made her way down the dark-paneled hallway in a daze. Andrew was thinking of leaving. He might decide to go back to Philadelphia, and she would never see him again. It felt like a sliver of glass had been shoved into her chest.

The idea hadn't ever occurred to her.

It struck her just how foolish that was. Of course he was considering leaving. He had reconciled with his family. He'd known for months now his job at the asylum wouldn't last. He had no reason to stay.

The fourth door on the left was supposed to be the bathroom. Amelia hadn't passed Emily on the way, so presumably she was still inside, but it didn't matter. Amelia didn't need it. All she'd needed was somewhere to be other than sitting at that table, watching as the mothers fenced and Jonas grew sloppy with wine. Standing alone in a hallway outside a closed door would do. But the bathroom door wasn't closed, and Emily was nowhere to be seen, so Amelia ducked inside and locked the door behind her.

Amelia should never have let Jonas talk her into coming tonight. This whole thing had been a mistake.

Those women had known within moments that there was something off about her. It was only because Jonas was with her that they hadn't already realized she had more in common with the women serving the meal than the women eating it. Amelia might be able to bluff her way through short interactions like the one with Mrs. Danbury, but there was no way she would be able to step permanently into this world and convince everyone she belonged. Everything about her—her work, her background, even her clothes and her hands—shouted that she didn't. That she never could. Even if she tried to hide it, she would inevitably slip up and reveal something that would leave her, and by extension Andrew, disgraced. Amelia couldn't do that to him. She had pulled away from him because of it, and tonight proved she'd been right to do it.

She wasn't even the same species as these women. They were as showy and dependent as parakeets with clipped wings. Their enclosures might be elaborate, Amelia thought as she looked at the checkerboard marble of the bathroom floor and the ornate fixtures, but they were cages nonetheless. She might be a common sparrow, but she had the whole of the sky.

She looked in the mirror and almost laughed at the overblown pretension. Best not to get too carried away by it. A great many sparrows got eaten by crows or had their nests knocked out of trees and windowsills by bored boys with sticks. Life was all one sort of risk or another; if you were lucky, you got to pick the one you preferred.

Amelia sighed. She couldn't stay in the bathroom all night, so she patted water on her face, dried it on one of the plush white towels, and stepped back into the hallway. A row of windows looked out over a garden, where Emily sat on a bench, her back to the house.

Amelia found the door and stepped outside.

Emily turned as she approached. "You couldn't stand it either?" she asked.

Amelia gave her a rueful smile. "What gave me away?"

Emily shrugged. "You're out here, aren't you? Join me if you like." She patted the bench beside her.

Amelia sat. The night was far from cool, but the ferocious heat of the day had abated. The back garden was large, with a high brick fence and several good-sized trees for shade. Crickets chirped amongst the shrubbery, and roses bloomed somewhere nearby, their perfume heavy in the humid air. There was a tranquility to the garden that eased some of the strain from her shoulders.

A moment passed before Emily pulled a small lacquered case from a pocket and flipped it open to reveal a neat row of hand-rolled cigarettes. "Would you like one?" she asked breezily.

"No, thank you, but you go ahead," Amelia said, amused. If this girl was trying to shock her, she would have to do better than that.

Seeming surprised by her lack of reaction, Emily put a cigarette between her lips and struck a match on the side of the bench. She lit the tip and regarded Amelia through narrowed eyes as she smoked. "So why are you here?" she asked finally.

"Here in the garden, or here at this dinner?"

"Either one." Emily blew a stream of smoke from one corner of her mouth.

Amelia shrugged, not feeling like going to the bother of figuring out the "right" answer. "Sidney—the younger Mr. White—invited us to dinner. I'm told there were three empty seats to fill, so he filled them with friends. I'm in the garden instead of at the table because it didn't seem to matter if I stayed." It was the truth. Not all of the truth, certainly, but enough. She glanced at Emily. "Your turn."

"Oh, I'm in the garden for the same reason."

"Really? Your mother won't mind?"

Emily laughed. "Up until the last year or so, Mother would have come to drag me back inside long before now. But she's finally given up, thank heavens."

"Given up?"

"On getting me married off," Emily said in a matter-of-fact tone. "I'm on the shelf. Too old, too plain, and too many strange notions to make me much of a prospect. It's all on Penny now, poor thing." There was a pause before she spoke again. "You called the younger Mr. White by his given name. I take it you know him well?"

"Fairly well," Amelia said cautiously. "Although he's more my brother's friend than mine." Again, far from the complete truth, but not a lie.

"Both his mother and mine badly want him to marry Penny. They've practically reserved the church." Emily took another pull on her cigarette and looked steadily at Amelia. "It's a terrible idea, of course. It's clear he's already taken."

Amelia straightened. "Oh, no. I don't—That is, we're not—"

"I know," Emily said. "I didn't mean you. I meant your brother."

"I'm sure I don't know what you mean," Amelia replied, on her guard at once. Her voice was ice.

Emily gave her a sideways look. "I spent a year in Paris. I know an *amitié charnelle* when I see one."

Amelia didn't speak French, but it was easy enough to guess what the phrase meant. She was flummoxed for a moment, unable to work out how best to respond. Emily seemed remarkably un-scandalized. She spoke of it casually, as if it were of no great importance to her.

Emily went on, appearing to pay no attention to her dilemma. "My mother's youngest aunt lives there on the 9th *arrondissement*. They let me stay with her since she's a respectable widow." She grinned. "But she's been there long enough to have developed very *continental* sensibilities. It was the best year of my life. I didn't want to come back." She straightened with a sigh. "So, if Mr. White isn't an option, maybe Penny would do better to go after the young doctor. He seems like a decent sort."

"He is," Amelia said stiffly.

Emily peered at her, then nodded. "Hmm. Well, maybe not him, after all. But I'd like to see her with someone who would treat her well. She's not actually stupid, you know. She's just never had the chance to be anything else. They let me go away to school, but they didn't like what it did to me—gave me all these radical ideas."

She waved the hand holding the cigarette, drawing an abstract shape in the air with the smoke. "As if there's anything strange about wanting to be in charge of one's own life. I don't want to stand in a church and promise to obey anyone against my own better judgment. I don't want to keep house and tend babies and organize teas and be content with whatever scraps of the world some man is willing to allow me to have."

It was so close to what Amelia herself had been thinking a short time before that she found herself nodding along. It was too bad there was so little chance of their becoming friends. Amelia could grow to like her.

Emily gave her a wry smile. "Anyway, they couldn't stop me from scaring men away by speaking my mind, and I was never as pretty as Penny. They aren't going to take any chances with her. They're going to pick her husband for her and get her married to him as quickly as they can, and it will never occur to her to say no, so that's why I came to dinner. I don't trust my parents not to overlook a terrible temper or a wandering eye in favor of a good pedigree and a healthy bank account. Someone has to look out for her."

"And what about looking out for yourself?" Amelia was curious. "Surely you aren't going to be content staying in their home as a spinster."

Emily made a face. "Of course not. My grandfather left Penny and me some money. It's in a trust. We don't have access to it until we turn thirty—or marry, whichever comes first. I can wait a few more years for my share."

"What will you do then?" Amelia asked.

Emily stubbed out the remains of her cigarette and turned her face up to blow out the last of the smoke. "Whatever I want," she said with a smile.

∽

This was a mistake, Jonas thought again as he emptied his glass. The butler stepped forward to refill it at once, and Jonas let him, despite the little voice in his head warning him to slow down. Two cocktails—three, technically, counting the one Amelia had set aside and he'd discreetly retrieved—plus he'd already forgotten how many glasses of wine. They were halfway through the meat course, a beef tenderloin in a heavy cream sauce. There would be some sort of liqueur with dessert, and probably an offer of brandy in the parlor afterward. They had to work later, and if Jonas arrived at the club wobbly and flushed, he'd have to spend the first half of the night dodging Sabine, who expected her staff to exercise some degree of self-control—or, at the very least, not to turn up for their shifts cockeyed—and the second half with a headache and a sour stomach, wishing he could crawl into bed. But he hadn't expected it to feel like this.

When the idea for the dinner invitation first occurred to him, it had seemed more like a clever bit of mischief than anything else. A way for Sidney to introduce his lover to his parents without their knowing it, a way to throw Amelia and Andrew together again, and a way to disrupt this particular attempt at matchmaking. Like killing—or at least bruising and harrying—several birds with one exceedingly well-placed stone. But almost as soon as they'd walked into the house, Jonas had been struck by a surge of emotion he'd never expected, and it had taken him until halfway through the meal to identify it: he was seethingly, roilingly jealous.

Not of the pretty child at the other end of the table, who blushed when Sidney spoke to her and had no idea his smiles were of the sort prompted by watching a kitten pretend to hunt. It was the sense of *plausibility* that clung to their every interaction. They barely knew one another, but they could marry tomorrow and no one would ever describe their relationship as anything but legitimate. Penelope would have a husband who could never love her with his whole self, but it wouldn't matter. She could touch his arm in public, refer to him in familiar terms without raising eyebrows, and know that no outside force—neither church, nor state, nor public scorn—could take that away from her. She could have something Jonas never could, and his envy was almost overpowering.

That was part of the reason why it drove him mad that Amelia continued to treat any relationship with Andrew as an impossibility. In the starkest terms, it wasn't. The potential was there—anyone with eyes could see it. The way she went still when he said he might go back to Philadelphia, and the way he watched her as she left the room. Oh, it was there, and it frustrated him to no end that she kept denying it. At her core, she was afraid. Jonas understood.

He had spent years keeping his emotions under control. It was a necessity in his line of work, and he'd been good at it. Then Sidney White walked into the club, and inside of a month Jonas had cut his own heart out and served it up on a platter. He didn't regret it for a moment, not really, though tonight was harder than he would have thought. The reality was there would always be tremendous pressure on Sidney to marry. He was the only son of a wealthy and well-regarded family. Every day of his life there would be some desperate mother flinging yet another girl into his path, hoping she would be the one to catch him.

And marriage was, in fact, the best camouflage for men like the two of them. There were such things as confirmed bachelors, men of status who declared they meant never to marry. It was tolerated as an eccentricity, but they were watched more closely for any hint of "unnatural behavior." The safest thing for Sidney to do was to propose to some nice girl and settle into the sort of tranquil domesticity Jonas had always scorned, but would now give his eyeteeth to have.

It was not fair. To anyone. But he could go around kicking rocks over it as much as he liked. It wouldn't do any of them any good. He gave himself a mental shake as Amelia and Emily came back into the room and moved to reclaim their places at the table. As Emily moved behind him, Jonas caught an unmistakable whiff of cigarette smoke, and he glanced at her, surprised. Before he could do more than wonder at it, Mr. Sheffield, who had been concentrating on his dinner with impressive single-mindedness, suddenly spoke.

"What's this I hear about your firm being involved in the Holloway case?" He looked between Mr. White and Sidney. "That doesn't seem like the sort of thing I'd expect to find you doing."

Mr. White pursed his lips. "The firm is not involved. Sidney has taken it upon himself to represent the boy."

All the Sheffields looked at Sidney, who looked back at them with equanimity. "I was asked by someone close to the family if I could help in the early stages. I agreed."

"I think that is admirable," Emily said. It was the first time she'd spoken since they sat down.

Mr. Sheffield snorted. "Of course you do."

"Emily has some very . . . modern . . . views," Mrs. Sheffield interjected with an uncomfortable smile.

"I don't know what this country is coming to," Mr. Sheffield grumbled. "Women wanting the vote. Workers going on strike. And now this. I don't know why they'd even bother with a trial. Didn't he confess?"

Jonas couldn't stop himself. "Of course he confessed. Anyone would have after what they did to him."

"What do you mean? What did they do to him?" Penelope asked.

"They beat him half to death after they caught him." Such bluntness was frowned upon in the presence of young ladies, and the mothers' mouths tightened as Penelope's eyes went round.

"They beat him?" She sounded shocked.

Mrs. White gave Jonas a chastising look and patted her arm. "Now, now, dear, I'm sure that's an exaggeration. And besides, everyone knows Negroes don't feel pain like we do."

Jonas barely managed to stop himself from flinging his wineglass against the wall at that, but before he could form a response, Andrew's voice cut in. It was polite, but the line of his jaw was hard as he spoke from across the table.

"That's a common belief, but there's no evidence it's true. Negroes have the exact same system of nerves and muscles as white men."

"That may be," said Mr. White. "But why couldn't it be true even so? They're certainly different enough from us in other ways."

Jonas considered the two inches of wine left in his glass. The hell with it. They wouldn't make the difference. He downed them. "And what might those be?"

Sheffield gave an irritable sigh. "Everyone knows they're less developed than the white man, somewhere above an animal, but with less moral sense, less work ethic, less intelligence than us. It follows they'd be less sensitive to pain."

"Oh, I don't know," Jonas said, flinging away the last shreds of his self-restraint. "I met a Negro doctor just this morning, and he seemed intelligent enough to me. And goodness knows there are no end of immoral, lazy, stupid white people. You can't even gather ten in a room without running into at least one." He said the last blandly enough that no one could accuse him of a direct insult, yet the words themselves hung there, bait on a barbed hook, just waiting for one of the other nine people in the room to bite.

Emily caught his eye and gave him a tiny salute with her glass.

"A Negro doctor," said Mrs. White, in a tone that made clear she was deliberately choosing to focus on that part of his statement and expected everyone else to do the same. "Why, I never heard of such a thing. Though I suppose it makes sense for them to have their own doctors. That way like can tend to like."

Jonas was about to say that Amos was half white, which might make tending to him complicated under that policy, but before he could speak, Sidney caught his eye for a pair of seconds before glancing away. His expression was neither angry nor pleading, but something about it made Jonas close his mouth. He was suddenly unbearably tired.

He had asked Sidney for his help, and Sidney had agreed, despite low odds of success, probable damage to his reputation, and increased friction with his family. If Jonas kept talking, he would make it worse. He would not change these people's minds. The sentiments they'd expressed were rather more common than not. If he kept going, kept pushing the conversation into places that made them uncomfortable, Sidney would be the one to pay for it.

Jonas wanted to reply with something cutting. Something that would shock and shame and silence them. Instead, he took a deep breath, scraped together every shred of forbearance he had left, and said, "An interesting point. I do imagine they prefer being treated by one of their own."

Mrs. White gave him a tight smile and said brightly, "Well then. I believe it's time for dessert."

❧

The final twenty minutes of dinner were near-silent, and Andrew was crushingly grateful to be able to plead an early morning and decline the offered after-dinner brandy.

"We need to be going as well," Jonas said on the heels of his refusal. No one begged him to reconsider.

Sidney stepped forward from where he had been standing beside Penelope. "Let me walk the three of you out. Please excuse me for a few moments," he said to the others.

The Whites and Sheffields made their goodbyes. To Jonas and Amelia, they were stilted, their voices and expressions covered in the thinnest veneer of civility. To Andrew, their courtesy was notably more robust, and the obvious disparity made it all the more awkward.

They all released simultaneous sighs as the front door closed behind them, then broke into quiet, self-conscious laughter as they exchanged knowing glances, whatever discomforts they were feeling with one another temporarily overcome by mutual relief.

"Let's step across the street," Sidney suggested quietly, a wry smile still on his face. "The parlor windows are just there, and I wouldn't be surprised if there was some interest in our conversation."

As he spoke, one of the windows he'd indicated was raised from the inside, and Mrs. White's voice could be heard proclaiming the evening air quite pleasant.

Sidney merely shook his head, his eyes glancing heavenward, and led them across the street, where a black steel fence surrounded a large, heavily shaded park. A plaque affixed to the bars beside the gate read PRIVATE PROPERTY, NO TRESPASSING. Andrew blinked in surprise as Sidney withdrew a key from his pocket and unlocked the gate, ushering them inside. Standing ahead of Andrew, Jonas looked at Amelia, raising one eyebrow. They stepped through the gate together and began avidly scanning their surroundings. Andrew followed, puzzled by their reaction.

It was a quiet, pretty space, with large trees and attractive plantings that remained lush and green despite the hot, dry weather. Someone kept it all well-watered, obviously. A nice park, but nothing about it seemed to warrant such a response.

"What am I missing?" he asked.

They looked at one another, then back at him.

"This is Gramercy Park," Amelia said, as if that were explanation enough.

Andrew must have looked blank, because Amelia sighed. "It's been here since the 1830s," she said. "And it's always been private. You have to have a key to enter, and you only get a key if you live in one of the houses around it. The very expensive houses around it. Neither of us has ever been inside."

"Rabble need not apply," Jonas said in a lofty tone. He wasn't drunk, but anyone who knew him would be able to tell he wasn't entirely sober, either. "There was a proposal a few years ago to run a cable car through it. You should have heard all the screeching."

"My parents were some of the loudest screechers," Sidney said. "My father was ready to fight to the death, legally speaking. The residents here are . . ."

"Elitist?" Jonas suggested. "Pompous? Over-privileged? Stuffy and self-important?" The words were harsh, but the delivery was teasing, suggesting this was part of a long-running, half-serious argument.

"All of those, yes," Sidney said, his tone one of amused exasperation. "But it's good for us at the moment, because we're not likely to be disturbed, and when I go back inside I can explain the delay by saying you asked for a tour. Happens all the time. Now," he said, turning serious. "We need to talk about the case."

They strolled along the neat, empty paths, taking turns relaying for one another what they'd learned that day. Jonas and Sidney naturally gravitated toward one another, leaving Andrew to walk beside Amelia. After a momentary hesitation, he offered his arm, and, after another hesitation, she took it.

Jonas spoke first, laying out the case Rhodes had made for Ginny's murder being only one of several committed by the same man.

"He offered to take me to visit the families tomorrow, so I'm going to—"

Sidney interrupted. "No. I need you at the coroner's inquest."

"Aren't you going?" Jonas asked.

"I'm not allowed to be there," Sidney said. "They'll call witnesses—not just the coroner, but others, too. We need to know who they are and what they say."

"Do you want me to bribe someone from the jury? Or a clerk?"

"No," said Sidney, sounding horrified. "Especially not after I've very publicly associated you with the firm. I want you to loiter in the hallway and watch who goes in and out and try to get their names. Chat with them if you get the chance. Once you know who they are, we can go and interview them later. There's no rule preventing that."

"Fine," Jonas said. "Then who's going to go with Rhodes?"

Sidney glanced at Amelia.

"No," Jonas said at once.

Amelia sighed. "Someone has to go. It might as well be me. Besides, the families—the mothers, especially—are more likely to talk to me than to a man. And speaking of men." She withdrew a card from her pocket and handed it to Sidney. "This man was at the Alston's house today." She told them what Miles had said about him.

"I'll look into it tomorrow," Sidney said, putting the card in his own pocket.

They'd made a full circuit of the park by then, and as they began the second, Sidney asked Andrew to tell them about the results of the postmortem. Amelia's hand tightened as he recounted the salient points of the examination. When he confirmed there was no evidence of sexual interference, she let out a breath beside him, and her posture relaxed.

"The coroner seems likely to return a finding of poisoning," he concluded. "But I'm skeptical. I would have liked to check the stomach contents, at least. And I want to know what that powder is."

Sidney spoke. "I drafted a petition after we spoke this afternoon asking for the defense to be provided with a copy of Amos's confession, along with copies of all photographs from the postmortem and a sample of the powder for our own testing. We need an expert. Someone who can do the analysis quickly and whose name is respected enough that the court would have to listen if it turns out to be something that helps Amos. There can't be more than a few such men in the city. Can you take responsibility for identifying and contacting them with the request?"

"I'm expected on the island tomorrow," Andrew said, "but the other doctors are probably the best place to begin the inquiries. They'll know all of the big names, and I can make telephone calls at the same time."

"All right," Sidney said. "That's the beginning of a plan, at least. Jonas, you'll need to be at the courthouse by nine at the latest. Amelia, if you'll come to my office, we can chat about your strategy before you meet Rhodes. I'm glad you all got a good dinner tonight, because we're not going to have time to eat over the next—"

"Oh," Andrew said, startled. "I forgot. Sidney, I don't think I remembered to tell you this earlier, but your mentioning food made me think of it. Ginny had a shard of candy stuck in her hair. Peppermint candy."

Sidney and Jonas exchanged a significant look.

"What?" Andrew looked at them.

"Rhodes told us this morning—this was after you left," Jonas said to Amelia, "that the police found a broken stick of peppermint candy beside the back gate. It seems he wasn't lying about his sources."

"It's good to have confirmation," Sidney said. "But it doesn't help identify the killer. 'He has candy in his pocket' isn't exactly damning evidence."

"Polly mentioned sending candy to Amos when I was there earlier today," Amelia said.

There was an uncomfortable pause.

"Well," Sidney said eventually. "It doesn't mean anything, but hopefully it wasn't peppermints."

The four of them were quiet for another long moment, the only sound that of their feet on the packed gravel of the path, before Jonas shot a glance over his shoulder at Amelia, and a wordless communication passed between them. Jonas drew Sidney off onto a separate path, leaving Andrew alone with Amelia beneath the trees.

They didn't speak, the silence between them growing less comfortable as the seconds passed. Finally, Andrew could bear it no longer. He stopped and turned to her. "I'm not certain of the right thing to say here," he said. "I suspect etiquette would dictate I say nothing of substance at all and behave as though we are pleasant acquaintances and nothing more."

Amelia drew back, her face going guarded, as if she feared whatever he was about to say.

Andrew rushed on, hoping to get it all out before she told him to stop or simply walked away. "But the books don't take into account situations like this. I know you don't want—That you aren't—That we aren't—"

God, he was babbling. Andrew drew in a breath and clamped down on his emotions. "We're going to be working together, at least for the next few days. It's going to be difficult enough without our being uncomfortable around one another. I don't want that. We need to be able to trust one another. We were friends, I thought, on the island. Before—" He cleared his throat. "I would like to be again, if we can. I won't seek more. If you think—"

"Yes," Amelia interrupted. "Friends. I would like that." She turned and began walking back toward the gate, taking the same path as Sidney and Jonas.

Andrew followed, trying to feel relieved. He should feel relieved. Amelia said she wanted to be friends. Except he didn't believe her. That same sense of separation, of distance, still lay heavy on him.

As they neared the gate, he began looking for Sidney and Jonas, but they weren't anywhere he could see. Perhaps they'd already gone back through the gate and were waiting on the other side. Andrew looked at Amelia, who wore a wry, amused expression.

"What—" he began, but she interrupted him with a sharp, low whistle aimed at one of the largest trees.

Deep beneath the low-hanging branches, a shadow stretched and split. The leaves rustled as first Jonas, and a moment later Sidney, emerged from the gloom, both flushed and slightly more rumpled than the last time he'd seen them. Jonas was unabashed, while Sidney wore an expression of mild chagrin. Andrew couldn't suppress a startled laugh, and Amelia glanced back at him with the first fully genuine smile he'd seen from her since their breakfast celebration months before.

Sidney straightened his jacket and held the park gate open for them. Andrew's momentary feeling of ease evaporated as they exited. He was not the only one to sense the change; all four of them fell out of the natural pairings they'd drifted into and resumed the decorous distance required for propriety's sake. They stood on the sidewalk, their reluctance to walk away from one another palpable.

At last Sidney squared his shoulders and bade them farewell, turning toward his parents' house with a sigh. A curtain twitched in the window as he crossed the street. Amelia took Jonas's arm and tugged him away, giving Andrew a guarded nod as she did. Andrew watched as they left, all bound by ties, both chosen and not, pulling them in different directions.

∽

What had begun as an apology for his behavior at dinner had quickly turned into more, and the drunken, reckless part of Jonas was heartily sorry he and Sidney had been interrupted so soon. The park was lovely. And private. Even that brief moment together had raised his spirits. Perhaps they could go back by themselves another time.

Surprisingly, Amelia didn't rib him about it on the way back to the club, though whether it was because she correctly sensed he was in no mood for teasing or because she was lost in her own thoughts, he didn't know. She needed to change clothes before their shift, so they separated on the sidewalk. As she disappeared into the mouth of the alley leading to their apartment, Jonas mounted the club's front steps and rapped on the door.

Tommy opened it. "Boss lady wants to talk to you," he said in greeting. "Told me to send you up soon's you got here."

Jonas grimaced. There went his plan to avoid Sabine until he was fully sober. "Do you know what she wants?"

"I don't," said Tommy, who lowered his voice as he went on. "But she was lookin' pretty sour when she came through."

Jonas sighed. Keeping her waiting would only make her temper worse, so he walked straight through the still-empty main room and made his way up to the second-floor parlor she used as an office.

Sabine looked up from her desk when he tapped a knuckle against the door jamb, and her mouth tightened as she looked him over. "How much have you had?"

Damn it.

"Hardly anything," Jonas assured her as he walked to his chair, careful to make certain he neither swayed nor slurred. "It was a perfectly respectable dinner party."

She made a disbelieving noise, but didn't push the issue. "That's good, because I'm going to need you on your toes tonight. You're going to have to cover the whole place yourself."

"Why? Where's Gunnar?"

Sabine made a notation on a paper before she answered. "I let Gunnar go."

"What?" Jonas blurted.

"I've hired a replacement," she continued, paying no attention to his outburst. "He starts next week, but he'll be in later tonight to get the lay of the land. You'll need to show him around."

Jonas waited for her to say more, but she merely raised an eyebrow. "That will be all."

The evening grew worse from there.

The club opened and began to fill, but even compared to recent weeks, it was a harder-drinking, more restless crowd than usual. All anyone wanted to do, it seemed, was talk about Ginny Holloway. Between drinks they traded lurid details gleaned from the papers, shared bits of gossip they'd picked up from God only knew where, and lamented the sad state the city was coming to that something like this could have happened.

And, of course, they savaged her supposed killer.

Jonas lost track of how many times he heard someone say hanging was too good for him. That they wouldn't feel safe in their beds until he was dead. That it was no better than one could expect from a mongrel. Half-Negro, you know—though that wasn't the word most of them used—and add to it the Irish influence, and it was no wonder.

The only mercy was Miles wasn't there to hear any of it. He'd taken the night off to be with his family. However, he wouldn't be able to afford to stay away long. Sabine was a fairly generous employer, but altruism never made anyone's fortune. She wouldn't keep him on staff if he didn't work. Miles would have to face it all without reacting.

And none of it was going to get better as more details trickled out. The evening editions had printed Amos's name, but nothing more about his family. It was only a matter of time. Jonas hurriedly scanned the papers as the patrons cast them aside. Rhodes's word, so far, at least, seemed to be good. There was an article in the *Sun*, but it was no worse than any of the others. He and Amelia weren't mentioned, and Sidney's statement was accurately quoted.

By midnight, the club was full, and the press of bodies meant it was warmer indoors than out. The tang of perspiration—never sweat, not among as rich a crowd as this one—began to compete with the smells of rich food and heavy perfume and cigar smoke. Jonas, his temples throbbing, made his way to Amelia's room, eager to find a few moments of peace.

It was not to be. Amelia was in a waspish temper, having been propositioned by a client. Jonas suppressed a sigh as he listened to her fuming. It was worse tonight because of Andrew. She was already convinced she wasn't good enough for him, and somewhere in her mind, she thought if she could be so easily taken for a whore, then it must be true.

It was ridiculous. They worked in a place where many of the staff did, in fact, take money in exchange for their favors. It was reasonable to expect that occasionally someone would be interested in Amelia's. It wasn't worth getting offended over. She, like everyone else, was free to respond to such offers as she liked. Sabine's philosophy was that a lack of enthusiasm for the work made for sub-par whores. It wasn't true—they'd both seen enough to know that even those who plainly detested the work never seemed to lack for clients—but Sabine's edict made the club a better place to work than most.

Jonas knew better than to tell her she was overreacting or speculate aloud as to why, but there was a limit to his own patience, so he escaped back into the hallway as quickly as he could.

Sabine called out to him as he passed the door to her room. "Jonas."

In contrast to earlier, this time she sounded almost . . . nervous. Not a word he'd ever associated with the self-assured, iron-willed woman. He stopped and turned. Standing beside her was a slight, roughly dressed man with a pugnacious thrust to his jaw and flat black hair so at odds with the tone of his skin that it had to be dyed.

"This is Dermot," she said. "He's taking over for Gunnar."

"How d' ye do, lad?" Dermot thrust out a hand, his heavy Irish accent marking him as a recent arrival.

Jonas warily took the hand, which was as ridged as a walnut shell, as he looked the man over. He was several years older than Jonas, with a hard-looking, weather-beaten face and a wild, mad light in his eyes that more than made up for his lack of bulk. A chill touched the back of Jonas's neck. It was a warning that said here was a man who would hurt you on the least excuse and never have a moment's disquiet over it.

Neither conscience nor consequences would bear on his behavior. Here was a man who was dangerous. Jonas's heartbeat accelerated.

Dermot was making his own reciprocal inspection of Jonas, and the grin that pulled at the corner of his mouth said he recognized the threat as mutual.

Good.

"Welcome," Jonas said, making no attempt to smile. "If you'll give me a few minutes, I'll be ready to show you the place." Almost unwillingly, he turned his back to the pair, his skin crawling, certain Dermot's eyes were boring into his back.

His stomach churning, Jonas turned at once down the hallway to the toilets. Some cold water on his face might help. He was only halfway there when running footsteps thudded on the wood floor behind him. Jonas's chest tightened, and a pulse of heat ran up his spine. He spun, fists coming up, ready to defend himself from the expected attack.

The young waiter skidded to a stop, eyes wide and palms up-raised.

"What do you want?" Jonas said, his voice raspy. He was barely able to make himself drop his hands to his sides. They tingled. There was a ringing in his ears and a metallic taste in his mouth. Spots danced in front of his vision.

"Ah, Lily needs you upstairs," he stammered. "It's another one of . . . You know."

Jonas closed his eyes and took a deep breath. He sent the waiter on his way and made himself move toward the stairs. His vision cleared as he climbed, but the roiling inside him got worse.

Lily, petite and red-haired, was a popular chorus girl who enthusiastically solicited invitations to the rooms upstairs. Usually, she was willing to indulge the men in their fantasies. But lately . . .

"Third one this week," she said, her face set in disgust as Jonas approached her. She stood outside the door in nothing but her shift, a strap of which had fallen off of one freckled shoulder. "I halfway think I ought to do it when they ask. We both know there are places they could go for the real thing. But Mother Mary help me, I just can't."

"I'll take care of it," Jonas said, brushing past her into the room.

An obviously drunk man sat on the bed in his undershirt. He looked up blearily as Jonas entered. "Ginny?"

"It's time for you to leave," Jonas said. God knew he wasn't one to judge people for their pleasures, but some things were not to be tolerated.

"I said I'd pay double!" he protested.

Jonas hoisted him upright. "She's not interested."

The man began to struggle. "I wouldn' do 'er any harm. I jus' wan'—"

Jonas put one hand on his shoulder. With the other, he twisted the man's arm up behind his back. "We're all aware of what you want," he said, feeling an overwhelming desire to twist the arm out of its socket like a wing off a roast chicken. He forced himself to stop an inch short of that point, far enough to hurt, but not far enough to maim. The man let out a pained yelp, and Jonas dragged him out of the room and toward the back stairs, thinking as he did it that he should have gone ahead and gotten blind drunk after all.

# 8

I t was far too early when Amelia left the apartment on Tuesday morning. She hadn't gotten to bed until nearly four, and it was now only just past nine. What sleep she had gotten had been uneasy, with anxious thoughts popping into her mind each time she began to drift off.

The dinner had been one step shy of a disaster. And her shift at the club, which might have allowed her to take her mind off of it, had been marred by Jonas's foul mood and her last client's insulting proposition.

And now she was going to spend several hours visiting the families of murdered children with a man she'd never met. A man who would be only too willing to use any information she inadvertently gave him for his own purposes. She had to be on her guard, but her guard, in truth, was feeling rather battered at the moment.

After the asylum, she would have laughed in the face of anyone who suggested she get involved with another murder case. But Tommy asking for their help had tipped over the first of a string of dominoes. There'd been no obvious moment to stop them, and now here they were, not merely involved, but knowing if they walked away further deaths would be at least partly on their heads.

And as much as that fact should have been enough to drive every other concern from her mind, Amelia was guiltily aware it was not. She'd spent more of her evening than she wanted to admit thinking about Andrew. Being around him the night before had been hard. The plain truth of it was she didn't want to be his friend. It would be easier if he weren't being so damned reasonable about the whole thing. If he'd been cold or sullen or had tried to argue, then it would be easier to keep him at arm's length. If he would just be less . . . decent. Her mouth twisted in a wry, private grin at the notion of wishing a man worse than he was. God knew most of them didn't need that sort of urging.

Amelia tried to refocus as she neared the corner where Jonas had been meant to meet Rhodes. A man she assumed must be the reporter stood there, looking much as Jonas had described him. Tall and whipcord-thin, he was inexpensively dressed, with a prominent Adam's apple and a pair of sharply inquisitive eyes, which widened when she offered him her gloved hand.

"You must be Mr. Rhodes," she said. "I'm Miss Matthew. I'll be accompanying you today."

"I thought Vincent was going to be my companion today."

Amelia shook her head. "Mr. White needed him somewhere else this morning. You get me instead."

"Well," he said with a grin. "Who am I to object to such an attractive substitute?" He held out an arm with a wink. "Shall we?"

Amelia accepted the offered arm and gave him the bland smile she used for overly familiar clients at the club. If he thought her susceptible to flirtation, he would be sorely disappointed. "I suppose so."

Undaunted, he kept up a stream of small talk on the way to the elevated train, all of it in the same relaxed, intimate tone, as if they were friends of long standing. Amelia played along, answering the questions that didn't matter and turning aside those that did with practiced ease. He was good, she decided as they boarded. It would be all too easy to forget what he was. It was no wonder he set Jonas's teeth on edge.

There was an abandoned newspaper on one of the seats, and Amelia flipped through its pages as they trundled east toward the Brooklyn Bridge. A small advertisement at the bottom of the page under the heading "Clairvoyants" caught her eye.

*"Mme Rose has returned from her summer residence at Crescent Beach, near Boston, and can now be consulted on all affairs of life at her home, Ivy Cottage, 22 Elm Place. Office Hours 10 A.M. to 8 P.M."*

Madame Rose must not be doing too badly, if she could afford to keep regular hours and a house of her own. Perhaps she and Jonas should come over some day and meet her. Amelia had never met anyone who possessed a gift like her own—not that it was likely Madame Rose did. She sighed. Having a mentor to help her master her abilities would be preferable to the slipshod trial and error methods she'd been using so far.

"Checking out the competition?"

Amelia looked up to find Rhodes regarding her with a quizzical eye.

"Something like that."

"It's an interesting line of work you're in," he said. "How does one go about becoming a fortune-teller to the rich and slightly scandalous?"

There was that tone again. He managed to make the question sound like nothing more than friendly curiosity. "I expect it's like anything else," Amelia said. "Sometimes you fall into things and they work out."

She turned the page. Rhodes took the hint, and they rode for a few moments in blessed silence. Brooklyn was expanding at a prodigious rate, and a significant portion of the paper was advertisements for new houses, mostly three- to four-story brownstones. Most boasted they were *"trimmed with select hardwoods"* and had *"tiled bathrooms with exposed plumbing and every modern convenience."* Several mentions of *"electric burglar alarms," "onyx fireplaces,"* and *"magnificent locations"* later, Amelia closed the paper, wishing she had $5,000 to spare.

As they crossed onto the Brooklyn Bridge, she set the paper aside and leaned toward the window.

Rhodes perked up. "First time across?"

Amelia shook her head. "I've been twice before. Jonas was here for the opening," she added.

"But not you?"

"No." When the bridge opened in May 1883, Amelia had been only nine years old, still some three years away from leaving the Foundling to join Jonas on the streets. "But he told me all about it afterward. How they cut the ribbon and Emily Roebling rode across—ahead of President Arthur and the governor, even."

In truth, Emily Roebling, wife of the bridge's chief engineer, had earned the right. She had managed most of the construction after her husband was crippled early in the project. Washington Roebling had been struck down by Caisson disease—Amelia gathered it had something to do with breathing pressurized air while underwater—as he oversaw the digging of the bridge's massive footers, which had to be sunk deep into the riverbed.

For more than a decade, he watched through a telescope while his wife directed the work. When it was done, she rode across holding a rooster, a symbol of victory. Amelia had always suspected the woman, who had undoubtedly bought a new dress for the occasion, couldn't have been thrilled about having nervous poultry on her lap, symbolism or no.

"I missed the opening," Rhodes said. "I was in bed with the chicken pox that week. But I was here for the Elephant Walk."

"Really?" Despite her desire to keep him at arm's length, Amelia couldn't help but be interested. A year after the bridge's opening, amid lingering concerns about its safety, showman P.T. Barnum had offered to prove the bridge was sound by marching a line of elephants from Manhattan to Brooklyn. That was one sight she sorely regretted missing.

"Really. I was fifteen and already working for the *Daily Eagle*—mostly as a runner, although sometimes when the typesetter was hungover, he let me help. I tagged along with one of the reporters, so I was there to count all twenty-one elephants and seventeen camels as they stepped off the bridge, Jumbo in the lead," he said.

The grin he flashed this time seemed genuine, and Amelia returned it. "I've seen the elephants at the Central Park menagerie," she said. "I imagine seeing that many of them walking along the street would be quite a sight."

"And smell," he said, waving a hand in front of his nose and making a face. Amelia laughed.

As they passed the midpoint of the bridge, Amelia peered out, mildly disappointed the day was too hazy for the Liberty statue to be visible but enjoying the view nonetheless.

A few minutes later, they disembarked in Brooklyn and boarded the Kent Avenue streetcar. It was too crowded for talking about the case, so they spent another thirty minutes in idle conversation as they made their way to Greenpoint. Despite herself, Amelia found she was enjoying Rhodes's company.

When they reached their stop, he led her along streets that looked little different from New York's. "We're going to the Rudlyks' first," he said as they turned onto a block where the smell of baking hung heavy in the air. "After that I'll take you to meet the Jankowskis."

"What about the Nowaks?"

Rhodes shook his head. "The Nowaks moved to Chicago a year after Paulina died—there were some cousins settled out there. Thought they could make a fresh start."

They stopped in front of a door over which a sign read PIEKARNIA. A smaller sign, on the building's side, read DOM KAPIELOWY, with an arrow pointing into the alley.

"This is the Rudlyks' place," Rhodes said. "They live in the apartment above, their bakery is the front, and they rent out the back. Right now it's a bath house."

He held the door open for her, and she stepped into a tidy storefront. The air was thick with the smell of butter and sugar tinged with cinnamon. A glass display case held pastries and breads, and a sturdily built, rosy-cheeked woman stood behind a counter. She smiled as she saw Rhodes, then shifted her eyes to Amelia. "*Najwyższy czas, żeby kogoś przyprowadzić. Ładna, ale zbyt chuda dla niemowląt.*"

To Amelia's surprise, Rhodes laughed and replied in the same language. "*Na pewno masz coś, co ją tuczy.* Coffee?" he asked, turning to Amelia.

"Please."

He said something else in Polish, then nodded toward one of the little tables.

"So," Amelia said once they were seated. "'Peter Rhodes?'"

"Piotr Rodek, technically, but that doesn't make for as appealing a byline. Born six months after my parents arrived from Krakow."

"What did she say when we came in?"

Rhodes grinned. "That it's about time I brought a pretty girl around, but you're too thin for babies."

Amelia glanced in the woman's direction and lowered her voice. "Is she Ina's mother?"

"No. Marya opens the bakery early, then goes to Mass mid-morning after things slow down. She'll be back in half an hour or so."

The woman approached with a tray holding not only their coffee but also a plate of sweets. She set them down on the table with a wink and walked away.

"They make the best raspberry *kolaches* in the city," Rhodes said, pointing at a small cookie made of folded pastry dough. It was dusted with sugar and had a thumbprint of ruby jam in the center.

Amelia ate one, then reached for a second. "All right," she said after swallowing the last bite. "We need to talk about the cases. Tell me everything you told Jonas yesterday."

He took her quietly through it all, spreading the children's pictures on the table and glancing at his notebook as he recounted the details of their disappearances. Amelia caught a glimpse of a rough-sketched map as he flipped through the pages.

"What's that?"

"It's a map of where the first three children lived, and where their bodies were found," he said, turning it so she could see. Three dots formed a backwards L, each with a cross a few blocks away. He pointed at the northernmost dot on the sketch, then at the cross nearest it. "This is Paulina. Then Markus." His finger moved to the westernmost dot and cross, before moving east again to the hinge of the L and the last cross. "And finally, Ina. They were all found within a few blocks of where they disappeared. I've started another for Ginny in Manhattan." He flipped to a second page. The dot and cross on that page were further apart than those on the first map.

Amelia stared at the markings, willing them to offer some sort of clue. "Ginny was taken at night," she said finally. "Were any of the others?"

"Broad daylight."

"And no witnesses?"

Rhodes hesitated. "One. Paulina Nowak's little brother was with her when she disappeared. Her mother sent her for a pound of potatoes and told her to take Yitzak along. He was barely two, but he definitely saw something."

"What did he see?"

"No one is certain. All of this is third-hand, you understand. I never got to talk to the Nowaks personally. I didn't even know about Paulina until I started digging after Markus was taken. The parents barely spoke any English. They relied on Paulina for that. But they did contact the police, and they managed to get across to them that their daughter was missing. According to the report, when the police asked Yitzak what happened to his sister, he said the broom man took her."

"The broom man?"

Rhodes shrugged. "That was all they could get out of him. There was a street sweeper in the neighborhood. An old man. Lived with his granddaughter and her husband. They questioned him and searched the house, but it turned out he'd been in bed with an attack of rheumatism that day. The granddaughter might have been willing to lie for him, but a neighbor had been in to see him too, with some salve she made. He couldn't have done it."

"And no one saw anything with the others?"

Rhodes shook his head. "They just vanished. I've always thought—"

He cut himself off as the front door opened and a woman stepped inside. Marya Rudlyk, undoubtedly. She was an older, plumper version of her lost daughter. She looked pleased to see Rhodes, but the light left her face as her eyes dropped to the pictures on the table.

"Marya," Rhodes said, rising and clasping the woman's hands in his. "This is Miss Matthew. She's helping with the investigation."

"Good morning, Piotr. Miss Matthew, is good to meet you," she said, her English heavily accented but understandable. "Let me check on Sofia, then we talk."

She switched to Polish as she spoke to the other woman, stripping off her hat and gloves as she did. She returned to them a moment later, carrying her own cup of coffee.

"I'm so sorry for your loss," Amelia said as Marya took her seat. There was no sign that Ina's spirit remained with her mother, and though Amelia steeled herself before shaking the woman's hand, she saw nothing.

Marya nodded. "Thank you. We miss her. Every day, we miss her. This boy they arrested, did he hurt my Ina?"

"No," Amelia said. "That's why I'm involved. He couldn't have had any connection to the children in Brooklyn."

Rhodes took the lead, asking Marya in a surprisingly gentle voice to recount the day Ina went missing. Their tenants in the back shop had been in the process of moving out of the space, so there had been an unusual amount of activity. Ina had been everywhere underfoot, so her mother sent her outside to play. Her face grew more lined and more gray as she spoke of the moment of realization, of the desperate searching. No one had seen anything. Ina had been there one moment and gone the next. Days later, the discovery. Marya wiped tears from her eyes.

Amelia's throat ached in sympathy. She was almost sorry they'd come. She'd learned little and forced this woman to sift through a horrifically painful memory. They left shortly thereafter, Rhodes accepting the bundle of pastries Marya pressed on him and promising to come see her again soon.

"Show me where the bodies were found," Amelia said abruptly as they walked away from the bakery. Maybe one of the children's spirits lingered in the place their body had been left. The thought of such an encounter was less than appealing, and the thought of making the attempt in front of Rhodes was almost enough to stop her from trying. But she couldn't afford to waste the opportunity.

The vacant lot where Ina Rudlyk's body had been abandoned was narrow and strewn with garbage. "Give me the photograph," Amelia said, holding out a hand to Rhodes as she peered into the gloom.

"Why?" Rhodes asked.

"Just do it," Amelia snapped, then glanced at him and tried to soften her tone. "If anything . . . happens . . . just pull me away and wait."

He opened his mouth, then apparently thought better of whatever he was about to say and closed it again, frowning.

Amelia tried to ignore his presence behind her as she held the photograph. "Ina Rudlyk, come to me," she muttered under her breath. There was no itch in her chest, and no wisp of silvery mist appeared. There was no sign the girl's spirit lingered in that depressing place, and Amelia was glad of it.

Rhodes eyed her as they walked north toward the wretched little alley where Paulina's body had been found, but he didn't speak, and he handed over the next photograph without comment. Again, Amelia attempted the summons, and again, there was nothing at the site.

As they walked toward the spot where Markus's body had been found, Rhodes's demeanor was tense and uncertain, as if he waged some internal battle. When Amelia put out her hand for the sketch of the boy, he didn't move to retrieve it for her.

Instead, he gave her a searching look, his mouth a tight line. "This . . . Whatever this is," he said, waving a hand in her direction. "It isn't necessary. Not on my account."

"I'm not doing it on your account," Amelia said evenly.

"Then you really do believe you can—" He cut himself off before finishing the question, but the tone of his voice left no doubt of his opinion. The reporter had thought her a fraud. Now he thought her slightly mad.

"I don't need you to believe me," Amelia said. Her cheeks warmed from a combination of embarrassment and anger. An anger she was aware was unjustified, which only irritated her further. "I need you to give me that picture and let me get on with what I do."

Rhodes hesitated, then held the sketch out to her. Amelia made a concerted effort to calm herself, then took it and called for the spirit of the murdered boy, not sure if she hoped more that he did or didn't come. After a long moment of frustration, she sighed and stepped back. Three failures in a row.

Rhodes didn't meet her eyes as he took the sketch back. He spent a long moment looking at it before tucking it away.

A sudden suspicion bloomed. "Who drew that?" Amelia asked.

"I did."

"It's very good. Is it from a photograph?"

He hesitated, still not looking at her. "It's a copy of a sketch I did earlier."

She looked at him, surprised. "You knew Markus?"

"Yes," Rhodes said. "Daniela—his mother—has been friends with one of my sisters since they were children."

"This isn't just a story to you, is it? You actually care about these children." Too late, she heard the surprise in her own voice and recognized the naked insult she'd offered.

Rhodes's eyes narrowed. "I grew up with six brothers and sisters over on Freeman Street. Any of us could have been one of these children. I cared about these children before anyone ever heard the name Ginny Holloway. They deserve to have their killer found, and I will do everything in my power to make that happen. And yes," he went on, passion in his voice, "I also care about the story. I've worked hard. I'm a damned good reporter. This story ought to be on the front pages, in the biggest type that will fit. And I want to be the one who puts it there." He looked at her defiantly, as if waiting for her censure.

"I apologize for the implication," Amelia said, raising one hand in surrender. "It was unfair of me."

They stood in awkward silence.

"I understand, you know," Amelia said after a long moment. "What it's like to have your motives questioned and your origins held against you." Her natural reluctance to reveal personal information warred with her desire to prove she was sympathetic to his struggle. "Jonas and I grew up at the Foundling," she said finally, using the common name for the city's Catholic orphan asylum.

"Oh?"

An edge of Rhodes's inquisitive tone was back, but Amelia ignored it. "How far to the Jankowskis' is it from here?"

"Not far." Rhodes hesitated. "I'd prefer if you didn't . . . I don't want to upset Daniela with . . ." He waved at the vacant lot.

"I can't promise that," Amelia said. "Whether or not I . . . It's unpredictable."

"Then perhaps we'd better not go at all."

Amelia stood, torn. She would just as soon skip the visit herself. But it was her last chance to make contact with one of the Brooklyn victims. "Look," she said finally. "I can't promise nothing will happen. But I can promise not to push anything to happen. I won't try to call him in front of her."

Rhodes looked as if he would argue, then visibly stopped himself. "All right. Let's go."

Six blocks later, Daniela Jankowski answered the door when Rhodes knocked. She was hugely pregnant, and her forehead was beaded with sweat. The raucous sound of multiple children came from inside the apartment behind her.

"Piotr," she said, pulling him down to kiss his cheek. He had to bend forward over the curve of her belly. She looked at Amelia.

"This is Miss Matthew," Rhodes said.

"Well, come in, both of you."

The apartment was tiny and spotless, with Rhodes's original sketch of Markus framed on one wall. Four children regarded the visitors curiously. They ranged from a girl of about eight to a tiny boy who staggered across the room on unsteady legs. He stuck two fingers in his mouth as he regarded them with dark, solemn eyes.

"Ruta, give them their lunch while we talk outside," Daniela said, leading them to the fire escape.

"Are you sure you can make it out the window?" Rhodes said teasingly.

"Hush, you," she said, slapping him gently on the arm.

Daniela's story was much the same as Marya's, as was the expression on her face when she spoke about Markus. He was there, and then he was gone.

"Those days he was gone were the longest days of my life," she said. Her face was sad, but her eyes were dry. "I read about Virginia Holloway every day with a knot in my stomach. I knew what her mother was going through."

Rhodes spoke. "Can you—"

There was a clatter and a wail from inside. Daniela turned, but Rhodes put a hand on her arm. "I'll take care of it." He clambered back through the window, leaving the two women alone.

Amelia seized her opportunity. "Daniela, do you have anything of Markus's I could borrow? A personal item? I might be able to—It could help." It was her last chance, and she wasn't going to let it pass her by, whether Rhodes liked it or not.

To Amelia's surprise, Daniela didn't ask questions, only shook her head. "About a month after Markus died, there was a fire. We all got out, thanks be to Heaven, but we lost everything." She glanced back in at Rhodes, who appeared to be doling out candy to the children from a bag. Daniela smiled. "He's a good man. Spent all those days Markus was missing helping with the search. And he loves children. All of mine treat him like their favorite uncle."

Her tone, even without the glance she gave Amelia as she spoke, was an immediate tell. She was matchmaking. Amelia rose with a friendly smile and behaved as if she hadn't noticed. They went back inside, where Rhodes hastily tucked the bag of candy back into his pocket, as if the peppermint-scented exhalations of four children didn't give him away.

At the door, Daniela shook Amelia's hand and pulled Rhodes in for another hug. "God love you for trying so hard."

"I'm going to find out who did it, Daniela," he replied. "Whatever it takes."

# 9

So Rhodes behaved himself?" Jonas asked.

They were walking west, and Amelia raised her hand to block the late afternoon sun. She should have worn a hat with a wider brim. "He was very pleasant. I'm not sure how useful it was, though. I'm not even certain he's right about all four children having the same killer. I know Ginny resembles the others," she said as Jonas started to speak. "And there's the matter of their all having been missing for several days before they were killed. But the others were raped and strangled. Ginny was neither. The others were found near where they'd been taken. Ginny was moved halfway across the city. I just don't know."

"At least you were doing something," Jonas said. "I sat outside the courtroom for four hours, and all I got was this one lead."

They were on their way to speak to Martin Steele, the owner of the laundry where Amos worked. Along with the coroner, the police officer who had discovered Amos with the body, and a woman Jonas thought was probably the Holloways' housekeeper, Steele had been called to give evidence at the inquest that morning. Sidney deemed it vital they find out what he'd said.

After a momentary pause, Jonas spoke again, in an overly casual tone. "Interesting news last night from Andrew. Did you know he was thinking about going back to Philadelphia?"

"No, but it's not surprising," Amelia said, feeling his eyes on her. "There's no reason he should want to stay."

"Isn't there?"

She didn't reply.

Jonas didn't give up. "He'd stay if you asked, and you know it."

Amelia didn't meet his eyes. "I don't know it. And even if I did, what would be the point? You saw him with those people last night. He's part of their world, not ours."

Jonas scoffed. "He came here to get away from that world. The club is full every night of people getting away from that world. I've never gotten the impression he wanted to rush back. Be honest, you pushed him away because you're scared."

"I did not," she said. "I just realized it wouldn't work."

"Why? Sidney and I work. You and Andrew could too, if you wanted it enough."

"Then maybe it means I don't," she said, in a tone meant to end the conversation.

Jonas sighed.

Amelia thought about what he'd said as they walked. Sidney's family was wealthy, and Jonas didn't mind. On the contrary, he was happy to enjoy the largesse. Therefore, Amelia should be able to do the same. But it was different somehow. Jonas could never be Sidney's acknowledged partner. As much as that fact disadvantaged them, it also freed them. What did a little thing like their relative status matter, when they were already violating a much greater taboo? Their relationship would remain secret. No Society matron would ever observe, in a disdainful tone, that Sidney had lowered himself by the connection, or raise a knowing eyebrow if Jonas made some small faux pas.

Both she and Jonas had observed the rich long enough to be able to ape them in casual interactions, but their facade would never survive the scrutiny she would invite as Andrew's . . . what, exactly? Amelia wasn't even certain what she was contemplating. His companion? His wife? She shook off the question. It didn't matter. He deserved more than she could give him. She would make herself miserable trying to be something she wasn't and hurt Andrew when she failed. She'd made the right decision in turning away, no matter what Jonas said.

It wasn't a happy thought, and she was relieved when they arrived at the laundry as it gave her a reason to stop dwelling on it.

Steele's Mechanical Laundry was a two-story brick building only a few blocks from the Hudson, and the smell of the river was faint but perceptible outside the gates. Beneath the name was the familiar logo, a stylized gold-painted S in a split shield quartered in red and white, almost like a coat of arms. A graveled drive made a horseshoe around the main building, with loading docks visible on either side. A line of wagons—their beds enclosed to protect their cargo from dirt and weather—led to the nearest dock, where a hard-faced, balding man sweated through his shirt as he scowled down at a clipboard.

"Good afternoon," Jonas called.

He looked up at their approach. "Be with you in just a minute," he said, his voice almost drowned out by a new clatter as a pair of boys pushed two large metal carts out onto the dock. The horses didn't startle at the noise. They stood placidly, swishing their tails to drive the flies away as the boys unloaded the contents of the wagon onto the carts. The driver handed over a paper, and the man with the clipboard scribbled something with a pencil. The skin of his hands and forearms was tinged an odd, bluish color, as if he wore gloves. "You're checked in, Johnny. Head on around. There's a delivery ready to go back out."

The driver clucked to the horses, and with a creak of the wheels and the jangle of harnesses, they vanished around the back of the building.

"How can I help you?" the man asked, sparing them only a glance as he waved the next wagon forward.

"We were hoping to speak with Mr. Steele," Jonas said.

"In his office," the man said. He indicated the doorway behind him as the boys pushed the cart back inside. "Through there and up the stairs. Tell him Park North is running late."

Inside the building, the air was sweltering, hotter than outside and heavy with damp. Almost as overwhelming was the noise, an echoing cacophony made up of shouts, clanging metal, and the sound of dozens of machines all chugging away. A narrow set of steel stairs led up to a landing with a single closed door.

Jonas knocked.

"Come in," a voice called, barely audible.

They walked through the door and immediately halted in bafflement. The room should have been stifling, situated as it was above an enterprise that produced so much heat. Instead, it was noticeably cooler. A mechanical hum filled the air, and Amelia's attention was immediately drawn to what seemed to be its source: a steamer trunk–sized cabinet along one wall with a pair of large fans that appeared to be connected to its top. Both whirred away, their blades creating a distinct breeze, though they alone couldn't account for the lower temperature.

That contraption alone would have been enough of a marvel, but it was hardly the only one. The opposite wall held a pair of long tables with a door between them. The first was covered with mechanical parts: coils of wire, bits of metal, and what looked like another fan, this one disassembled. A schematic was tacked to the wall beside it. Adjacent to the first table was another, this one full of what looked like equipment for chemistry experiments: glassware in various shapes, a little gas burner, and a row of jars full of substances she couldn't identify. A man stood pouring something from one beaker to another, his back still to them.

Amelia glanced at Jonas. He was greedily taking it all in, his eyes as wide as a child's. She cleared her throat, and the man turned at the sound, his eyes widening when he saw them. He wore a stained pair of kidskin gloves, Amelia presumed to protect his hands from the chemicals.

"My apologies," he said. "I was expecting Himes."

"Is that the fellow downstairs with the clipboard?" Jonas asked, tearing his gaze away from the glassware.

"Yes. My floor manager."

"He said to tell you Park North is late."

Steele drew a heavy watch from his pocket, clicked open the cover, and grimaced. "That's going to throw the rest of the shift off. But I suppose it can't be helped. What can I do for you?" He looked between Jonas and Amelia as he tucked the watch away. The end of the fob was a gold shield, enameled in red and white. Just like the business logo. He had to have had it custom made.

"I'm Jonas Vincent, and this is Miss Matthew. We're working with the lawyer defending Amos Alston, and—"

The man drew back, his guard coming up at the name. "I'm not going to talk about that. It has nothing to do with me."

"Oh, we know," Jonas hastened to assure him. "But he worked here, so we wondered if anyone had noticed anything unusual, or if he had any particularly close friends here. If we could talk to a few of them, then—"

"No," the man said definitively. "I have a business to run, and I can't have you wandering around in the middle of things, bothering my workers and dragging my name into all of this."

"We aren't trying to drag you further into anything," Jonas said, "I promise. But I know you testified before the grand jury yesterday, and—"

"I thought you looked familiar," Steele exclaimed. "You were there, in the hallway."

"I was," Jonas said. "I'm trying to gather as much information as I can about the evidence against Amos. If you could just tell us what questions you were asked and what you told them, we'll be out of your way."

Steele frowned, considering. "Fine," he said with a sigh. "It wasn't much. They asked me how long Amos had been working for me. I told them a little over a year. They asked if he'd ever helped with deliveries and pickups, and I told them yes. They asked if the Holloways were customers of ours, and I said yes to that as well."

Amelia's heartbeat accelerated as Steele spoke. Jonas, though his expression remained politely inquisitive, stilled beside her. They had assumed Amos couldn't have had any connection to Ginny Holloway.

Steele went on, oblivious to their sudden tension. "And finally, they asked if Amos had ever helped out on the route that ran by their house, and I told them he had."

Dismayed, Amelia looked at Jonas. He still appeared calm, but the hardness in his jaw said he was anything but, though his voice was steady when he spoke. "Was there anything else?"

Steele shook his head. "Nothing. They thanked me for my cooperation and dismissed me. And I don't mind telling you that I was happy to go," he added. "I hate having my name associated with something so terrible."

Steele launched into an explanation of how he'd started the business out of a rented back room and made it thrive through his own hard work. Amelia kept a polite expression on her face, but her mind was wholly occupied by the revelation that Amos could have known Ginny Holloway.

"—things you have to do to keep a business running! Never a day off, and—"

Amos had known the victim. Amos, who carried candy and had been found crouched over her body. Amos, who had confessed.

"—still drive a wagon myself, time to time, when we're short of hands. Why—"

It still didn't mean he was guilty. There were still questions that—

*I told you to be careful. Now look what you've done.*

Amelia, already unsettled, felt the blood drain from her face as the disembodied words floated through the air around her. A woman's voice. She couldn't stop herself from looking wildly around the office for the spirit. She hadn't seen or felt anything when they entered. And she'd never heard one of them before. Was this some new manifestation of her gift? What if she was about to be possessed? If she—

Her eyes fell on Jonas. He was also turning his head, looking as wide-eyed as she felt.

Steele burst out laughing. "I'm sorry. I should have warned you. I'm so used to it by now I don't even notice, but it is unnerving the first few times."

"What is it?" Amelia asked, her heart only beginning to settle back into her chest from where it had leapt into her throat.

Steele gestured to a grate high on the wall, one she hadn't noticed until he pointed it out.

"It's a trick of acoustics," he said. "Let me show you." He turned toward the door on the far wall, gesturing them to follow.

Amelia gasped as they stepped through the door. They stood on a high metal catwalk, at least twenty feet off the ground. She groped for the railing, disoriented. Spread out beneath them was a cavernous room of bare concrete and metal.

"This is the drying room," Steele said, pride in his voice. "All my own design."

"How does it work?" Jonas asked, his fascination apparent.

With evident pride, Steele pointed out the huge vents and fans set in the walls and the system of steel bars attached to pulleys and chains in rows along the ceiling. Half a dozen young workers pushed carts loaded with wet linens through the room. Several turned cranks to lower the bars, while the others began using clips to secure the edges of the damp linens to them. When they were full, they were cranked back up, exposing all sides of the cloth to the fans and keeping it off the floor.

"I purposely built tall," Steele said, gesturing for them to step back into his office. "I'd like to get out of the household laundry business altogether, except for a select few clients, of course. Hotels and restaurants—they generate a lot of linens that constantly need to be washed. I can dry a hundred pieces at once, and they wrinkle less this way, too."

"But what about the voice?" Amelia asked. "Where did it come from?"

"It came through the ductwork," Steele said. "There's one particular spot out on the floor. If someone is standing there, their voice comes through that grate sounding like it's right next to you. Scared me half to death the first few times it happened, until we realized. But the system works so well it's a small price to pay."

"It's brilliant," said Jonas.

"It's the future," Steele said, obviously pleased by the praise. "And it's not my only innovation." He indicated the tables. "We don't use tubs and wash-boards here, not anymore. All electrical machines, and I designed most of them myself. I'm even working on my own formula for the soap—it'll be gentler on fabrics but still get them clean. And then the cooling cabinet, of course," he said, pointing toward the contraption. "Not much to do with the laundry business, but lots of interesting applications. There's no ice involved—it uses compressed ammonia."

"I'd love to see how it works," said Jonas, glancing at Amelia.

She recognized her cue and smiled. "Is there a lavatory I might use while the two of you are chatting? I'm sure it would all be over my head anyway," she said with an intentional simper.

Steele gave her directions, then turned eagerly to Jonas, having already forgotten about her. Perfect. Amelia walked past the door that would have taken her out to the lavatory and instead headed for the main floor of the laundry. Perhaps two dozen workers toiled away in appalling heat, emptying carts, loading machines, and feeding wet laundry through mechanical wringers. Perhaps two-thirds were Negroes. Most of the rest had the rangy, underfed look of recent immigrants. The girls had their collars and sleeves unpinned. Scarves covered their hair. The boys had handkerchiefs folded and tied around their foreheads. All of them dripped with sweat, and none of them met Amelia's eyes, though they darted curious glances in her direction when they thought she wasn't looking.

She wouldn't have long. She needed to find someone who knew Amos and might be willing to talk to her about him. Amelia focused on a pair of Negro boys loading laundry into one of the machines. They appeared to be about Amos's age, but when she approached, they became visibly nervous, answering her questions in as few words as possible while avoiding looking at her. Yes, they knew Amos. No, they didn't know anything about the routes he'd ridden or whether he'd known Ginny Holloway, though shrouded in fear and mistrust as their voices were, she couldn't tell if they were lying.

She gave up and handed them one of Sidney's cards. "If you think of anything, or have anything you think we need to know, you can go to this address and show this card. It's important," she added when neither of them reached for it. She waited until one of them tucked it into a pocket before she moved on to a trio of girls—two Negroes and one olive-skinned Italian—folding finished laundry and wrapping it in brown paper. They all admitted to knowing Amos when pressed, but none of them volunteered anything further.

Amelia chewed her lip, then changed tactics, asking more general questions about the laundry and how it worked. Away from the frightening topic, they opened up. Dina was the oldest, rail thin, with hair in two stiff braids. Her sister was Orla. The Italian, Maggie, had a single heavy braid pinned up beneath a kerchief.

"It's hard work," Dina said, "but Mr. Steele pays a decent wage. Better than some other places I've worked, where they try to short you."

"And I suppose his inventions help," Amelia commented.

Orla snorted.

Amelia raised an eyebrow. "No?"

"He's always got a new one to try," she explained. "Sometimes they work. Sometimes—"

"Sometimes they fly to pieces and we all drop down on the floor with our hands over our heads," finished Dina, grinning.

"And it's not just the machines," Maggie added. She raised her hands, and Amelia's eyes went to a ring of yellowing, half-healed bruises around her forearm.

"Did Mr. Steele do that?" Amelia asked, shocked.

"Oh," Maggie said, embarrassed. "No. Don't mind that. I meant my hands."

Trying not to frown, Amelia focused on the girl's hands. Now that it had been pointed out, she could tell they were discolored.

"From the bluing," Orla said, lifting her own hands. "It don't show much on us, and it's not too bad on her, but every white person here got blue hands. Some special bluing he makes us use. He's always got a new jar of somethin' or other he wants to add to the water. Says it'll get things cleaner. Remember that one a while back?" she asked the other two.

Dina reached for a new sheet of paper. "Near about knocked you out every time you got more than a whiff of it. But it could be worse," she said. "He keeps his hands to hisself, which is more than you can say for some of 'em."

The girls exchanged glances, and Maggie darted a quick, sour look toward the loading dock, where Himes was still directing wagons. "Ain't that the truth," she muttered.

Amelia grimaced in sympathy. Girls like this had little recourse when men like Himes made advances. They needed their jobs. Dina caught her look. "It ain't so bad, miss," she said. "We just warn the new girls and try to stay together."

Amelia decided it was time to try coming back to Ginny again. "Were you all working the day the news about the kidnapping came out?"

They went quiet again, and she feared she'd lost them. She took another of Sidney's cards and set it on the table. "I'm working with some people who are trying to find out what happened. If you know anything, anything at all, you can come to this address. It could be important."

Maggie looked down at her hands, but the sisters looked at one another, as if silently discussing whether or not to say anything. Finally, Dina spoke. Her voice was low, and Amelia had to lean forward to catch the words. "He was late that morning."

Amelia's heartbeat accelerated. "Amos was? The day Ginny went missing? You're certain it was that same—"

She was interrupted by a horrible, echoing crash from the drying room. All of them ran toward the door.

Inside, one of the pulley systems appeared to have failed. A tangled jumble of chains and metal lay in the center of the room, the cloth it had held now crumpled beneath it. Three workers stood around it. Steele and Jonas were on the catwalk, looking down at the mess. Steele's face was red, whether from anger or embarrassment, Amelia couldn't tell.

A shout came from behind her. "What the hell happened?" Himes rushed past Amelia, headed for the three workers. He shoved one so hard the boy fell down, then slapped another on the side of the head. The sound of the strike echoed in the open space. He pulled back his arm again, but before he could hit the third worker, Steele's voice cracked like a whip.

"Mr. Himes."

Himes stopped his assault to look up at his boss, who nodded toward Amelia. Himes looked in the direction he indicated, and his face flushed scarlet when he saw her standing among the workers.

Up on the catwalk, Jonas said something to Steele that Amelia didn't catch, then shook his hand and came down the stairs toward her as if unruffled by the incident. He took her arm and guided her back toward the exit. On the way, Amelia glanced back toward the table where she'd stood with the girls. The card she'd left there was gone.

∞

Once they were on the sidewalk, Jonas strode away from the laundry gates, too agitated to notice Amelia was all but trotting alongside him until she hauled back on his arm with an exasperated noise.

He grimaced and slowed. "Sorry."

They'd gone another block before Amelia voiced the question that had been plaguing him since the moment Steele acknowledged that Amos might have known Ginny.

"What if he did it?" The words hung in the air.

"He couldn't have." He meant for the denial to sound confident, but it came out weak. Unconvincing.

"Couldn't he?" Amelia's voice was leaden. "He couldn't have done the three in Brooklyn. Fine. But we already know there are differences. What if that was a different killer? Amos had a connection to Ginny. What are the chances that he'd also be the one to stumble across her body? And he confessed, Jonas. He—"

"They beat him," he objected. "Anyone would have confessed."

"Yes, anyone would have," Amelia said. "That doesn't mean it couldn't be true."

"What about the assault? Amos confessed to it, but the autopsy showed Ginny wasn't assaulted."

Amelia looked grim. "The autopsy showed she wasn't raped. That doesn't mean there couldn't have been some sort of molestation. We haven't seen the confession. We don't know exactly what he did or didn't confess. And maybe," she went on, forestalling Jonas's reply with a raised hand. "Maybe you're right. Maybe he didn't touch her and that part of the confession was false. But now we know he could have known her. And some of the girls told me he was late to work the morning Ginny went missing."

Jonas brushed that bit of news aside. "She was held somewhere after she was taken. Amos doesn't have anywhere he could have kept her."

"That we know of. Jonas, I'm not saying it's certain, but we jumped into this so quickly we never asked ourselves if he might have done it. We assumed he was innocent. I don't think we can keep doing that."

Jonas felt ill. Miles said Amos was innocent. Tommy said he was a good boy. Jonas had trusted their judgment and never bothered to use his own. He'd taken the case to Sidney, knowing it would be difficult for him, believing he was doing a good thing. "All right," he said finally. "We need to talk to Miles and Polly again."

They reached 6th Avenue and turned toward the Alstons' home instead of heading back to their apartment. Sarah answered the door when they knocked and greeted them before returning to the stove, where something was simmering.

Polly sat in the main room beside a basket of mending, Silas playing on a blanket beside her feet. She looked up as they entered, hope on her face. "Any news?"

Jonas glanced at Amelia. "We're not sure," she said.

"Is Miles here?" Jonas asked.

Polly shook her head. "He left early. He wanted to take another basket over to Amos before he went to work. My brother and sister-in-law were here, and she brought some of the cookies Amos likes." She inspected her stitches, then bit off the thread. "Some sort of Polish things," she added. "I can never remember the name."

Amelia stiffened beside him. "*Kolaches?*" she asked.

"That's it," Polly said as she reached into the basket and came out with a shirt. A palm-sized flap of fabric was missing from one sleeve. "That boy," she said, poking a finger through the hole. "I don't know if I can save this one."

The shirt was the striped broadcloth worn by waiters at the club, though this one was faded from repeated washings. Amos must get his father's cast-offs.

"Where do they live?" Jonas asked. "Your brother and his wife." He made his voice deliberately casual.

"Over in Brooklyn. Greenpoint," Polly said.

The words were drops of icy water down his back. Amelia had gone still.

"Her family is there," Polly went on, oblivious to the sudden tension in the room. "So that's where they settled after they got married. My mother liked to have had a fit over it. You'd have thought Michael was moving to a foreign country. I told her, 'Mam, they have a bridge. You can get over to see them as often as you like!' She's a nice girl, though."

Jonas couldn't ask the next question. It felt as though his tongue had been cemented to the roof of his mouth. Amelia managed, though. "Does Amos spend a lot of time with them?"

"He did, up until he started working. After that there wasn't as much time."

Every word felt like a hot needle shoved into Jonas's chest. Amos had spent time in the same neighborhood where the first three victims had lived.

Polly looked up from her mending and caught the glance they were exchanging. "What? Why are you asking that?"

"I spent the morning over in Greenpoint," Amelia said slowly.

"Why?" Polly demanded.

"We found out about some children there. They were . . . taken. Like Ginny Holloway."

"Other children?" Polly looked between them, realization spreading over her face. "You can't think Amos had anything to do with them. Or with Ginny. I told you, he was here all night." Her words were defiant, but there was something frightened in her eyes. She darted glances back and forth between them, and her knuckles were white where they clutched her mending.

The feeling in Jonas's chest intensified. Polly displayed every sign of an honest person telling a lie.

"Polly," he said softly. "We have to know what happened. Did you actually see or hear Amos the night before last, or are you saying that to protect him?"

"I know my son," Polly snapped back, her chin thrust out. "He didn't do this terrible thing. He was here. All night."

Behind Polly, Sarah, who stood beside the stove, went still and pressed her lips together.

Amelia saw it too. "Sarah? If you know something, we need to know what it is."

The girl shot an anguished look at her mother, who had twisted in her chair to look at her daughter.

"He wasn't," Sarah said, her face crumpling. "I'm sorry, Mama, but he wasn't here."

"What do you mean?" Polly asked. Her face had gone gray.

"He's been sneaking out at night. At least a couple of times a week for the last year or so."

Polly's voice was aghast. "Why didn't you tell us?"

"I didn't want to get him in trouble."

"Do you know where he goes?" Jonas asked gently.

"Not exactly," Sarah said. Her eyes darted to her mother and away again before she went on. "I followed him once. He didn't know I was there."

"You were out alone in the middle of the night?" Polly's voice was horrified. "Mother Mary, Sarah, what were you thinking? Anything could have happened to you."

Sarah shrank beneath the scolding, her shoulders curling in toward her chest. "It was just that once. I wanted to know where he was going."

Jonas prodded her on. "And?"

Sarah hesitated. "I'm not sure. There's a building next to a bar over on Watts Street. One of the ones they stopped without finishing. He went down the alley beside it. I didn't follow him—he'd have been mad if he saw me. But he couldn't have gone inside. It's all boarded up. So I don't know where he went after that."

There was a long moment when no one spoke.

"No," Polly said finally, her voice as flat and firm as before. "It still doesn't matter. Amos wouldn't—"

"Polly," Amelia began, "if he wasn't here, then we—"

"No." Polly put up a hand. "You listen to me, both of you. I don't care what you think you know, or what you've found. Amos did not hurt those children—any of them. I know my son. I carried him." She put a hand on her belly. "Right here, same as this one. When he was born the midwife took him from my body and laid him right over my heart. There are things about being a mother that you can't know until you are one. You think you understand. But you don't. I know my son. He did not do this terrible thing."

"I know you believe that," Jonas said. "But we have to consider—"

She looked up at them. "I will not. And if you're going to, then I don't want you in my house anymore. Leave."

# 10

When Andrew arrived at Sidney's office early on Wednesday morning, he found the lawyer at his desk, massaging his temples with the heels of his hands.

"What's wrong?" Andrew asked.

"Jonas was here earlier," Sidney said. "He was on his way to investigate another lead. But he and Amelia discovered some things yesterday they thought I ought to know."

He outlined the facts the pair had uncovered as Andrew listened, growing increasingly uncomfortable.

"Do you think it means Amos is guilty?" he asked when Sidney fell silent.

"I don't know," Sidney said. "It doesn't matter. I owe him whatever aid I can render either way. On the other hand . . ." He sighed. "Do you have time for a cup of coffee before you leave for the island?"

Andrew consulted his pocket watch. "I do."

Sidney called Morris with the request, and the efficient secretary appeared only moments later with a silver coffee service.

"I also have these," Andrew added as Morris set the tray on the desk. He pulled a stack of envelopes from his bag and set them on the corner of the desk. "I made a list of eleven chemists in the city who have the ability to analyze the powder found at the autopsy and the reputation to hopefully make the court listen.

"I found telephone numbers for four of them. Three declined to become involved. I left a message for the fourth, and his assistant promised a response today. I've written requests to the others. I thought you might be able to make sure they're delivered this morning."

Sidney gestured for him to give the envelopes to Morris. "Send them by messenger," he said to the secretary, who nodded and left.

Andrew served himself and relaxed into one of the supple leather chairs, vaguely surprised all over again by how much he liked the young lawyer. On the surface, it was a ridiculous feeling. They had a tremendous amount in common. They were both educated men from similar backgrounds, and it hadn't taken them long to realize they had a certain similarity of personality.

But everything in his background and education had taught him men with Sidney's tastes were deviants, moral degenerates who were to be at best pitied and at worst despised. As Andrew sat in the well-appointed office, however, drinking excellent coffee and listening to him give quiet, authoritative instructions to a subordinate, it was impossible to view him as such. He was a peer. Someone with whom Andrew could envision forming a friendship. It was another way in which meeting Amelia had upended his view of the world. She'd told him he was acquainted with many more such men than he'd realized. It had left him looking around rooms and wondering at the secrets people kept.

"To return to the subject," Sidney said, "it shouldn't matter to me if Amos is guilty, but, in this case, it would be a comfort if he is, since there's so little I can do to save him."

"It's that bad?" Andrew asked. "It seems as though you're doing a lot."

"I'm not doing nearly as much as I'd like."

"Such as?"

Sidney's voice was blunt as he leaned back in his chair. "The police took statements from everyone at the party that night. I don't even have a list of names yet, let alone copies of the statements themselves. Ideally, I'd re-interview every one of the guests and their servants, along with anyone any of them can recall seeing in the vicinity of the Holloway house that day. I'd investigate the backgrounds of all the Holloway servants.

"I would look into Mr. Holloway's past business arrangements and personal affairs. But there's no time. We have to focus on the things we can do quickly and hope we get a lucky break somewhere. We're working with almost nothing.

"I haven't even been able to get anything more from Amos himself. I went back to see him yesterday, to make sure they'd moved him and had a doctor in and so on. They'd given him morphine to set his arm, I don't even think he knew I was there, and he was in no shape to answer my questions. Not that I think it matters for our immediate purposes." He spoke like a man who knew he had a losing hand but had to play it anyway.

"You don't think there's any hope of stopping the transfer?"

Sidney sighed again and leaned back in his own chair. "I think in forty-eight hours Amos Alston is on a train and as good as dead." He sounded infinitely weary as he went on. "I write contracts for a living. I've never had a case where a life was at stake. Knowing that everything I do is likely not enough is a terrible feeling. Although I suppose doctors are familiar with it," he added.

Andrew grimaced. "Indeed we are, and it never gets easier. I regret your having to experience it. At least no one has ever been angry with me for trying to save a patient. Is your family any more resigned to your involvement?"

Sidney snorted, and a wry smile pulled at one corner of his mouth. "My father has moved past anger into pretending it isn't happening. And my mother is more preoccupied with the failure of her dinner party to produce an immediate engagement. She's already planning her next attempt."

Andrew chuckled. "Shall I keep my schedule clear? I'm always happy to help thwart unwanted matrimonial attempts. That's another experience with which I am familiar."

"A little less complicated in your case, though. You could at least theoretically find someone you wanted to marry that your family would approve of."

"I suppose so," Andrew said, feeling less like smiling.

Sidney must have noticed, because he went on hurriedly. "In any case, don't forgo plans on my account. I don't think the three of you will—"

He broke off as there was a rap at the door, and Morris entered again with a parcel in his hand. "A courier just brought this for you. It's from the District Attorney's office."

Sidney took it from him and untied the wrapping as Morris left.

Andrew leaned forward. The package contained a sheaf of documents, photographs from the postmortem, and a stoppered vial with a tiny quantity of powder in the bottom.

"This says that's a third of what was collected," Sidney said, reading the note. "The coroner's office will use another third to run their own tests, and a third will be kept in reserve in case there is a discrepancy. That seems a reasonable approach. Now all we need is someone to agree to do the testing."

Another rap at the door drew their attention. Amelia entered, her eyes flickering to Andrew. To Andrew's surprise, she was accompanied by an unfamiliar man.

"What are you doing here?" Sidney's voice was sharp. Andrew glanced at him in time to see him slip the vial into his pocket and flip the stack of photographs over. "I gave you your quote already. I'm not saying more."

Andrew straightened and examined the stranger more closely. This must be the reporter. The way Jonas had talked about him, Andrew had expected someone altogether more devious-looking. Instead, he had a disarming smile, which he deployed as he stepped into the office.

"Peter Rhodes, *New York Sun*," he said, offering his hand to Andrew.

When Andrew introduced himself, Rhodes's face brightened. "The doctor who attended the postmortem. Excellent."

"How did you know that?" Sidney said, sounding annoyed.

Rhodes glanced at him. "I told you before: I have good sources." He turned back to Andrew. "I understand you disagree with the coroner's finding of poison. I'd love to talk to you about your observations."

Andrew didn't need Sidney's help to know how to answer. "Absolutely not."

"Never mind about that," Sidney said. "Why are you here?"

"I met Mr. Rhodes outside," Amelia said. "He says he has another proposition for us."

Her voice, and indeed, her whole manner toward Rhodes was less antagonistic than Andrew would have expected, given what he'd heard about the reporter. He wondered exactly what had happened during the previous day's outing to make them so friendly.

"Well?" Sidney asked, looking at Rhodes.

"I'm going to meet with Mrs. Holloway this morning," Rhodes said casually, pretending to ignore the thunderstruck silence his announcement left in its wake.

"She actually agreed to talk to you?" Amelia sounded as shocked as Andrew felt.

Rhodes shrugged. "I can be very persuasive. I thought we might make another trade. I'm certain she wouldn't talk to someone so publicly associated with Alston's defense," he said, looking at Sidney. "But I could take Miss Matthew with me." He glanced at Andrew. "Strikes me she might like to talk to you too, Doctor, if you're available."

"And what would you want in return?" Sidney's voice was wary.

"I want to know about whatever that was you just hid away in your pocket, for starters. Evidence in the Holloway case?"

Sidney didn't even flush. "What else?"

"A quote from the good doctor would do nicely."

There was another silent negotiation. Finally, Sidney glanced at Andrew and dipped his chin in a nod.

"Very well," Andrew said.

Rhodes smiled. "Perfect. We need to be going. Are you coming, Doctor?"

Andrew's eyes went to the hand Rhodes put on Amelia's elbow. "Yes," he said without thinking.

"Thrilled to hear it."

"I need to make a telephone call first," Andrew said.

"Well, why don't we go ahead and get a cab. We'll wait for you out front." Rhodes gestured for Amelia to precede him through the door, then winked at Andrew and Sidney as he closed it behind him.

"I thought you had to work today," Sidney said, the slightest hint of amusement leaking through his tone.

Andrew gave him a rueful grin and shrugged as he reached for the telephone. "The job ends in a few weeks anyway. What are they going to do? Fire me?"

∽

What was it, Amelia wondered, that made some silences comfortable while others were so agonizing? Silence was silence. There shouldn't be *kinds*. There were, however, and the one echoing inside the cab was excruciating. Even Rhodes, with his carefully nonchalant demeanor, looked edgy. Andrew's expression was mild, but his posture betrayed his tension.

Amelia tried to tell herself that visiting the grieving mother of a murder victim while working on behalf of the accused was reason enough for anxiety, but it was no good. Andrew's face had hardened as soon as Rhodes identified himself, and when Rhodes had taken her elbow, she hadn't imagined the flicker of emotion on Andrew's face. He was jealous. It made her feel . . . all sorts of things she didn't have time to pick through. She fidgeted with her handbag, trying to think of something to say, then started as Rhodes spoke from beside her.

"I hear you visited the laundry yesterday afternoon."

Equal parts grateful for the opening and impressed at how quickly he learned of such things, Amelia's voice was over-eager as she replied. "We did."

"Did you learn anything?" Rhodes leaned toward her, and out of the corner of her eye she caught Andrew's jaw tightening.

She forced herself to coolness. "Maybe. We aren't certain what any of it means. It's an interesting place, though."

"I hear Steele is something of an amateur inventor."

Amelia nodded. "Jonas was fascinated by his machines."

"Supposedly he's using a lot of them in the business. That's all to the good, if they make it easier. Laundry work is miserable."

"It is," Amelia agreed. Her arms and back still ached from Monday's turn at the scrub board. "I'd rather do almost anything else."

"Spoken like someone who has spent some time with her hands in a washtub," Rhodes said with a grin.

Amelia nodded. "Everyone had to take a turn helping with laundry at the Foundling. And one of the worst punishments, the one they saved for when they really wanted to make an impression, was doing all of the Sunday linen by yourself."

"Oof," Rhodes said.

"Exactly. It took all week. It was meant to break you. The boilers and tubs are all down in the basement. There would be a mound of linen taller than you were. All the scrubbing and rinsing and wringing, then hanging it all over the boiler pipes to get dry. And then you had to iron it and wrap it in white paper and carry it all up to the vestry and put it in the cupboards so it didn't get dirty."

She let out a sudden laugh. "There was one week—coincidentally, the week before the bishop was scheduled to visit—Jonas got caught doing something, and that was the punishment they set for him. It wasn't his first time. The rest of us were cleaning the whole building and the church with all of the nuns standing over us the whole time. They looked in on Jonas a time or two, but he looked to be working as hard as the rest of us, and it wasn't his first trip to the tubs, so they didn't have anyone watching him closely."

"Did he not do it?" Andrew asked. It was the first time he'd spoken since they got underway.

"Oh no, he did it," Amelia said. "He gathered every bit of white cloth he could find—both altar cloths, the nuns' good wimples, the priest's best robes. He washed it all very carefully, but he used an entire bottle of Mrs. Stewart's in the rinse. And he let it soak for a full day."

Rhodes laughed, but Andrew only raised a questioning eyebrow. Amelia thought of the neatly folded laundry waiting for him outside his bedroom. Of course he had no idea what it took to get it there.

"Mrs. Stewart's is a kind of laundry bluing," she said.

He still looked confused.

"White linens tend to turn yellow and dingy over time," she explained, trying not to sigh. "Using a tiny bit of blue dye in the rinse water counteracts it. But it's extremely concentrated—you only need a little, and you have to dilute it before you add it to the water. An entire bottle poured into the washtub . . . Well, when they opened up those parcels to get ready for the Mass that morning, every bit of the linen was robin's egg blue. All of it." Rhodes was still grinning, and finally Andrew joined him as Amelia went on. "And it was too late to do anything about it. I will never forget the look on the bishop's face. They whipped him for it, but to this day he says he's not sorry." She sat back against the seat, the atmosphere softened. The last few minutes of the trip passed in a silence far more pleasant than it had been.

The Holloway home was a massive granite edifice situated only a few blocks from the "Triple Palaces" built for the granddaughters of Cornelius Vanderbilt. A wide half-flight of stairs led up to a pair of ornate wood doors, each of which held a somber wreath of black crepe, a reminder that the house was in mourning. Rhodes wasted no time, mounting the stairs and employing the heavy bronze knocker with enthusiasm before Amelia and Andrew were halfway to the landing.

A tall, cadaverously thin butler with jowls as droopy as softened candle wax answered the door. "May I help you?"

"Mr. Peter Rhodes here to see Mrs. Holloway," he said, presenting a calling card with a flourish.

The butler gave him a piercing glare. "Mrs. Holloway is in mourning. She is not receiving callers." He managed to convey genteel outrage at the notion.

Amelia waited for Rhodes to say Mrs. Holloway was expecting them. Instead, he gave the man a brash grin. "She'll want to see us." He pointed at Andrew. "That's the doctor who examined her daughter's body. And that," he added, finger swinging toward Amelia, "is the city's most celebrated medium. She's here to call Virginia from the other side so her mother can talk to her. Do you think she'll thank you for sending them away?"

The words were as galvanizing as a lightning bolt. Rage sizzled down Amelia's spine as she understood what Rhodes had done. There had never been any appointment. He'd lied to them. Used them. The feeling of betrayal was especially sharp. She glanced at Andrew. The shock on his face was giving way to an anger every bit as molten as her own.

The butler hesitated, his expression betraying a hint of anxiety. "You may remain in the front parlor while I inquire."

Her wits too scattered to form a coherent response, Amelia found herself trailing along behind Rhodes and staring at a point between his shoulder blades as the butler escorted them through a massive marble foyer. If she could have burned him to a cinder in that moment, she would have done it. Her embarrassment was nearly as scalding as her fury. He'd been pleasant company the day before, and though she knew better, she'd allowed her guard to drop.

The parlor was as grand as she might have expected, with silk-upholstered furniture and the gleam of brass and silver everywhere. The carpets were deep and the drapes heavy. A silenced grandfather clock and a massive gilt mirror covered in black cloth further testified to the family's recent bereavement.

The instant the door closed behind the butler Amelia rounded on Rhodes. "How dare you?" she said from between gritted teeth, her voice barely louder than a whisper.

Rhodes raised an eyebrow. "I got us in. There's no way she would have agreed to speak to me if I'd introduced myself as a reporter." He showed no trace of remorse. If anything, he sounded pleased with himself.

Andrew's voice was strangled. "You lied to us."

"You don't have to remain part of it," Rhodes said. "The door is right there. You're welcome to leave if you like. But you won't," he went on as Andrew and Amelia looked at one another. "You want to talk to her, and this is your chance. You won't get another."

The urge to march out the door and slam it behind her, to show him she wouldn't be lied to, wouldn't be used, was staggering. Amelia yearned to throw his smug confidence back in his face. But he was right, loath though she was to admit it. This was too important an opportunity to pass up, no matter how it had been obtained. And there was a little voice in the back of her mind, telling her it was no worse than a great many of the things she had done when she thought it necessary.

Amelia bit down on her anger. She paced the length of the room once, twice, trying to master herself. When she thought she could speak coherently, she stopped in front of him. "Very well. What's done is done." She turned toward the door. "We're here. We can't waste the opportunity."

She took a deep breath. "I'm going to ask for the powder room and try to talk to a couple of the servants."

A maid in a black armband directed Amelia to a door hidden behind the stairs. The powder room was just inside, but Amelia bypassed it, continuing down the hallway. The kitchen was probably back here somewhere, and there would be no better place to find servants congregating. Cooks always knew all the household gossip, since everyone had to eat and tended to think well of the person who fed them. Halfway down the hall, however, another open door caught her attention. Amelia peered inside. It was a tidy little parlor with a comfortable-looking chair covered in flowered chintz. A small writing desk against one wall, stacked with account books and papers. A door in the back stood partly open, revealing a sliver of a similarly neat bedroom.

The housekeeper's quarters. The domain of an upper servant in a wealthy home—space to herself, a place to do the household accounts or write letters. Amelia checked the hallway in both directions, then ducked inside before she had a chance to think better of it. She wouldn't stay long. Just a quick poke through the papers on the desk. The housekeeper would likely have been the one to make out the list of names for the police. Right there on top, that might well be a guest list. She lifted a hand.

"What are you doing in here?"

Amelia whirled, yanking her hand away from the sheet of paper. A woman—obviously the housekeeper herself—stood in the doorway. She wore a black dress of good quality and a heavy chatelaine at her waist. Her graying hair was tucked into a neat roll, and her bright blue eyes snapped with anger.

"I was—"

"I know what you were doing. Higgins came to me to ask if he should disturb Mrs. Holloway on your behalf." She scoffed. "A medium. I never heard anything so ridiculous. Speaking to the dead. Our Ginny is in Heaven, the little angel, not floating around haunting people."

Telling this woman she'd seen Ginny standing beside her own corpse wouldn't help. Amelia kept her mouth closed as the woman went on, her tone scathing.

"How dare you come into a house of mourning with your lies? To dangle such a thing before a grieving mother when all along you know you're a fraud? And snooping around in my rooms, to boot." The woman advanced on her as if intending to physically remove her, and Amelia fell back beneath the onslaught, though the woman was not much larger than she. "Tell me why I shouldn't call the police and have you thrown in jail for trespassing and harassing a grieving family? Have them tell the whole world you're nothing but a thief and a liar."

Amelia's face flamed. Damn Rhodes for getting her into this in the first place, and damn herself for being so feckless as to get caught. This woman was angry enough to actually call the police. Amelia had no justification for being in her rooms, and the family was well-connected enough that they probably could see her—and maybe Andrew and Rhodes as well—jailed. She flailed about for some way to rescue the situation.

"I can prove I'm not a fraud," she blurted, then wanted to clap her hand over her own mouth. That was a terrible idea.

The housekeeper snorted. "And how do you think you'd do that? Going to read my palm? Maybe you've got your crystal ball in your pocket?"

"No." Amelia straightened, trying to gather the scraps of her dignity around her as her heart pounded. "But if you have someone you've lost, I could contact them for you. You could see I'm not pretending."

Her palms grew damp even as she made the offer. The people who came to her of their own volition wanted to speak to their lost one, and it made them willing to believe they were, even when all Amelia was doing was reading their own cues. That wouldn't be enough this time. Even if Amelia gave the performance of a lifetime, this woman wouldn't believe it. It would have to be undeniably real. And there was no guarantee she would be able to call anyone at all. She hadn't managed anything yesterday, even with three murder victims who should have wanted to speak. And this woman didn't have a visible spirit around her. Amelia suppressed a grimace. The alternative was to fall to her knees and beg. She could always do that later if it came to it.

The housekeeper was considering the offer, though. Her forehead had softened into a thoughtful frown, rather than the furious scowl she had been wearing.

Amelia pressed ahead. "Your parents? A brother or sister? If you have something that belonged to them, that would help."

The housekeeper's hand went involuntarily to her chest. Touching something beneath her dress. "All right," she said abruptly. "I'll give you your chance. But I warn you, I'll know if you try to lie to me."

"I won't," Amelia said, unsure whether or not the promise itself was a lie. Committed, she pointed at the chintz chair, trying not to let her hand tremble. "Why don't you sit there?" She drew the wooden chair away from the writing desk and sat facing the other woman, so close the fabric of their skirts brushed. "I'll need to touch whatever the object is."

Warily, the housekeeper drew a chain from beneath the neck of her dress. On it was a small silver St. Christopher's medal. She lifted the chain over her head and held it out to Amelia.

"Hold it in the palm of your hand," Amelia said.

Wordlessly, the housekeeper complied.

Amelia stripped off her glove and placed her own palm over the medal, sandwiching it between their two hands. Usually she asked for a name before attempting something like this, but it would be more impressive if she could find it for herself. If it worked. Amelia closed her eyes and focused on the feel of the medal against her hand. She reached out, seeking.

The first few times Amelia had channeled spirits it had been inadvertent. They were the ones who had form, the ones so eager to speak that they'd overtaken her. As she gained control, she'd first learned how to keep them at bay. Only after that had she learned how to invite them in. Some of the weaker ones needed coaxing. She hadn't even known she could pull them from the other side until it happened at the club one night, completely by accident. A man had come hoping to speak to his business partner. He had no shade lingering about him, and Amelia had expected to have to pretend. But to her surprise, when she called him, he came.

She had done it several times since, but never under such pressure. And never without a name to call. "Come to me," she said, hoping that whoever had owned this medal, their connection to it—and to the woman who now owned it—would be enough. She stretched her awareness as far as it would reach, seeking the elusive sensation of an approaching spirit.

There.

At the edge of everything, something flickered. Amelia reached for it. *Come. She's waiting for you.* Who was it?

"Padraig O'Mallon," she murmured as the spirit touched the edge of her consciousness. The housekeeper's hand flinched beneath hers. Amelia ignored it, all her focus on her task. Bringing him across felt like pulling molasses through a straw. Every instant it seemed as though she would lose her grip and he would slide away again. Finally, finally, she had him, though the connection was tenuous. She wouldn't be able to hold him for long.

"*Bláth beag,*" he said through Amelia's lips. *Little flower.* Amelia knew what it meant because Padraig did. She—they—opened her eyes.

The housekeeper—*Sally, her name is Sally O'Mallon*, Padraig thought—had gone pale. "Da?" she whispered, her own eyes gone so wide the whites showed all around.

"*Sea*, love. I'm here." His voice—Amelia's voice, its tones and cadences changed by the man who shared her mind—roughened as he went on. "I canna stay long. But tis good to see your face. When I put you on that boat with St. Christopher round your neck, I didn't think it would be the last time we'd be together."

"I know." Sally's eyes welled. "But it was for the good, Da. I missed you and Mam, but I've done well."

"Indeed you have. I always knew you would. My little maid all grown up and carryin' the keys to the castle."

Amelia's head ached with the strain of holding him there, and Padraig grimaced. He squeezed Sally's hands. "This isn't my place. I have to go. But I'm proud of you, Sally O'Mallon. Goodbye, love."

"Goodbye, Da." The woman's voice was a whisper.

Amelia dragged in a breath as Padraig slipped away, her head pounding like a hollow drum hammered by a mallet. She pulled her hands away from Sally's—Mrs. O'Mallon's—and pressed her palms to her temples, trying to still the throbbing.

The housekeeper dug through a pocket for a handkerchief, then dabbed at her eyes with a shaking hand. She didn't look at Amelia as she busied herself looping the chain back over her head and tucking the medal away. "I never thought something like that could happen," she said when she'd finished. "But . . . it was real?"

Amelia didn't dare nod. Her head would fall off her shoulders if she did. "It was real."

"And you can do the same thing for Mrs. Holloway? Let her say goodbye to Ginny?"

Even as the woman said it, it occurred to Amelia for the first time what a tenuous notion it was. Even if she could successfully channel the girl's spirit—and there was no guarantee, not when pulling Padraig from the other side had taken so much out of her—there was little likelihood of repeating the heartwarming scene she'd just witnessed. Ginny was a frightened child. A *recently murdered* frightened child, at that. There was no telling how she would behave if Amelia summoned her.

"Maybe," Amelia said in answer to Mrs. O'Mallon's question.

The housekeeper seemed to think that was good enough. "I'll send her maid up to her. She's abed, poor thing. Hasn't hardly been up since Ginny went missing. It will take her a bit of time to get presentable for company. I'll take you back to the parlor to wait."

"Would you mind if we stayed here for a few minutes? My head always aches afterward." Amelia gave her a wan smile, not having to try to look unwell.

"I suppose that would be all right." Mrs. O'Mallon directed a maid to go to Mrs. Holloway, then returned to her chair.

"I'm sure it's been a terribly sad time for the whole household," Amelia said after a moment.

"Oh, just dreadful," she replied. "Our poor little darling. I just can't hardly believe she's gone."

"Were you surprised at who they arrested? I heard he made deliveries here for the grocer." It was an old trick, getting a detail wrong. Most people liked being the ones to correct you, and they were less suspicious if you seemed not to already know. Usually they said more than they would otherwise.

Mrs. O'Mallon was no exception. "Not the grocer. He delivered the laundry sometimes. It's so shocking. He seemed like a nice enough boy. Respectful. Not too forward, you know. Not like some of them. Ginny liked him. Always ran out when she saw the laundry wagon coming."

Amelia tried not to sag at the confirmation that Amos had known Ginny. Mrs. O'Mallon's next words were another blow.

"If he was there, he usually had a piece of candy for her. He must have dropped one that night when—" She stopped. Most likely the police had told her not to talk about the candy.

"Such a tragedy." Having gotten most of the information she'd been after, she let out a little sigh. "Thank you for letting me rest. I'm sure you're busy." She pushed herself to her feet.

Mrs. O'Mallon likewise rose and started for the door. Amelia lingered a few steps behind her, intentionally veering toward the desk where she'd seen what had looked like a guest list. Mrs. O'Mallon turned into the hallway far enough ahead of her to give Amelia an opening. She darted out her hand and snagged the sheet of paper, hastily folding it into her pocket. She felt bad about her deception, but could think of no way to ask for the list that wouldn't make Mrs. O'Mallon suspicious. It would undo all the goodwill she'd earned if the woman found out Amelia was working for the defense. Besides, she thought as the headache thrummed in her temples, she'd already paid a fair price for it.

Andrew sprang from one of the sofas as she reentered the parlor. "Amelia, are you all right?"

Amelia grimaced. She hadn't had access to a mirror, but his response suggested the effort she'd spent in channeling Padraig showed.

Rhodes lounged on the other sofa, seemingly at ease, as Andrew helped her to a chair.

Amelia still held the glove she'd removed in one hand, and Andrew's eyes narrowed as she worked it back on. "What happened?"

"I convinced the housekeeper to talk to me," she said shortly. "Amos knew Ginny. He gave her candy when he delivered the laundry. And I got a copy of the guest list from the party."

Rhodes straightened. "Let's see it."

"No," Amelia said shortly. Her head still ached too much for her to feel charitably toward him. He pressed his lips together, but didn't reply.

It was another ten minutes before the door opened again, revealing the lady of the house, accompanied by a maid.

All three rose to greet her, Amelia more slowly than the men.

The papers had described Cassandra Holloway as a great beauty and a gracious hostess. She may have been, but bereavement had stripped her of any elegance. She wore fine black silk and held a creased, black-edged handkerchief in one hand. Her face was pale and puffy, and her eyes had an unfocused sheen. Lines of grief had etched themselves so deeply into her face that it was hard to imagine what she might have looked like only weeks before. Her husband had two older boys by his first wife, who were away at school. But Ginny had been this woman's only child.

Amelia studied the area around her, wondering if the girl's spirit clung to her mother, but there was nothing.

Etiquette dictated none of them should speak until spoken to by their hostess, but after an awkward pause, it became apparent she would not—or could not—perform the necessary courtesies.

Andrew stepped forward. "Mrs. Holloway. I am Dr. Andrew Cavanaugh. Please allow me to extend my deepest condolences for your loss."

She started. "Thank you. Welcome, all of you. Please, sit." The invitation was mechanical, an automatic response trained into her until she didn't need to think the words in order to say them.

They reclaimed their seats as she sank into the chair opposite Amelia. There was another long pause.

"Can you tell me what happened to my daughter?" she asked abruptly. "Did she . . . Did she suffer?" The last few words were barely more than a whisper, and her face crumpled as she brought the handkerchief to her eyes.

Andrew's own face was sympathetic. "I can't tell you exactly what happened, but there was no sign Ginny suffered. There was no overt sign of violence, or of . . ." He hesitated. It was likely no one had ever used the word 'rape' in front of this gently reared woman, and he clearly didn't want to be the first. "Interference," he said finally.

Mrs. Holloway closed her eyes, pressing her handkerchief to them and saying nothing.

Rhodes chose that moment to speak. "If I may, there are other ways of revealing what medical science cannot." He indicated Amelia. "Miss Matthew is renowned for her ability to speak with the spirits of the dead. I'm certain she would be willing to attempt to speak with your daughter."

Though she'd known it was coming, Amelia could not suppress a surge of anxiety at the offer.

Mrs. Holloway turned her devastated gaze on Amelia. "It would mean the world to me, Miss Matthew." Her voice broke on the last word.

There was nothing else Amelia could say. "Of course, Mrs. Holloway." She took a deep breath and closed her eyes. She wouldn't try to call the girl. No one would need to know.

Before she could so much as exhale, Rhodes spoke up.

"I've heard that many mediums have greater success if they can touch something belonging to the deceased," he said, turning to Mrs. Holloway and ignoring the glare Amelia shot him. "Do you have something of Virginia's—a personal item—that Miss Matthew could use?"

"Of course," Mrs. Holloway said. She stood. "Please, come with me."

There was no way Amelia could object.

Mrs. Holloway led them up the stairs, the possibility of speaking with her daughter again seeming to lend her new energy.

They stopped outside a room on the second floor. Mrs. Holloway swung the door open and ushered them inside.

"This is Ginny's room."

It was all pale, pretty colors, with a canopied bed covered in ruffles and nursery rhyme prints on the walls. A cat in a lace ruff played a fiddle for an audience of dancing mice, while a dish with a face ran holding hands with a similarly humanized spoon. A shelf of books and another of toys filled the remaining walls. It was so unlike anything Amelia had ever known, let alone experienced herself as a child, that it made her breathless. A loved child had slept here.

Rhodes, damn him, looked at it all as if he were trying to memorize it. He couldn't very well take notes without giving himself away.

"We've left all of her things as they were," said Mrs. Holloway. "Except . . ." She turned to the maid. "Bridget, would you fetch Clara from my room, please?"

The maid nodded. She returned a moment later, and as soon as Amelia's eyes fell on the doll in her hands, the familiar itch began in her chest. It was well-worn, its yarn hair tied in tails with trailing green ribbons that matched its ruffled dress.

As Mrs. Holloway took the doll from the maid, the air beside her swirled, and Ginny's spirit appeared with a suddenness that made Amelia suppress a gasp. Even as her mother held the doll out toward Amelia, Ginny was sliding over Amelia's skin, pressing against the boundaries of her mind. Her emotions were a discordant symphony of terror and longing and confusion, and as Amelia touched the doll, even with her gloves on the volume intensified a hundredfold.

Ginny's being exploded into her mind, and what little was left of Amelia knew the girl was a hairsbreadth from pushing her out. A spike of her own fear, a different texture from Ginny's in a way she would never be able to explain to another soul, stabbed through her. She could not, must not let it happen. Not here, not like this, in front of the child's mother. Ginny wanted to wail her child's terror through Amelia's mouth, into her mother's ears, and if Amelia let it happen it would shatter this woman forever.

Barely aware of anything happening around her, Amelia fought back, trying to reclaim the ground of her own mind. Ginny clung and howled as Amelia pushed forward, step by desperate step. Amelia didn't know how much time had passed, couldn't spare the energy to worry that the others were watching, couldn't—

"What is the meaning of this?" The loud, masculine voice cut through everything. Ginny's spirit flinched, and in the scant second of advantage it bought her, Amelia managed to force her own fingers open. The doll fell to the carpeted floor with a thud, and Amelia shoved Ginny entirely away. The spirit vanished.

A man stood at the head of the stairs, his face thunderous.

"Darling," Mrs. Holloway said, starting toward him. "They're—"

Her husband looked past her, his eyes focusing on Rhodes. "You," he said, his voice a snarl. His wife reached him then, and he curled one arm protectively around her. "You come into my home and harass my wife at a time like this. You've always been scum, Rhodes, but even from you, this is low."

Amelia looked at Rhodes in shock.

Holloway motioned to his wife's maid, who hurried to her mistress's side and began to gently urge her back down the hall. Holloway stepped to one side, allowing the large footman behind him on the stairs to move past him. "Get that man out of my house," he said, looking from Rhodes to Andrew and then to Amelia, marking them all with eyes turned dark with fury. "Get them all out."

"No need for that," Rhodes said casually. "We're leaving." He walked toward the stairs. Andrew bent to retrieve the doll from the floor and handed it to the maid as she and Mrs. Holloway passed them.

"Please, Miss Matthew," Mrs. Holloway said, reaching out to grasp Amelia's arm. "Did you—"

Amelia shot a glance at the men, then lowered her voice. "Ginny is at peace. She loves you very much. She knows you'll grieve for her, but she wants you to find peace as well." The lie was all she had to offer, so she offered it with every bit of sincerity she possessed.

Mrs. Holloway shuddered, and fresh tears came to her eyes. "Thank you." She squeezed Amelia's arm once and allowed her maid to lead her away.

# 11

Jonas stood outside a motley collection of tenements on Watts Street, surveying them in grim disapproval.

He was more than familiar with the various classes of accommodations, having lived, or squatted, in all of them in his time. The really old ones, governed by barely any law at all, were often former row houses chopped up into apartments, sometimes with new-built stories stacked atop the originals like a child's teetering block tower. Where there had originally been a back garden, there was usually a second building, newer but even more shoddily constructed than the first. Built without a thought for the safety, hygiene, or comfort of the residents, they were among the most squalid dwellings in the city, where overcrowding and filth drove out all but the most desperate.

The Tenement Act of 1867 had made a feeble attempt to improve conditions, mandating the construction of fire escapes and at least one toilet or privy for every twenty people. It also decreed that every room must have a window, which might have been a nice addition if it had specified that the window had to face the outdoors. It didn't, so landlords set the five-story red brick buildings flush against one another and cut windows that faced into the unlit interior hallways. Having satisfied the letter of the law, they continued renting rooms that were just as cave-like, but now offered even less privacy than before.

Another effort at reform, in 1879, was meant to put an end to such shenanigans, but, as so often happened, a bid to make things better merely made them bad in a different way. Buildings constructed since then were roughly dumbbell-shaped. When built in a row, the outer edges were still flush, but the middle sections now had a narrow air shaft, enabling the inclusion of windows that did, technically, open to the outside. The amount of light they let in was laughable, and, owing to the common use of the shaft as a dumping ground for all manner of noxious refuse, the air they admitted was frequently dank and foul. Worst of all, when fires broke out, the air shaft acted like a giant chimney flue, drawing the flames upward and frequently igniting upper apartments and the adjoining building as well.

The ones along this section of the street were particularly sorry specimens. Several appeared to have been in various stages of construction before being abandoned, almost certainly because whoever had been building them had been caught in the cascading bank failures that had begun earlier in the year. Thanks to Sarah's description, Jonas had no trouble finding the one she'd seen Amos near. It had, thanks to some fortunate quirk of fate, a narrow alleyway running between it and the old-law building beside it, meaning the people who would someday live in the middle part of the dumbbell might actually get some benefit from their windows. Now, however, everything was boarded up, and the alley Sarah said she'd seen Amos disappear into was choked with weeds and trash.

Jonas was on the front stoop examining the sturdy chain on the door when a voice called from the sidewalk behind him, "Ain't nothin' worth seein' in there."

He turned. A man in a dirty shirt and worn dungarees stood looking at him. Judging from his red face and unfocused gaze, he'd wandered out of the bar next door.

"You live around here?" Jonas called back.

"Over there, if you can call it livin'." The man gestured approximately in the direction of one of the old buildings.

"Have you ever seen a boy around this building? A light-skinned Negro, thin, about this tall?" Jonas held his hand up to roughly his own armpit.

The man shrugged. "Couldn't say. Seen a lot of people around."

"Any of them living in this particular building?"

Now he cackled. "Ain't nobody livin' in that building."

"Really? No one?" Jonas didn't bother to hide his disbelief. The idea of a vacant building with no squatters was hard to imagine, especially right now.

The man snorted, hearing his skepticism. "You just try to go in. You'll see." He turned and stumbled back into the bar.

Jonas watched him go, then gave the chain an experimental tug. It held tight. He walked to the mouth of the alleyway and poked a toe through the trash collected at its mouth. He had to turn nearly sideways to fit, at least through the first and last sections, but eventually it spit him out in a courtyard strewn with garbage and reeking of rot and cat piss.

Even now a pair of the animals were growling and hissing at one another beside the back fence. Startled by his appearance, they looked away from one another and stared at him, their ears laid flat and their tails lashing like whips, before the smaller cat turned tail and ran, slipping through a gap in the boards. The larger, a ragged gray tom missing half an ear, made no move to follow, but settled onto his haunches, watching Jonas warily through flat yellow eyes.

"You leave me alone, and I'll do the same for you," he told the cat, then turned his back on it.

There was no back stoop, only a door three feet off the ground with a trio of boards nailed across it. But in contrast to those on the front door, these wiggled when he tested them. It only took a moment to work them free and boost himself onto the narrow sill. He pushed the door open, foot already lifted to step through, then grabbed the sides of the doorway to keep himself from falling as vertigo swept over him and his balance tottered.

The building was almost hollow inside. There was no floor. A few joists remained, spotted with nail holes where floorboards must have once been, but the wide spaces between them yawned open into the basement, at least a ten-foot drop. Jagged-looking piles of debris littered the bottom.

There were no walls, only a few studs where walls would have been—the important ones, he assumed, the ones necessary to keep the building from falling. In the center of the room a pair of naked, saw-toothed boards—the outer edges of what should have been the stairs—angled upward. Bracing his hands on the door jamb, Jonas leaned in and twisted at the waist to peer upward into the gloom. Enough sunlight made it through the narrow cracks between the boards on the windows for him to count. One, two, three floors' worth of windows before his sight line was cut off by the still-intact floor of the fourth story.

No wonder the man said no one came in here. The builder must have stripped the interior to frustrate squatters. It was an effective deterrent. There were plenty of other options in the city—near-complete buildings that didn't all but guarantee you'd fall to your death before reaching an actual room. Jonas was about to pull his head back out of the building and concede that Sarah had been wrong about seeing Amos here, or perhaps she'd been right, but had seen Amos go into the alley as a shortcut to somewhere on the adjacent street—when a hot breeze blew against his back and something in the building moved at the edge of his vision. He scanned the empty interior. There. On a corner of one of the stringers, up at the top, near where it met the nonexistent second floor, was a scrap of something. Jonas frowned, trying to bring it into focus in the dim light. Pale. Another gust, and the thing fluttered. It looked like cloth.

Probably it was nothing. But the longer he looked at it the more it bothered him. It shouldn't be there. It would nag at him if he walked away. He needed to get a closer look.

Jonas turned his attention to the joists, perhaps two inches wide and set two feet apart. He didn't like his chances of making his way across them. He glanced around, his eyes coming to rest on the planks he'd pulled from the door. That might do it. Jonas clambered back down to retrieve them, then one by one he laid them across the joists before pulling himself back up. He stepped gingerly out onto the makeshift platform, taking care to make sure his weight was distributed properly. Picking up the rearmost plank and putting it down in front of him as he went, it took him five minutes and twice that many splinters to cover the distance from the door to the bottom of the stairway. It was beyond cumbersome, and he'd sweated through his coat by the time he got there. He took it off and hooked it over a nail sticking out of one of the remaining wall studs.

Jonas took a deep breath and studied the boards where the stairs should have been, visualizing his next moves. His leapfrog method should still work, but it would be trickier going upward. He laid the planks over the first three gaps and stepped. After a little experimentation, Jonas found it easiest to crouch on the second plank and brace himself against the third while retrieving the first. Slowly, one deliberate step at a time, more on his knees than his feet, he made his way toward his target. From a few feet away, he could tell he was right: it was cloth, caught on a bent nail, the edges frayed. He stretched, reaching for it, and was just able to grasp the end between his two longest fingers. With a little yank, he tore it free from the nail.

Jonas held it in a beam of light and examined it, rubbing it between his fingers. Good-quality broadcloth, worn but clean. It had a faint gray chevron pattern that made his mouth tighten in a line. It looked very much like the one on the shirt Polly had been mending the afternoon before. He suspected that if he held this swatch of fabric against the hole in that shirt, they would match.

Amos had been here. Recently.

But for what purpose? Jonas had been a fifteen-year-old boy. He knew they didn't need a reason to do foolish, dangerous things. But sneaking out to come climb this building in the dark was extreme. He looked up toward the fourth floor, then dropped his head with a grimace, deeply hating the idea of going further. But Amos had to have a reason to come here, and there was nowhere else it could be. They had to know what was up there. And they didn't have any more time to waste. He was here, he'd figured out a way to do it, therefore he had to.

Grimly, he began climbing again. Mechanically, he placed, stepped, braced, reached, lifted. He coughed dust from his throat, and his sleeves grew filthy with the sweat and grime he wiped from his face. Place, step, brace, reach, lift. The same series of motions, over and over, as he passed the second floor. His back began to ache from the constant crouching, but he went doggedly on. Halfway up the third story, however, he placed, stepped, braced, and reached, but as he lifted the trailing plank in his right hand, his left arm, which had remained weak since the shooting, spasmed. It knocked the topmost plank, the one he was meant to be bracing against, sideways. It slid too far over the edge, and its own weight flipped the other end up toward his head.

Reflexively, Jonas jerked away from it, and the weight of the plank still in his right hand pulled him off balance. He dropped it and flailed, grabbing at anything, legs and knees, arms and elbows all scrabbling for purchase. Visions of his body lying twisted and shattered across the joists below flashed through his mind. Would the fall be enough to kill him, or would he lie there in agony for hours before dying? Would anyone hear him if he screamed for help? There was no telling how long it would take for anyone to come looking. The rats would certainly get there first.

He caught himself on the rough boards and barked a curse as the two lost planks tumbled end over end, their downward progress marked by loud bangs, until they finally came to rest somewhere far below him. He knelt on the only remaining plank, lungs working like a bellows, his heart beating like a kettledrum. When he finally stopped shaking, Jonas evaluated his situation, deciding the one remaining plank was worse than useless. He couldn't stand on the narrow edges of the boards while leaning down for it, and even if he only used it on the stairs above him, as a thing to brace against, he'd need both hands to lift it to the next step, leaving him balancing on those same narrow edges. Better to use hands and feet on the edges and keep three points of contact.

He stepped onto the inch-wide boards, grasped a higher one with his left hand, and used his right to heave the now-useless plank over the edge to join its companions. Gritting his teeth, Jonas began to clamber upward. *It's like climbing a ladder,* he thought. *If it were broken in half. And then turned so the rungs faced the wrong way. And propped over a three-story drop.* The dust tickled his nose. Sweat dripped into his eyes. He didn't dare look down.

It was only half a flight, but it felt as though it took an hour. Jonas heaved himself gratefully onto the intact landing of the fourth floor and lay on his back, his whole body trembling, resolutely not thinking about how the hell he was going to get back down now that he was up here. His hands were bloody and stinging where the rough wood had gouged them. He sat up and fished for his handkerchief, then tore it into strips and bound them around his palms, using his teeth to pull the knots tight.

Finally, he pushed himself to his feet, ready to search for the reason Amos Alston had come here. There were four apartments to a floor, each of them narrow, three-roomed, and identically laid out. He found what he was searching for in the third apartment. An old mattress tick, stuffed with straw, was in one corner. A battered tin bucket with a handle sat in another. A lidless earthenware chamber pot. An oil lamp. Jonas picked it up and shook it. There was oil in the reservoir. There were also two things he couldn't immediately identify in the dim light. He moved to the window. As he suspected, the boards covering it were merely propped into place. He removed them and looked out. He was in the narrow middle section of the building, facing the featureless wall of the old tenement next door. Thanks to the wide outer edges of the building, this window was essentially invisible from both the street and the building behind it.

Jonas turned back to examine the two unknown items and stopped, staring at the floor. Grayish powder, thicker in some places than others, was streaked and striped across the floorboards. Grimly, he knelt and scraped a quantity of it into a pile, then tipped a palm full of it into his pocket, wondering if he'd found the source of the powder trapped in Ginny Holloway's nightgown.

That done, he picked up the first of the unidentified items. It was some sort of rope and pulley system. He examined it for a moment until he thought he understood how it worked. Then he reached for the bundle of canvas, already suspecting its purpose. He laid it out on the floor, turning it this way and that, until he was satisfied he was correct.

A bucket had a handle. A rope could be tied around it and used to haul it up from the ground. But not everything could be easily lifted that way. Amos might have wanted to bring things up that couldn't be secured by a rope and a square knot. The chamber pot, for instance. He'd probably brought that up wrapped in this homemade canvas web. Along with any number of other things Jonas could think of.

Including the one that turned the sweat coating his body cold. Jonas stood in Amos Alston's secret lair and imagined the boy, the son of a man he respected, designing this system, then sneaking out of his home in the middle of the night to use it to bring Ginny Holloway into this lonely, secure little prison.

# 12

Andrew's face flamed as they were ushered out of the house by the glowering footman. The last time he was so unceremoniously removed from a place, he'd been six years old and had just been discovered in the kitchen pantry with his face smeared with that evening's dessert.

On the sidewalk, Amelia whirled on Rhodes. "Why does Mr. Holloway know who you are?"

"I've done some stories about corruption in the city government. His name came up a while back." Rhodes shrugged. "I tried to get an interview."

Andrew found his voice. "Does that mean you followed him around and badgered him?"

The reporter made a face. "Badgered is such an ugly word." He stepped toward the curb and raised a hand to flag down a cab.

If Andrew had been disconcerted by the apparent friendliness between Rhodes and Amelia before—and he had, he'd been shocked when she'd so casually mentioned the Foundling in front of the reporter—he was immeasurably relieved by the look she threw him now. It was an unworthy thing to dwell on under the circumstances, and he was embarrassed by his own pettiness.

Coming here at all had been a ghastly mistake. They'd intruded on a family in the midst of their grief, had gained nothing but a list of people Sidney had already told him they didn't have time to question, and, worst of all, had exposed that poor woman to the reporter's prying eyes. No doubt his melodramatic account of the grieving mother's lonely days would sell hundreds of papers. It made Andrew sick to have been a part of it, however unwittingly.

And they'd done it all on behalf of a boy who looked increasingly guilty.

Amelia made a disgusted sound and turned away, massaging her forehead. It jolted Andrew out of his own outrage and reminded him of what he'd seen pass over her face when she held Ginny Holloway's doll, as well as what she said as she passed Mrs. Holloway on their way out.

Andrew stepped to her side and lowered his voice. "Ginny was there, wasn't she?"

Amelia gave him a tight nod.

"But you kept her out?"

Again, she nodded.

"Why?" he blurted, hearing the dismay in his voice but unable to suppress it.

Amelia looked startled at his outburst, but her expression turned stony as he went on. "She wanted to talk to her mother, and you prevented it."

A cab had pulled to a stop beside the curb, and without replying, Amelia spun on her heel and strode toward it. Rhodes opened the door and held out a hand for her, but she brushed past him and climbed in without looking at him. He started to step in after her, but she put out a hand, palm out.

"I have no interest in being anywhere near you right now." She looked past him to Andrew. "Either of you." She reached for the door, slammed it, and rapped the ceiling of the cab. Her back was stiff as it pulled away.

Rhodes stared after her, then chuckled and raised his hand for another cab. Within a minute, another had stopped, and they climbed aboard. Rhodes whipped a pencil and notepad from his pocket and began scribbling.

Andrew looked on in distaste, but said nothing. There was no point. Instead, he looked out the window. Amelia's action troubled him. He knew, as well as anyone, what comfort and peace her gift could give. Amelia had helped Andrew say goodbye to his sister. She'd chosen to withhold that opportunity from Mrs. Holloway. Whispered words of comfort weren't the same thing as actually being able to speak to your lost loved one. It felt to Andrew like a betrayal of something sacred. Perhaps it was irrational, but that made it no less true.

He wrestled with the feeling all the way back to Sidney's office, where Morris met them at the door with the news that there were sandwiches and coffee waiting. Amelia, seated on the sofa beside Sidney, was evidently no less angry after her solitary ride. She barely looked at either of them when they walked through the door.

Sidney regarded Rhodes with contempt. "Did you enjoy pulling that little stunt?"

Rhodes shrugged. "I got a look at the mother, which no other reporter in town has managed. It wasn't a total loss."

Andrew ignored him and claimed a seat beside Amelia on the sofa. She didn't look at him.

"Why?" he asked.

Her voice was so low he had to strain to hear it. "You have to ask? You've seen what it can be like, when they're . . . distraught."

It was true. The first time Amelia had channeled his sister, Susannah had been hysterical. Uncontrollable.

Amelia went on. "She would have taken me over, and it would have been horrible. Do you think I should have let it happen? Let Mrs. Holloway hear her daughter screaming in fear? Do you think that would have been any comfort?"

"No. You're right. But . . ." Andrew trailed off, conflicted.

Amelia wouldn't let it go. "But what?"

Andrew fought a war with himself over whether to say the words. "You lied to her. She wanted to talk to her daughter, and you lied to her." He knew he was being unfair even as he said it. The choice had been between a devastating truth and a comforting lie. He couldn't say she'd made the wrong one.

"Cassandra Holloway didn't need to hear her daughter sobbing for her," Amelia said, and Andrew wilted in the face of her certainty.

"You're right," he said, raising a hand in surrender. "I'm sorry." He started when Sidney spoke next, having all but forgotten the others were listening.

"Mrs. Holloway may not have needed to hear what Ginny had to say," Sidney said, "but we did. That was likely our best chance. I hate to ask you to do it, but do you think you could contact Ginny again?"

Rhodes barked a disbelieving laugh.

They ignored him.

"I don't know," Amelia said, her voice tired. "I suppose I can try."

Andrew drew the green ribbon from his pocket. The one he'd surreptitiously taken from Ginny Holloway's doll before handing it back to the maid. "Would this help?" He offered it to Amelia, and a complex series of emotions flashed over her face.

"Why did you—" She trailed off.

"I don't know." It was true. It had been an impulsive act, with no real thought behind it. They stared at one another for a moment before Amelia dropped her eyes from his face to the ribbon in his hand. She licked her lips.

Rhodes's voice was incredulous. "Don't tell me both of you actually believe in this horseshit."

Amelia's eyes snapped toward the reporter, and her face bloomed red with anger as she sprang to her feet. "Fine," she said through gritted teeth. "If you want to hear from Ginny Holloway, then be my guest." She tore off her glove in one violent motion and flung it aside, then clenched her bare fist around the ribbon dangling from Andrew's hand.

It was immediate.

Amelia gasped, her face going slack and blank for the merest instant before terror overtook her features. Her mouth opened, and the sound that came from her throat was impossible to mistake for anything other than the high, thin wail of a frightened child.

Every hair on Andrew's body stood at attention. Rhodes took an unthinking step back.

Amelia's hands flailed in front of her as if warding them away, and her eyes darted around the room, wide and round in terror. "Where am I? Where's my mama? I want my mama!" Tears spilled down her cheeks, and she breathed in jerky little gasps between sobs.

Rhodes looked from Amelia to Sidney and Andrew, his expression caught between fear and suspicion. "What is this?"

Amelia—Ginny—flinched away from his voice with a cry. She grew more frantic as the seconds passed, her breathing more ragged, her body curling in on itself. Any moment, she was going to start screaming, and Andrew had no idea how they would get her to stop. They had to do something. Andrew took a deep breath and tried to sound reassuring. "Ginny."

Amelia's head swiveled toward him. "Who are you?" Her voice was choked. "What happened to me?"

"My name is D—Andrew," he said, stopping himself from using his title. Lots of children were afraid of doctors. He went on in the gentlest tone he could manage. "No one is going to hurt you now. Can you tell us what you remember about that night? There was a party."

She shook her head—in confusion, not refusal. "I wanted to see. I went outside. The man was there. He gave me a candy. And then . . ." She began to tremble.

"Which man? Did you know him?"

"He said he was my friend, " Ginny whispered. "But he—" She broke off and began keening again, the sound piercing Andrew to his core.

"Was he—" he tried to ask, but stopped as the keening grew in volume. Ginny put her hands over her ears and closed her eyes. Tears streamed from beneath her lids. She began to rock back and forth.

Andrew pressed his lips together and glanced at Sidney, who shook his head. It was no good. Carefully, the two of them stepped toward her, and Andrew reached for the end of the ribbon. He drew it from between her fingers, and as the end fell free, Amelia's face went blank again, her eyes rolling back.

Sidney, prepared for it, caught her as she fell. Andrew dropped the ribbon and moved to help him guide her back onto the sofa as she gasped, her eyes blinking back into focus. She moaned and cradled her head in her hands.

Rhodes started like a rabbit at the sound. His face was white and sheened with sweat. "I . . . Ah." He began to back toward the door, then muttered something under his breath, turned, and all but fled.

Amelia let out a jagged laugh. "I take it my demonstration was convincing," she said. She pressed her palms to her temples and grimaced. "I shouldn't have done that angry. My control wasn't good."

"Do you remember it?" Andrew asked.

"No. She pushed me right out." She accepted the glass of water Sidney handed her with a trembling hand, drained it, and handed it back to him.

"You should eat something," he said.

"Not right now, thank you," she said. "You go ahead."

Andrew had just polished off his second sandwich when the door of Sidney's office burst open, making them all jump.

Jonas stormed into the room. His clothes were filthy, his hair disarranged, and sweat had run tracks through the dirt on his face. He held a sheet of newsprint in his hand, and he looked utterly enraged. "That lying little bastard. I knew it. Look at this. Look what he did." He all but flung the paper toward them, then stomped toward the whiskey decanter on the table. He poured himself a healthy slug and downed it, then followed it with a second as Andrew picked up the paper from the floor.

It was a midday extra edition of the *New York Sun*. HOLLOWAY FIEND'S OTHER VICTIMS? The headline blared. Below it were two bylines. The first was unfamiliar, but the second . . .

Andrew licked his lips and began to read aloud. "Reporters for the *New York Sun* have uncovered shocking evidence that the murderer of Virginia Holloway may have been practicing his foul trade on the city's children for years."

Numb horror spread throughout the room as he went on. The article spared nothing. Not the names of the other victims. Not the Alstons' names nor the street they lived on. And not their involvement. Sidney's name was mentioned, as was the name of the firm. Both Amelia and Jonas were named, she as "a young woman who claims to be able to converse with the dead" who was "known to work out of a private room in a Greenwich Village club notorious for the indulgence of every sort of vice," and Jonas as "her protector, said to be her brother, who accompanies her everywhere."

Andrew glanced at her as he finished that bit. Amelia's face was stricken. The article had all but named her a whore and Jonas her procurer. She dropped her eyes from his, and he cleared his throat and continued reading.

Amos Alston was described as a "menacing youth the size of a full-grown man with an unusual fondness for children" who was "believed to have been acquainted with the victims, the true number of which remains thus far unknown." The article concluded with a call for further investigation and "charges in as many other killings as he is believed to have perpetrated."

Sidney's face was appalled. "We'll be lucky if they don't storm the jail and lynch him after this."

"I'm afraid the story isn't the only bad news," Jonas said. He told them about the house and the things he found inside.

Sidney's face went harder as he spoke. When he got to the powder, Sidney reached into his desk drawer and silently handed over an envelope. Jonas turned out his pocket into it, coating the lush blue carpet in pale dust in the process, but enough went into the envelope.

"That was an incredibly foolish thing to do," Sidney said when Jonas had finished. "You could have been killed."

"We needed to know," said Jonas, making a vaguely apologetic gesture.

"And now we do." Sidney sat with a sigh. "We know Amos Alston had a place he could have hidden Ginny Holloway and that he came up with a fairly ingenious way to move items—possibly people—in and out without being seen. It makes it less of a stretch that he could have also figured out a way to move her from her house. And now there's another unknown powder. If it matches the powder from the postmortem, we'll have fairly conclusive evidence that we're working on behalf of someone who murdered four children." He opened the desk drawer as he spoke and withdrew the vial they'd been sent by the District Attorney's office.

All four of them clustered around the desk as he spilled a bit of the powder from the envelope onto the dark wood of the desk and set the vial beside it. There was a long beat, the sense of a held breath, as they peered downward.

Amelia was the first to speak. "I can't tell."

Andrew let out a breath. She was right. The two samples weren't identical, but they weren't so obviously different as to make it clear they couldn't be the same substance.

"All right," Sidney said, straightening. "I suppose—" He stopped at a tentative rap on the door. "Yes?"

Morris poked his head inside, looking hesitant—and no wonder, since he had to have overheard essentially everything that had happened over the last hour. "I just got this from one of the clerks." He held up a small white rectangle, a business card. "He says a girl on the sidewalk asked if he worked here, then handed him this when he said yes and walked away. He brought it to me. I went straight out to look for her after I read it, but she's gone, whoever she was."

Sidney held out a hand for it, and Morris handed it over and withdrew. Sidney looked down at it, and the play of expressions over his face was something to behold. "Of course," he said, pinching the area between his eyes as if developing a headache. He held it out for the rest of them to read. It was Sidney's business card, and on the back was written, in a spiky, uneven hand *I NO AMOS DINT DO IT.*

There was a long pause, and Jonas sounded entirely fed up when he finally spoke. "I've had enough. We've been chasing our tails for two days. There's at least one person who knows for certain whether or not Amos Alston killed Ginny Holloway. We need to go back to The Tombs and ask him."

# 13

Little as she wanted to go back to the jail, Amelia wanted even less to be left behind while the men went to get answers, which turned out to be what all three of said men tried to suggest. She had channeled two spirits in the previous hours, they argued, so she should go home and rest and leave them to talk to Amos. It rankled, and she replied in a tart tone that she had as much right to go as Jonas, who currently looked more like an inmate than a visitor, or Andrew, on whom Amos had never before set eyes. In the end, all four of them crowded irritably into the cab and set off for Five Points.

No one felt much like talking, so Amelia had plenty of time to contemplate the many ways in which she felt absolutely wretched. Her head still ached. She was somehow both hungry and nauseated. Worst of all, though, was the feeling of having been a fool. Jonas had been right. They never should have allowed Rhodes anywhere near the case. There was no telling what he would write now that she'd allowed her anger with him—and with Andrew—to goad her into channeling Ginny Holloway. He'd been frightened, but she had no doubt he'd manage to recover enough to write about the experience. And there was nothing—not one single thing—any of them could do about it.

They reached The Tombs, and Sidney led them to the boys' cells. The cells were cleaner and lighter than the one Amos had been in on Monday, but he was still held away from the other inmates. Moving stiffly, the boy struggled up from where he had been lying on his cot as they entered, his good arm pressing against his ribs. The other was splinted and held in a sling. His face had been cleaned, though if anything it looked worse now that there had been time for the bruises to bloom. He wore a clean shirt and pants, but there was no evidence of candy or magazines in the cell, so if Polly had sent a care package, not all of it had reached her son. Amos watched them file into the cell through wary eyes.

"Amos, do you remember meeting me on Monday?" Sidney began.

Amos nodded slowly. "You're th' lawyer." His jaw remained swollen, but his speech, though mushy, was intelligible.

"I'm your lawyer," Sidney said, emphasizing the second word.

"M' father's been," he said. "Says it's all right to talk to you."

Sidney nodded. "Good. This," he said, indicating Andrew, "is Dr. Cavanaugh. I've asked him to come and make sure your medical needs have been seen to. Would you mind if he examines you?"

Amos gave him a half-shrug, and Andrew stepped forward. His exam was thorough and gentle, though that didn't stop Amos from wincing at times. "The arm is splinted correctly," he said when he'd finished. "It should heal well enough. The jaw is deeply bruised, but not broken, and the eyesight seems undamaged. Your ribs are what worry me most right now. I know it hurts," he said, "but you need to concentrate on breathing as deeply as you can. We don't want you getting pneumonia."

Assured that, for the moment, Amos was in no danger, Sidney turned to business. "Amos, you're in a great deal of trouble. The four of us have been investigating, and I need to ask you some questions about what we've found. It's important you tell me the truth. No one here will use anything you say to hurt you, but I can't help you if you lie. All right?"

Amos shrugged. "I guess so."

"Did you know Virginia Holloway?"

"A little," he said.

"Did you ever give her candy?"

"A few times."

"Do you make a habit of giving away candy to children on your routes?"

"'S not a habit," Amos said, his tone aggrieved. "If there's kids out when I make a delivery, sometimes I give 'em a piece."

"Were you at the Holloway house at any time during the day or the night Ginny went missing?"

"No." The boy's voice was definite.

"When she went missing, did you tell anyone you knew her?"

"Not right off," Amos said. "I din' know at first that I did know her. But everybody was talkin' about it. When they put that drawin' in the paper was the first time I knew. I told a couple of people."

"Who?"

"Jus' some people at work. Nobody."

It was the first hint of evasion Amelia had seen from him. She nudged Jonas, and he glanced at her and gave a single nod. He'd noticed it, too.

Sidney didn't press. "What happened the morning you found the body?"

"I was walking to work, jus' like every other mornin'. I saw somethin' white laying in the road, and when I got closer I saw . . . a hand." The boy swallowed hard. "I couldn't hardly believe it. I bent down t' look. I knew who it had to be, even before I uncovered her face. Very next second the policeman was blowing his whistle, and I jus' started running. I knew what they'd think, me squatted down by her like that. I thought if I could get home, I'd be safe."

"That's quite a coincidence," Amelia said from her place beside the door. "You finding the body."

Amos looked at her. "You think I'm lyin'?"

"No one is saying that," Sidney said. "But the prosecution will point it out, and we have to have an answer a jury will believe."

"I don't have one," Amos said. "Not for that." He seemed to sink down into the bunk.

"How about an answer for what I found at the house on Watts Street?" Jonas asked abruptly. "Do you have an answer for that?"

Amos sat up as though jolted, winced in pain, then immediately tried to hide the reaction. "I dunno what you're talkin' about."

"That's a lie," Sidney said calmly. "It's my job to help you whether you're guilty or not, but I can't do that if you tell me obvious falsehoods. Is Watts Street where you kept Ginny Holloway after you took her?"

Amos leaned forward, then winced again. "No. I never did anything to Ginny Holloway, I swear. The house on Watts don't have anything to do with that. It's where I meet—" He cut himself off.

"Where you meet whom?" Sidney asked. When Amos didn't speak, he sighed and reached into his pocket. "Someone came to my office this afternoon and left this." He showed the boy the business card. "Someone says they know you are innocent. If there's someone out there who can prove that, we need to know who it is."

Amos closed his eyes and pressed his lips together. "I can't."

Sidney leaned forward and put his hand on the boy's shoulder. "This is your life we're talking about. Based on the case the prosecution has now, you're going to be convicted. They won't care that you're fifteen. They'll send you to the electrical chair and congratulate themselves for it. Whoever it is you're protecting, they wouldn't want that. If there's something you can tell me that could possibly help me stop it, you have to do it."

"If I tell you, he'll kill her," Amos blurted.

Her. Amelia thought of the handful of cards she left at the laundry and the girls she'd seen working there. It could have been any of them. But a sudden suspicion overtook her. If Amos was involved with one of them, why was it so important to keep it a secret? Boys had sweethearts; there was nothing unusual about it. Unless they feared someone's disapproval. An image of the pretty, dark-haired girl with the bruised hand print on her arm came to Amelia's mind. The one who had lowered her eyes when Amelia mentioned Amos. What was her name? "Maggie," she said suddenly. "You're talking about Maggie."

Amos drew in an audible breath, but didn't deny it.

Jonas pressed him. "You meet Maggie at the house on Watts Street?"

Amos's shoulders dropped. "It's safe there. If you've seen it, you know."

"Safe from whom?" Sidney asked.

"Her father," Amos said. "He's drunk most all the time, and mean. He saw us talking at the laundry, and he whipped her bloody after. Told her to stay away from me. But we—" Amos looked away, uncomfortable.

"There's no way he could climb it. So we go there sometimes. And when it's bad at home, she brings her little brother with her."

"Do you pull them both up with the pulley?" Jonas asked.

Amos shook his head. "Maggie's a better climber than me. But Giorgio's too little. First couple of times, I took him up on my back, but it threw my balance off. Almost fell. So we needed another way."

"Where did you get the block and tackle?" Sidney interjected.

"Maggie stole it. Her father works over at the docks." Amos made a noise of derision. "When he works at all. He brought it home one night to fix. One of the wheels was stuck. She took it while he was passed out and brought it over to the house. He was mad when he couldn't find it the next morning, but she swore up and down he'd never brought it home with him, and finally convinced him. I fixed it and rigged it up with the sling."

Jonas spoke again. "And what's the powder all over the floor?"

"Rat poison," Amos said. "Wouldn't think the filthy little bas—" He caught himself with an apologetic glance at Amelia. "That they'd bother to climb up that high. There's plenty of garbage on the ground. But they did. So I spread some around."

Amos's easy explanations had the ring of truth, and they left Amelia feeling curiously unmoored. Over the past two days, her suspicion of his guilt had grown. It had made it easier to bear the fact that they likely couldn't save him.

"Were you there with Maggie the night Ginny Holloway was taken?" she asked, her heart thudding inside her chest. Not because she doubted his answer, but because of what it would mean.

"Yes."

Amelia let out a shaking breath. Amos was innocent. And he was almost certainly doomed.

# 14

Jonas regarded the tenement building where Maggie Caruso lived with distaste. They'd come directly there after leaving The Tombs, splitting up from Sidney and Andrew, who had gone back to the office to wait, agreeing too large a delegation would likely frighten the girl and prevent her from talking. Amelia, having already met Maggie, was the obvious choice for this errand. Equally obviously, she couldn't go alone. Besides, she and Jonas were better suited to handling themselves in this kind of neighborhood.

The entire block had a sagging, dissolute air, but this structure was particularly unappealing. It couldn't be more than ten years old, but, built in haste from the cheapest available materials and no doubt packed full of people ever since, it was already visibly decaying. Amelia stood beside him, and from the expression on her face, she was no more charmed by the place than he.

The noise of children playing drifted toward them from around back. The building's younger residents could be a good source of information, and perhaps less guarded than the adults. He exchanged a glance with Amelia, and in wordless agreement, they walked past the cracked front steps and through the alley toward the back. The courtyard was square, with lines of drying laundry crisscrossing from the fire escapes above and casting fluttering shadows over the packed dirt. Bedraggled pigeons pecked at the ground. Half a dozen ragged children squatted in a rough circle, absorbed in a game of marbles, while off to one side another pair, younger, used a stick to poke at a dead rat. None of them seemed to notice the eye-watering stench coming from the row of over-full privies along the back fence.

The children went quiet at the sight of the strangers standing amongst them.

"I'm told Maggie Caruso lives here," Jonas said, trying to ignore the smell.

The biggest boy turned from the marble game to assess them. "What's it to you?" he asked after a moment, his tone pure insolence. He turned his back on them as the game resumed.

Jonas fought the sudden urge to grab the boy by the neck and shake him like a terrier shaking a rat. He didn't have time to fence with this ragged little—

Amelia put a hand on his arm, and Jonas realized he'd been grinding his teeth. He took a deep breath—regretting it at once as the stink of the outhouses seared his lungs—and tried to affect an air of unconcern. He knew how this worked. The boy who'd spoken was the ringleader. None of the others would speak to them now until he allowed it. Jonas watched as the marble game progressed, the boys sharing a chipped clay cosher. Most of the marbles in the circle were similar, hard-baked clay in shades of gray and brown. But there was a trio of clear glass spheres, two blue and one green, nestled in among them. They clearly belonged to the ringleader, and despite the fact that they were in the circle, they were clearly off-limits—none of the boys aimed at them.

The outcome of the game was a foregone conclusion, and the ringleader was about to drop his winnings into a dirty cloth pouch when Jonas spoke. "How about a game? Keepsies. If I win, you answer my questions."

The boy considered. "What do I get if I win? You got a bag of marbles in your pocket you're willing to lose?"

Jonas fished a nickel from his pocket and flipped it in the air. The coin caught a stray beam of light and flashed as it tumbled, every child's eyes following its arc. Jonas caught it and pinched it between two fingers.

The boy grinned. "Easiest nickel I'll ever make. I'll even let you have first shot."

The children gathered around as Jonas knelt beside the circle, privately mourning the probable ruin of his pants, and lined up his shot. He'd been a fairly good marble player at one time, but it had been years, and there was a good chance he was about to make a fool of himself. His first few shots were nothing remarkable. His opponent was good but overconfident. As the game went on Jonas got better, and the advantage began to tilt in his direction. The boys shouted and cheered—a couple of them for him, which earned them furious scowls from their leader. Even the two younger ones left the rat to come and watch. Jonas won the game with a shot that was pure luck, and he scooped up his winnings as his opponent sat back on his heels, his jaw tight.

"Fair's fair," he said roughly. "Ask your questions."

"Does Maggie Caruso live here?"

"Yeah."

"Is she home?"

The boy looked over his shoulder at one of the little ones. "Giorgio. Go fetch your sister," he ordered, sending the child scrambling up the stairs on twig-thin legs.

A minute later, there was movement in the doorway. The man who stepped out looked like a prizefighter gone to seed. His head nearly brushed the top of the door frame, and his shoulders were wide and corded with muscle. But beneath them, his stomach strained at his dirty undershirt. Black hair sprouted in tufts from the neck and armholes. His face was puffy and unshaven, and the eyes above the flattened, crooked nose were bloodshot and suspicious.

A girl peeked out of the doorway behind him, her hand on the little boy's shoulder. Jonas glanced at Amelia and raised an eyebrow. Maggie? She nodded once, and Jonas turned back to the trio.

The man scratched at his belly with a meaty hand. "Who're you?" His eyes darted around the yard. The children shrank beneath his gaze and began to melt away, most of them disappearing around corners until the only one left was the biggest. He stood back, watching as if the proceedings had suddenly become a great deal more interesting.

Jonas looked up at the man. "We're here to talk to Maggie. Who are you?"

"I'm her father. You wanna talk to her, you tell me why."

Jonas glanced at the girl. The expression on her face begged him to be careful what he said. "We were told she works at Steele's Laundry with Amos Alston," he said finally. "We're talking to people who know him."

Caruso coughed, a phlegmy sound, then spat out a yellow gob of something. It landed in the dirt beside Jonas's shoe with an audible plop. "My Maggie don't know nothin' about that baby killer. He was sniffin' around her a while back, but I put a stop to it right quick." He cracked his knuckles. "She knows better now. We got troubles enough. I'm not havin' her bringin' no *moolie* babies home."

Jonas's eyelid twitched at the slur.

Caruso glanced over his shoulder at his daughter. "Get on back upstairs."

Maggie shrank away from him, but before she vanished, she caught Jonas's eye behind her father's back and tilted her head toward the front of the building. Jonas didn't respond.

"Takes after her mother, that one. Needs a crack across the mouth once in a while to keep her in line."

Amelia spoke for the first time since they'd entered the courtyard. "Where is her mother?"

Caruso snorted. "Bitch up and died on me. Two years ago."

"We're sorry for your loss," Jonas said.

"Ah, she was a worthless slut anyway." Caruso looked at Amelia. "Means I got a vacancy. You come to apply for the position?" He gave her a leering grin, revealing stained and broken teeth.

"I think not," Amelia said, her tone leaving no doubt about her disdain.

Caruso's face twisted, and he took a step forward. "Someone ought to teach you not to be so high and mighty."

"It won't be you," Jonas said. "If you take another step, I will break your legs. We'll be leaving now."

Guiding Amelia ahead of him, he kept an eye out behind them as they made their way back through the alley to the sidewalk. They waited fifteen minutes before Maggie stepped out the front door.

"I can't talk long," she said. "I told him I had to come back down to use the privy."

"All right. We'll be quick," Jonas said. "Did you leave this?" He withdrew the card that had been delivered to Sidney's office.

Maggie nodded.

"How do you know he didn't do it?" Amelia asked.

"I just do," she said.

"That's not good enough, Maggie," Jonas said gently. "Whatever you know, you need to tell us."

Maggie darted a look back at the door, then grimaced and lowered her voice. "I was with 'im. The night that little girl got taken."

"In the building on Watts Street?" Jonas asked.

Maggie started. "If you already know, why are you making me say?"

Jonas ignored the question. "Why that building, specifically?"

"Have you been there?"

"Yes," Jonas said.

"If you've seen it, you know why. Once you're up top, you're safe."

"How often do you need somewhere safe to go?" Amelia asked.

Maggie looked down and scuffed a toe of her shoe against the sidewalk. "Couple times a week, usually. And always on paydays."

"And you're certain you were there the night she was taken?"

Maggie hesitated. "Yes. Giorgio and I went over after dinner. It was a payday, and Pop hadn't come home yet. I knew what that meant. Amos can't come til everyone at his house is asleep. But he got there about midnight. He never could have done it."

"You're sure he never left."

"I'm sure."

"You little slut."

Jonas started and turned as Caruso's growling voice came from behind him. The man stepped from the shadowed doorway into the sunshine, his face enraged, his hand wrapped around a narrow wooden rod as long as his forearm.

Maggie cowered away from him as he drew it back.

"Sneaking around under my nose with that—" He swung the stick, a short, sharp blow, and it landed across Maggie's shoulder blades with a meaty thwack that drowned out the last word. The girl let out a cry of pain and covered her head with her arms in anticipation of another strike, which Caruso was already drawing back to deliver.

Jonas stepped between Maggie and her father, close enough to smell stale beer and unwashed flesh. "Enough." Caruso was quicker than Jonas anticipated, slipping to one side and grabbing Maggie by the hair. He lashed her across the back, then gave her a shove that sent her sprawling. "Get back inside. I'll deal with you later." He turned to Jonas. "And you. Come here with this uppity slit and threaten me?" He smacked the club into his palm and grinned. "I'm going to enjoy putting you on your back, but not as much as I'll enjoy it when she's on hers."

Crimson rage boiled through Jonas at the threat, and he took a careless stride forward.

Caruso whipped the club out in a fast, hard swing. Jonas dodged, a beat too slowly, and the end of the weapon clipped him painfully in the ribs.

The next swing was wild, and Jonas slipped beneath it and snapped a punch at Caruso's throat. Caruso gagged and staggered back, and Jonas wrenched the club from his grasp. He brought it down in a vertical arc. He both heard and felt the crack as Caruso's left collarbone snapped. Caruso roared in pain but didn't fall, swinging a wild right at Jonas's head and landing a glancing blow on his cheekbone.

Jonas grabbed Caruso by the front of his shirt and drove him backwards into the side of the building. A wild, dark rush of euphoric rage spilled through Jonas's body. He wanted to hurt the man, wanted to see him bleed, watch him suffer. Caruso snapped his head forward into Jonas's. Roaring filled Jonas's ears. Red washed over his vision, and what few threads of restraint remained snapped. His fists drove like pistons into Caruso's face and body. The man's face was a bloody mess, and still Jonas went on hitting him, unable to stop himself, not wanting to stop himself, wanting to turn the bastard into so much meat.

From somewhere far away came the shrill sound of a police whistle and the thud of feet pounding against the sidewalk behind him. A heavy arm came around Jonas's throat, and his whole body went wild, terror and fury and blinding rage, and he wheeled on the new attacker with nothing left of the world but the fight.

# 15

By the time Amelia got back to Sidney's office, she'd managed to calm herself enough to explain what had happened. Sidney and Andrew listened in growing horror as she described Caruso's attack and Jonas's unhinged response.

"I've never seen him lose control like that," she said, pacing across the floor. "It was like he'd gone mad. Several of the neighbors had to pull him off the policeman, or I think Jonas would have killed him. Another pair arrived with a wagon and took them both away."

When she'd finished, Sidney put both his hands flat on his desk and closed his eyes for a long moment. Then he stood and began loading his briefcase, swearing with impassioned creativity all the while.

"They'll have taken him to The Tombs," he said when he'd run out of invective. "There's probably no way I can get him out tonight, but I'll see what I can do."

"Are you all right?" Andrew asked her as Sidney stalked from the office.

"I'm fine." She dropped onto the sofa, abruptly exhausted.

"So before the fight, Maggie confirmed Amos's story?"

Amelia nodded without looking at him. "He's innocent, and we're all but out of time to do anything about it."

Andrew drew a breath to reply, but before he could speak, Morris rapped at the door and stuck his head inside.

"There's a boy out front. He says he has information about the Alston case, but he won't come inside, and he won't tell me whatever it is. He says he was told to only talk to 'somebody as was personally involved with the case.'" Morris's careful diction was at odds with the ungrammatical phrasing.

Amelia closed her eyes. "What now?" She rose and brushed past Morris, heading for the door and aware that both men had fallen in behind her. She reached the front of the office and peered out. Standing on the sidewalk out front was a grimy, raggedly dressed child in a newsboy cap. He appeared to be about eight years old, but could just as easily have been an underfed eleven. He stood shifting from foot to foot, as if whatever information he had to convey was too important to let him remain still.

Amelia opened the door, and when the boy saw the three of them crowding in the doorway, he backed away, his eyes widening.

"Stay back," she said quietly to the two men. "Don't scare him away." She came through the door and took two steps toward him. "You know something about—"

She got no further. He barreled toward her, and in the strange, elongated second before he slammed her to the ground, Amelia had time enough to be first shocked at his attack, then puzzled that his expression was not menace, but rather one of wide-eyed horror. There was a crack, and something stung her cheek a fraction of an instant before the impact with the sidewalk knocked the breath from her lungs for the second time in an hour. Only in the aftermath did she hear Andrew and Morris shouting, and only after they had pounced on her and dragged her—and her erstwhile assailant—back inside did she realize the sound had been a gunshot, and that the office's large, plate glass window now sported a nickel-sized, spiderwebbed hole in the dead center of where she had stood.

# 16

Morris held the newsboy in Sidney's office.

Numb in the aftermath of her near miss, Amelia allowed Andrew to lead her into the firm's tiny bathroom, where he gently cleaned the blood from her cheek. His eyes serious, he leaned in toward her as he finished. For a wild instant of mixed panic and exhilaration, Amelia thought he meant to kiss her. Instead, he stopped, his face only inches from hers.

"I don't see any glass in the cut," he said after a long second. "And I don't think it will scar." He stepped back, opening a space between them.

"Oh," she said, and hearing the deflated tone in her own voice, she tried again. "That's good."

"Does your head ache?"

"No. My shoulders hurt, but that's all. It could have been so much worse. If he hadn't pushed me out of the way . . ." Amelia stopped, her throat dry. She had nearly been killed. The enormity of it washed over her, and her head swam. She staggered.

Andrew had an arm around her in an instant. "It's all right. I've got you. Deep breaths."

When she was certain she wouldn't fall, she pulled away from him, unnerved by his proximity. Or, possibly, by how much she liked it. He let her go.

"That boy pushed you away because he knew someone was about to shoot," Andrew said as he turned on the tap, and Amelia noticed that despite the steadiness of his voice, his own hands trembled as he held them beneath the stream. "And he was the one who called you outside in the first place. The police will be here soon. Hopefully they'll be able to get some information out of him."

"I want to talk to him first," Amelia said.

The newsboy's name turned out to be Walter.

"Don't hardly anybody call me that, though," he said as he sat on the sofa in Sidney's office. "Mostly I go by Wink." The boy affected a casual pose, but his nervousness showed as he glanced at each of them in turn, looking rather small and helpless as Morris stood over him with a grim expression and crossed arms.

Amelia didn't relax. A knife was as sharp in a small hand as a large one. But if he wanted her dead, all he'd had to do was nothing. She put a hand on Morris's arm, then stepped past him and sat on the other end of the sofa. Call it a compromise.

"Wink," Amelia said, looking him directly in the eye, "we need you to tell us what just happened."

The boy grimaced. "Well, it's like this. This afternoon I was sellin' papers over in Chelsea—I got a real good spot, over on 8th—and I was just about sold plumb out of the afternoon edition when this feller turns up'n tells me he's got a job for me if I want it, it won't take long and it'll pay. I thought he wanted . . . Uh, well, beggin' your pardon, miss, but it ain't unusual for us newsboys to get unnat'rul suggestions, if you know what I mean."

Amelia blinked, then made a "go on" gesture, and Wink swallowed. "Well, I tell 'im I ain't into that kind o' work. An' he says how it ain't like that, and if I'll meet him at the corner a couple blocks from here and do one thing, he'll pay me a dollar before and another one after. Weren't goin' to turn that down, was I? So I meet him, and he says all I got to do is knock on your door here and say I got somethin' to say about the Alston case and get someone to come out. So that's what I done." His face and tone turned indignant. "He didn't say it might be a gal."

"So you knew he intended to shoot whoever came out?" Morris demanded. "And you only intervened because it happened to be Miss Matthew?"

Wink had the grace to look abashed. "He didn't *say* he was goin' to shoot anyone, but I saw the gun. Thought maybe he only meant to scare whoever it was. I didn't ask. Ain't a good idea to get mixed up in other people's business. But a feller can't be goin' around lettin' gals get shot at, no matter whether anybody means to hit 'em."

Amelia sighed. "I suppose I have to thank you for that bit of chivalry. Whoever it was might have as easily chosen someone with fewer scruples. Can you tell us what this man looked like? How he spoke? Have you ever seen him before?"

Wink's answers were not particularly helpful—there were many tall, dark-haired men in the city. He had been dazzled by the prospect of wealth, and the man who had offered it seemed to have taken care to appear nondescript in both person and dress.

When they'd wrung as much information out of the boy as they could, they warned him not to move and withdrew a little distance away.

"Maybe the police will be able to get more out of him," Andrew said.

"I don't want to tell the police about him," Amelia said. The memory of Amos Alston's battered face was too fresh in her mind to contemplate handing another child over to their charge.

"Are you certain?" Morris asked. "He was part of it, even if he did back out at the end."

Amelia nodded. "I know. But he didn't personally mean us any harm."

"It's your decision," Andrew said. Then he sighed as if he'd only just realized something. "But if we're not going to hand him over, we'll have to keep him with us, at least for a little while."

"Why?" Amelia asked.

Morris answered. "Because he's the only person who saw this man, and he's the only person who could recognize him if he tries again."

"You really think he might?" she asked. "You don't think this was a case of someone getting riled up by the newspapers and deciding to put a scare into Amos Alston's lawyer?"

"Maybe," Morris said, "but there's no way to know. There is a murderer out there, after all. He probably reads the papers, too. Not only that, Wink can't walk out of here alone, either. He saw whoever this was. I suspect if the first bullet had hit you, there would have been a second coming for Wink."

He was right. Amelia made a sour face. "Well, he'll have to stay with one of you. I have to work tonight."

"You can't do that," Andrew said immediately. "It's not safe."

"I have to," she said. "Sabine's already going to be angry enough about Jonas. I can't leave her with an empty room. Besides, it's not as though I was the actual target. He told Wink to ask for anyone connected with the case. He was ready to shoot at whoever stepped outside. There's no reason to think I'm in any particular danger from him."

"You're the *only* one in danger from him right now," Andrew said as Morris nodded along. "Jonas and Sidney are beyond his reach for the moment, not that he's likely to have any idea where they are. The awning above the door means I doubt he got a good look at Morris or me. My name hasn't been in the papers. Yours has, along with the fact of where you work. Until we have reason to believe otherwise, we have to act as if he's specifically after you."

The two men were implacable, and twenty minutes later, after ascertaining that Wink lived with his parents and eight siblings in a Five Points back tenement and would not be missed for a day or so, Amelia found herself in a cab with both Andrew and the boy in tow. She had no idea what she was going to do with either of them.

Her first stop was the back door of the club's kitchen.

"You aren't bringing him in here," the cook said, wrinkling her nose at the sight of Wink. "Not til he's been deloused, at any rate."

"Fine," Amelia said with a sigh. "Can we at least have something to eat? And can you ask Tommy to come back here?"

The cook hurriedly made up a parcel of food while a busboy went to fetch Tommy, who appeared a minute later.

"Miz Amelia," he said, looking at the odd trio. "Everythin' all right?"

"Not hardly," she said, before quickly explaining.

Tommy's eyes widened when he heard Jonas was in jail, and he looked wholly horrified when she admitted how close she'd come to being shot.

"So both of them need to be inside the club tonight," she finished. "Andrew can be a guest, and we can put Wink somewhere unobtrusive—he just needs to be able to see who's coming in. But they need clothes, and I was hoping you could help."

"Miz Sabine's not gonna like any of that," Tommy said as he looked them over.

"I'm not exactly thrilled about it myself," Amelia snapped, out of patience. She caught herself and sighed, then put a hand on his arm. "I'm sorry. None of this is your fault."

Tommy let out a humorless chuckle. "Might say it's all my fault. I'm the one who brought you into this mess to start with." He looked appraisingly at Andrew and Wink, then nodded once. "I'll see what I can do."

He ducked back inside, and Amelia led Andrew and Wink across the courtyard and up the stairs to her apartment. Strange as it was to have the boy with them, it bled away some of the awkwardness she would have felt at inviting Andrew inside. He looked around the narrow front room with interest, though there was not much to see. A heavily scratched table with a pair of chairs, a square coal stove in the corner, and a small icebox were the only contents. Amelia put the sack of food on the table, and Wink's gaze turned to it with a gleam she recognized from her own frequently hungry youth. She separated out a few items for herself and Andrew, then pushed the rest toward the boy. "Help yourself."

After they ate, Amelia went to bathe and dress, nervously emerging from her bedroom thirty minutes later wearing décolleté blue silk and false curls at the back of her head.

Wink's eyebrows went up, and he let out an appreciative whistle. "Don't you clean up a sight." Amelia mentally revised her estimate of his age upward.

Andrew gave him a light cuff to the back of the head. "That's not how you compliment a lady." He turned to her. "But you do look lovely."

Amelia's cheeks heated, and she was grateful when a knock at the door gave her an excuse to turn away from him.

Ever the miracle worker, Tommy had procured clothing that was close enough to pass for appropriate in dim lighting. Andrew put his on without complaint, though it was clearly inferior in quality compared to what he'd worn to dinner Monday. Wink, after much grumbling, submitted to being scrubbed and dressed in stiff black trousers and a starched white shirt, though he drew the line at the tailed coat. "I ain't wearin' that," he said flatly. "I'll look like a nob. Too hot for it, asides."

"Fine," Amelia said. "You're meant to stay out of sight anyway. Come on."

The three of them made their way down the stairs, and Andrew offered Amelia his arm as they crossed the courtyard. She accepted with a feeling of dreamlike inevitability and held her breath as two heretofore separate parts of her life folded in on one other.

⁓

Andrew walked into the club's main room with a keen sense of anticipation. He'd been here once before to speak with Jonas. But that had been in the daytime, when the place was empty and the windows had been thrown open to the air and light. The decor had been little different from that of any other well-to-do home—though Society matrons tended toward more chaste subjects for the art on their walls. Tonight, however, the building hummed with something more primal. More eager. The brass front of the bar was polished and shining, while rows of crystal glassware sparkled behind it, ready for the kiss of liquor. A trio of showgirls, wearing feathers and pearls and little else, rehearsed on a small stage.

One glanced over at them and laughed, and Andrew followed her gaze to see Wink eyeing them with brazen interest. The girl's laugh attracted the attention of the other two, and they broke off their ribald song and left the stage to meet them.

"Who do we have here?" the first girl asked, looking at Andrew. She was pretty, with masses of dark curls and a wide smile. Her outfit left no detail of her figure to the imagination, and the generous expanse of pale bosom visible above her neckline swelled alarmingly with each breath. After the first, unavoidable eyeful, Andrew desperately tried to keep his focus on her face. Wink made no such effort, waiting with bated breath for the seemingly inevitable moment when her breasts would break free from their precarious containment.

The girl didn't seem remotely concerned. "This your fella?"

Andrew felt Amelia stiffen beside him. "No. We're . . . friends."

"Friends, huh?" She gave Andrew a smile full of invitation. "I like making new friends. I'm Delilah. If you're going to be around later tonight, maybe you'd like to buy me a drink?"

"I, ah," Andrew said, thoroughly at a loss. He'd never had to manage a polite response to a bold solicitation from an attractive, half-naked woman while standing right beside the woman he was actually interested in.

"I'll buy you one," Wink offered hopefully from his other side. "I have a dollar."

Delilah grinned at him, the seductive look dropping from her face. "Well, maybe I'll take you up on that. I think Joey keeps lemonade behind the bar." She ruffled his hair.

"Sabine's not going to like you bringing a kid in here," one of the other girls said. "And where's Jonas?"

"Jonas won't be in tonight," Amelia said. "And Wink won't be any trouble." She looked at Andrew. "If you wouldn't mind getting him situated, I think Tommy's set up a spot for him by the front."

Happy to escape, Andrew snagged Wink by the sleeve and towed him away. There was a latticed folding screen with a stool behind it in a corner near the door. Wink should have an excellent view of everyone who came through.

"Long as I can see the stage, I'll be happy," Wink said, peering through the lattice.

"This is serious," Andrew told him. "You have to pay attention. If you see the man from this afternoon, tell Tommy at once."

Wink didn't reply, his eyes still on the girls.

"Are you listening?"

"Yeah, yeah, I heard you," Wink said. "That Delilah sure is a jammy one, ain't she?"

"She's very pretty," Andrew conceded. "Now stay out of sight. I'll check in with you in a while."

He left the boy and crossed back to Amelia, who had just turned from the chorus girls.

Delilah blew him a kiss over her shoulder as they walked away.

"Where would be the best place for me to be?" he said to Amelia, half in desperation.

"You've got options. I'll show you around." She led him upstairs, Andrew avidly taking everything in, aware his interest came not from the club itself—he was not a stranger to risqué nightlife, though his enthusiasm had largely waned after his school days ended—but from the glimpse it offered into another facet of Amelia's life. Here was something that had been, until now, mostly hidden from him.

There were two rooms with billiard tables covered in heavy green felt, two card rooms, with round tables and comfortable leather chairs, and a pair of private dining rooms—including the one where he'd met with Jonas the previous spring. Finally, beside the back stairs at the end of the hall, Amelia opened the door to a small room with heavy hangings on the walls. A pair of velvet-upholstered chairs faced one another across a narrow table on which sat a large, smoked glass orb and a deck of tarot cards. Something about the room was at odds with the exuberant welcome of the rest of the place, but Andrew couldn't put his finger on precisely what.

"You should go back downstairs," Amelia said after a moment. "I should get ready, and it's better if Sabine doesn't see you up here before opening."

A bell chimed, and she straightened. "That's the five-minute warning. You'd better go."

"What's on the third floor?" he asked, pointing at the stairs.

A tiny pause. "It's all bedrooms," she said without looking at him.

"Oh. Well. I'll, um." Andrew tried not to look as if he were fleeing, cursing himself for having been so obtuse. Of course that was what was up there. Downstairs, he headed directly for the bar, and someone must have told the bartender he was a friend, because he waved away Andrew's money. "First one's on the house."

The doors opened, and for the first hour, Andrew hung back as the club began to fill with well-heeled carousers. He had more than a few school friends and acquaintances who had settled in New York, and though he wasn't unduly worried about running into any of them, kept a wary eye on the crowd, just in case. He ordered a second drink as the chorus girls, Delilah among them, took the stage. She looked in his direction and winked as they began their performance, which seemed to involve a great deal of bending forward. Andrew wasn't the only man there holding his breath, but he was probably the only one who was relieved when they finished without incident. There were scattered shouts and applause, and the girls left the stage and began a circuit through the crowd, stopping to talk or drink with customers.

It wasn't long before the first of them disappeared up the stairs with a portly man in an expensive suit. He spotted Delilah on the lap of a young dandy, her arms looped carelessly around his neck as she laughed. Waiters wove adroitly through the crowd carrying trays of drinks, and the sheer curtains began closing on the cushioned alcoves along the back wall. Some of the men dining together appeared to be only friends, while others were very obviously more. Andrew would have bet everything he had that none of the women there were the wives of the men they accompanied. They wore too much rouge and fluttered lashes darkened with kohl at men two decades older than them. None of it was entirely surprising, though Andrew did do a double-take when another showgirl headed for the stairs, this time leading a couple.

He made his way over to check on Wink, who was trying to look everywhere at once.

"They really got everythin' here, don't they?" the boy said in undisguised glee.

The night passed. Andrew grew numb with noise and alcohol. He politely declined several sexual overtures. He moved to the second floor when he could no longer tolerate the relentless gaiety of the first. He played billiards and sat in on hands of cards until the sums being wagered climbed to breathtaking heights and he was forced to withdraw. It was all revelry and frenetic energy and vulgar excess. Andrew could remember a time in his life when he would have found it mesmerizing. Now, it felt like an assault.

Somewhere around two o'clock in the morning, he found himself outside Amelia's door. It was closed, so she must have a client. He leaned against the wall to wait. Delilah approached with a man in tow, and he stepped aside to allow them access to the stairs. She gave him a long look as she passed, and to his surprise, returned alone a minute later.

"What are you doing back here?" he asked. "I thought you were . . ." He trailed off, his muddled brain unable to come up with the right way to finish that sentence.

Delilah smiled, genuine and amused. "He only needed me for cover. He's in with one of the boys now."

"Oh."

"So," she went on, stepping off the bottom step and pressing closer to him. She went up onto her toes to speak into his ear. "That means I'm entirely free at the moment. For that drink. Or maybe more."

Her breasts were soft against his arm, her breath sweet against his cheek, and Andrew was suddenly, almost painfully, aware of the nearly monastic life he'd been leading for the past year. There was enough alcohol in his veins to cocoon him in relaxed warmth and soften his inhibitions.

But not quite enough to completely eradicate them. With an enormous effort of will, he shook his head. "I can't."

"Too bad," she said, running a finger along the lobe of his ear and making a shudder run through him.

The door to Amelia's room opened, and a man stepped out, nodding to them as he passed. Through the open door, Andrew could barely make out Amelia's silhouette, but it was enough to bring him back to his senses. He pulled away.

Delilah followed his glance, and her expression turned knowing. "I see. Friends. Well, you know where to find me if you change your mind," she called over her shoulder as she sauntered past him toward the main stairs.

The heat in his blood had not fully dissipated as he stumbled into Amelia's room, and after the clamor of the rest of the club, the sudden quiet was disorienting. With the door closed, the only light came from a single gas lamp, and it took a moment for his eyes to adjust.

Amelia sat behind the table, her skirt spilling over the sides of the chair, the silken folds shimmering in the flickering light. Shadows played over the delicate bones of her face, throwing them into sharper relief. The neckline of her gown appeared positively demure in contrast to the flagrant displays he'd seen over the past hours, but it still revealed an expanse of skin as smooth and lustrous as pearl.

Andrew's throat was dry when he swallowed, wondering if she had any idea what a lovely tableau she made.

It had always struck him as odd that a place like this, so dedicated to encouraging everyone who stepped through its doors to lose themselves in the present, should employ someone whose function it was to help those self-same revelers look to their pasts and futures. Why did people come to this place and seek out this room? The line from the liturgy came unbidden to mind: "In the midst of life we are in death," and a hazy, inebriated understanding came to him. The debauchery of the rest of the club was the defiance of mortality. But to feed that defiance, to keep it burning, there had to be a reminder. Amelia and her work in this little room were that reminder. The contrast. Not only between life and death, but between quiet and clamor, subtlety and garish display.

She stood and stepped around the table. "Enjoying your evening?"

Her voice was tart, and it took his gin-muddled brain a moment to recognize why. She'd seen him with Delilah. And she hadn't liked it.

She was jealous.

Sudden euphoria filled his chest. She didn't want to be only friends, not any more than he did.

Impulsively, he held out a hand, palm up. "Tell my fortune?"

Amelia blinked at him. "How much have you had to drink?"

"More than I ought to have, I'm sure. Read my future."

"Why?"

Andrew shrugged. "Why not?"

She half-laughed, then reached for his hand. She held it gently.

"What do you see?" Andrew's voice was low.

"No less than what anyone who knows you would expect. A distinguished career. Lives saved, suffering averted."

"Is that all? I'd hoped for more. Isn't there something called a love line? Can't you read that one?"

Amelia's voice was barely audible. "I'm sure that's in your future. With someone . . . right for you. But I can't tell you who that is."

"How disappointing," Andrew said. "I think I could do a better job reading a palm than that." Made fearless by the realization that she still cared for him, he caught her hand in his and tipped it up. He stroked the lines of her palm with one gentle finger, not speaking, then lifted her hand, his eyes on hers, and pressed his mouth to the soft skin of her wrist. Her pulse quickened beneath his lips, and she sucked in a breath.

When she didn't pull away, Andrew reached out to trace a line from the corner of her mouth down the side of her neck and across the top of her shoulder, an echo of the caress in his office those months before. They'd been interrupted, or he might have followed it then with what he did now, which was to slide an arm around her waist and draw her closer. He dropped his mouth to the soft place behind her ear, and then to her neck, where he grazed the flesh with his teeth and tasted the salt of her skin.

Andrew's blood pounded in his ears, and Amelia's breathing was ragged as he moved to cover her mouth with his.

"No."

Her eyes were still closed, and the word was barely more than breath, but it landed against him with the force of a slap. He rocked back.

"What?"

Her cheeks were hectic with color. "I said no."

Andrew let go of her and stepped back. "I don't understand." He couldn't keep the hurt and bafflement from his voice.

Her own voice was full of regret as she turned away. "I know."

# 17

Wink was the only one who was cheerful as they crossed back to the apartment an hour later under the light of the heavy yellow moon. "I'm beat," he announced as they walked through the door. "And I can't wait to get out of this get-up."

Amelia pointed. "Jonas's room is that one." She glanced at Andrew without meeting his eyes. "The two of you will have to share."

"Won't bother me none," Wink said. "I pig together with three brothers at home." He disappeared through the door, leaving her alone with Andrew in the dim front room.

Amelia spent an agonizing few seconds looking at him, wishing desperately there was a way she could explain that telling him no might have been the hardest thing she'd ever done, in terms of sheer willpower required. And that she could still feel the place on her neck where his mouth had been. But if she told him, he would want to know why she'd done it.

And she couldn't bear to tell him.

Instead, she dropped her eyes and went to her room, where she stripped and lay restlessly awake, alternately visualizing Andrew lying only feet away and Jonas on a bunk in a cell. Those competing thoughts were almost enough to drown out the fact of her near death by gunshot only a few hours before, as well as the fact that in a little over twenty-four hours, Amos Alston would be taken from the Tombs and put on a train to Sing Sing. Everything they'd done in the past three days had gotten them nothing. They were going to fail—had already failed, if she were going to be honest about it.

Amelia had given up on trying to sleep by the time the sun rose, and she was sitting in the front room staring at nothing when there was a firm knock on the apartment door.

Sabine stood on the other side.

"Good morning, Amelia. May I come in?"

"Of course." Amelia stepped back, and her employer swept into the apartment.

She filled the little room, even in her plain morning attire, and didn't wait to be invited to sit, pulling out both chairs and gesturing for Amelia to take one as she seated herself on the other. Amelia complied. One generally did, when Sabine gave a direction.

Sabine looked around the room, uncharacteristically wistful. "I'd forgotten how small this place was. I lived here, you know, when I first opened the club." She nodded in the direction of the washroom. "I had it put in when I did the plumbing for the main building. I couldn't have privies fouling up the backyard, not with the kind of clients I meant to attract. But I admit, I was glad to have the excuse to do it."

"We've certainly appreciated it," Amelia replied.

There was a pause, and when Sabine spoke, there was regret in her voice, though her words were blunt. "I'm letting you and Jonas go, and I'm giving you two weeks to vacate the apartment."

"What? Why? Because Jonas missed last night? Just like that, we're out?"

Sabine half-laughed. "Just like that? Amelia, it's been more than six months since either of you were anything like a good value to me. Ever since you got hurt back in February, which, I'll grant you, wasn't entirely your fault—although you had no business out in that alley to begin with."

Amelia tried to speak, but Sabine forestalled her, raising a well-manicured hand. "And Jonas stopped working to look after you. And then," she went on, tapping the table for emphasis, "then you up and vanished, and Jonas was useless, with his worrying and hunting all over the city. I might have let him go then, but for his silver tongue. And then you turn back up without a word of explanation, and I take you back, thinking you'll make it up. But you've taken fewer clients and worked shorter nights ever since. You turn people away! You don't turn people away in this business," she said. "And Jonas. He's been barely keeping himself together, and now he's gone and gotten himself arrested for assaulting a police officer!"

"How do you—"

Sabine looked at her as if she were simple. "I pay off half the cops in this damned city. Did you think I wouldn't hear about it?"

Amelia only looked at her, unable to form a response.

Their voices had been enough to rouse Andrew, who emerged from Jonas's room, his shirt rumpled and unbuttoned. Wink blinked sleepily in the doorway behind him.

Sabine glanced at them, unfazed, and went on, her words precise. "I've made all the allowances I can make. More than I should have. Our arrangement was beneficial, but it isn't working any longer."

She stood, and, numb, Amelia stood with her.

Something like regret flickered behind her eyes, but her face did not change. "I'm sorry it's come to this."

As the door closed behind her, Amelia melted back into her chair. She looked around at the apartment that had been her home for the last two years. The best one—by far—she had ever known. And now it was gone.

∽

Amelia was pale and quiet on the way to Sidney's office on Thursday morning. Andrew felt gritty-eyed and wan, as much from the smoke and noise as from the alcohol.

When they arrived, Morris told them Sidney had been in that morning and had already left again for the Tombs. Jonas would be appearing in police court later that day, and Sidney was optimistic about getting him released. When informed about the shooting, he had promised to take precautions. He left instructions for Andrew to keep seeking a chemist to analyze the samples. Amelia should stay out of sight.

Wink slumped in a chair and scuffed his toe against the carpet during this discussion, but brightened when Morris offered that there was a box of leftover pastries in the clerks' office. They left, and Andrew was alone with Amelia for the first time since she had rejected his advance the night before.

He would not ask why. He would not. Disappointment and confusion ate away at him like acid, but he would not beg her to explain.

Amelia didn't look at him as she spoke. "Don't you have to go to the island today?"

"When I called yesterday I said I'd be out the rest of the week." He hesitated. "I'm sorry about your job. And the apartment."

"Thank you." She was subdued.

"I'm sure it will work out, though. You'll find something else."

She barked out a bitter laugh. "Landing at Sabine's was the luckiest thing that ever happened to us."

"Maybe. But especially now that I've seen it, I can't help thinking you're both too good for the place."

Amelia eyed him. "Because what goes on there is sordid and dishonest, and you think we're better than that?"

Andrew groped for a response. "I'm not sure I would have put it so bluntly, but yes. I suppose so."

Amelia tipped her head back against the sofa cushion. "You don't understand. What we do at the club is the most honest work we've ever done. If you'd known us before, you'd never have—" She cut herself off with a grimace.

"I would never have what?" Andrew asked, sensing that whatever she'd been about to say was the most important bit.

She shook her head. "It doesn't matter."

"It sounds as though you think it does."

There was a long pause, and when Amelia spoke, her voice was that of someone too tired to bother with further evasion. "It upset you when I lied to Mrs. Holloway, even though it was for a good reason."

"Yes. But I do understand why you did it. It was a kindness."

"That time it was. But that sort of kindness is a luxury I haven't often been able to afford. I've lied to hundreds, maybe thousands of people. I've taken their money and lied to them about their futures or their investments or their marriages or their dead loved ones, and none of it was about kindness. It bothers you to know that about me, doesn't it?"

Her words so closely echoed the thoughts he'd had in the aftermath of their visit to the Holloway house that he couldn't deny it. "Yes. Some."

"Those sorts of lies . . . They're the barest sliver of the things Jonas and I have done in order to survive. You don't—" She cut herself off with a grimace.

"Is that why you . . ." Andrew stopped. He had sworn to himself he would not ask. But she seemed to be trying to offer an explanation, and he could not let it pass. "Is that why you pulled away from me last night? Why you declined my invitations earlier this summer? Because you think I wouldn't approve?"

"You wouldn't." She sounded certain, but went on before he could argue. "But it was also because I realized that even if we . . . care for one another, it isn't enough. We're not the same. Not compatible."

"How can you be so certain of that?"

She sighed. "Who does your laundry?"

"What?" he asked, thrown by the sudden change of topic.

"Who does your laundry?" she repeated. "It's a simple question. Does your Mrs. Danbury send it out, or is there someone in the house who does the washing?"

"I don't know," he said, baffled by her insistence. "It's included in the price of the room. I never thought about it."

Amelia's smile was sad. "Of course you haven't. Your whole life, you have been accustomed to leaving your laundry, having it disappear and returned clean and folded without another thought on your part."

"And that makes us incompatible?"

"It makes us almost different species."

"Because I don't know anything about laundry?"

She spoke patiently, as if explaining something to a small child. "Because you have expectations I can't meet. You don't even know you have them, but you do. Eventually, no matter how much you cared for me, I would disappoint you."

"That's not fair," he said. "I've never asked you to be anyone but who you are, and—"

"But that's just it. You think you know who I am, but you don't."

"Then tell me," he said, louder. "Tell me, and let me decide for myself. You don't get to decide for me what I do or don't need. Or what I could or couldn't forgive."

"That's exactly what I mean about expectations," Amelia said, her own voice rising in turn. "There's one right there. The idea that I would ask you for—or you would have any right to grant or withhold—your forgiveness for anything I've done. The assumption that I'm sorry about any of it, or I wouldn't do it all again if I had to. You've only seen the thinnest sliver of my life. And even if you somehow managed not to care about any of it, your family still would."

"My family?"

"You've reconciled with them, and I'm glad for you, but—"

"My family doesn't have anything—" Andrew tried to say.

"—I can't live in that world. I know what they—"

"—to do with this. I—"

"—expect for you, and it isn't me. They'll want a blushing virgin with a family that—"

"—don't want—wait. Are you not—" Andrew, startled into a foolish degree of bluntness, managed to stop himself, but not quickly enough.

"A virgin?" Amelia looked him dead in the eye, and he had to force himself not to squirm beneath her gaze. "No. I'm not. Why? Are you?"

He felt himself flush. "I hardly think that's relevant."

"Why not? Because there's no expectation of virginity in men, but for some reason it's different for women?"

The truth of her statement was so obvious there was no way he could argue.

A bitter smile pulled at the corner of her mouth. "You see? We found an expectation for me to disappoint, and it didn't even take that long. There would be plenty of others, if we looked. I've lied and stolen and swindled, and yes, I sold what was mine to sell when that was the price of surviving one more day. Jonas and I did whatever we had to do. Most of it wasn't pretty. And I won't apologize for it. Not to you or anyone else."

Andrew stared at her, too shocked to respond. Amelia glared back, her face flushed and defiant.

He wasn't sure how long they would have stood there if Morris hadn't knocked on the door.

"Mr. Rhodes was here," he said after he poked his head inside. He glanced between them as though aware something serious had happened, although Andrew was certain they hadn't raised their voices enough to have been overheard. "I wouldn't allow him inside," he went on. "He insisted I give you this." He held a note out to Amelia, who took it reluctantly.

She unfolded it, and her face went white.

"What is it?" Andrew asked, stepping toward her.

Amelia handed him the note without a word.

Andrew looked down. A rough sketch of a child's face looked back at him, something in the few spare lines conveying the pointed chin and the curl to the hair. Beneath the drawing was a single sentence, but it was enough to pour ice water into his veins: *Anna Moretti, age 4, discovered missing this morning from her home on Bond Street.*

# 18

I t was early afternoon when the bailiff rapped on the bars of the cell.
"Time to go face the judge, boys."

Jonas hauled himself to his feet and held out his hands for the cuffs
almost eagerly. He'd spent an absolutely miserable night and morning
sitting upright on a bench in a cell with a dozen other men, more than a
few of whom were passed out in pools of their own vomit. On the whole,
he preferred them to the ones who were awake. The unconscious drunks
were at least peaceful. The others were angry. None of them had bothered
him, but the need for vigilance had been exhausting. Worse, it had left
plenty of time for self-recrimination.

He didn't think he'd ever been so embarrassed. He didn't know what
had come over him. Caruso was a bully who'd needed to be taught a
lesson, but Jonas knew that wasn't what he was doing. He would have
beaten the man to death if no one had intervened. And not because of
the things he'd done. But because that volcano of rage that had been
seething inside of him for months had finally erupted.

All the times he'd snapped at Amelia or Sidney, all the times he'd
twisted arms a little too far—they'd been warning rumbles, signs of the
coming explosion. He'd ignored them. Because it felt good. That was
what he hadn't wanted to acknowledge until now. It felt good to let go,

to let himself be swept away. To be outside of himself, freed from the constant weight of being in his own mind.

Jonas rubbed his face with his cuffed hands as he was prodded into line with the other men and led down a narrow hallway.

He didn't even remember hitting the police officer. When the footsteps pounded up from behind him, it was as if every nerve in his body had been jolted with electricity. He'd already been mad with rage, all restraint gone, and the new opponent only added fuel to the fire. A wash of red had blotted out the world. He would have tried his best to destroy anyone who'd touched him.

That reality left him chilled to the core. If Maggie had gotten in his way, tried to stop him, or God forbid, Amelia. He imagined Amelia's fragile bones cracking beneath his fists and wanted to vomit.

Everything from the first punch until a few minutes after he'd been thrown into the police wagon was a blur. He hadn't even felt the blows of the nightstick when they'd hit, although he certainly felt them now. Jonas grimaced. There had been some blood in his urine stream that morning, and the whole of his back and shoulders ached as if . . . Well, as if they'd been repeatedly hit by a club. He stretched his neck to the side until something popped. He'd had worse in his life. He would heal. The question was, where would he be doing that healing? Exactly how much trouble was he in?

The courtroom was packed and oven-warm. It stank of sweat and sour breath and unwashed bodies. Every available seat was taken, and people lined the walls three-deep. Jonas winced. So many more people here to witness his disgrace than he'd expected. His eyes picked out Sidney, standing among the throng at the back, and despite his tight jaw and stiff posture, Jonas couldn't stop his shoulders from dropping as his insides went liquid in relief.

Rhodes was also there, to his displeasure. Damn the man. How did he manage to be everywhere, and what would he print now?

Jonas was shoved into a holding area with the admonition that only the extremely unwise caused trouble here. It was three long, uncomfortable hours until his name was finally called.

He was led before the judge, who looked down at the papers in front of him and read aloud. "Vincent, Jonas. Two counts of assault with great bodily harm. One of the victims was a police officer." The judge looked at him with a gimlet eye.

Sidney stepped forward from where he stood along the wall, and the judge's eye shifted to him questioningly.

"Sidney White, Your Honor, representing Mr. Vincent in this matter."

"Really," the judge said, raising an eyebrow. Sidney was the best dressed person in the courtroom by a mile, his suit well cut and obviously expensive. He looked as out of place as a peacock among a flock of pigeons, but he didn't appear to notice, his voice clear and confident as he went on.

"We've reached an agreement with both victims for restitution, and as a result the District Attorney has agreed to withdraw the charges." He held up a sheaf of papers, and the judge nodded to the bailiff, who retrieved them and brought them to him.

He fanned through them, frowning. "These appear to be in order, though I must say I disapprove. Assaulting a police officer isn't something we can tolerate. But it appears it isn't my decision. The charges are dismissed. I don't ever want to see you here again, Mr. Vincent."

"Yes, Your Honor," Jonas said. His voice was raspy from disuse.

"Next case," the judge called, and Sidney turned without a word and strode back down the aisle.

Jonas was delayed by the need to have the handcuffs removed, and by the time he was free, Sidney had left the courtroom. Jonas followed.

Sidney was waiting in the hallway. "We're taking the back exit," he said when he saw Jonas, then turned and began pushing his way through the throng. Jonas followed.

"Vincent!" The shout came from behind him. Jonas glanced back. Rhodes was fighting against the crowd, trying to reach him. Jonas turned away and redoubled his efforts, making it out the back door only a moment after it closed behind Sidney.

He stood in the alley, gulping in deep breaths of hot, stagnant city air. It stank, as always, of smoke and horse manure, but it was still the cleanest thing he'd breathed in more than a day.

Sidney still didn't look at him.

"I'm sorry," Jonas said to his rigid back.

"We'll discuss it later," Sidney said without turning.

Before Jonas could reply, the courthouse door opened behind them and Rhodes burst out, almost panting. "I have to talk to you both."

There was still something inside him that wanted to teach the reporter a lesson, but the split skin over his knuckles and his general exhaustion argued against it. He sighed. "What do you want?"

"Another child has been taken," Rhodes said bluntly.

Sidney spun toward the reporter as an electrical charge went up Jonas's spine. They listened in horror as Rhodes explained. The girl had disappeared either late the previous night or early that morning—no one was sure. The photograph her family had given the police left no doubt she'd been taken by the same man who killed the others.

"And that's not all I've been working on," Rhodes went on. "I got a tip from a source about the shooting, and—"

Jonas interrupted. "What shooting?"

Rhodes glanced at Sidney. "I didn't have a chance to tell him yet," Sidney said.

"Tell me what?" Jonas demanded.

"Amelia is fine," Sidney said quickly. "But someone took a shot at her outside my office yesterday."

Jonas ground his teeth. Amelia could have been killed, and where had he been? Cooling his heels in a cell. "Who did it?"

"That's what I'm trying to tell you," Rhodes said. "My source says some of the private detectives Holloway hired when Ginny went missing are still in town. A couple of them were in a bar last night, flashing a roll of cash."

"You think it was them?"

"I think it's possible. I think everyone involved in this case needs to be careful. There are hard feelings in the city, especially after yesterday's article. Which," he went on, putting up a hand as Jonas scowled at him, "I did not write."

Jonas couldn't stop himself from making a derisive noise.

"I mean it," Rhodes said. "My notes were in my desk. Another reporter went through them and took it all to my editor. I knew he was getting impatient, but I swear I didn't know anything about it until it was done."

There was a beat as the three of them looked at one another. "Is there anything else?" Jonas asked finally.

Rhodes deflated a bit. "No. I just wanted to make sure you knew. About . . . all of it."

They watched him walk away, then Sidney sighed. "Come on."

"Is Amelia really all right?" Jonas asked as he followed Sidney. "Where is she?"

"Andrew was going to stay with her last night. He was meant to be talking to chemists today, so she's probably at the office with Morris." Sidney's voice was level, but now that it was just the two of them again, it was as though he'd remembered he was angry. They emerged onto the sidewalk two blocks away from the courthouse, and Sidney raised a hand for a cab.

When one pulled up, Jonas hauled himself aboard with a grunt of discomfort. He was going to be sore for days.

"Thank you for getting me out," he said quietly as the cab pulled away from the curb. He didn't know exactly what Sidney had done, but he expected it involved a thick envelope of cash. That was one more thing he owed and couldn't afford to pay back.

"It wasn't easy," Sidney said. "There were a dozen witnesses. You'd have gone to prison, and there wouldn't have been anything I could do about it."

"It was Caruso who started—"

"No one gives a damn about Caruso," Sidney said, his calm demeanor shattering. "He's a menace and the neighbors all know it. Not a one of them would have admitted to seeing anything if his case against you were tried. But the policeman is another matter. You cracked his jaw-bone and knocked out two teeth. You're lucky he wanted money more than he wanted to see you in jail. And you're lucky the District Attorney knows who I am. As it is, between this and Amos, I've used up every bit of goodwill I have with De Lancy. At this rate, I'm going to owe his grandchildren favors." He was silent for a long moment. "You could have killed those men," he said finally.

"I would have killed them," Jonas said, his voice barely more than a rough whisper. "I know. I don't . . . I'm so sorry."

Sidney looked at him. "I'm worried about you. You've been different since you were shot. The moodiness and the nightmares. The fighting. The drinking."

"I know," Jonas said again. "I don't know what's wrong with me. I've been hurt before without being this way. My arm isn't even that bad anymore. It's just . . . My head can't seem to let it go. I keep . . . Remembering isn't the right word. It doesn't describe what it's like. I can't stand having my back to a room or having anyone approach me from behind.

"And the nightmares—they're so real. And sometimes it's like I'm dreaming even when I'm awake. I hear something, or smell something, and it's like I'm right back there on that street. Right in the middle of it. Feeling the gun against my spine and hearing the hammer cock and waiting for the bullet. And I never know what's going to set it off. I'm always waiting for the next time. I know I've been short-tempered, with you and Amelia both. It's like the rage is always there, waiting. I went after Caruso, and giving in to it felt . . ."

"Good?"

Jonas made a helpless gesture. "Not even that. Just less bad. For a little while." He sighed again. "I'm sorry I put you in this position. Not a good look for my first week on the job. I assume I'm—"

"Fired? Oh, yes. Very much so," Sidney said. "You absolutely cannot show your face at my office again or my father will have my hide."

Jonas snorted. "Well, I didn't much think I was cut out for the law anyway."

Sidney smiled faintly, and they rode on for several minutes without speaking. "We'll get through it," he said eventually, reaching for Jonas's hand.

The touch untied the knot in his chest. "I love you, you know," Jonas said abruptly. It was the first time he'd spoken the words aloud, and the rush of fear and euphoria that filled him as they left his mouth was dizzying, though not as dizzying as what happened next.

"I do know," Sidney said. "I love you, too."

It was one of the most exhilarating sensations of his life. Jonas wanted to bathe in it, to drink it in and hold onto the feeling. If he could have stopped time and frozen the moment in place forever, he would have done it, instantly.

But as it always did, time moved on, and reality intruded as the cab pulled to a stop in front of Sidney's office.

Sidney sobered. "Damn it. I have to go in." He visibly pulled himself together, straightening his shoulders, then climbed out. "Hold a moment, please," he called up to the driver. "He'll be going on." He looked up at Jonas, leaning out the window of the cab. "Go home," he said. "Get bathed and changed. I'll send Amelia in a cab."

Jonas nodded, glancing down the block as he did. Andrew was coming toward them.

One look at the set of his shoulders and the barely hidden distress on his face was all it took to know he had failed.

Sidney followed his glance, reading the same news.

Andrew came level with them, and his expression lightened a hair when he saw Jonas. "That's one thing gone right, at least," he said.

"I take it you had no luck," Sidney said.

Andrew shook his head. "I managed to speak to seven of the eleven on the list. I've just come from Columbia College. There was a chemistry professor there I hadn't managed to speak to yet and had some hope of, but he turned me down the instant he heard what it was about."

"Wait," Jonas said. "A chemistry professor at Columbia. His name wouldn't happen to be Fraser, would it?"

The cab driver called down. "You getting off here? I'm not going to sit here and wait while you lot jabber."

"Keep your shirt on," Jonas shouted. He looked down at Andrew. "Well?"

"Yes," Andrew said. "Haywood Fraser."

Jonas felt a grin spread across his face. "Get in."

"What?" said Andrew, looking baffled.

"Get in," Jonas said again, swinging the door open. "We're going to ask him again."

# 19

Andrew looked at Jonas as the cab pulled away from the curb, waiting for an explanation, but Jonas merely smiled and said nothing.

"Fine. Don't tell me." Andrew flung himself back against the seat cushion, unreasonably annoyed. Nothing about the past twenty-four hours had been easy; why should this be any different? He'd watched Amelia nearly be murdered. He'd spent most of the rest of the night trying to prevent another attempt while trying to keep a grip on the slippery little urchin who had set them up. He'd barely slept, then, within an hour of rising, somehow walked into the most mortifying argument of his life—the crux of which he'd been chewing over all day without coming to any sort of internal resolution. Another child was missing. He'd spent the day having doors slammed in his face. And now Jonas was grinning like the Cheshire cat instead of explaining why he was dragging Andrew all the way back across the city for another try at a man who'd ejected Andrew from his office almost before he'd finished making the first request.

On second thought, maybe his annoyance wasn't unreasonable after all.

"How was your evening? I suppose you've been told the rest of us spent ours dodging bullets?" Andrew didn't make much effort to hide his irritation.

"I heard," Jonas said, the smile melting from his face, replaced by a look of mingled guilt and embarrassment.

Andrew squeezed his eyes shut and sighed. "That was unkind of me. I apologize."

"It's all right," Jonas said wearily. "It's only the truth. I lost control and made things harder for the rest of you at exactly the wrong time. I'm sure Sabine was furious, too."

Andrew grimaced, realizing Sidney hadn't known, so he couldn't have told Jonas about their firing and imminent eviction. "I'm afraid it was worse than that," he admitted. He gave a selective accounting of the morning's events, leaving out his argument with Amelia.

Jonas took the news stoically. "Amelia will take it hard. We had a good run there. But everything ends, eventually. I'm glad you were there last night."

"It was no hardship. Although I'd boil your sheets before I slept on them again, if I were you. I'm not sure I managed to drown all the vermin."

Jonas half-chuckled and rubbed at his face, and Andrew noticed for the first time how exhausted he looked. He had dark circles beneath his eyes—the kind that didn't develop over the course of a few stressful days. It occurred to Andrew that he'd been so caught up in seeing Amelia again—and in watching her and Rhodes, if he were being honest—that he hadn't paid much attention to Jonas. His cheekbones seemed sharper. He'd lost weight in the last few months. Andrew frowned, thinking about what Amelia had told Sidney about the fight, and about the look they had exchanged.

"How is your arm?" he asked, a suspicion beginning to grow in his mind.

"Recovered," Jonas said shortly.

"Any weakness or continued pain?"

"The muscle aches occasionally, but I wouldn't say it's painful. And it spasms sometimes—the way it did in the house on Watts yesterday."

Andrew let a beat pass. "You said you lost control yesterday. Has that been happening more lately?"

Jonas looked guarded. "What do you mean?"

"Well, have you noticed any change in your moods? Any nightmares or trouble sleeping? Anything like that?"

"Why?" Jonas asked, straightening. "Did Amelia say something to you? Or Sidney?"

Ah. So there had been. Andrew didn't speak for a long moment, trying to decide how to proceed. "Have you ever heard anyone talk about something called 'soldier's heart'?" he asked finally.

Jonas glanced at him, caught off guard by the sudden change in subject. "No."

"It's something I came across while reading about mental afflictions. I had an uncle—my father's brother—who fought for the Union in the war. When I read about soldier's heart it reminded me so powerfully of him. I'm convinced he suffered from it. He had nightmares for years after he came home. Bouts of rage and melancholy that didn't seem connected to anything."

Andrew glanced at Jonas, who was looking out the window, concentrating on nothing in a way that made Andrew feel sure he was actually paying close attention to every word. "And he had sudden episodes where he felt as if he were back in the middle of a battle. Some of them were triggered by obvious things: he hated thunderstorms and fireworks. But he also couldn't tolerate the smell of camphor. When he caught cold, he'd cough himself half to death rather than have a plaster on his chest. Apparently, it happened to a lot of men, on both sides."

There was a long pause. Finally, Jonas spoke. "I didn't go to war."

"No." Andrew shrugged. "But war isn't the only way to have a frightening, life-threatening experience. You felt many of the same things a soldier might feel—it was just concentrated into one event. It doesn't seem so far-fetched to me that there would be similar effects. Or that they would linger."

Jonas slumped. "I feel like I'm going mad. And the whole thing feels so ridiculous," he said. "I'm fine. I lived. My arm healed. There's no reason I should still be so shaken. And by the silliest things. A grown man shouldn't go to pieces because someone walks up behind him."

"Most of the time, when someone walks up behind you, it's harmless, and you know that," Andrew said. "But part of you remembers that once, someone walked up behind you, and you came to great harm. At some level, the association is logical. We understand so little about the way the mind works. Why are some people prone to melancholy, even when there seems to be no reason? Why do some people have bouts of mania? We don't know. Perhaps we will someday, but for now it remains a mystery."

"So there's no cure? For this soldier's heart? I might be this way forever?"

"I don't know," Andrew said frankly. "It's possible. There's no medicine I can give you. No powder or tincture or surgery. But some of the veterans did improve over time. I suspect some of them had a natural resilience, while others had particular things that made them want to get better." Andrew hesitated. "And I suspect those who made room for the changes in themselves probably found some relief. I know I have always found it to be the case that letting hurts fester without acknowledgment makes them worse."

"What about your uncle? Did he get better?"

"No," said Andrew. "He never talked about the war, or about any of the aftereffects. He tried to carry on as though nothing were wrong. Everyone around him did the same. Eventually he drank himself to death, far too young." He turned to look at Jonas directly. "You have people who care for you. They worry for you and want to help you. Let them. And try to be patient with yourself. That's the best advice I can give you."

Jonas nodded without looking at him, and Andrew turned to look out his own window to give him a moment.

They were nearing the grounds of Columbia College, and Andrew fought the urge to ask Jonas once again why they were here. Generally speaking, he trusted Jonas's judgment, even if he was occasionally shocked by his methods. Hopefully, given everything they'd just talked about, Jonas wasn't planning to resort to violence to convince Fraser to cooperate.

The cab let them off outside the building that housed Fraser's office, a castle-like red brick structure on 50th Street. Andrew had left it no more than an hour before, and he couldn't help but be pessimistic as he mounted the stairs for the second time that day. Fraser had been emphatic in his refusal to become involved. Jonas, on the other hand, appeared supremely confident. He was wearing, as usual, a well-cut and up-to-the-moment suit, but it was creased and dirty. He looked, and smelled, like a man who had been wearing the same clothes for two days in the middle of summer and had spent the intervening night in a jail cell. His hair was disheveled, and there was an obvious bruise on his jaw. The students they passed were giving him wary looks and making certain to step out of his path.

Andrew sighed and gave in to his impulse. "You're not planning on threatening him, are you?"

Jonas shook his head. "Persuasion only."

"In that case, you might want to duck into a washroom for a few moments."

Jonas glanced down at himself and grimaced. "Good idea. Do you happen to have a comb?"

Andrew did. Jonas disappeared into the next washroom. He emerged ten minutes later, his face and neck washed, and the worst of the dust brushed off his clothes. His hair was tidy again.

"Now, where is Fraser's office?"

Andrew pointed to the door at the end of the hallway.

"All right," Jonas said quietly as they approached. "You go in first."

Andrew hesitated, and Jonas made a little shooing motion.

Andrew shot him a look, then rapped on the door.

"Come in," said Fraser's sharp voice.

Fraser, a hale-looking middle-aged man with an impressive set of side-whiskers, looked up from behind his desk as Andrew entered, and a look of distaste twisted his features. "You again? My answer is the same. I'm not interested in being involved in this case."

"Not even as a favor to me?" said Jonas from the doorway behind him.

Fraser looked past Andrew, and his face drained of color. He gripped the edge of his desk with both hands, his eyes darting from Jonas to Andrew and back again. "You . . . you can't be here." The man could barely speak. "Do you know what will happen if . . ."

"Nothing is going to happen," Jonas said. "But we do need someone to do this analysis, and quickly. Tonight, in fact."

"But a murder case," Fraser gabbled. "I can't have my name associated with—"

"Saving an innocent boy from the electrical chair?" Jonas asked. "Why not?" He stepped further into the office, and Fraser's eyes followed him as if they were on a string. "There are worse things you could be known for."

There was no hint of implication in his voice, but Fraser blanched nonetheless.

"Please," Jonas said after a long pause. "I'd be very . . . grateful."

After a long, silent moment, he tightened his jaw and put out a hand. "Fine."

Jonas stepped back as Andrew withdrew the stoppered vial from his pocket and handed it over.

With a professional challenge to focus on, Fraser began to regain his equilibrium. He held the glass tube between his thumb and forefinger, eyeing the tiny quantity of powder in the bottom. "I'm not going to be able to do much with such a small amount. I'll have to be selective in which tests I use. Can you give me any additional information that might be useful?" He looked directly at Andrew, apparently having decided to pretend Jonas was no longer there.

"You may have read that the coroner returned a verdict of poison. But I have my doubts," Andrew said. "There was no examination of the stomach contents, and the presentation was not classic for any of the common poisons. This material was found trapped in a fold of the victim's clothing. Anything you can tell us about what it is and where it could have come from would be useful."

"All right," Fraser said. "I'll do what I can. Where shall I send the results?"

"Send them to the club," Jonas said from the doorway. "You know the address."

Fraser didn't look at him.

"Thank you for your help," Andrew said awkwardly. He waited until they were back on the sidewalk to speak again. "I take it that Fraser is . . . ah . . ."

"A client? Yes, for more than a year now," Jonas said. "Normally I wouldn't be so indiscreet about it. But desperate times. Do you mind if we walk part of the way back? I've been in a cage all day. I'd like to stretch my legs."

"That's fine," Andrew said faintly. They'd gone a block before he spoke again, his discomfort making his voice strange. "So even though you and Sidney are . . ."

"Together?"

"Yes," Andrew said. He couldn't quite believe he was intentionally initiating this conversation, but Jonas's nonchalant tone and his own raging curiosity drove him forward. "Despite that, you're still . . . working?"

"Yes. Some."

"And Sidney doesn't mind?"

Jonas gave him a sideways glance. "He minds, but not for the reason you assume. He'd be perfectly happy for me to stop working completely and let him support me. Obviously he could afford it, and it would make it easier for us to see one another. But I have to know I can make my own way. Always. I can't be dependent on someone else. But to Sidney it feels like a lack of trust."

"Isn't it?"

Jonas gave him a rueful look. "I should have known you'd see it the same way he does."

"What does that mean?" Andrew couldn't help but let a tiny bit of offense creep into his voice.

Jonas stopped on the sidewalk and turned to him. "Have you ever been hungry? Not 'worked through lunch' hungry, or 'sent to bed without supper' hungry, but really, deeply, hungry? A long string of days without enough to fill your belly even once? Willing to rummage through the garbage, willing to eat a pigeon or a rat if you could manage to catch one? That sort of hungry?"

"No."

"Then you can't know," Jonas said simply, and began walking again. "That kind of poverty scars you as surely as a knife. You can't understand what it's like to claw your way out and how terrifying it is to know that with a little bad luck, you could fall back in. You can't let your guard down, can't get too comfortable. There's no such thing as feeling completely safe. You have to keep your claws sharp. If you stop paying attention and let them go dull, they won't be there when you need them. If you let someone else pay your way, well, when they stop, you might find out you've forgotten how to do it yourself. Sidney is one of the finest people I've ever known. I trust him more than anyone except Amelia. But trust is dangerous. That's why it's so precious. The more of it you give to someone, the more they can hurt you."

Andrew said nothing, trying to imagine living that sort of life as a child. He couldn't do it. Even when he'd fallen out with his parents and left Philadelphia, he'd been an adult with a set of skills they had paid for him to acquire—skills that would always be in demand. And he'd always known he could go back. If he fell, angry or not, they would catch him. Of that he was certain.

"It's not your fault you can't understand," Jonas said a moment later, as if he'd heard Andrew's thoughts. "You and Sidney both grew up in families with money. Life was predictable. Your future, however you imagined it, was good—something certain, worth looking forward to. Clear paths, and all of them went somewhere appealing. Amelia and I didn't have that. The sorts of futures the two of you saw, those were a myth to us. A fable for children. We never bothered to imagine them. We dreamed of enough to eat and a steady roof over our heads. You know the two of us now, when we have a life that looks enough like yours that if you squint it could pass for the same thing. But it's not. We remember being hungry. We remember scavenging newspapers to put inside our clothes in the winter. We remember all of it well enough to know not to let our claws get dull."

"And so, you still take clients."

"A few. I'm able to be selective. Sabine's is a better place to work than most that way. It's not technically a brothel. Sabine makes her money from the food and drink and the gambling. She takes a cut of Amelia's earnings. And she gets the money from renting the rooms on the third floor. You keep whatever you make once you're inside. You can make a comfortable living, if you're good." Jonas gave Andrew a direct look. "And I am." The words were a statement of pure fact, without a trace of boastfulness.

Andrew had no idea what he was meant to say to that. They walked another block in silence—awkward on his own part and apparently unconcerned on Jonas's—as he tried to find a reasonable way to bring up the topic that had taken on an outsized significance in his mind. Finally, he gave up on subtlety. "Amelia told me she also . . . worked that way. For a time."

Jonas eyed him. "She told you, did she? And what did you say?"

"Not much," Andrew admitted, looking anywhere but at Jonas. "She said it, and then a minute later we found out there was another child missing. We didn't really talk anymore after that."

"And how do you feel about it?" Jonas asked, looking at him intently. "You know something more about her life now. What does it mean to you?"

Andrew struggled to explain. "I don't know. It's as if she isn't—"

"If you're about to say it means she isn't what you thought she was, then I suggest you reconsider, or I'll knock every one of your teeth out of your head. And I won't feel bad about it." Jonas's voice was blandly polite, but the sincerity of the threat was evident in the set of his shoulders.

Andrew snapped his mouth shut, flushing at the realization that those words, or others very like them, had, in fact, been about to come out of his mouth. He took a long moment. "I just . . . I didn't expect it, that's all. As long as I've known her, she's been fairly emphatic that she wasn't . . ."

Jonas shrugged. "She's not. Now. It was a temporary necessity."

"But?" Andrew prodded, both wanting and not wanting to know more.

Jonas hesitated for a long moment. "It shouldn't matter," he said finally. "If you care for her, it shouldn't change anything either way. And if you want to know the details, you'll have to ask her. But I'll tell you this much: she has complicated feelings about it. It wasn't something she'd ever planned on doing. We'd agreed on it right from the start. I can take care of myself. But it's more dangerous for women—being alone in a room with a man you don't know, who believes that as long as he pays, he's entitled to take what he wants from you. We'd seen what happened to some of them. The ones who'd been beaten, the ones who'd gotten pregnant and had to take their chances with some old woman in a back room.

"We were getting by, so it wasn't worth the risk. But then—" Jonas cut himself off, then glanced at Andrew and sighed. "It was several years ago, the year before we went to work at Sabine's. It was the middle of winter.

We were living in a room in a back tenement, and I came off worst in a fight. It hasn't happened often, but that time there were three of them, and they caught me by surprise.

"One of them had a lead pipe. He swung it right at my head, too, the bastard. Broke my collarbone and a couple of ribs. They robbed me and left me in the gutter. I wound up getting pneumonia. We were already living close to the bone, and now there I was laid up, and she was trying to pay for better food and visits from the doctor, in addition to rent and coal for the stove so we didn't freeze to death.

"We'd split off from our crew not so long before and there were still some bad feelings there, so she couldn't go to them—not that any of them had any money either. She picked a few pockets, but it's harder in winter. Finally, the rent was due and there wasn't anything else to do. We knew lots of girls in the life. Amelia went to one of them, and she arranged it. Once I was up and back to work, she stopped."

"You make it sound so straightforward."

"Why shouldn't it be?"

Andrew shrugged, unsure how to answer.

"Your world says she should have been willing to let me die, and to starve herself, with her so-called honor intact. She wasn't, and you'll have to pardon me for saying I'm glad of it."

"You said she has complicated feelings about it. How does she feel about the fact that you still . . ."

Jonas made a wobbling "sort of" gesture with one hand. "You're aware of the Whitman quote about contradicting oneself? And containing multitudes?"

Andrew gave a half smile. "Yes."

"That's Amelia on this subject. She spent her whole childhood being told about the saints—all of them women, you'll notice—who preferred gruesome forms of martyrdom to the loss of their precious virginity." Jonas snorted. "Fairy stories, but they get in your head, even when you don't really believe them."

"But they didn't get into your head?"

"Oh, I'm committing a mortal sin whether I get paid for it or not, so I might as well take the money," Jonas said cheerfully. "And all the sanctimony is ridiculous. There are only sellers because there are buyers lined up every night. Let's cross over to Broadway here and take the streetcar the rest of the way."

Andrew mulled that over as they boarded a crowded car and rode south. He couldn't deny what Jonas said was true. There were buyers lined up every night.

There was a time when he'd been one of them.

When he had first arrived at college, he'd found a slip of paper tucked in among his things. Written in his father's handwriting was the address of a discreet house on a side street in a pleasant neighborhood. He'd been too mortified to go for several months, but, when it transpired that a number of his classmates had the same information, half a dozen of them had gone out drinking one night before making their way there.

An attractive woman had proceeded to relieve Andrew of his virginity in the most expeditious manner possible. He'd gone back as often as his student's budget would bear for the next year or so, but eventually had come to understand that he preferred his own hand to the knowledge that his partner's degree of enthusiasm was directly correlated to her price.

In his later years, he'd had discreet relationships with several women, all of them respectable widows, women of means who didn't want to marry again but weren't averse to having a man in their beds occasionally. The most recent had ended when he became engaged to his former fiancée, with whom he'd shared nothing more intimate than a kiss on the cheek. He'd never dreamed of attempting more. Because she was a lady, and the rules were different with ladies.

But the lines got blurrier the longer you looked at them. The widows had been ladies, too, and they'd insisted on discretion, because their reputations would have been damaged—though not ruined—if the relationships had become generally known. Andrew had complied, because he knew the rules as well as they. But how, precisely, was it different than visiting a high-class brothel or even keeping a mistress? No money exchanged hands, but he couldn't deny there was something transactional about those relationships. There'd been warmth. Affection even. But there was an unspoken understanding on both sides that each had something the other wanted.

At any rate, Andrew had no high ground from which to cast stones at Amelia. Whatever she'd done, she'd done it to buy Jonas's life. He'd had no such noble purpose. The longer he thought about it, the worse he felt. For all his high-minded thinking about how he admired Amelia's courage, her willingness to flout convention, it appeared he was more parochial than he'd realized. He'd thought himself enlightened, but he hadn't reacted that way. A hot flood of shame washed over him. When he got a chance to talk to Amelia, he had to apologize. It might not matter, but he would do it anyway. Because she was right. He was a fool.

# 20

Amelia sat in the main room of Miles and Polly's house with Sarah and Silas as Miles got ready for his shift.

"You do what Doc said and stay off your feet," Miles called back to Polly as he came out of their bedroom, his suit freshly brushed and his shirt gleaming white. His voice was gentle, despite the tightness in his shoulders. "Let Sarah and Miz Amelia help you."

Amelia didn't hear Polly's response. The woman had been politely avoiding her since she'd arrived an hour before, just as it began to get dark. Amelia had spent the day trying to stay out of the way at Sidney's office, and had finally asked Morris to bring her here. He'd seemed relieved to be rid of her. Politely, of course. She would have preferred to go back to her apartment, but she'd promised she would not go anywhere alone. And she wanted to make things right with Polly, if she could.

"Thank you for stayin'," Miles said to her. "Any word on Jonas?"

"Nothing yet," Amelia told him. "He and Mr. White should be back any time. I hope."

It felt odd, not having anywhere to be that night, and in the wake of Miles's departure Amelia found herself unable to settle. Her mind was too full. All her worries—about Jonas and Amos and Andrew—competing against one another.

Finally, Amelia made herself go to Polly. She couldn't do anything about the rest of it, but she could try to set one thing right.

"May I come in?" she asked from the doorway.

Polly, sitting in a rocking chair with her feet propped on a stool and a pile of knitting atop the mound of her belly, glanced up at her. "If you like."

"What are you working on?" Amelia asked, gesturing at the yarn looped around the needles.

Polly spread the half-finished piece with a sigh. "A blanket. We don't need it—we've got plenty left from when the others were babies. But it helps to keep my hands busy. Makes it easier not to think."

The silence descended again.

"Polly, I'm sorry," Amelia said finally. "I'm sorry we couldn't help Amos. And I'm sorry for suspecting him. We were wrong. But at the time—"

"At the time, you thought the colored boy might be guilty."

"That didn't have anything to do with it," Amelia exclaimed, shocked at the implication.

"Didn't it?" Polly looked up at her. Her eyes were hard. "I've been that boy's mother for fifteen years. I've seen how it is. How when he played with the Irish boys on the block, he was always the one who got called out for being too rough, even though he wasn't doing anything the other boys weren't. How his white teachers seemed surprised when he got an answer right, or punished him for something I know they would have overlooked in a white child. That's not even mentioning the kind of things people say in front of me before they know who I'm married to." Her hands shook as she made the next stitch.

"I know people can be awful," Amelia said. "But I would never—"

"No, you don't use ugly words or talk about how they ought to know their place. But I notice you asked me to call you by your first name, but Miles and Tommy are still saying 'Miz.'"

Amelia gaped at her for an instant before mortified realization swept over her.

Polly was right.

"I don't know what to—" She broke off as Polly made a sound in the back of her throat, then grimaced and dropped a hand to cradle the bulge of her stomach.

Amelia straightened and took a step toward her. "What is it? Are you all right?"

Polly waved her off, her mouth tight. A long moment later, she relaxed and blew out a breath. "I'm fine. I've been having pains off and on for the last month. It's normal," she added as Amelia stepped forward in alarm.

"Are you sure? Should I go and fetch Dr. Landry?"

Polly shook her head. "No point. I'm several weeks away yet."

Shouts came from outside, and Amelia turned toward the window again. Before she got there, there was a thump and a wail from the outer room. Polly glanced at the door, then moved to push herself to her feet with a sigh. "Silas ought to be in bed."

"Let me," said Amelia. But before she'd taken more than a step, the window exploded inward. Amelia flinched away and had an instant to be shocked at the idea of being shot at a second time before her mind registered something—*a bottle,* she thought dimly—had smashed against the wall. Amelia caught a whiff of something sharp as flames rolled outward from the impact with a muffled *whump.* They spread over the wall and reached up for the ceiling.

Some of the bottle's contents had spattered the bed, and little sprouts of flame rose from a dozen different spots on the quilt.

Polly struggled out of her chair with a cry and dragged it from the bed, using its own weight to muffle the sparks, then looked around her as if trying to decide which part to attack next.

The flames were already taking hold of the old, dry beams above their heads. Amelia grabbed Polly by the wrist and hauled her toward the door. "It's too late. We have to get out!"

From the outer room came the sound of more glass breaking, followed by the children's screams.

Faster than Amelia would have thought possible in her condition, Polly whirled, still clutching the quilt, shoved past her, and dashed toward the sound. Amelia was hard on her heels.

Another pair of bottles had come through the windows, and the front half of the room was ablaze. The curtains billowed as they burned. Puddles of fire rippled over the floor and licked at the walls.

Sarah, her eyes wide with terror, stood frozen in the center of the room, holding Silas by the hand. The toddler saw his mother and pulled free of his sister's grip. He lurched toward Polly, his arms held out to her, heedless of the danger. The hem of his nightdress swept through a patch of burning liquor on the floor and caught like the wick of a candle.

He screamed as the flames kissed his legs, a high, thin sound of terror and pain.

Polly flung herself at him and knocked him to the ground, beating at the flames with the quilt and her bare hands.

Black smoke was already boiling against the ceiling. Amelia doubled over, coughing, as it stung her eyes and throat.

Polly began to rise, clutching a shrieking Silas high against her chest over the curve of her stomach.

Amelia grabbed her arm. "Stay down," she wheezed in her ear. She pointed to the back door. Polly nodded, her face drawn, and began crawling toward the rear of the house. Amelia, staying low, hooked an arm around Sarah's waist as she passed and dragged the shocked girl along with her.

Mere seconds had passed, but the room was already an inferno. The flames moved faster than anything Amelia had ever seen. Fire leapt from place to place, swallowing a chair here and a wall there, growing as it consumed. It roared and crackled around them, the heat astonishing. The thickening smoke boiled ever lower, forcing them first to their knees, and then onto their bellies in search of breathable air. The ceiling had vanished from sight, but the sound of the timbers cracking was clear enough.

Amelia could no longer see anything. She crawled toward what she thought was the back door, dragging Sarah, hoping Polly and Silas were still moving. She didn't have the breath to call out for them. She feared with every terrified beat of her heart the roof would collapse and trap them all inside. She bumped into something hard at the same moment a crack like a lightning strike came from the roof. Amelia clutched Sarah to her and rolled beneath the kitchen table, the whole world made of fire, raining down around her.

# 21

After stopping at Sidney's office with the news of Fraser's agreement and finding Amelia had left for the Alston house, Andrew and Jonas boarded another streetcar and headed off to collect her. Andrew was worried about what sort of reception he might receive, but he couldn't bear to let their argument fester if he could avoid it.

A block from their stop, the smell of smoke began to tinge the air.

He glanced at Jonas, uneasy. "Something's burning."

The bells began to sound a moment later.

"That sounds like the Judson bell," Jonas said, tensing beside him. "From the church on the south side of the park."

They exchanged a look and moved toward the front of the car. Not panicking, not yet. Fires happened. A saloon. Or one of the half-finished tenement buildings that dotted the neighborhood. Perhaps a workman had been careless. God forbid, not one of the completed ones. Andrew imagined a fire in one of the over-packed buildings. Dread coated the inside of his chest in a layer of ice.

They stepped down from the streetcar and hurried in the direction of the Alstons' house, moving faster as the smell of smoke grew stronger. By the time they were a block away it was clear: Minetta Lane was ablaze.

At least six separate columns of smoke were visible, and the sounds of terror and frantic activity carried to them on plumes of furnace-hot air.

They broke into a run and turned the corner to chaos.

People ran in every direction, dodging wagons, hauling buckets of water. A trio of sweating, soot-covered men were dragging a pumper-wagon toward the lone hydrant at the far end of the street. Four more struggled beneath the weight of coiled rubber hoses.

Partway up the block, a tenement blazed. Flames gouted from the shattered first-floor windows as people spilled down the fire escape and out the front doors. Someone had found a ladder and was helping people clamber out through a side window on the second floor. Andrew's heart stuttered. If people on the upper floors were cut off from the fire escapes, the toll would be grisly.

Just east of the bend in the street another house burned. A bucket brigade had formed, though it was obviously too late to do more than attempt to keep it from spreading. At the house beside it, a pair of men were frantically hauling furniture out the front door to a waiting wagon, which was hitched to a stamping, shying draft horse, its eyes rolling in terror. A teenage boy had a desperate grip on its bridle. There was a loud crack from the burning house, and part of the roof collapsed with a deafening crash, sending sparks flying into the sky as the flames leapt higher. The horse reared with a scream, tearing the bridle from the boy's hands and wheeling away from the flames. The wagon overturned, blocking the street and strewing splintered furniture and glassware everywhere.

People surged away from the animal's flailing hooves, and Jonas swore as he and Andrew tried to shove their way through the sudden choke point.

They broke through to the other side, and Jonas stopped abruptly and let out a sound of horror. Andrew looked at him, then followed his gaze. The house he was staring at was an inferno.

"No," Andrew said, his knees going weak. That couldn't be the Alston house. Flames roared from the broken front windows, and the roof was fully engulfed. Even as they watched, the front half of the house groaned and folded in on itself with a crash. They broke from their trance at the same moment, racing through the street, their feet crunching over shattered glass and debris.

Andrew's heart thundered in his ears as he scanned the street. *Please, don't be in that house. Please be out here somewhere.*

There was no sign of Amelia anywhere.

"Around back," Jonas shouted. "There's another door!"

The alley beside the house was impassable, so they darted around a neighboring house instead, vaulting a low fence into the Alstons' backyard.

The back of the house looked relatively unscathed thus far, though smoke boiled through every crack and the roof popped ominously.

Jonas started for the door.

"Wait," Andrew shouted.

"We've got to get in! What if they're trapped inside?"

Andrew seized a pair of blankets hanging from the clothesline and dunked them in the waiting washtub.

"Take this!" He shoved one sodden cloth at Jonas and threw the second over his own head and shoulders.

"Now!" he shouted.

Jonas had barely waited for his shout. He hit the door at a run, Andrew right behind him. As it burst open, black smoke roiled out. They plunged inside.

Andrew crouched just inside the door, desperately trying to get some sense of the layout. He couldn't see, couldn't breathe. The heat was incredible, the smoke so dense that Jonas, who couldn't be more than a foot away, had been swallowed up by it. The wet wool over his head began to steam immediately, and he couldn't hear anything over the roar of the fire and the cracking and heaving of wood.

"Amelia!" he shouted. Andrew dropped the to the floor and crawled forward, casting around with his hands, knowing that even if he managed to find something, there was a good chance it would be a corpse.

At the same moment his hand brushed against something yielding and cloth-covered—an arm or leg, he couldn't tell which—his forehead thunked into something hard.

He grunted in pain, then seized the limb he'd found and pulled. "Here," he shouted, choking on smoke. "Help me!"

Somehow, Jonas found him, and an instant's gap in the curtain of smoke showed them the four prone bodies tangled together beneath the kitchen table. None of them were moving.

Dropping the blanket, Andrew hooked one of Amelia's arms over his shoulders and grabbed the little boy by a fistful of his nightshirt. Jonas took the woman and girl. They crawled toward the exit, dragging the four limp bodies with them.

If they'd been any further from the door, they'd all have been lost. As it was, Andrew's vision was graying by the time they reached the yard, and both he and Jonas remained on their hands and knees, the heat of the flames still roasting their backs, coughing so hard they could barely stop long enough to suck in another breath of the relatively cleaner air.

Amelia, Polly, and Sarah began to stir, adding to the chorus of coughing. Silas, however, remained still. The little boy wasn't breathing, and the pulse in his neck was thready beneath Andrew's shaking fingers. He laid Silas flat on the packed dirt of the yard and tipped his head back as Polly scrabbled toward them, panic on her face. Andrew clamped his mouth over the child's and breathed into his lungs. Once. Twice.

"Breathe," he muttered, his whole focus on Silas's unmoving chest.

Andrew was about to lean down again for another breath when Silas convulsed. He coughed once and dragged in a ragged, rattling breath. He tried to cry, but it triggered a spasm of coughing. Polly reached for her son, tears making clean tracks through the soot smudging her face.

Andrew sat back on his heels and closed his eyes in relief.

"We need to get away from the house before the rest of it collapses," Jonas said, and Andrew opened his eyes, having nearly forgotten the fire raging behind them. He nodded and pushed himself to his feet.

∽

Amelia sat against a wall across the street from what had been the Alstons' house. It was a pile of burning timbers now. Looking at it, it seemed a miracle any of them had made it out alive.

Of course, they nearly hadn't. Her lungs ached, and her brain felt as though it were wrapped in cotton wool. She couldn't tell if she wanted to cry, sleep, or scream. Someone had tried to kill them. Had wanted to kill a pregnant woman and her children, had been willing to burn down these people's homes, risking God only knew how many lives. The city was angry, and Rhodes's article had given them a list of targets. But this level of indiscriminate violence shocked her.

Across the street, a saloon burned, the sound of bursting liquor bottles added a tinkling accompaniment to the noise of the street. It was full of people, some crying as their homes burned, some still desperately trying to quench the flames, others, incredibly, watching as though they were at a most entertaining circus.

Jonas crouched on one side of her, and Polly sat on the other, Sarah and Silas huddled beneath her arms. Sarah's eyes were glazed with shock, and Silas cried and squirmed away from Andrew and Dr. Landry as they tried to examine the burns on his legs.

"What happened?" Jonas asked.

Amelia tried to answer, but the attempt triggered another coughing fit.

Landry answered instead. "I was on the sidewalk when they came through. Men on horseback, wearing masks. At least half a dozen of them. Bottles full of liquor and fuel oil. Everything dry as dust and nothing in the rain barrels."

"Where are the fire brigades?" Andrew said.

Cold fury was evident in Landry's voice. "They may come, eventually." He shook his head. "They're loading ambulances on Bleeker. I've sent four on already—burns, broken bones. At least twelve dead that I've seen—one of them stabbed."

"Stabbed?" Jonas said.

"Probably nothing to do with the fire," Landry said. "Likely someone took advantage of the situation to settle a score. These are largely superficial," he said, tearing away the burned bottom portion of Silas's nightdress so it wouldn't touch the tender skin. "But they do need to be cleaned and dressed. And I don't like the sound of his lungs."

Silas whimpered, and Polly brushed a hand over his head, then hissed between her teeth.

"Polly," Landry said, "let me see your hands."

She held them out, and he gently took hold of her wrists and turned her palms upward. "Hmm. They're not bad. But ointment and bandages would help. And I want you off your feet."

"Do you want to take them over to Bleeker?" Andrew asked.

Landry shook his head. "Not if I can help it. If they go to the hospital, they'll separate them and send Silas to the colored ward."

"No hospital," Polly said. Her voice was a croak.

"Take everyone to my house," said Landry, fishing a key from his pocket and handing it to Jonas. "It's only a few blocks from here. Polly and Sarah know where it is. There are supplies there to dress the burns. I need to stay—there are still too many people we've got to get to the hospitals. But all of you should get off the street and rest." He turned to Andrew. "Dr. Cavanaugh, would you be willing stay here and help?"

"Of course," said Andrew, sounding baffled. "It hadn't crossed my mind to do anything else."

A faint hint of a smile touched Landry's face. "Good." He stood. "You all go on ahead. We'll be there when we can."

Andrew began to rise to follow Landry, then paused. He looked at Amelia, and a flicker of some emotion crossed his face. It was gone before her poor, overtaxed brain could decipher it. He pushed himself to his feet, following the other doctor back out into the maelstrom of the street.

"All right," said Jonas. "I'll take Silas, and Polly, you can lean on me if you need. Amelia, can you and Sarah manage together?"

Amelia nodded and struggled to her feet, reaching out a hand to the girl.

The five of them began to make their way down the sidewalk, weaving around the piles of debris and skirting the still-burning buildings. At the end of the block, a group of men were trying to connect a second pumper wagon.

One of them spied Jonas and called out, "We could use another man here. We've got the hoses connected, but not enough hands!"

Jonas shot an agonized look at Amelia. "Can you manage? If we don't get it doused . . ."

"Go. We'll be fine," she rasped. It ended in another fit of coughing. When she managed to stop it, Jonas transferred Silas into her arms and gave Sarah the key.

"I'll come find you as soon as I can," he said, and a moment later, he'd been swallowed up by the throng around the hydrant.

They kept going. The clamor and smoke were disorienting, and Amelia put one foot in front of the other feeling as though she were moving underwater.

They turned the corner and came upon a row of bodies laid out on the sidewalk, hastily draped with whatever was at hand. A brightly embroidered shawl covered the head and upper torso of a man. An empty flour sack hid most of the much smaller form beside him. Amelia covered Silas's eyes against the sight and forced her own gaze forward, refusing to allow herself to look for spirits. There was nothing she could do for them now. The living had priority.

No one paid them any mind as they shambled along, soot-streaked and reeking of smoke. Amelia paused every few steps to hitch Silas higher onto her hip with a little grunt of effort.

"That's the house, up there," Sarah said at the end of the next block. "The one with the bell by the gate."

"Thank God," Amelia muttered. Silas was a stout little thing, and his hurt made him wriggle and twist on her hip, looking for his mother. Amelia's arms quivered from the strain of carrying him so far.

But they'd made it. They could clean themselves up, tend to their burns, and then—

Polly gave a sudden gasp from behind her. Amelia turned. Polly was looking down, the hem of her dress dripping and a dark puddle spreading on the sidewalk between her feet.

# 22

The protective bubble of detachment burst as Amelia stared at Polly, aghast, waiting with a faint hope borne of desperation for Polly to tell her not to worry, that it wasn't what she thought.

Seconds stretched as Sarah looked between them, her eyes huge in her soot-streaked face.

Silas broke the spell. He whimpered, and Polly straightened.

"We can't stand out here," she said, her tone matter-of-fact. "Let's get inside." She stepped around Amelia, opened the gate, walked through. Amelia followed. Sarah put the key in the lock and opened the door.

The doctor's home had a faint medicinal scent and the spare, utilitarian feel of a bachelor's quarters—but one of neat, orderly habits, at least. The only ornamentation was a woven tapestry hanging on one wall, depicting an enormous tree with wide, spreading branches. The vivid colors were almost too much for Amelia in her suddenly hyper-aware state, so she averted her eyes and set Silas on the worn settee beneath it. She stretched the joints of her arm.

"What do we need to do?" Amelia's voice pierced the silence, and she heard the thread of panic running beneath the rasp of the smoke.

"Why don't you get some water warming so we can wash while I tend to Silas. I'll—" Polly paused to cradle her belly with one hand, her face tightening. She didn't speak for a long moment, bending slightly forward and breathing deeply through her nose. After a moment, Polly straightened, blew out a breath, and continued as though there had been no interruption. "I'll take a look through Doc's supplies and get what we'll need."

Amelia barely suppressed a snort. What they *needed* was someone to run for Andrew and Landry, and quickly.

Her incredulity must have shown on her face, because Polly chuckled. "I've done this three times myself and been there for no telling how many others. Everything will be fine."

She laid a reassuring hand on Amelia's bare forearm, and time stopped as a tangled swirl of visions spun through Amelia's mind, overlapping one another, overwriting the reality in front of her.

Polly lay writhing in pain on a bed in an unfamiliar room. Polly lay smiling down at a swaddled bundle cradled in the crook of her arm. Polly lying blank and sightless, her face white and slack in death.

With a gasp, Amelia wrenched herself back into the present, shuddering. She made herself breathe slowly, trying to force the images from her mind. Moving jerkily, she stepped away from Polly and stumbled to the door of what she supposed was the doctor's bedroom, already knowing what she would find.

The room was exactly as she had just seen it, and she felt an instant's vertigo—she'd never experienced one of her visions in such close proximity to reality. The experience was unsettling. It was almost as if yet another vision was attempting to lay itself over what she'd already seen. The empty, neatly made bed was a stark contrast to the rumpled, sweated birthing bed in her mind.

Dread coiled in Amelia's stomach. That night, in that room, Polly would reach a fork in her destiny. She was passing through what Jonas had once called the Valley of the Shadow—and Amelia had no idea how to lead her safely out. It was the worst sort of vision, the most useless of her gifts: certain foreknowledge of danger and no notion of how to avoid it. Any of the outcomes she had seen were possible. Polly's life depended on the choices made in the coming hours. Anything any of them did—or failed to do—could be the deciding factor.

"Amelia?"

Polly's voice shook Amelia from her stupor. She turned back to the main room to find Polly looking at her with a quizzical expression. Amelia faced the first choice of the night: whether or not to tell Polly what she'd seen. She made it without more than an instant's reflection.

"I'll get the water heating." She brushed past the other woman without looking at her.

The stove was cold, but there was coal in the box and matches on the shelf above it. Amelia's hands shook as she twisted newspapers for kindling, wondering as she worked if she'd already made the key mistake. Would knowing what Amelia had seen cause Polly to change something about the next hours? And if she did, would it be a change for the better, or the worse? Amelia made a noise of frustration as the third match broke. She clasped her shaking hands in her lap and tried to breathe. She had to stop this. Second-guessing every move would drive her mad. She got the fire lit on the fourth try and sat back on her heels, staring at the flame as the edges of the newspaper blackened and curled.

"Miss Amelia?" Sarah touched her shoulder.

Amelia started, suddenly aware it wasn't the first time the girl had tried to get her attention. Amelia looked at her. Perhaps she should send Sarah to fetch help. Andrew and Landry hadn't said which hospital they were going to. But there had to be a local midwife. Someone who could help. Someone who knew something—anything at all—about delivering babies. Someone who could take the responsibility from her shoulders.

But one look at the hollow-eyed girl was all it took to know she couldn't do it. Sarah had been through as much as any of them, and the streets were still chaos. Someone had already tried to kill her tonight, along with the rest of her family. Who was to say the danger was past?

Perhaps Amelia should go herself. But even as she finished the thought, Polly grunted and bent to breathe again, this time staying in the position a shade longer and frowning as she straightened.

Amelia didn't know how much time they had, but it didn't seem abundant. She couldn't send Sarah out, and she couldn't leave her here alone with a mother who was, by the looks of it, going to have a baby quite soon, and who might well die doing it. They were on their own.

Amelia had never been so terrified in her life.

But it didn't matter. The future would come. What had to be done had to be done.

Amelia squared her shoulders. "All right. The fire is lit. What's next?"

Twenty minutes later, they'd all washed their hands and faces, the doctor's bed had been remade with clean sheets over several layers of newspaper, and Silas's burns had been dressed. With Polly's urging, he swallowed a tiny dose of laudanum in a cup of water.

"I wouldn't normally." Polly set the cup on the table, watching the little boy's eyes as they began to drift closed. "But best if he can sleep through this next bit."

*Lucky boy.* Amelia shook herself. Such thinking served no purpose. A queer, detached calm settled over her.

"What else do we need?"

"More hot water," Polly said. "Towels. Ties for the cord and something to cut it. Those need to be boiled." She stopped, and her face went tight again as another contraction swelled. They were coming closer together, and this one seemed worse. Sweat beaded her forehead by the time she spoke again.

"I'm going to walk around a little. Why don't you two see if there's anything to eat."

Amelia looked doubtfully at the icebox, certain the knot in her stomach wouldn't allow her to eat. But there was a brimful pitcher of something cold sitting on the shelf. She poured some and took a sip—some sort of tea. Ginger, lemon, and mint. Amelia drained the glass in a long, desperate draught, soothing her throat, washing the taste of fire from her mouth. She poured some for Sarah, then took a second cup to Polly, who had begun making a steady, meditative circuit of the main room, pressing a hand to her lower back as she walked and focusing on a point in the far distance.

She took a single swallow from the cup. "Tastes good," she commented without much interest, handing it back just before the next spasm hit. She doubled over and made a low, pained noise.

"Mama?" Sarah's voice was anxious.

"I'm all right, baby," Polly said when she could speak again.

"Shouldn't you lie down?" Amelia asked.

Polly shook her head and resumed her plodding route. "Better if I can keep walking for a bit. Moves things along."

Amelia bit back a reply. Moving things along seemed like precisely the wrong goal. Andrew and Landry might return in time if things would only move a little more slowly.

Her thoughts must have shown on her face. Polly gave her a wry grin. "No use trying to get away from it. The only way out is through."

An hour passed. Polly paced the length of the room until Amelia thought she might wear a groove in the floorboards. Sarah perched on the settee beside Silas, stroking his hair and watching her mother anxiously. During the last few contractions, Polly had stopped her walking and leaned forward to press her hands against the wall, rocking her lower body as if trying to soothe the baby inside her to sleep.

Now, she beckoned to Amelia. "When this next one comes, take your fists, put them in the lowest part of my back, and push. Hard as you can."

Amelia did as she instructed.

"Harder," Polly gasped.

Amelia pressed, lifting onto her toes and pushing most of her weight down onto the taller woman. She repeated the exercise through half a dozen more contractions, each longer than the one before. Eventually, just as Amelia's arms were beginning to shake with the strain, Polly announced she was ready to lie down.

Sarah made to follow them, but Polly shooed her back. "Stay with your brother."

"But Mama—"

"Do as I say," Polly snapped, then softened her tone as she continued. "Get the towels and warm them on the stovetop. Keep swapping them out so they're always warm but not hot."

She turned to Amelia. "Bring a basin of warm water and some disinfectant."

Amelia hurried to do as she instructed. The sweet, chemical smell of the disinfectant-laced steam tightened her throat as she hurried back to the bedroom, trying not to slosh the water onto the floor in her haste.

In the bedroom, Polly had undressed and was struggling onto the bed in nothing but her shift. "I don't want to scare her. I sent her to my mother while I was having Silas. Scrub your hands," she went on in the same breath, her eyes focused on the far distance. "All the way up past the wrists."

She leaned back on her hands and arched her back as another contraction hit. This one pulled a ragged cry from between her teeth.

Amelia pinned her sleeves back and hurriedly scrubbed her hands, her whole body tensing with sympathy as she watched Polly struggle against the pain.

"Won't be . . . much longer," Polly said, panting.

Amelia found herself panting along with Polly, her chest tight, her body moving almost without her as Polly motioned toward the foot of the bed.

"I have to push now," Polly gasped.

Amelia knelt between Polly's open legs, newspapers crackling beneath her knees. She skimmed atop a sea of terror. It stretched in every direction, waiting to swallow her, but she forged ahead, hoping as long as she didn't look down, she wouldn't fall in. Eons passed between each breath. Her hands moved automatically in response to Polly's instructions, now issued in gasps between sounds of pain. Amelia wiped sweat from her own forehead until the rolled cuffs of her smoke-blackened sleeves grew wet with it.

After what felt like an eternity, a patch of dark, wet curls the size of a dollar coin appeared between Polly's legs as she strained, then disappeared again as she relaxed.

"I see it," Amelia said. "It's coming."

"Once the head is out," Polly panted, "support it with your hands but don't pull. It's—" She broke off as her face twisted, and her whole body clenched as she bore down again.

Amelia gasped as the baby's head began to emerge. She put a hand beneath the hot, slick roundness as Polly dragged in a breath and pushed again. Amelia watched, transfixed, as first one shoulder and then the other appeared. Then, with a disconcerting suddenness, the rest of its body slipped out, along with a gout of bloody liquid, and Amelia was holding a purple, floppy, disturbingly slippery baby in her hands.

"It's a girl," she said in awe, as the baby drew in her first breath and let out a hiccuping wail.

Polly dropped her head back onto the pillow. "Tie the cord in two places," she said. "Then cut it in between them."

Amelia did as she instructed, moving with careful deliberation, irrationally afraid she would hurt the baby. When she finished, she wrapped the baby in a towel and handed her to her mother.

Polly settled the infant on her chest and gazed down at the crumpled, gnome-like little face with a tired smile. "Hello, little miss," she said, cradling the baby's head with practiced ease. She looked up at Amelia. "Can you see the afterbirth coming yet?"

"There's more?" Amelia blurted, appalled.

Polly let out a low chuckle. "Yes. But the hard part's over. If you can't see anything yet, we've probably got a little time. Why don't you tell Sarah to come meet her sister?" She turned her attention back to her new daughter, and Amelia slid from the bed and left the room, feeling limp as a dishrag.

Sarah was hovering outside the door. Amelia sent her in and went to wash up. Her face was streaked with grime and soot. Her hairline was wet with sweat, and her dress, already singed by the fire, was stained with blood and fluid. She found a cloth and scrubbed the worst of the mess off.

She poured water into the basin and dipped her hands in, thinking as she did of Polly's hands stroking the damp curls on the baby's head.

Her own mother might have done that once. Amelia went still. All Amelia had ever known of her own birth was that she'd been brought to the Foundling when she was less than a day old. Strange that she'd never considered what must have come before. But her mother, whoever she was, had been a real person. Had carried Amelia inside her body, had sweated and struggled and cried out to bring her into the world, only to give her up. In the moments between birth and relinquishment, had she cupped her newborn daughter's head and looked down into her face? And if she had, what did she feel? Love? Despair? Indifference? Amelia had never wasted time daydreaming about it. She came from a world where no one had a mother; she wasn't special. At the Foundling, it was Jonas, who'd had his mother for the first few years of his life, who was the oddity. He never spoke of her, but Amelia knew that despite his own strident apostasy, he kept her rosary beads in a box beside his bed.

Amelia dried her hands, then sat on the end of the settee where Silas slept, watching his breathing. Amelia had never craved motherhood for herself, had never cooed over new babies brought to the Foundling like some of the other girls. Now she wondered: What was it like to look at a being you had created from your own blood and bone? To know, without an instant's doubt, that you would spend your own life to save it? To risk Polly's anguish at being unable to help her son or Cassandra Holloway's half-mad grief at the loss of her daughter?

Footsteps outside the front door interrupted her thoughts. Amelia stood, tensing, then slumped back onto the settee in relief as Dr. Landry entered. Andrew followed behind him. She stared at them and nearly laughed. Of course they would arrive now.

Amelia relayed the evening's developments in a few sentences, and Landry headed back immediately to check on Polly.

Andrew lingered beside the settee as the silence stretched between them, growing more pointed with every passing second. Amelia felt the impulse to fill it, then quashed it with a flash of irritation, recognizing where it came from. Etiquette said it was a lady's job to smooth social interactions. Well, etiquette could go hang. She was exhausted, she was not responsible for Andrew's comfort, and she was not going to waste her time pretending to be something he already knew she wasn't. They were past that now. And if Andrew couldn't even be bothered to fill the awkward silence he had created, then Amelia would be damned if she would—

"I owe you an apology," he said abruptly, cutting her off mid-thought.

Amelia looked up in surprise. "What?"

"I was wrong. I was judgmental, and I had no right to be. I created a picture of you in my own mind, and then blamed you for not living up to it. I'm sorry."

Amelia's irritation drained away, replaced by sadness. "It was an honest reaction, though, wasn't it?"

He shrugged helplessly. "Yes. That doesn't make it any more reasonable."

She leaned back against the settee and looked at him. "Reasonable or not, it was what you felt."

"In that moment, it was. But when I thought you were in that house, I—"

Before he got out another word, Sarah burst from the bedroom, her face frantic. "Doc says come quick!"

A chill raced up Amelia's spine as she and Andrew sprang from the settee and ran to the bedroom. He beat her there and was already beside the bed when she stopped in the doorway with a gasp. In the minutes since she'd left the room, a sizable puddle of blood had formed on the newspaper-covered mattress between Polly's legs. Polly's face was pale, her lips purplish in the lamplight.

Landry glanced back at Amelia. "Was she bleeding like this just after the birth?"

Amelia shook her head in mute horror.

Landry's expression darkened. "Increased bleeding, and no sign of the afterbirth." He moved to Polly's side as he spoke, cupping his hands around her still-distended abdomen and massaging as though he were kneading bread.

Each press of his hands pushed more blood out onto the sheet, and Polly grunted in pain. After a full minute of this, he stopped.

Andrew spoke, his tone as tense as Landry's. "No movement?"

Landry shook his head.

"What does that mean? What's happening?" Amelia asked.

"There are large blood vessels that feed the placenta—the afterbirth," Andrew explained. "Usually, it's expelled shortly after the baby, and the womb clamps down and closes the vessels off. But sometimes, if it's too tightly attached, it doesn't happen on its own."

Landry was unbuttoning the cuffs and rolling his sleeves up past his elbows. He glanced at Andrew. "Have you ever done a manual removal?"

"Not on my own." The two men exchanged a look.

Landry took a deep breath. "Sarah, take the baby into the other room."

"But I—"

Polly interrupted, her voice weak but calm. "Give me a kiss, then do as the doctor tells you."

Sarah, looking stricken, pressed her lips to her mother's forehead, then gathered the baby into her arms and left the room.

Landry turned to the basin of water Amelia had used and dumped in more disinfectant. He began vigorously scrubbing his right hand and arm.

"Open my bag," he said to Amelia. "There's a black metal box inside. Get it out and open it, but don't reach inside. Set it right here, next to the basin."

Amelia did as he instructed. Inside the pouch were two rolls of what looked like thin rubber.

Landry thrust his scrubbed hand into one of them and began rolling it up his arm.

"Halstead gloves," Andrew said approvingly. "I've read about them, but haven't seen a pair."

Landry nodded. "I read the publication he released and had a pair made. I boil them between uses. I've seen good results. Polly," he said, turning to the woman on the bed, "we've got to get the afterbirth out. Do you understand what that means?"

Polly nodded, her breathing shallow and rapid. Her eyes were frightened.

"I need you to relax as much as you can and not fight. You," he said to Amelia, all deference gone, "loop your right arm under her right knee. Pull it back and hold it. Put your left hand on her shoulder. Hold her down. Cavanaugh, take her left."

Amelia did as he instructed. The next few minutes were the stuff of nightmares.

Amelia watched in horror, somehow unable to look away, as Landry inserted not merely his fingers, but the whole of his hand and much of his forearm into Polly's body. He did something with his hand, tearing a ragged scream from Polly's throat and making her buck against Amelia's grip.

"Hold her," Landry snapped.

With a half-sob, Amelia leaned the whole of her weight onto Polly's shoulder as Landry worked. The room was stifling. Polly's screams stopped only long enough for her to draw another breath. Blood. There was so much blood. Amelia's stomach lurched. The room began to swim around her.

Andrew's voice cut through the fog like a whip. "Amelia. You cannot faint. Look at me. Focus on me."

With a supreme effort of will, Amelia wrenched her eyes up to his and kept them there. His face was tight, but his gaze was as immovable as an oak tree, never for an instant shifting away from her. She anchored herself to it, matching her breathing to his, tracing the planes of his face with her eyes, studying color and texture and shape, trying to stay outside of herself, until finally, Landry withdrew his hand, bringing with it an enormous mound of tissue traced with purple veins. He tipped the gruesome thing onto the sheet with barely a glance and began to massage Polly's abdomen again, his still-bloody hand printing a macabre tattoo on her skin.

The bleeding began to slow almost immediately.

At a nod from Andrew, Amelia lowered Polly's leg to the bed. Without waiting to see if they had further need of her, she stumbled from the room blind and breathless, her body nerveless and numb.

Sarah hovered outside the door, drawn taut as a wire. She seized Amelia's arm in a ferocious grip. "Is my mother alive?"

Amelia managed to nod. Sarah rushed past her into the bedroom.

Amelia staggered back to the basin, where she washed again, her hands, her face and neck, with a mechanical precision. Then she poured another cup of the doctor's ginger tea and made herself drink it, a swallow at a time, rolling the liquid over her tongue, letting the cold bite of it wake her. Her heartbeat thudded in her ears.

The birth itself had looked painful, but it was nothing—nothing—to what Polly had just endured. And what if Amelia was the one who had forced it on her? What if there was something she could have done to prevent that from happening? Her legs wouldn't hold her any longer, and she slid down onto the floor and sat with her back against the wall. She hadn't seen this possibility in her premonition. Had it been there, buried somewhere between the others, or had she pulled herself out of it too quickly? If she'd paid more attention, allowed it to continue, would she have seen something she could have done differently?

She had no idea how long she'd been there when Landry and Andrew emerged from the bedroom.

"—want her to have a saline infusion, at least, and skilled nursing for a couple of days," Landry was saying. "I'm going to find a wagon to take her."

As Landry left the house, Andrew lowered himself to the floor beside her.

"Will she live?" Amelia's voice was hollow.

He hesitated. "Probably. She's lost a lot of blood, and there's some risk of infection. But Landry seems to be good at his job. I don't know of anyone who could have done better."

They sat for a long moment without speaking.

"Was that my fault?" Amelia said, finally giving voice to the question. "Was there something I should have done during the birth? To keep it from happening?"

"No," Andrew said, sounding surprised. "It's a complication that happens for some women. No one knows why. Landry said there have been signs from the beginning that something wasn't right with Polly's pregnancy. There's nothing you could have done."

The tight band around Amelia's chest let go, and she gasped out the sob she hadn't known it was holding back. She tried to smother it with her hand and turned her head away, embarrassed. She felt him draw nearer.

"Please don't hide from me," Andrew said quietly. "I regret more than anything that I ever made you feel you had to. I didn't see it before. But tonight, when I realized you were in that house . . ." He swallowed hard; his voice was hoarse when he went on. "There was nothing I wouldn't have done to know you were safe. Nothing. I understood, then."

Amelia's breathing was a series of great shuddering gasps. Her whole body trembled, a reaction not only to the unmistakable emotion in Andrew's voice but to the tension and terror of the last few days, everything there'd been no time to feel now spilling out. She found herself huddling into him, and he drew her into his arms and tucked her head against his shoulder. Amelia clung to him, gripping fistfuls of his shirt in her hands, and he held her as she shook. Finally, she began to quiet. Andrew's arms were still around her, his heartbeat strong and steady beneath her ear.

When he spoke again, his breath was warm against her temple. "All the parts of your life—all the things you've done, all the things you've experienced—they're what made you who you are, and I would never want you to be anyone else." He spoke with such certainty, such total assurance, that Amelia blinked away tears again as he moved to pull away.

She didn't let him.

Amelia lifted a hand to his cheek, trapping him and drawing his mouth toward hers. Andrew hesitated, as if giving her one last chance to pull back. She closed the distance. There was nothing tender in the kiss; it was a thing born of need and impatience, greedy and seeking. She tasted smoke and mint. His hands slid along her back as Amelia twined her arms around his neck and pressed into him, her blood pounding in her ears. He made a sound and pulled her into his lap, one hand coming up to cup the back of her head. She gasped against his mouth.

The front door swung open, and they both froze as Landry strode through. The doctor checked for a startled instant, then obviously decided to take no notice of the embrace.

"I have the wagon," he said, managing not to look directly at them without appearing to be avoiding it. "But no one to drive it. Dr. Cavanaugh, I'll drive, if you can stay in back to monitor Polly."

"Ah, certainly," Andrew said as Amelia tried to discreetly ease herself back down to the floor.

Landry gave a brief nod. "I'll go and get Polly ready to go." He walked past them and into the bedroom.

"Well. That was . . . unexpected," Andrew said after a long pause.

"Which part?" Amelia asked.

He snorted. "The entirety of the last four days, if you want to be literal about it." He stood, somewhat reluctantly, Amelia thought, then reached down a hand to her.

She let him pull her to her feet, and warmth flooded her chest when he didn't let go of her hand. She looked up at him, waiting to feel awkward and feeling instead a sense of wonder. There were a thousand things that could still go wrong for them, but for this still, small moment, everything was right.

# 23

As Andrew and Landry carried Polly out to the waiting wagon, the baby tucked into the crook of her arm, Landry cautioned Amelia and Sarah not to leave the house.

"The streets are still unsettled—all sorts of people are out wandering around. I've left word to let Miles know you're here if they see him. And Jonas already knows. So one of them ought to be along eventually. Don't open the door for anyone else. We shouldn't be gone more than an hour or so."

The quiet after they left was deafening. Amelia found herself unable to settle. She'd kissed Andrew. The last few days had cracked the wall she'd built between them, and tonight had left it in rubble. She didn't know what came next, but there was no going back. They could no longer pretend—to themselves or others—that they were friends and nothing more. Trying to distract herself from the apprehension that realization provoked, Amelia set herself to cleaning up the mess they'd made of the doctor's home. The bedroom had obviously seen the worst of it. Amelia did what she could, throwing out the stained newspapers and dirty water and putting the sheets out to soak in a washtub of cold water in the back garden. The stains probably wouldn't come out, but perhaps they could be repurposed.

While she was washing up, Silas woke, fretful and in need of a new diaper.

Sarah grimaced. "I guess all his diapers burned up. I hate to use anything of Doc's."

"No help for it," Amelia said, handing over one of the towels Sarah had been warming for the baby.

Sarah folded it and pinned the makeshift diaper in place. "I ought to see if he wants to eat anything." Silas wailed and reached for her as she rose.

"I'll do it," Amelia said hastily.

Sarah picked him up, and Silas quieted, putting two pudgy hands on her cheeks and looking at her with a quizzical expression. He babbled a few syllables. They sounded like mush to Amelia, but Sarah replied as if she understood. "No, it's nighttime. Not time to play."

Amelia brought a cup of milk and a bit of bread she'd found in the kitchen, but after a few sips, Silas decided he didn't want any more. He tucked his head beneath Sarah's chin, and she swayed with him, trying to lull him back to sleep. "Aren't those pretty colors, Silas?" Sarah asked, pointing at the woven tapestry hanging above the settee. "What's this one?" She pointed to a red stripe.

"'et," he said sleepily.

Sarah put her finger on the orange disk of the sun, and to Amelia's ears the sound Silas made was incomprehensible.

"That's right," Sarah said. "Orange."

She pointed to a blue patch.

"Broo." Another pair of soft breaths, and he was asleep.

Sarah eased him back down onto the settee with a yawn of her own. "Beg pardon," she said. "I don't know when I've been so tired."

They settled into a pair of the doctor's chairs, both of them sagging with weariness. Within a few minutes, Sarah was asleep, her chin on her chest. Amelia's body was likewise exhausted, but her mind was still abuzz after the frantic activity of the last hours. It skipped from one thought to the next without pause. Andrew and the kiss. The fire. The need to find a new place to live. Polly and her baby. Mrs. Holloway and her grief. Amos and their failure to save him. Anna Moretti and their inability to uncover any trace of her.

Amelia sighed. There'd been so much to do over the last few days, so much information to gather, that there had been little time to sit and think about what any of it meant. They knew Amos was innocent. Maggie said he'd been with her when Ginny was taken.

Ginny had been lured with candy. Had the others? Was that how he took them? It seemed impossible that five children could somehow be taken without a single witness other than Paulina Nowak's little brother. Amelia looked at Silas, sleeping on the settee. Paulina's brother hadn't been much older. It was no wonder he couldn't tell the police anything helpful. Even if he had, they probably wouldn't have understood—

Amelia sat bolt upright, her heart pounding. They wouldn't have understood him. They *hadn't* understood him, not any more than she could understand Silas when he spoke. "Broom man" never had made any sense. What had he been trying to say? Silas said "broo" when he meant "blue." But "blue man" wasn't much better. There weren't any such thing as blue men, so—

Wait. Amelia's breath caught as pieces began to fall into place. There *were* blue men. Or at least . . . What would it sound like if Silas tried to say "blue hands"? Probably much like "broom man" to someone unaccustomed to his speech. The people who worked at the laundry had blue hands—the white people, at least. She didn't know how many white men worked there, but any one of them could drive a laundry wagon into any part of the city without attracting a second glance. Any one of them could have ridden with Amos before and known he gave candy to children along the route. She thought of Himes, with his wandering hands and his ready violence. Maybe he was the one.

Amelia stood, trembling. Even now, the unknown man had Anna Moretti. She stalked across the floor, barely aware of anything around her, almost deranged with the need to share the discovery. To do something. Jonas was still somewhere battling the fire. She could go and fetch him. Tell him what she'd realized. But what good would that do? She had no idea how to find their suspects. Didn't know where they lived. Didn't even know their names or how many of them there were.

There had to be records at the laundry. Amelia could go and, what? Break in and make a list? Why not? She'd broken into plenty of places before.

Amelia shook Sarah awake and explained.

"You're leaving?"

"Only for a little while," Amelia said, in a hurry to be gone. "If any of the men get back before me, tell them I've gone to the laundry. Lock the door again behind me."

Sarah clicked the bolt closed behind her as Amelia hurried into the night, determined. She would get what they needed, and when the men returned, they would hunt down this monster and put an end to his evil.

∞

The fires were out, but smothering heat rose from the rubble, and a thick haze of smoke still choked the air of Minetta Lane. Jonas had hauled lengths of canvas hose and worked the hydraulic pumps until his back shrieked in protest and his arms felt as though they might fall off. He was so drenched in sweat and covered with soot that the two had mixed to form a sticky black paste over much of his body. He sat leaning against the wall of an undamaged building and considered sleeping right there rather than dragging himself upright and walking home.

The excited shouts and darting figures had begun to taper off, but there were still plenty of people on the streets. The newly homeless had mostly been taken in by neighbors or gone on their own to seek shelter with family elsewhere in the city. Jonas wondered vaguely where Miles and his family would go, then jerked upright at the realization that he hadn't seen Miles since all this started. Both he and Tommy would be at work, and if they'd heard what happened, they would have been here by now. So they didn't know. Someone needed to go tell them. Miles especially, being that his house was gone and Polly and the children were at Landry's, a fact of which—Jonas's sluggish brain reminded him—only he was aware. So he might as well go, and then he could wash off all this muck and fall into bed. Tommy could walk Amelia back from the doc's.

He shoved himself to his feet, groaning at the ache of his stiffening muscles, and began walking home. He was at the end of the street less than a block away, almost within sight, when someone called from behind him.

"Vincent? Is that you?"

Jonas wanted to groan again. It was Rhodes's voice, and Jonas couldn't think of anyone he wanted to see less right then. "What are you doing here?" He began walking toward the corner.

Rhodes followed. "Where else would I be? 'Arsonists Destroy Home of Accused Killer' is a great story." The reporter walked along beside him for a pair of blocks, Jonas too tired to either send him on his way or ask him what else he wanted.

"I would have kept my word," Rhodes said finally. "I wouldn't have used any of what was in my notes."

Jonas didn't respond.

"Do you believe me?" Rhodes asked finally.

Jonas stopped with a sigh. The club was almost in sight, and his bed called to him like a siren. "Do you care?"

"Yes."

"Then fine, yes, I believe you, for whatever that's worth."

His voice was more tentative than Jonas had ever heard it. "Will you tell Amelia?"

"Tell her yourself," Jonas said irritably.

"All right. I will."

"Great. Wonderful. Now go away and leave me alone. I'm so tired I could die."

Rhodes gave him a jaunty little salute, some of his old insouciance returning, and walked away.

Jonas watched him go and shook his head, then turned back toward the club.

Tommy was at the door, and his already impeccable posture straightened as he saw Jonas approaching. "Are you all right?"

Jonas nodded wearily. "You heard all the commotion?"

Tommy nodded. "The bells and such. Where was it?"

"Minetta."

Tommy's eyes widened, but Jonas went on before he could speak.

"Everyone got out, but Miles's place is gone. Amelia is with them at Landry's house. I'm sorry to leave you to tell him, but I'm half-dead." Jonas began to turn.

"Wait." Tommy thrust a hand into his inner breast pocket and pulled out an envelope. "Someone came by not an hour ago and left this for you."

On the outside of the envelope, written in heavily overlined letters, was *JONAS VINCENT—URGENT*. Fraser's reply. It had to be. He'd forgotten over the past few hours. He took the envelope from Tommy and ripped it open. Inside were two sheets of paper. One was a laboratory report listing a number of scientific tests and the names of chemical compounds Jonas didn't recognize and, in several cases, couldn't pronounce. The other was a note, brief and unsigned.

*The analysis proved easier than I imagined. The sample in question is a mixture of two different particles: larger, whitish crystals and smaller grayish-blue ones. Under analysis, the white crystals proved to be plain sodium carbonate, most often used in washing soda and other cleaning agents. The other particles are predominately ferrous ferrocyanide, more commonly referred to as Prussian Blue, although this sample contains impurities, lending it the dingy, grayish color rather than the brilliant blue one would find in a purer form. It can, in theory, be used to make prussic acid, which you may know as cyanide. Despite that connection, however, I do not believe this sample is of a pure enough form to manufacture the poison. Prussian Blue itself does have several other uses, most often in pigments and as the primary agent in some types of laundry bluing. Given its addition to the sodium carbonate, I would tend to assume, in this instance, that it is the latter.*

*The attached report contains the list of tests I conducted and the results I obtained. I trust this satisfies the terms of our agreement.*

Washing soda and laundry bluing.

His exhausted brain struggled to put it together. Amos worked at the laundry. He hadn't taken Ginny, but she'd somehow wound up with laundry detergent in her nightgown.

Amos hadn't taken her, but someone else from the laundry had. There were those outbuildings. She could have been held there.

If he was right, Anna Moretti could be there even now.

Abruptly awake, Jonas stood frozen for a moment, considering what to do next. There was no question; he was going to the laundry. But going alone would be foolish. He needed another pair of eyes, at least. He glanced at Tommy, then discarded the notion. It might be dangerous, and Tommy wasn't a young man. And, another corner of his mind reminded him, if they found Anna there, or her body, someone else would need to testify to it. Better for all of them if it were a white man.

Jonas spun. "Rhodes," he bellowed, jogging in the direction the reporter had gone moments before. "Rhodes, can you hear me?"

He'd gone no more than half a block when he came upon the other man hurrying in his direction. "Vincent! What is it?"

Jonas grabbed the man by the arm and began dragging him along. "Come with me. We have to hurry."

"Where are we going?"

"I'll explain on the way. If I'm right, then I know where you can find a story that will get you on the front page of any paper in the city."

# 24

The laundry was deserted, the quiet an eerie contrast to the bustle it had contained during her previous visit. Gravel crunched beneath her feet, the sound unbearably loud in the darkness, so she abandoned the wagon path in favor of the packed dirt of the yard.

An electric light mounted above the door created a round puddle of light in front of the main entrance. Amelia skirted it as best she could, moving quickly around the side of the building.

The loading bay door was open.

Amelia went still, straining for any hint someone else was there. Nothing. She crept up the stairs to Steele's office and tried the handle of the door. Locked. She bent to put her eye to the mechanism. Even in the dark, she could pick it. It was worth checking the other door—the one in the drying room—first, however. She'd learned that lesson after once spending a tense fifteen minutes picking a door lock only to discover an open window once she was inside the house.

Amelia eased back down the stairs and stepped out into the main floor of the laundry. Water dripped from somewhere within, but there was no other sound. It wasn't as viciously hot as it had been during their earlier visit, when all the machines were running, but the air was oppressive, heavy with damp and smelling of starch and hot metal.

The shadows pressed against her, and a shudder rippled down her spine.

She made her way toward the drying room door. It was ajar. Barely visible within was a hanging garden of damp linens, the chains holding them making tiny mouse-like squeaks as a phantom breeze caused them to sway.

She was only steps from the door when another sound intruded: the unmistakable crunch of footsteps on the gravel drive.

Instinctively, with one long stride, Amelia leapt through the open door of the drying room. As she crossed into the darkness, she heard the laundry door open behind her. She ducked behind the first row of hanging linens as a light clicked on in the outer room, her heart pounding, waiting for the shout, certain she had been seen. Footsteps moved across the floor outside. A masculine cough. The half-open door cast a skinny rectangle of illumination across the smooth concrete. A shadow moved through it, and the drying room door swung closed.

Amelia swallowed a yelp and froze as the room was plunged into absolute blackness. She stood, willing her eyes to adjust. But the vents were closed. No light penetrated the chamber. The back of her neck prickled. She fought rising panic as the velvet darkness pressed against her until she felt she would smother in it.

She closed her eyes against it, clapped a hand over her nose and mouth until she could swallow the panic down. Amelia counted her breaths, talking herself back from the edge. She was being irrational. She was not a child, to be afraid of the dark. It could not hurt her. She was fine. She was undiscovered. She would wait a moment, then make her way to the office as she had planned. She would find whatever information she could and take it back to the others.

Minutes crept past. No sound reached her from outside the room. Finally, Amelia could stand it no longer. An instant after she made up her mind to move, in the fraction of a second before she began to do so, something scraped across the concrete floor, a sound so stealthy she might have imagined it.

She knew she had not.

It was a footstep, and it had come from the direction of the door. It had come from inside the drying chamber.

Horror swept over her. He hadn't accidentally closed her in. He had seen her. He had trapped her. And he was here with her, alone in the dark.

# 25

Terror overwhelmed her good sense. Amelia spun on her heel and
sprinted in what she thought was the direction of the staircase. A
heavy, clammy shroud wrapped itself around her before she'd gone
more than a step, and she flailed against it with a little cry, reeled
away and kept going, only to encounter another, and another, all of
them choking and damp as they slapped and clung against her face
and body. The hanging linens. They were all around her. She batted
them away, utterly disoriented. Dread settled over her. In the course
of her panicked flight, she'd lost track of her direction. She no longer
had any idea which way she was facing, or where in the enormous
room she was—how near the walls, the staircase, or the door where
he waited. If he was still waiting. If he hadn't used her long moment
of distraction to move toward her.

The realization all but crushed the air from her lungs, and she let out a
wheezing gasp. It cut through the darkness, loud as a scream. She clapped
her shaking hands over her mouth and nose, trying to muffle the sound.
But there was nothing she could do to stop the gentle creaking of the chains
overhead. She'd set them swinging when she ran, and their noise was a
path that would lead him right to her if he chose to take it. She strained

her senses, trying to see, trying to hear if he was coming. For a long moment, there was nothing. And then he spoke.

"How did you find me?"

She didn't recognize the voice.

It was quiet, but it bounced off the walls and ceiling, distorted by the hanging cloth, coming from everywhere and nowhere all at once. It was low. Rough. Harsh as a rasp running over her flesh. She shivered.

"It's upsetting," he went on. "I didn't expect it. But here you are. And you're much too old to be of any real interest to me. Still . . ." A deep inhalation. "This has possibilities."

A chain squeaked somewhere to her right.

Amelia gritted her teeth, fighting the impulse to run again. She couldn't. If she ran—if she even moved—she would set another chain to squeaking. He would hear it and know where she was. But she couldn't just stand here. She still reeked of smoke. If she didn't move, he'd eventually find her by smell alone.

"I've never done this with one of my little ones," he said, and the pleasure in his voice made a shudder ripple through her. "But perhaps I'll try it. Hunting them through the darkness. Feeling their fear. And then, when I find them . . ."

He went on, in a voice so thick with anticipation that her stomach twisted in disgust. She wanted to jam her hands over her ears, to block out that horrible voice and its catalog of obscenities. But listening was the only way she could tell how close he was, so she forced herself to concentrate, trying to focus on the sound of the words, their direction and volume, without allowing their meaning to penetrate.

As he moved, he set the chains to swinging, just as she had, and within a minute it was clear he was getting closer.

She had to move. Even if it gave her away, she had to, or else stand still and allow him to walk right into her. Amelia reached out into the darkness with one shaking hand, an inch at a time, trying to make her touch feather-light. If she could find the nearest bit of cloth, if she could determine which direction it faced without moving it, perhaps she could find a clear path through them. If she could make it to the edge of the room, put her back against a wall, maybe she could avoid him long enough for someone to come. Or even find the door. Amelia doubted she could outrun him if it came down to it, but anything was better than fumbling through the dark, waiting for him to find her.

Her fingers brushed cloth. Not gently enough. There was a tiny metallic noise. Barely audible, even to her. Amelia held her breath.

Silence.

He'd heard it. He was close.

Amelia's muscles tensed. He was going to find her. There was nothing she could do to stop him. In the next few seconds, she would feel his hand brush against her skin and clench tight. She would fight him. For all the good it was likely to do, she would fight. She was no child. She would make him pay a price for taking her life. Higher than he'd paid for the others. Paulina. Markus. Ina. And Ginny. Ginny, whose spirit had held onto the terror and confusion of her last moments.

A spark appeared in the dark, and Amelia only barely smothered another gasp, imagining a struck match, a flame touched to a lamp wick. He had grown impatient and decided to end the chase. But it was too silvery, too soft and pale for flame, and as it grew and brightened, as the features began to resolve, Amelia understood what was happening. Before she'd had time take another breath, Ginny Holloway's spirit stood before her, drawn into being by Amelia's gift and her own connection to this man.

A footstep scraped the concrete again, and Amelia's heart stuttered in her chest as an indistinct form stepped into the open space at the end of the row. The head swiveled toward her, features lost in the shadows, but after a long, silent moment, he stepped sideways again, obviously still relying on sound to guide him.

He couldn't see Ginny, or the nimbus of light around her.

When he was out of sight, Ginny beckoned to Amelia, then slipped between the hanging curtains. Startled, Amelia hesitated. She'd never had a spirit do anything like this before. But as Ginny moved further away and the light began to dim, Amelia shook herself alert and followed. At the moment, there were more important considerations.

Carefully, so carefully, Amelia trailed behind Ginny through the maze of hanging linens. The gentle glow banished the dark in a circle around her. Not far enough to see more than a few feet, but far enough that Amelia could keep moving without touching the linens. She didn't know where Ginny was leading her. It wasn't a straight line, so perhaps they were circling away from their pursuer.

Help would come eventually. If Amelia could keep away from him, she could survive this. There was profound relief in the thought, but on its heels came something else. A flicker of furious anger. Now that it seemed survival was possible, it was no longer enough.

She wanted him to pay.

This man—this monster—had murdered children. He'd stolen their futures to sate his appetites and counted it as no more than what he was due. He thought nothing of their terror and pain, or of their families' anguish. He allowed an innocent boy to be blamed for his crimes, and would see him die for them with perfect serenity. And he wanted to kill her. Everything Amelia was and everything she might become, all of it was meaningless to him. He would take all of it away from her.

And she wanted it. All of it. She wanted more years with Jonas, to watch him flourish. She wanted more time to understand herself, to develop her gift and discover all the ways she might use it. And she wanted to know what she and Andrew could be to one another now that she'd finally stopped being too afraid to find out.

He would take it away. Amelia wanted to tear him apart with her bare hands. She wanted to spring at him, to bring him down like an animal and rip out his throat with her teeth in recompense for all the pain he had wrought and the time he had stolen.

Caught up in this new realization, Amelia almost tripped over a pile of debris. She caught herself and moved close enough for Ginny's light to fall fully over the jumbled metal. Broken chains and steel bars and bits of pulley—the remnants of the mechanism that had let go during their earlier visit. It oriented her. She was in the corner of the drying room farthest from the door, on the opposite wall from the staircase. With that knowledge and Ginny's presence, she could make her way out. She could escape.

Amelia stared at the hunks of twisted metal, rage bubbling through her. She leaned down and carefully removed one of the heavy metal crossbars that lay atop the jumble. She couldn't entirely prevent it from making a series of small metallic noises. They would give him a clue to her location. But she grasped the metal bar in a two-handed grip and set her feet, her back to the corner, as Ginny stood pale and silent at her side. She had light. She had a weapon.

He would come. And Amelia would be ready.

# 26

"There's the main building, plus two good-sized outbuildings behind it. Anna is probably in one of those," Jonas told Rhodes as they neared the Steele Laundry property. "We'll each search one. Watch your back."

They sprinted through the shadows past the main laundry building and split up on the path behind it. Jonas waited to make certain Rhodes was able to get into his building before trying the door of the other one and finding it unlocked. He stepped carefully inside. Amelia would be furious with him for excluding her from this search, but Jonas would accept that as the cost of knowing she was safe at the doctor's house.

From the mechanical hum, the space had clearly been electrified. Jonas searched the walls near the door for a switch, but hesitated before turning on the lights. He didn't remember seeing windows, but he hadn't been looking. But the building was easily half as large as the main laundry and crammed full of work benches and half-assembled machinery. There were too many nooks and crannies to check in the dark. He held his breath as harsh white lights flickered to life.

There were at least twenty different iterations of cooling cabinets, some plugged in and running, others standing open and quiet with their inner works on display. Steele was clearly experimenting with different materials and methods. They ranged from the size of a bread box to one nearly the size of a carriage—almost large enough for a man to walk inside. Other machines, including some Jonas couldn't even discern the purpose of, were shoved back against the walls, either abandoned or merely waiting their turn for Steele's attention.

Methodically, he began to search behind all of the machines and in the closed-off storage spaces, listening as he did for any sign that anyone was there or that Rhodes had found anything in his own search. He'd reached the back of the warehouse and found nothing when he caught himself looking at several of the larger cooling cabinets. An awful, morbid thought struck him. Steele had explained that they had to be well-sealed to function. A live person would smother inside, but an operational one would be an ideal place to store a body. With great trepidation, Jonas began opening each of them, one at a time, and was relieved to reach the end of the row without finding anything.

He turned and hurried toward the door, his hip accidentally bumping into the side of one of the partially disassembled cabinets. A panel sheared off the front and fell to the concrete floor with an ear-shattering crash. Automatically, Jonas bent to replace it.

And found himself eye to terrified eye with Anna Moretti.

The girl lay curled inside the cabinet in a fetal position. A gag covered her mouth, and she was bound by the hands and feet. For an appalled instant, Jonas could only stare, then he straightened, ripped the lid open, and reached for the child, who shrank away in fear.

"Shh," Jonas said. "It's all right. I'm taking you home." He lifted her from the cabinet, untied her, and hefted her into the crook of one arm. "Quiet now," he said. "I need to listen."

Outside the building, he carefully scanned for any sign of movement. Nothing.

A figure moved through the block of light coming from the window. Rhodes. He'd apparently finished searching his outbuilding and had moved on to Steele's office. Jonas mentally cursed him for turning on the light and jogged toward the main building, Anna bouncing against his hip. He climbed the stairs to the office, ready to bawl Rhodes out for his lack of caution.

Instead, he opened the door and found the reporter standing as if turned to stone in the middle of the floor, his eyes wide, his face white and horrified.

"Rhodes," Jonas said, "what in the hell are you do—"

"Shhh," Rhodes hissed, desperation and terror evident in the sound. "Don't you hear it?"

"Hear wh—" Jonas began, then cut himself off as he did hear it.

A voice. Sibilant, unearthly, and saying things that made his hair stand on end. It took him a long second to remember the vent in the wall and realize the voice was coming from the drying room. When he did, he all but tossed Anna into Rhodes's arms and hurtled toward the door. He flung it open as a shriek rang out, followed by a meaty thump and another cry.

Jonas groped for the light with numb fingers, and an instant later the whole vault flooded with illumination.

Linens danced on their hoists, undulating between him and the far side of the room, blocking his vision.

"Who's there?" called a voice, and Jonas had to clutch the railing of the catwalk as his entire body clenched in sudden, overwhelming disbelief and horror. He knew that voice.

Loose-kneed, he almost tumbled down the stairs to the drying room floor in his haste. He batted linens aside, setting the vault to echoing with the keening song of the swinging pulleys, until he emerged on the far side, where he stopped dead, his jaw going slack.

Amelia, both hands clenched around a length of steel rod and blinking in the sudden light, stood over the prone form of a man who lay face-down and bleeding on the concrete.

"Did I kill him?" she asked, panting.

Jonas knelt and put two fingers to the man's neck, noting distantly that she didn't seem surprised to see him.

"Still alive," he said, standing just in time to pluck the bar from her hands as her shoulders twitched as if she were about to draw it back and finish the job.

"He killed them all," Amelia said. "He admitted it."

"We heard," said Rhodes.

Jonas knelt again as the reporter approached. He put one hand on the unconscious man's shoulder and rolled him over. Martin Steele's slack face stared up at them.

# EPILOGUE

*One Week Later*

Amelia sat with Jonas in the main lobby of the law office, both of them holding glasses of champagne and watching in amusement as mildly inebriated clerks reeled past. Sidney was on the far side of the room, hemmed in by young associates. Overnight, they'd gone from being resentful of his place in the firm to according him near god-like status as the lawyer who had successfully represented the most notorious defendant any of them were likely to ever encounter.

That image, of the young lawyer zealously defending a client—even a seemingly guilty indigent Negro client—and standing fast in the face of violent threats and intimidation, had turned out to be wonderful advertising for the firm. Potential clients were streaming through the doors—so many that a new clerk had been hired to manage all the applications for their services. Mr. White's earlier opposition to Sidney's taking the case had been wiped from his memory, replaced by the unshakable conviction that he had always been supportive of his son's involvement. "Everyone deserves a defense, after all," one newspaper had quoted him as saying.

The door to the street opened, and Rhodes stuck his head inside. He saw Amelia and Jonas and gestured to them. They stood, Jonas catching

Sidney's eye and raising a hand to let him know they were leaving. They had another party to attend. Sidney had promised to join them if he could manage to extricate himself from this one, although that appeared unlikely at the moment.

Outside, they climbed into the cab waiting by the curb and sat in silence as it lurched into motion.

"Well?" Amelia said finally.

A grin split Rhodes's face. "Agreed to terms with the *Times* about an hour ago."

"Congratulations," she said.

After his bombshell story about solving the Holloway case, every paper in the city had begun trying to woo Rhodes into a permanent position. He had played them against one another brilliantly, parceling out subsequent stories among them until they all began bidding higher and higher in an effort to gain exclusive access. He'd always had his eye on the *Times*, and his pleasure at announcing his success was evident.

"They're going to let me keep investigating Edwin Holloway, too," Rhodes said.

Jonas snorted. "Good luck with that. You'll never be able to prove he had anything to do with the shooting. Or with the fires."

"Maybe not," Rhodes conceded, "but I'm going to give it my best shot."

Amelia had no doubt that was true. The reporter had already assembled enough bits of evidence to convince her of the link, even if it wasn't enough for the papers to risk publicly accusing the bereaved father of an attempt at vigilante justice. The most persuasive item was a sketch of the man who had paid Wink to lure Amelia out of Sidney's office. Rhodes had worked with the boy for more than an hour, and when he'd finished, Miles Alston identified him as the man who'd come to his house the morning of Amos's arrest. Several of Rhodes's "sources" identified him as one of the investigators Holloway had hired. Whether he'd been specifically paid to take certain steps or had acted on his own would be harder to prove. Rhodes was determined to try, however, and Amelia wished him luck.

"Of course you come out of all this on top," Jonas grumbled. There was no heat in his voice, however. He knew as well as the rest of them that despite all the work he, Amelia, Andrew, and Sidney had put into the case and the risks they had taken, they still would have failed to save Amos Alston's life without the reporter.

Even after Amelia gave a statement about what had happened in the drying room, and Jonas attested to what he'd heard through the vent—never mind the fact that he'd found Anna Moretti trussed like a goose in one of Steele's outbuildings—the district attorney had been hesitant to release Amos. He seemed loath to accept that his perfect suspect, one who knew the victim and had been found literally standing over her body, was in fact innocent, and that an upstanding citizen like Steele could be the monster he sought. Despite all the pressure Sidney could bring to bear, De Lancy was inclined to put Amos on the train to Sing Sing as scheduled and sort the whole thing out later. It was only when Rhodes threatened him with a story exposing Amos's treatment in jail and pillorying the DA's office for pressing the case in spite of everything they'd discovered that De Lancy relented. Amos was free by Friday afternoon.

"Oh, I don't think the two of you need to worry about your prospects," Rhodes said. "You're all the rage. You're going to be telling fortunes and channeling the dead in every front parlor on Fifth Avenue, if that's what you want."

Amelia grimaced. The Holloways had spoken to a reporter—not Rhodes, of course—and Cassandra Holloway had talked at length about how much comfort Amelia had given her. Her social circle had taken notice. If Amelia and Jonas did decide to go out on their own, they wouldn't lack for clients. There were a great many factors to consider, and they didn't even have a new place to live yet, but at least it didn't seem likely they'd wind up on the streets.

"Any word on Steele?" Jonas asked.

"No change," Rhodes said. "It's giving the DA fits, trying to figure out whether he's faking or not."

The laundry owner had been taken to the hospital with what turned out to be a fairly significant injury to his head. He was alive, but seemed to have entirely lost his reason, babbling incoherently and drifting into an abstracted half-awareness whenever police tried to speak to him. The evidence against him ensured that if he was faking, he would have to do it for the rest of his life to avoid a date with the noose.

"They're keeping him handcuffed to the bed in a locked ward for now," Rhodes went on. "If he's faking, having to live that way is some punishment, at least, even if it's not as much as he deserves. Either way, it's a shame he's not talking. I have questions."

"Not so many questions, surely," Amelia said. They'd already pieced together much of what had happened.

A search of Steele's workshop had turned up several jars of caustic-smelling liquid. Under analysis, it proved to be similar to ether, albeit far stronger and with some additional toxins threaded through its chemical structure. A cloth soaked in the stuff and pressed to her face would explain the burning Andrew had noted in Ginny's nose and throat. It would have been more than enough to knock out a child of her size. Indeed, Andrew had hypothesized it might well have killed her before Steele had ever gotten her back to the laundry.

"He could have miscalculated its potency or left the cloth on her face for too long," he said when he first put forth the idea the day after Steele was captured. "If Ginny was dead already when he took her out of the wagon, it would explain why there was no evidence of assault."

"But she couldn't have been dead that long," Jonas said. "Her body would have—" He stopped, grim understanding spreading over his face. "The cooling boxes. If Steele found her dead in his wagon when he got back to the laundry and didn't have time to go back out to dump the body that night, he could have put her into one of his cooling boxes. He had several that were large enough."

"I think that's exactly what happened," Andrew said. "Cold conditions at or near the time of death can result in bright pink lividity. I even mentioned it in passing at the postmortem, but it didn't occur to me to consider it as a possibility in this case. It would have slowed decomposition to the point where she would appear to have been dead for only a few hours when she was found."

It was a cheerless idea they all eagerly embraced. If Ginny had died only minutes into the abduction, then perhaps she experienced only a few moments of fear and confusion before the dark overtook her. It was a cruel sort of mercy, but it was what they had.

"And it might explain why he took the risk of abducting Anna when he did," Amelia said thoughtfully. "He'd been . . . frustrated . . . by Ginny's death. The compulsion was still there, so he took another child."

"I would still like to ask him why he chose those particular children," Rhodes said now.

It seemed they were destined to wonder. A search of Steele's belongings had turned up a worn photograph of a young girl who looked very much like the victims. The style of her hair and clothing suggested it had been taken at least twenty years before. There was no name or photographer's mark on the print, and so far, all inquiries into Steele's past had turned up nothing. Was she a family member? An early victim?

"And why did he take such a chance by abducting Ginny?" Rhodes went on. "No one was looking for him until then."

It was true. Steele might have continued to evade scrutiny for years if he had continued to confine his activities to poor immigrant children, which itself was an indictment that Rhodes had explored at length in several of his articles. But Steele had to have known that snatching a child like Ginny Holloway would lead to an uproar.

"I think it was an impulsive act," Jonas said. "He saw her for the first time earlier that day, when he delivered the linens for the party. He came back that night, and when he saw his chance, he took her."

"He couldn't have known she'd be outside wandering around," Rhodes said.

Jonas shrugged. "Maybe he didn't. Maybe he saw her that afternoon and it made him want to go out hunting that night. He drove by the Holloway house, saw her, and couldn't help himself. And then when she was discovered missing and all hell broke loose, it dawned on him what sort of risk he'd actually taken. He'd made a mistake, and he was afraid of making another one by taking her body back out in the wagon. It took him several days to work up the nerve to do it."

"And then one of his very own employees just happened to be the one to find the body? That's awfully coincidental," Amelia said.

"Not as much as it seems at first," Jonas countered. "He dropped Ginny's body on one of the main streets in between the laundry and a neighborhood where more than a few of his workers live, and he did it at exactly the same time of day his employees would be on their way in. It's not so surprising that one of them would find the body. If he'd been more thoughtful, he'd have dropped her somewhere else. He might have been a brilliant inventor, but he's not actually that skilled a criminal. He got away with it for as long as he did because no one cared enough to look for him."

They lapsed into silence, each lost in their own thoughts, until the cab pulled to a stop outside Tommy and Mrs. Franklin's house, where the buzzing noise of conversation came through the open front door. Inside, the front room was crowded with friends and neighbors. Maggie, holding Giorgio's hand, stood talking to another girl. The kitchen table, which had been pushed back against one wall, was fairly groaning with food, and Wink paused in the act of filling his plate to give them a nod of greeting.

Miles sat beside Amos in a back corner.

The boy had been subdued since his release, though he seemed to be doing better as the days passed. He would never be who he had been before, however. The last remnants of his childhood had been stripped away, leaving a solemn almost-man behind. Sarah, Silas on her lap, sat on his other side. All of them made as if to stand as Jonas and Amelia approached, but Amelia waved them back down. She took the chair beside Sarah and gave the girl a squeeze.

"How are you?"

"All right," the girl replied. "The apartment is pretty crowded, but we're managing."

Miles had decided he would not rebuild the house on Minetta Lane. The land was too valuable, or would be, if he could hold onto it until the economy improved and people began building again. For the time being, his family was living in the three-room apartment above a dry-goods store six blocks away. It was cramped, but it would do until something better came along.

"Where are the guests of honor?" Jonas said. "I thought we'd be the last to arrive."

"Should be here any minute," Miles said. "Doc said they were—" He broke off as he looked past them at the doorway. He stood, a wide smile splitting his face.

Landry, carefully supporting Polly, stood on the threshold. Behind them, Andrew held the baby in the crook of his arm. Polly had lost enough blood that she'd had to remain in the hospital longer than expected, but thanks to Landry and his miraculous glove there had been no infection, and she had recovered without incident. Both doctors had concurred she was well enough to be released, as long as she didn't over-exert herself for the next few weeks.

A cheer broke out as the guests noticed Miles striding across the room toward his wife, and well-wishers reached to hug Polly and coo over the baby as she made her way back to the rest of her family. She opened her arms to her children, and for a few minutes, the whole Alston family looked as if they'd forgotten anyone else was there. Polly folded Amos against herself, cradling him and making soothing sounds as he wrapped his arms around her, buried his face in her neck, and cried.

Amelia's own eyes stung, and she glanced away from the intimate scene, blinking. She met Andrew's gaze and couldn't help but smile. He, too, was teary-eyed. He smiled back.

"That's the way the wind blows, I see," Rhodes said into her ear.

Amelia started, not having realized he was so close.

He went on before she could respond. "I wish you the very best of luck. And who knows, maybe we'll see each other around." He gave her a wink and whistled as he disappeared into the crowd, a man content with his world.

"—have to find the right location," Andrew was saying to Landry as she approached.

"Miss Matthew," Landry said with a nod.

"Amelia, please," she said.

His chin dipped again, and something in the set of his shoulders softened. "Amelia. If you'll both excuse me, I'm starving." He nodded toward the table. "We can talk more later," he said to Andrew, then left them.

"What are you going to talk more about?" she asked.

"How we might go about starting a medical practice together," Andrew said. "I'll be finished at the asylum within the next month or so, and it's time I make some firmer plans. He's an excellent physician, and I think we could do a lot of good working together. The doctors at Bellevue have spent all week complimenting me on what a good job I did treating Polly. Most of them don't believe me when I tell them it was all Landry."

"I think that sounds like a wonderful idea."

"My mother will be disappointed," he said. "But I like New York, and I want to stay. For a while longer, at least."

"I'm glad," Amelia said.

A beat passed before Andrew spoke again. "There's a free concert in Central Park next Saturday. Would you like to go with me?" There was no pressure in his tone, no sense that the question was any weightier than its actual words, but it was a gauntlet thrown, nonetheless.

Amelia looked over at the Alstons, at Miles and Polly, who had taken a chance on one another, had set the cost against what they might create together and found happiness. She thought of Jonas and Sidney, who made the same calculation every day of their lives and chose one another each time. She thought of her own unknown mother and of Jonas's devotion to his barely remembered one. She thought of Polly's fierce defense of Amos and the tenderness on her face as she gazed at her new baby, even as her body quivered with exhaustion. She thought of Ginny Holloway's mother and her unfathomable loss.

Every sort of love brought risk along with it. It meant opening yourself to life in all of its wondrous, terrible permutations. Exhilaration and despair. Ragged grief and glorious, dizzying joy. You could not control the outcome. You could only decide if you would be brave enough to make the attempt.

Amelia smiled up at him. "I'd love to."

# ACKNOWLEDGMENTS

Writing a first book is a little like climbing a mountain in the dark. You have no idea where you're going, so you just keep fumbling your way upward and hoping you don't fall. Deciding to write a second book, it turns out, is like walking up to the base of that same mountain in broad daylight. It should be easier, but now you can see how far away the summit actually is and what a massive effort it's going to take to get up there again.

Fortunately, I had a lot of people cheering me on as I climbed.

The Arlington Writers Group was, as always, my lifeline. Your continued support and encouragement have meant more than I can ever say. Special thanks to Michael Klein, Sarah Blumenthal, Dale Waters, and Lori Sullivan for their invaluable comments on the early draft. The Unquiet Dead is a better book because of the four of you.

My thanks also to Alexia Howell for her thoughtful sensitivity read. A book so heavily reliant on themes of race and injustice written by a well-meaning white lady can go wrong in a lot of ways. Having Alexia's perspective on the choices I was making was crucial to getting it right.

There wouldn't be a book at all without the team at Pegasus. I am profoundly grateful to everyone there for allowing me to tell more of

Amelia's story, as well as to my tireless agent, Jill Marr, for her continued advocacy of my work.

Thank you to my therapist, Olivia Mancini, for helping keep me together though the chaos and uncertainty of the last two years. She listened to my book-angst and told me she was sure I could do it again—if that was what I wanted. And she (gently, repeatedly) pointed to all the signs that I was depressed and (gently, repeatedly) prodded me into doing something about it. There should be a thousand more of her. Please, if you're struggling, reach out to someone.

Thank you to everyone who read *A Deadly Fortune* and liked it enough to tell a friend or leave a review or send me an email. There's nothing more rewarding than hearing from a stranger that they enjoyed your book. I hope you enjoy this next chapter just as much.

Finally, thank you to my family. Mom, Dad, Sara, and especially Alex and Audrey, I love all of you so very much.